Masterpieces
OF
Mystery

Masterpieces
OF
Mystery

The Supersleuths

Selected by ELLERY QUEEN

CONTENTS

PHOTOGRAPH CREDITS: pp. 31, 194, 229, The Bettmann Archives, Inc.; pp. 139, 181, 245, The New York Public Library; pp. 52, 95, 212, 260, 290, 337, Wide World Photos, Inc.; p. 309, Alfred A. Knopf cr. Hal Boucher; p. 9, Radio Sun Times Library.

Why Charlie Chan Does Not Appear in this Volume

EDITOR'S NOTE: Charlie Chan is one of the very few world-famous detectives of fiction who have never appeared in short stories written by their creators. For example, Dashiell Hammett wrote short stories about Sam Spade and the Continental Op, but he never wrote a short caper about wisecracking Nick and Nora Charles; and S. S. Van Dine wrote novels about Philo Vance, but never a short exploit about his sophistic and sophisticated dilettante-detective.

We remember corresponding, back in the old "Mystery League" days, with Earl Derr Biggers, creator of Charlie Chan, and asking him—indeed, pleading with him—to write at least one Charlie Chan short adventure for posterity. But Mr. Biggers replied that if he could hit upon a really satisfactory short-story idea for Chan, he would not squander it on 6000-to-7000 words; he would expand the idea to a 60,000-to-70,000-word novel. It was an argument we could not demolish. Like his beloved little Charlie, Mr. Biggers was essentially a practical man. Nevertheless, readers the world over will always regret that Earl Derr Biggers failed to leave us a single short story about his Confucious-minded, Chinese-Hawaiian-American folk hero.

INTRODUCTION

DEAR READER:

This new series of hardcover anthologies is titled, without false modesty, MASTERPIECES OF MYSTERY. The volumes will contain some of the finest short stories, short-shorts, novelettes, and short novels of detection, crime, mystery, and suspense ever written. Volume One is subtitled *The Supersleuths*, and its master manhunters were chosen on the basis of three international polls conducted by *Ellery Queen's Mystery Magazine*.

As you may know, on November 13, 1972 the Central American country of Nicaragua issued a commemorative set of 12 postage stamps to celebrate the 50th Anniversary of Interpol, the International Criminal Police Organization. Also, as you may know, Nicaragua decided to use portraits of the 12 most famous sleuths of fiction, and asked *Ellery Queen's Mystery Magazine* to set up a poll to establish the dozen greatest detectives of all time.

Actually, three different polls were conducted, and as a result *EQMM* received 66 ballots from mystery critics and editors (the foremost in the world), 91 ballots from professional mystery writers (the best in the world), and 1090 ballots from mystery readers (the most devoted fans in the world).

Only one fictional detective was voted for unanimously by mystery critics, mystery editors, and mystery writers—not surprisingly, Sherlock Holmes. But, surprisingly, the vote for Sherlock Holmes by mystery readers was not unanimous—no less than 64 readers out of 1090 failed to rank Holmes as one of the 12 best and greatest. Surprising, indeed. (Surprising? Incredible!)

Here is the definitive list, a consensus of all the votes, of the 12 most famous detectives of fiction, the 12 greatest of all time, in order of critic-editor-writer-reader popularity:

A. Conan Doyle's Sherlock Holmes
Agatha Christie's Hercule Poirot

7

Ellery Queen's Ellery Queen
Rex Stout's Nero Wolfe
Erle Stanley Gardner's Perry Mason
Earl Derr Biggers' Charlie Chan
Georges Simenon's Inspector Maigret
Edgar Allan Poe's C. Auguste Dupin
Dashiell Hammett's Sam Spade
Gilbert K. Chesterton's Father Brown
Dorothy L. Sayers' Lord Peter Wimsey
Raymond Chandler's Philip Marlowe

The immediate runners-up were:

John Dickson Carr's Dr. Gideon Fell
Ross Macdonald's Lew Archer
Margery Allingham's Albert Campion

Further runners-up included:

J. J. Marric's (John Creasey's) George Gideon
Agatha Christie's Miss Jane Marple
S. S. Van Dine's Philo Vance

Ballots were also cast for:

Leslie Charteris' Simon Templar (The Saint)
Ngaio Marsh's Roderick Alleyn
Dell Shannon's Luis Mendoza
Carter Dickson's (John Dickson Carr's) Sir Henry Merrivale
Mickey Spillane's Mike Hammer
Ian Fleming's James Bond
Wilkie Collins' Sergeant Cuff
John Creasey's Inspector Roger West

This anthology, Volume One of MASTERPIECES OF MYSTERY, contains stories by 14 of the 15 top vote-getters in the three combined polls—14 of the 15 most famous and most popular detective heroes of fiction.

Happy reading!

ELLERY QUEEN

THE ADVENTURE OF
THE ABBEY GRANGE

BY A. CONAN DOYLE

Arthur Conan Doyle was born in Edinburgh on May 22, 1859. The Doyles were strong Roman Catholics and Conan spent nine years with the Jesuits. In 1881 he received his Bachelor of Medicine degree from Edinburgh University. His observations there of Joseph Bell, an angular, skilled surgeon whose strong point was diagnosis of occupation and character as well as disease, metamorphosed six years later into the character of Sherlock Holmes. Sir Arthur was knighted in 1902 for his defense of the British cause in *The Great Boer War*. He died in 1930.

IT WAS ON a bitterly cold and frosty morning, towards the end of the winter of '97, that I was awakened by a tugging at my shoulder. It was Holmes. The candle in his hand shone upon his eager, stooping face, and told me at a glance that something was amiss.

"Come, Watson, come, Watson, come!" he cried. "The game is afoot. Not a word! Into your clothes and come!"

Ten minutes later we were both in a cab, and rattling through the silent streets on our way to Charing Cross Station. The first faint winter's dawn was beginning to appear, and we could dimly see the occasional figure of an early workman as he passed us, blurred and indistinct in the opalescent London reek. Holmes nestled in silence into his heavy coat, and I was glad to do the same, for the air was most bitter and neither of us had broken our fast.

It was not until we had consumed some hot tea at the station, and taken our places in the Kentish train, that we were sufficiently thawed, he to speak and I to listen. Holmes drew a note from his pocket, and read it aloud:—

> Abbey Grange, Marsham, Kent,
> 3.30 A.M.
>
> MY DEAR MR. HOLMES,—I should be very glad of your immediate assistance in what promises to be a most remarkable case. It is something quite in your line. Except for releasing the lady I will see that everything is kept exactly as I have found it, but I beg you not to lose an instant, as it is difficult to leave Sir Eustace there.
> Yours faithfully,
> STANLEY HOPKINS.

"Hopkins has called me in seven times, and on each occasion his summons has been entirely justified," said Holmes. "I fancy that every one of his cases has found its way into your collection, and I must admit, Watson, that you have some power of selection, which atones for much which I deplore in your narratives. Your fatal habit of looking at everything from the point of view of a story instead of as a scientific exercise has ruined what might have been an instructive and even classical series of demonstrations. You slur over work of the utmost finesse and delicacy, in order to dwell upon sensational details which may exist, but cannot possibly instruct, the reader."

"Why do you not write them yourself?" I said, with some bitterness.

"I will, my dear Watson, I will. At present I am, as you know, fairly busy, but I propose to devote my declining years to the composition of a text-book, which shall focus the whole art of detection into one volume. Our present research appears to be a case of murder."

"You think this Sir Eustace is dead, then?"

"I should say so. Hopkins' writing shows considerable agitation, and he is not an emotional man. Yes, I gather there has been violence, and that the body is left for our inspection. A mere suicide would not have caused him to send for me. As to the release of the lady, it would appear that she has been locked in her room during the tragedy. We are moving in high life, Watson, crackling paper, 'E.B.' monogram, coat-of-arms, picturesque address. I think that friend Hopkins will live up to his reputation, and that we shall have an interesting morning. The crime was committed before twelve last night."

"How can you possibly tell?"

"By an inspection of the trains, and by reckoning the time. The local police had to be called in, they had to communicate with Scotland Yard, Hopkins had to go out, and he in turn had to send for me. All that makes a fair night's work. Well, here we are at Chiselhurst Station, and we shall soon set our doubts at rest."

A drive of a couple of miles through narrow country lanes brought us to a park gate, which was opened for us by an old lodge-keeper, whose haggard face bore the reflection of some great disaster. The avenue ran through a noble park, between lines of ancient elms, and ended in a low, widespread house, pillared in front after the fashion of Palladio. The central part was evidently of a great age, and shrouded in ivy, but the large windows showed that modern changes had been carried out, and one wing of the house appeared to be entirely new. The youthful figure and alert, eager face of Inspector Stanley Hopkins confronted us in the open doorway.

"I'm very glad you have come, Mr. Holmes. And you too, Dr.

Watson. But, indeed, if I had my time over again, I should not have troubled you, for since the lady has come to herself, she has given so clear an account of the affair that there is not much left for us to do. You remember that Lewisham gang of burglars?"

"What, the three Randalls?"

"Exactly; the father and two sons. It's their work. I have not a doubt of it. They did a job in Sydenham a fortnight ago, and were seen and described. Rather cool to do another so soon and so near, but it is they, beyond all doubt. It's a hanging matter this time."

"Sir Eustace is dead, then?"

"Yes, his head was knocked in with his own poker."

"Sir Eustace Brackenstall, the driver tells me."

"Exactly—one of the richest men in Kent—Lady Brackenstall is in the morning-room. Poor lady, she has had a most dreadful experience. She seemed half dead when I saw her first. I think you had best see her, and hear her account of the facts. Then we will examine the dining-room together."

Lady Brackenstall was no ordinary person. Seldom have I seen so graceful a figure, so womanly a presence, and so beautiful a face. She was a blonde, goldenhaired, blue-eyed, and would no doubt have had the perfect complexion which goes with such colouring, had not her recent experience left her drawn and haggard. Her sufferings were physical as well as mental, for over one eye rose a hideous, plum-coloured swelling, which her maid, a tall, austere woman, was bathing assiduously with vinegar and water. The lady lay back exhausted upon a couch, but her quick, observant gaze, as we entered the room, and the alert expression of her beautiful features, showed that neither her wits nor her courage had been shaken by her terrible experience. She was enveloped in a loose dressing-gown of blue and silver, but a black sequin-covered dinnerdress was hung upon the couch beside her.

"I have told you all that happened, Mr. Hopkins," she said, wearily, "could you not repeat it for me? Well, if you think it necessary, I will tell these gentlemen what occurred. Have they been in the dining-room yet?"

"I thought they had better hear your ladyship's story first."

"I shall be glad when you can arrange matters. It is horrible to me to think of him still lying there." She shuddered and buried her face in her hands. As she did so, the loose gown fell back from her forearms. Holmes uttered an exclamation.

"You have other injuries, madam! What is this?" Two vivid red

12

spots stood out on one of the white, rounded limbs. She hastily covered it.

"It is nothing. It has no connection with this hideous business to-night. If you and your friend will sit down, I will tell you all I can.

"I am the wife of Sir Eustace Brackenstall. I have been married about a year. I suppose that it is no use my attempting to conceal that our marriage has not been a happy one. I fear that all our neighbours would tell you that, even if I were to attempt to deny it. Perhaps the fault may be partly mine. I was brought up in the freer, less conventional atmosphere of South Australia, and this English life, with its proprieties and its primness, is not congenial to me. But the main reason lies in the one fact, which is notorious to everyone, and that is that Sir Eustace was a confirmed drunkard. To be with such a man for an hour is unpleasant. Can you imagine what it means for a sensitive and highspirited woman to be tied to him for day and night? It is a sacrilege, a crime, a villainy to hold that such a marriage is binding. I say that these monstrous laws of yours will bring a curse upon the land—God will not let such wickedness endure." For an instant she sat up, her cheeks flushed, and her eyes blazing from under the terrible mark upon her brow. Then the strong, soothing hand of the austere maid drew her head down on to the cushion, and the wild anger died away into passionate sobbing. At last she continued:—

"I will tell you about last night. You are aware, perhaps that in this house all the servants sleep in the modern wing. This central block is made up of the dwelling-rooms, with the kitchen behind and our bedroom above. My maid, Theresa, sleeps above my room. There is no one else, and no sound could alarm those who are in the farther wing. This must have been well known to the robbers, or they would not have acted as they did.

"Sir Eustace retired about half-past ten. The servants had already gone to their quarters. Only my maid was up, and she had remained in her room at the top of the house until I needed her services. I sat until after eleven in this room, absorbed in a book. Then I walked round to see that all was right before I went upstairs. It was my custom to do this myself, for, as I have explained, Sir Eustace was not always to be trusted. I went into the kitchen, the butler's pantry, the gunroom, the billiard-room, the drawing-room, and finally the dining-room. As I approached the window, which is covered with thick curtains, I suddenly felt the wind blow upon my face, and realized that it was open. I flung the curtain aside, and found myself face to face with a broad-shouldered, elderly man, who had just stepped into the room. The window is a long French one, which really forms a door leading to the lawn. I held my bedroom candle lit in my hand, and, by its light, behind the first man I saw two others, who were in the act of entering. I stepped back, but the fellow was on me in an instant. He caught me first by the wrist, and then by the throat. I opened my mouth to scream, but he struck me a savage blow with his fist over the eye, and felled me to the ground. I must have been unconscious for a few minutes, for when I came to myself, I found that they had torn down the bellrope, and had secured me tightly to the oaken chair which stands at the head of the dining-table. I was so firmly bound that I could not move, and a handkerchief round my mouth prevented me from uttering a sound. It was at this instant that my unfortunate husband entered the room. He had evidently heard some suspicious sounds, and he came prepared for such a scene as he found. He was dressed in his shirt and trousers, with his favourite blackthorn cudgel in his hand. He rushed at the burglars, but another—it was an elderly man—stooped, picked the poker out of the grate, and struck him a horrible blow as he passed. He fell with a groan, and never moved again. I fainted once more, but again it could only have been for a very few minutes during which I was insensible. When I opened my eyes I found that they had collected the silver from the sideboard, and they had drawn a bottle of wine which stood there. Each of them had a glass in his hand. I have already told you, have I not, that one was elderly, with a beard, and the others young, hairless lads. They might have been a father with his two sons. They talked together in whispers. Then they came over and made sure that I was securely bound. Finally they withdrew, closing the window after them. It was quite a quarter of an hour before I got my mouth free. When I did so, my screams brought the maid to my assistance. The other servants were soon alarmed, and we sent for the local police, who instantly communicated with London. That is really all that I can tell you, gentlemen, and I trust that it will not be necessary for me to go over so painful a story again."

"Any questions, Mr. Holmes?" asked Hopkins.

"I will not impose any further tax upon Lady Brackenstall's patience and time," said Holmes. "Before I go into the dining-room, I should like to hear your experience." He looked at the maid.

"I saw the men before ever they came into the house," said she.

"As I sat by my bedroom window I saw three men in the moon-light down by the lodge gate yonder, but I thought nothing of it at the time. It was more than an hour after that I heard my mistress scream, and down I ran, to find her, poor lamb, just as she says, and him on the floor, with his blood and brains over the room. It was enough to drive a woman out of her wits, tied there, and her very dress spotted with him, but she never wanted courage, did Miss Mary Fraser of Adelaide, and Lady Brac-kenstall of Abbey Grange hasn't learned new ways. You've ques-tioned her long enough, you gentlemen, and now she is coming to her own room, just with her old Theresa, to get the rest that she badly needs."

With a motherly tenderness the gaunt woman put her arm round her mistress and led her from the room.

"She has been with her all her life," said Hopkins. "Nursed her as a baby, and came with her to England when they first left Australia, eighteen months ago. Theresa Wright is her name, and the kind of maid you don't pick up nowadays. This way, Mr. Holmes, if you please!"

The keen interest had passed out of Holmes' expressive face, and I knew that with the mystery all the charm of the case had departed. There still remained an arrest to be effected, but what were these commonplace rogues, that he should soil his hands with them? An abstruse and learned specialist who finds that he has been called in for a case of measles would experience some-thing of the annoyance which I read in my friend's eyes. Yet the scene in the dining-room of the Abbey Grange was sufficiently strange to arrest his attention and to recall his waning interest.

It was a very large and high chamber, with carved oak ceiling, oaken panelling, and a fine array of deer's heads and ancient weapons around the walls. At the further end from the door was the high, French window of which he had heard. Three smaller windows on the right-hand side filled the apartment with cold winter sunshine. On the left was a large, deep fireplace, with a massive, overhanging oak mantelpiece. Beside the fireplace was a heavy oaken chair with arms and crossbars at the bottom. In and out through the open woodwork was woven a crimson cord, which was secured at each side to the crosspiece below. In releas-ing the lady, the cord had been slipped off her, but the knots with which it had been secured still remained. These details only struck our attention afterwards, for our thoughts were entirely absorbed by the terrible object which lay upon the tiger-skin hearthrug in front of the fire.

It was the body of a tall, well-made man, about forty years of age. He lay upon his back, his face upturned, with his white teeth grinning through his short, black beard. His two clenched hands were raised above his head, and a heavy, blackthorn stick lay across them. His dark, handsome, aquiline features were convulsed into a spasm of vindictive hatred, which had set his dead face in a terribly fiendish expression. He had evidently been in his bed when the alarm had broken out, for he wore a foppish, embroidered night-shirt, and his bare feet projected from his trousers. His head was horribly injured, and the whole room bore witness to the savage ferocity of the blow which had struck him down. Beside him lay the heavy poker, bent into a curve by the concussion. Holmes examined both it and the indescribable wreck which it had wrought.

"He must be a powerful man, this elder Randall," he remarked.

"Yes," said Hopkins. "I have some record of the fellow, and he is a rough customer."

"You should have no difficulty in getting him."

"Not the slightest. We have been on the lookout for him, and there was some idea that he had got away to America. Now that we know that the gang are here, I don't see how they can escape. We have the news at every seaport already, and a reward will be offered before evening. What beats me is how they could have done so mad a thing, knowing that the lady could describe them, and that we could not fail to recognize the description."

"Exactly. One would have expected that they would have silenced Lady Brackenstall as well."

"They may not have realized," I suggested, "that she had recovered from her faint."

"That is likely enough. If she seemed to be senseless, they would not take her life. What about this poor fellow, Hopkins? I seem to have heard some queer stories about him."

"He was a good-hearted man when he was sober, but a perfect fiend when he was drunk, or rather when he was half drunk, for he seldom really went the whole way. The devil seemed to be in him at such times, and he was capable of anything. From what I hear, in spite of all his wealth and his title, he very nearly came our way once or twice. There was a scandal about his drenching a dog with petroleum and setting it on fire—her ladyship's dog, to make the matter worse—and that was only hushed up with difficulty. Then he threw a decanter at that maid, Theresa Wright, there was trouble about that. On the whole, and between

16

ourselves, it will be a bright house without him. What are you looking at now?"

Holmes was down on his knees, examining with great attention the knots upon the red cord with which the lady had been secured. Then he carefully scrutinized the broken and frayed end where it had snapped off when the burglar had dragged it down.

"When this was pulled down, the bell in the kitchen must have rung loudly," he remarked.

"No one could hear it. The kitchen stands right at the back of the house."

"How did the burglar know no one would hear it? How dared he pull at a bell-rope in that reckless fashion?"

"Exactly, Mr. Holmes, exactly. You put the very question which I have asked myself again and again. There can be no doubt that this fellow must have known the house and its habits. He must have perfectly understood that the servants would all be in bed at that comparatively early hour, and that no one could possibly hear a bell ring in the kitchen. Therefore, he must have been in close league with one of the servants. Surely that is evident. But there are eight servants, and all of good character."

"Other things being equal," said Holmes, "one would suspect the one at whose head the master threw a decanter. And yet that would involve treachery towards the mistress to whom this woman seems devoted. Well, well, the point is a minor one, and when you have Randall you will probably find no difficulty in securing his accomplice. The lady's story certainly seems to be corroborated, if it needed corroboration, by every detail which we see before us." He walked to the French window and threw it open. "There are no signs here, but the ground is iron hard, and one would not expect them. I see that these candles in the mantelpiece have been lighted."

"Yes, it was by their light, and that of the lady's bedroom candle, that the burglars saw their way about."

"And what did they take?"

"Well, they did not take much—only half a dozen articles of plate off the sideboard. Lady Brackenstall thinks that they were themselves so disturbed by the death of Sir Eustace that they did not ransack the house, as they would otherwise have done."

"No doubt that is true, and yet they drank some wine, I understand."

"To steady their nerves."

"Exactly. These three glasses upon the sideboard have been untouched, I suppose?"

"Yes, and the bottle stands as they left it."

"Let us look at it. Halloa, halloa! What is this?"

The three glasses were grouped together, all of them tinged with wine, and one of them containing some dregs of beeswing. The bottle stood near them, two-thirds full, and beside it lay a long, deeply stained cork. Its appearance and the dust upon the bottle showed that was no common vintage which the murderers had enjoyed.

A change had come over Holmes' manner. He had lost his listless expression, and again I saw an alert light of interest in his keen, deep-set eyes. He raised the cork and examined it minutely.

"How did they draw it?" he asked.

Hopkins pointed to a half-opened drawer. In it lay some table linen and a large cork-screw.

"Did Lady Brackenstall say that screw was used?"

"No, you remember that she was senseless at the moment when the bottle was opened."

"Quite so. As a matter of fact, that screw was *not* used. This bottle was opened by a pocket screw, probably contained in a knife, and not more than an inch and a half long. If you will examine the top of the cork, you will observe that the screw was driven in three times before the cork was extracted. It has never been transfixed. This long screw would have transfixed it and drawn it up with a single pull. When you catch this fellow, you will find that he has one of those multiplex knives in his possession."

"Excellent!" said Hopkins.

"But these glasses do puzzle me, I confess. Lady Brackenstall actually *saw* the three men drinking, did she not?"

"Yes, she was clear about that."

"Then there is an end of it. What more is to be said? And yet, you must admit, that the three glasses are very remarkable, Hopkins. What? You see nothing remarkable? Well, well, let it pass. Perhaps, when a man has special knowledge and special powers like my own, it rather encourages him to seek a complex explanation when a simpler one is at hand. Of course, it must be a mere chance about the glasses. Well, good morning, Hopkins. I don't see that I can be of any use to you, and you appear to have your case very clear. You will let me know when Randall is arrested, and any further developments which may occur. I trust that I shall soon have to congratulate you upon a successful conclusion. Come, Watson, I fancy that we may employ ourselves more profitably at home."

During our return journey, I could see by Holmes' face that he was much puzzled by something which he had observed. Every now and then, by an effort, he would throw off the impression, and talk as if the matter were clear, but then his doubts would settle down upon him again, and his knitted brows and abstracted eyes would show that his thought had gone back once more to the great dining-room of the Abbey Grange, in which this midnight tragedy had been enacted. At last, by a sudden impulse, just as our train was crawling out of the suburban station, he sprang on to the platform and pulled me out after him.

"Excuse me, my dear fellow," said he, as we watched the rear carriages of our train disappearing round a curve, "I am sorry to make you the victim of what may seem a mere whim, but on my life, Watson, I simply *can't* leave that case in this condition. Every instinct that I possess cries out against it. It's wrong—it's all wrong—I'll swear that it's wrong. And yet the lady's story was complete, the maid's corroboration was sufficient, the detail was fairly exact. What have I to put up against that? Three wineglasses, that is all. But if I had not taken things for granted, if I had examined everything with care which I should have shown had we approached the case *de novo* and had no cut-and-dried story to warp my mind, should I not then have found something more definite to go upon? Of course I should. Sit down on this bench, Watson, until a train for Chiselhurst arrives, and allow me to lay the evidence before you, imploring you in the first instance to dismiss from your mind the idea that anything which the maid or her mistress may have said must necessarily be true. The lady's charming personality must not be permitted to warp our judgment.

"Surely there are details in her story which, if we looked at in cold blood, would excite our suspicion. These burglars made a considerable haul at Sydenham, a fortnight ago. Some account of them and of their appearance was in the papers, and would naturally occur to anyone who wished to invent a story in which imaginary robbers should play a part. As a matter of fact, burglars who have done a good stroke of business are, as a rule, only too glad to enjoy the proceeds in peace and quiet without embarking on another perilous undertaking. Again, it is unusual for burglars to operate at so early an hour, it is unusual for burglars to strike a lady to prevent her screaming, since one would imagine that was the sure way to make her scream, it is unusual for them to commit murder when their numbers are sufficient to overpower one man, it is unusual for them to be content with a limited plunder when there was much more within their reach, and finally, I should say, that it was very unusual for such men to leave a bottle half empty. How do all these unusuals strike you, Watson?"

"Their cumulative effect is certainly considerable, and yet each of them is quite possible in itself. The most unusual thing of all, as it seems to me, is that the lady should be tied to the chair."

"Well, I am not so clear about that, Watson, for it is evident that they must either kill her or else secure her in such a way that she could not give immediate notice of their escape. But at any rate I have shown, have I not, that there is a certain element of improbability about the lady's story? And now, on the top of this, comes the incident of the wineglasses."

"What about the wineglasses?"

"Can you see them in your mind's eye?"

"I see them clearly."

"We are told that three men drank from them. Does that strike you as likely?"

"Why not? There was wine in each glass."

"Exactly, but there was beeswing only in one glass. You must have noticed that fact. What does that suggest to your mind?"

"The last glass filled would be most likely to contain beeswing."

"Not at all. The bottle was full of it, and it is inconceivable that the first two glasses were clear and the third heavily charged with it. There are two possible explanations, and only two. One is that after the second glass was filled the bottle was violently agitated, and so the third glass received the beeswing. That does not appear probable. No, no, I am sure that I am right."

"What, then, do you suppose?"

"That only two glasses were used, and that the dregs of both were poured into a third glass, so as to give the false impression that three people had been here. In that way all the beeswing would be in the last glass, would it not? Yes, I am convinced that this is so. But if I have hit upon the true explanation of this one small phenomenon, then in an instant the case rises from the commonplace to the exceedingly remarkable, for it can only mean that Lady Brackenstall and her maid have deliberately lied to us, that not one word of their story is to be believed, that they have some very strong reason for covering the real criminal, and that we must construct our case for ourselves without any help from them. That is the mission which now lies before us, and here, Watson, is the Sydenham train."

The household at the Abbey Grange were much surprised at our return, but Sherlock Holmes, finding that Stanley Hopkins had gone off to report to headquarters, took possession of the dining-room, locked the door upon the inside, and devoted himself for two hours to one of those minute and laborious investigations which form the solid basis on which his brilliant edifices of deduction were reared. Seated in a corner like an interested student who observes the demonstration of his professor, I followed every step of that remarkable research. The window, the curtains, the carpet, the chair, the rope—each in turn was minutely examined and duly pondered. The body of the unfortunate baronet had been removed, and all else remained as we had seen it in the morning. Finally, to my astonishment, Holmes climbed up on to the massive mantelpiece. Far above his head hung the few inches of red cord which were still attached to the wire. For a long time he gazed upwards at it, and then in an attempt to get nearer to it he rested his knee upon a wooden bracket on the wall. This brought his hand within a few inches of the broken end of the rope, but it was not this so much as the bracket itself which seemed to engage his attention. Finally, he sprang down with an ejaculation of satisfaction.

"It's all right, Watson," said he. "We have got our case—one of the most remarkable in our collection. But, dear me, how slow-witted I have been, and how nearly I have committed the blunder of my lifetime! Now, I think that, with a few missing links, my chain is almost complete."

"You have got your men?"

"Man, Watson, man. Only one, but a very formidable person. Strong as a lion—witness the blow that bent that poker! Six foot three in height, active as a squirrel, dexterous with his fingers, finally, remarkably quick-witted, for this whole ingenious story is of his concoction. Yes, Watson, we have come upon the handiwork of a very remarkable individual. And yet, in that bell-rope, he has given us a clue which should not have left us a doubt."

"Where was the clue?"

"Well, if you were to pull down a bell-rope, Watson, where would you expect it to break? Surely at the spot where it is attached to the wire. Why should it break three inches from the top, as this one has done?"

"Because it is frayed there?"

21

"Exactly. This end, which we can examine, is frayed. He was cunning enough to do that with his knife. But the other end is not frayed. You could not observe that from here, but if you were on the mantelpiece you would see that it is cut clean off without any mark of fraying whatever. You can reconstruct what occurred. The man needed the rope. He would not tear it down for fear of giving the alarm by ringing the bell. What did he do? He sprang up on the mantelpiece, could not quite reach it, put his knee on the bracket—you will see the impression in the dust—and so got his knife to bear upon the cord. I could not reach the place by at least three inches—from which I infer that he is at least three inches a bigger man than I. Look at that mark upon the seat of the oaken chair! What is it?"

"Blood."

"Undoubtedly it is blood. This alone puts the lady's story out of court. If she were seated on the chair when the crime was done, how comes that mark. No, no, she was placed in the chair *after* the death of her husband. I'll wager that the black-dress shows a corresponding mark to this. We have not yet met our Waterloo, Watson, but this is our Marengo, for it begins in defeat and ends in victory. I should like now to have a few words with the nurse, Theresa. We must be wary for a while, if we are to get the information which we want."

She was an interesting person, this stern Australian nurse—taciturn, suspicious, ungracious, it took sometime before Holmes' pleasant manner and frank acceptance of all that she said thawed her into a corresponding amiability. She did not attempt to conceal her hatred for her late employer.

"Yes, sir, it is true that he threw the decanter at me. I heard him call my mistress a name, and I told him that he would not dare to speak so if her brother had been there. Then it was that he threw it at me. He might have thrown a dozen if he had but left my bonny bird alone. He was forever ill-treating her, and she too proud to complain. She will not even tell me all that he has done to her. She never told me of those marks on her arm that you saw this morning, but I know very well that they come from a stab with a hatpin. The sly devil—God forgive me that I should speak of him so, now that he is dead! But a devil he was, if ever one walked the earth. He was all honey when first we met him—only eighteen months ago, and we both feel as if it were eighteen years. She had only just arrived in London. Yes, it was her first voyage—she had never been from home before. He won her with his title and his money and his false London ways.

If she made a mistake she was paid for it, if ever a woman did. What month did we meet him? Well, I tell you it was just after we arrived. We arrived in June, and it was July. They were married in January of last year. Yes, she is down in the morning-room again, and I have no doubt she will see you, but you must not ask too much of her, for she has gone through all that flesh and blood will stand."

Lady Brackenstall was reclining on the same couch, but looked brighter than before. The maid had entered with us, and began once more to foment the bruise upon her mistress' brow.

"I hope," said the lady, "that you have not come to cross-examine me again?"

"No," Holmes answered, in his gentlest voice, "I will not cause you any unnecessary trouble, Lady Brackenstall, and my whole desire is to make things easy for you, for I am convinced that you are a much-tried woman. If you will treat me as a friend and trust me, you may find that I will justify your trust."

"What do you want me to do?"

"To tell me the truth."

"Mr. Holmes!"

"No, no, Lady Brackenstall—it is no use. You may have heard of any little reputation which I possess. I will stake it all on the fact that your story is an absolute fabrication."

Mistress and maid were both staring at Holmes with pale faces and frightened eyes.

"You are an impudent fellow!" cried Theresa. "Do you mean to say that my mistress has told a lie?"

Holmes rose from his chair.

"Have you nothing to tell me?"

"I have told you everything."

"Think once more, Lady Brackenstall. Would it not be better to be frank?"

For an instant there was hesitation in her beautiful face. Then some new strong thought caused it to set like a mask.

"I have told you all I know."

Holmes took his hat and shrugged his shoulders. "I am sorry," he said, and without another word we left the room and the house. There was a pond in the park, and to this my friend led the way. It was frozen over, but a single hole was left for the convenience of a solitary swan. Holmes gazed at it, and then passed on to the lodge gate. There he scribbled a short note for Stanley Hopkins, and left it with the lodge-keeper.

"It may be a hit, or it may be a miss, but we are bound to do

23

something for friend Hopkins, just to justify this second visit," said he. "I will not quite take him into my confidence yet. I think our next scene of operations must be the shipping office of the Adelaide-Southampton line, which stands at the end of Pall Mall, if I remember right. There is a second line of steamers which connect South Australia with England, but we will draw the larger cover first."

Holmes' card sent in to the manager ensured instant attention, and he was not long in acquiring all the information he needed. In June of '95, only one of their line had reached a home port. It was the *Rock of Gibraltar*, their largest and best boat. A reference to the passenger list showed that Miss Fraser, of Adelaide, with her maid had made the voyage in her. The boat was now on her way to Australia somewhere in the south of the Suez Canal. Her officers were the same as in '95, with one exception. The first officer, Mr. Jack Crocker, had been made a captain, and was to take charge of their new ship, *The Bass Rock*, sailing in two days' time from Southampton. He lived at Sydenham, but he was likely to be in that morning for instructions, if we cared to wait for him.

No: Mr. Holmes had no desire to see him, but would be glad to know more about his record and character.

His record was magnificent. There was not an officer in the fleet to touch him. As to his character, he was reliable on duty, but a wild, desperate fellow off the deck of his ship—hot-headed, excitable, but loyal, honest, and kind-hearted. That was the pith of the information with which Holmes left the office of the Adelaide-Southampton company. Thence he drove to Scotland Yard, but, instead of entering, he sat in his cab with his brows drawn down, lost in profound thought. Finally he drove round to the Charing Cross telegraph office, sent off a message, and then, at last, we made for Baker Street once more.

"No, I couldn't do it, Watson," said he, as we reentered our room. "Once that warrant was made out, nothing on earth would save him. Once or twice in my career I feel that I have done more real harm by my discovery of the criminal than ever he had done by his crime. I have learned caution now, and I had rather play tricks with the law of England than with my own conscience. Let us know a little more before we act."

Before evening, we had a visit from Inspector Stanley Hopkins. Things were not going very well with him.

"I believe that you are a wizard, Mr. Holmes. I really do sometimes think that you have powers that are not human. Now, how on earth could you know that the stolen silver was at the bottom of that pond?"

"I didn't know it."

"But you told me to examine it."

"You got it, then?"

"Yes, I got it."

"I am very glad if I have helped you."

"But you haven't helped me. You have made the affair far more difficult. What sort of burglars are they who steal silver, and then throw it into the nearest pond?"

"It was certainly rather eccentric behaviour. I was merely going on the idea that if the silver had been taken by persons who did not want it—who merely took it for a blind, as it were, then they would naturally be anxious to get rid of it."

"But why should such an idea cross your mind?"

"Well, I thought it was possible. When they came out through the French window, there was the pond with one tempting little hole in the ice, right in front of their noses. Could there be a better hiding-place?"

"Ah, a hiding-place—that is better!" cried Stanley Hopkins. "Yes, yes, I see it all now! It was early, there were folk upon the roads, they were afraid of being seen with the silver, so they sank it in the pond, intending to return for it when the coast was clear. Excellent, Mr. Holmes—that is better than your idea of a blind."

"Quite so, you have got an admirable theory. I have no doubt that my own ideas were quite wild, but you must admit that they have ended in discovering the silver."

"Yes, sir—yes. It was all your doing. But I have had a bad setback?"

"A setback?"

"Yes, Mr. Holmes. The Randall gang were arrested in New York this morning."

"Dear Mr. Hopkins! This is certainly rather against your theory, that they committed a murder in Kent last night."

"It is fatal, Mr. Holmes—absolutely fatal. Still, there are other gangs of three besides the Randalls, or it may be some new gang of which the police have never heard."

"Quite so, it is perfectly possible. What, are you off?"

"Yes, Mr. Holmes, there is no rest for me until I have got to the bottom of the business. I suppose you have no hint to give me?"

"I have given you one."

"Which?"

"Well, I suggested a blind."

"But why, Mr. Holmes, why?"

"Ah, that's the question, of course. But I commend the idea to your mind. You might possibly find that there was something in it. You won't stop for dinner? Well, good-bye, and let us know how you get on."

Dinner was over, and the table cleared before Holmes alluded to the matter again. He had lit his pipe and held his slippered feet to the cheerful blaze of the fire. Suddenly he looked at his watch.

"I expect developments, Watson."

"When?"

"Now—within a few minutes. I dare say you thought I acted rather badly to Stanley Hopkins just now?"

"I trust your judgment."

"A very sensible reply, Watson. You must look at it this way: what I know is unofficial, what he knows is official. I have the right to private judgment, but he has none. He must disclose all, or he is a traitor to his service. In a doubtful case I would not put him in so painful a position, and so I reserve my information until my own mind is clear upon the matter."

"But when will that be?"

"The time has come. You will now be present at the last scene of a remarkable little drama."

There was a sound upon the stairs, and our door was opened to admit as fine a specimen of manhood as ever passed through it. He was a very young man, golden-moustached, blue-eyed, with a skin which had been burned by tropical suns, and a springy step, which showed that the huge frame was as active as it was strong. He closed the door behind him, and then he stood with clenched hands and heaving breast, choking down some overmastering emotion.

"Sit down, Captain Crocker. You got my telegram?"

Our visitor sank into an arm-chair, and looked from one to the other of us with questioning eyes.

"I got your telegram, and I came at the hour you said. I heard that you had been down to the office. There was no getting away from you. Let's hear the worst. What are you going to do with me? Arrest me? Speak out, man! You can't sit there and play with me like a cat with a mouse."

"Give him a cigar," said Holmes. "Bite on that, Captain Crocker, and don't let your nerves run away with you. I should not sit here smoking with you if I thought that you were a common criminal, you may be sure of that. Be frank with me and we may

26

do some good. Play tricks with me, and I'll crush you."

"What do you wish me to do?"

"To give me a true account of all that happened at the Abbey Grange last night—a *true* account, mind you, with nothing added and nothing taken off. I know so much already that if you go one inch off the straight, I'll blow this police whistle from my window and the affair goes out of my hands forever."

The sailor thought for a little. Then he struck his leg with his great sun-burned hand.

"I'll chance it," he cried, "I believe you are a man of your word, and a white man, and I'll tell you the whole story. But one thing I will say first. So far as I am concerned, I regret nothing and I fear nothing, and I would do it all again, and be proud of the job. Damn the beast, if he had as many lives as a cat, he would owe them all to me! But it's the lady, Mary—Mary Fraser—for never will I call her by that accursed name. When I think of getting her into trouble, I who would give my life just to bring one smile to her dear face, it's that that turns my soul into water. And yet— and yet—what less could I do? I'll tell you my story, gentlemen, and then I'll ask you, as man to man, what less could I do.

"I must go back a bit. You seem to know everything, so I expect that you know that I met her when she was a passenger and I was first officer of the *Rock of Gibraltar*. From the first day I met her, she was the only woman to me. Every day of that voyage I loved her more, and many a time since have I kneeled down in the darkness of the night watch and kissed the deck of that ship because I knew her dear feet had trod it. She was never engaged to me. She treated me as fairly as ever a woman treated a man. I have no complaint to make. It was all love on my side, and all good comradeship and friendship on hers. When we parted she was a free woman, but I could never again be a free man.

"Next time I came back from sea, I heard of her marriage. Well, why shouldn't she marry whom she liked? Title and money—who could carry them better than she? She was born for all that is beautiful and dainty. I didn't grieve over her marriage. I was not such a selfish hound as that. I just rejoiced that good luck had come her way, and that she had not thrown herself away on a penniless sailor. That's how I loved Mary Fraser.

"Well, I never thought to see her again, but last voyage I was promoted, and the new boat was not yet launched, so I had to wait for a couple of months with my people at Sydenham. One day out in a country lane I met Theresa Wright, her old maid.

27

She told me all about her, about him, about everything. I tell you, gentlemen, it nearly drove me mad. This drunken hound, that he should dare to raise his hand to her, whose boots he was not worthy to lick! I met Theresa again. Then I met Mary herself —and met her again. Then she would meet me no more. But the other day I had a notice that I was to start on my voyage within a week, and I determined that I would see her once before I left. Theresa was always my friend, for she loved Mary and hated this villain almost as much as I did. From her I learned the ways of the house. Mary used to sit up reading in her own little room downstairs. I crept round there last night and scratched at the window. At first she would not open to me, but in her heart I know that now she loves me, and she could not leave me in the frosty night. She whispered to me to come round to the big front window, and I found it open before me, so as to let me into the dining-room. Again I heard from her own lips things that made my blood boil, and again I cursed this brute, who mishandled the woman I loved. Well, gentlemen, I was standing with her just inside the window, in all innocence as God is my judge, when he rushed like a madman into the room, called her the vilest name that a man could use to a woman, and welted her across the face with the stick he had in his hand. I had sprung for the poker, and it was a fair fight between us. See here, on my arm, where his first blow fell. Then it was my turn, and I went through him as if he had been a rotten pumpkin. Do you think I was sorry? Not I! It was his life or mine, but far more than that, it was his life or hers, for how could I leave her in the power of this madman? That was how I killed him. Was I wrong? Well, then, what would either of you gentlemen have done, if you had been in my position?

"She had screamed when he struck her, and that brought old Theresa down from the room above. There was a bottle of wine on the sideboard, and I opened it and poured a little between Mary's lips, for she was half dead with shock. Then I took a drop myself. Theresa was as cool as ice, and it was her plot as much as mine. We must make it appear that burglars had done the thing. Theresa kept on repeating our story to her mistress, while I swarmed up and cut the rope of the bell. Then I lashed her in her chair, and frayed out the end of the rope to make it look natural, else they would wonder how in the world a burglar could have got up there to cut it. Then I gathered up a few plates and pots of silver, to carry out the idea of the robbery, and there I left them, with orders to give the alarm when I had a quarter of an hour's start. I dropped the silver into the pond, and made off for Sydenham, feeling that for once in my life I had done a real good night's work. And that's the truth and the whole truth, Mr. Holmes, if it costs me my neck."

Holmes smoked for some time in silence. Then he crossed the room, and shook our visitor by the hand.

"That's what I think," said he. "I know that every word is true, for you have hardly said a word which I did not know. No one but an acrobat or a sailor could have got up to that bellrope from the bracket, and no one but a sailor could have made the knots with which the cord was fastened to the chair. Only once had this lady been brought into contact with sailors, and that was on her voyage, and it was someone of her own class of life, since she was trying hard to shield him, and so showing that she loved him. You see how easy it was for me to lay my hands upon you when once I had started upon the right trail."

"I thought the police never could have seen through our dodge."

"And the police haven't, nor will they, to the best of my belief. Now, look here, Captain Crocker, this is a very serious matter, though I am willing to admit that you acted under the most extreme provocation to which any man could be subjected. I am not sure that in defence of your life your action will not be pronounced legitimate. However, that is for a British jury to decide. Meanwhile I have so much sympathy for you that if you choose to disappear in the next twenty-four hours, I will promise you that no one will hinder you."

"And then it will all come out?"

"Certainly it will come out."

The sailor flushed with anger.

"What sort of proposal is that to make a man? I know enough of law to understand that Mary would be held as accomplice. Do you think I would leave her alone to face the music while I slunk away? No, sir, let them do their worst upon me, but for Heaven's sake, Mr. Holmes, find some way of keeping my poor Mary out of the courts."

Holmes for a second time held out his hand to the sailor.

"I was only testing you, and you ring true every time. Well, it is a great responsibility that I take upon myself, but I have given Hopkins an excellent hint, and if he can't avail himself of it I can do no more. See here, Captain Crocker, we'll do this in due form of law. You are the prisoner. Watson, you are a British jury, and I never met a man who was more eminently fitted to represent one. I am the judge. Now, gentleman of the jury, you have heard the evidence. Do you find the prisoner guilty or not guilty?"

"Not guilty, my lord," said I.

"Vox populi, vox Dei. You are acquitted, Captain Crocker. So long as the law does not find some other victim you are safe from me. Come back to this lady in a year, and may her future and yours justify us in the judgment which we have pronounced this night!"

THE DREAM

BY AGATHA CHRISTIE

Agatha Christie was born Agatha Mary Clarissa Miller in Devon, England, on September 15, 1890. Her father, a New Yorker, died when she was a child and she was raised by her mother, who encouraged her from an early age to write stories and poems. Two of her fictional detectives, Hercule Poirot and Jane Marple, are among the most famous in the world. *Curtain* represents the peerless Dame Agatha's 86th novel and she has written dozens of short stories and plays, including *The Mousetrap*, now in its 24th year at the Ambassador Theater in London. She died on January 12, 1976.

HERCULE POIROT GAVE THE house a steady, appraising glance. His eyes wandered to its surroundings—the shops, the big factory building opposite, the blocks of cheap mansion flats.

Then his eyes returned to Northway House, relic of an earlier age of space and leisure, when green fields had surrounded its well-bred arrogance. Now it was an anachronism, submerged and forgotten in the sea of modern London.

Few people could have told you to whom it belonged, though its owner's name would have been recognized as one of the world's richest men. But money can quench publicity as well as flaunt it. Benedict Farley, that eccentric millionaire, chose not to advertise his choice of residence.

He himself was rarely seen. From time to time he appeared at board meetings, his lean figure, beaked nose, and rasping voice easily dominating the assembled directors. Apart from that, he was just a well-known figure of legend.

There were his strange meannesses, his incredible generosities, his famous patchwork dressing gown, now reputed to be twenty-eight years old, his invariable diet of cabbage soup and caviar, his hatred of cats. All these things the public knew.

Hercule Poirot knew them also. It was all he did know of the man he was about to visit. The letter in his coat pocket told him little more.

He pressed the bell, glancing as he did so at the neat wrist watch which had at last replaced the large turnip-faced watch of earlier days. It was exactly 9:30.

The door opened after just the right interval. A perfect specimen of the genus butler stood outlined against the lighted hall.

"Mr. Benedict Farley?" asked Hercule Poirot.

The impersonal glance surveyed him from head to foot, inoffensively but effectively.

En gros et en detail, thought Hercule Poirot to himself with appreciation.

"You have an appointment, sir?" asked the suave voice.

"Yes."

"Your name, sir?"

"M. Hercule Poirot."

The butler bowed and drew back. But there was yet one more formality before the deft hands took hat and stick from the visitor.

"You will excuse me, sir. I was to ask for a letter."

With deliberation, Poirot took from his pocket the folded letter and handed it to the butler. The latter gave it a mere glance, then returned it with a bow. Its contents were simple:

Northway House, W. 8

M. HERCULE POIROT.

Dear Sir: Mr. Benedict Farley would like to have the benefit of your advice. If convenient to yourself, he would be glad if you would call upon him at the above address at 9:39 tomorrow (Thursday) evening.

Yours truly,

HUGO CORNWORTHY,
Secretary.

P.S.: Please bring this letter with you.

The butler said, "Will you please come up to Mr. Cornworthy's room?" and led the way up the broad staircase. Poirot followed him, looking with appreciation at such *objets d' art* as were of an opulent and florid nature. His taste in art was always of a bourgeois nature.

On the upper floor the butler knocked on a door.

Hercule Poirot's eyebrows rose very slightly. It was the first jarring note. For the best butlers do not knock at doors, and yet, indubitably, this was a first-class butler.

A voice from within called out something. The butler threw open the door. He announced—and again Poirot sensed the deliberate departure from orthodoxy, "The gentleman you are expecting, sir."

It was a fair-sized room, very plainly furnished in a workman-like fashion. Filing cabinets, books of reference, a couple of easy chairs, and an imposing desk covered with neatly docketed papers. The only light came from a big green-shaded reading lamp which stood on a small table by the arm of one of the easy chairs. It was placed so as to cast its full light on anyone approaching from the door.

Hercule Poirot blinked, realizing that the lamp bulb was at least one hundred and fifty watts. In the armchair sat a thin figure in a patchwork dressing gown—Benedict Farley. His head was stuck forward in a characteristic attitude, his beaked nose projecting like that of a bird. A crest of white hair like that of a cockatoo rose above his forehead. His eyes glittered behind thick lenses as he peered suspiciously at his visitor.

"Hey," he said at last, and his voice was shrill and harsh. "So you're Hercule Poirot, hey?"

"At your service," said Poirot politely, and bowed.

"Sit down—sit down," said the old man testily.

Hercule Poirot sat down in the full glare of the lamp. From behind it the old man seemed to be studying him attentively.

"How do I know you're Hercule Poirot, hey?" he demanded fretfully. "Tell me that, hey?"

Once more Poirot drew the letter from his pocket and handed it to Farley.

"Yes," admitted the millionaire grudgingly. "That's it. That's what I got Cornworthy to write." He folded it up and tossed it back. "So you're the fellow, are you?"

With a little wave of his hand, Poirot said, "I assure you there is no deception."

Benedict Farley chuckled suddenly. "That's what the conjurer says just before he takes the rabbit out of the hat. Saying that is part of the trick, you know."

Poirot did not reply.

Farley said suddenly, "Think I'm a suspicious old man, hey? So I am. Don't trust anybody! That's my motto. Can't trust anybody when you're rich. No, no, it doesn't do."

"You wished," Poirot hinted gently, "to consult me?"

The old man nodded. "That's right. Always buy the best. That's my motto. Go to the expert and don't count the cost. You'll notice, M. Poirot, I haven't asked you your fee. Send me the bill later. I shan't cut up rough over it. Damned fools at the dairy thought they could charge me two and nine for eggs when two and seven's the market price. Lot of swindlers! I won't be swindled. But the man at the top's different. He's worth the money. I'm at the top myself; I know."

Hercule Poirot made no reply. He listened attentively, his head poised a little on one side.

Behind his impassive exterior he was conscious of a feeling of disappointment. He could not exactly put his finger on it. So far, Benedict Farley had conformed to the popular idea of himself, and yet Poirot was disappointed.

"The man," he said disgustedly to himself, "is a mountebank; nothing but a mountebank."

34

He had known other millionaires, eccentric men, too, but in nearly every case he had been conscious of a certain force, an inner energy that had commanded his respect. If they had worn a patchwork dressing gown, it would have been because they liked wearing such a dressing gown. But the dressing gown of Benedict Farley, or so it seemed to Poirot, was essentially a stage property. And the man himself was essentially stagy.

He said again, unemotionally, "You wished to consult me, Mr. Farley?"

Abruptly, the millionaire's manner changed. He leaned forward. His voice dropped to a croak.

"Yes. Yes. I want to hear what you've got to say—what you think. Go to the top! That's my way! The best doctor—the best detective—it's between the two of them."

"As yet, monsieur, I do not understand."

"Naturally," snapped Farley. "I haven't begun to tell you."

He leaned forward once more and shot out an abrupt question. "What do you know, M. Poirot, about dreams?"

The little man's eyebrows rose. Whatever he had expected, it was not this.

"For that, Monsieur Farley, I should recommend Napoleon's Book of Dreams, or the latest practicing psychologist from Harley Street."

Benedict Farley said soberly, "I've tried both."

There was a pause, then the millionaire spoke; at first almost in a whisper, then with a voice growing higher and higher.

"It's the same dream, night after night. And I'm afraid. It's always the same. I'm sitting in my room next door to this. Sitting at my desk, writing. There's a clock there, and I glance at it and see the time—exactly twenty-eight minutes past three. Always the same time, you understand. And when I see the time, M. Poirot, I know I've got to do it. I don't want to do it, but I've got to."

Unperturbed, Poirot said, "And what is it that you have to do?"

Benedict Farley said hoarsely, "At twenty-eight minutes past three I open the second drawer down on the right of my desk, take out the revolver that I keep there, load it, and walk over to the window. And then—and then—"

Benedict Farley said, in a whisper, "Then I shoot myself."

There was a silence; then Poirot said, "That is your dream? The same every night?"

"Yes."

"What happens after you shoot yourself?"

"I wake up."

Poirot nodded his head slowly and thoughtfully. "As a matter of interest, do you keep a revolver in that particular drawer?"

"Yes."

"Why?"

"I have always done so. It is as well to be prepared."

"Prepared for what?"

Farley said irritably, "All rich men have enemies."

Poirot remained silent for a moment or two, then he said, "Why exactly did you send for me?"

"I will tell you. First of all, I consulted a doctor—three doctors, to be exact. The first told me it was all a question of diet. He was an elderly man. The second was a young man of the modern school. He assured me that it all hinged on a certain event that took place in infancy at that particular time of day—three twenty-eight. I am so determined, he says, not to remember that event that I symbolize it by destroying myself. That was his explanation."

"And the third doctor?"

Benedict Farley's voice rose in shrill anger. "He's a young man too. He has a preposterous theory! He asserts that my life is so unbearable to me that I deliberately want to end it! But since to acknowledge that essentially I am a failure, I refuse in my waking moments to face the truth. But when I am asleep, all inhibitions are removed, and I proceed to do that which I really wish to do. I put an end to myself."

Poirot said, "His view is that you really wish, unknown to yourself, to commit suicide?"

Benedict Farley cried shrilly, "And that's impossible—impossible! I'm perfectly happy! I've got everything I want—everything money can buy! It's fantastic, unbelievable, even to suggest a thing like that!"

Poirot looked at him with interest. Perhaps something in the shaking hands, the trembling shrillness of the voice, warned him that the denial was too vehement. He contented himself with saying, "And where do I come in, monsieur?"

Benedict Farley calmed down suddenly. He tapped with an emphatic finger on the table beside him.

"Because there's another possibility. And if it's right, you're the man to know about it! You're famous, you've had hundreds of cases—fantastic, improbable cases! You'd know if anyone does."

"Know what?"

Farley's voice dropped to a whisper. "Supposing someone wants to kill *me*. Could they do it this way? Could they make me dream that dream night after night?"

"Hypnotism, you mean?"

"Yes."

"It would be possible, I suppose," Poirot said at last. "It is more a question for a doctor."

"You don't know of such a case in your experience?"

"Not precisely on those lines, no."

"You see what I'm driving at? I'm made to dream the same dream night after night, night after night, and then one day the suggestion is too much for me, and I act on it. I do what I've dreamed of so often—kill myself!"

Slowly, Hercule Poirot shook his head.

Farley said, "You don't think that is possible?"

"Possible?" Poirot shook his head. "That is not a word I care to meddle with."

"But you think it improbable."

"Most improbable."

Benedict Farley murmured, "The doctor said so, too." Then, his voice rising shrilly again, he cried out, "But why do I have this dream? Why? Why?"

Hercule Poirot shook his head.

Benedict Farley said abruptly, "You're sure you've never come across anything like this in your experience?"

"Never."

"That's what I wanted to know."

Delicately, Hercule Poirot cleared his throat. "You permit," he said, "a question?"

"What is it? What is it? Say what you like."

"Who is it you suspect of wanting to kill you?"

"Nobody. Nobody at all."

Poirot persisted, "But the idea presented itself to your mind?"

"I wanted to know if it was a possibility."

"Speaking from my own experience, I should say, no. Have you ever been hypnotized, by the way?"

"Of course not. D'you think I'd lend myself to such tom-foolery?"

"Then I think one can say that your theory is definitely improbable."

"But the dream, you fool—the dream!"

"The dream is certainly remarkable," said Poirot thoughtfully. "I should like to see the scene of this drama—the desk, the clock, the revolver."

"Of course. I'll take you next door."

Wrapping the folds of his dressing gown round him, the old man half rose from his chair. Then suddenly he resumed his seat.

"No," he said. "There's nothing to see there. I've told you all there is to tell."

"But I should like to see for myself."

Benedict Farley snapped out, "There's no need. You've given me your opinion."

Poirot shrugged. "As you please." He rose. "I am sorry, M. Farley, that I have not been able to be of assistance to you."

Benedict Farley was staring straight ahead of him.

"Don't want a lot of hanky-pankying around," he growled out. "I've told you the facts; you can't make anything of them. That closes the matter. You can send me in a bill for a consultation fee."

"I shall not fail to do so," said the detective dryly. He walked toward the door.

"Stop a minute." The millionaire called him back. "That letter—I want it."

Poirot's eyebrows rose. He drew out a folded sheet and handed it to the old man. The latter scrutinized it, then put it down on the table beside him with a nod.

Once more Hercule Poirot walked to the door. He was puzzled. His busy mind was going over and over the story he had been told. Yet in the midst of his mental preoccupation, a nagging sense of something wrong obtruded itself. And that something had to do with himself, not with Benedict Farley.

With his hand on the doorknob, his mind cleared. He, Hercule Poirot, had been guilty of an error! He turned back once more.

"A thousand pardons! In the interest of your problem, I have committed a folly! That letter I handed to you—by mischance I put my hand into my right-hand pocket—"

"What's all this? What's all this?"

"The letter that I handed you just now—an apology from my laundress concerning the treatment of my collars." Poirot was smiling, apologetic. He dipped into his left-hand pocket. "This is your letter."

38

Benedict Farley snatched at it and grunted. "Why the devil don't you mind what you're doing?"

Poirot retrieved his laundress' communication, apologized gracefully once more, and left the room.

The butler was in the hall below, waiting to let him out.

"Can I get you a taxi, sir?"

"No, I thank you. The night is fine. I will walk."

Hercule Poirot stopped a moment on the sidewalk, waiting for a pause in the traffic to cross the busy street.

A frown creased his forehead. "No," he said to himself. "I do not understand at all. Nothing makes sense. Regrettable to have to admit it, but I, Hercule Poirot, am completely baffled."

The second act followed a week later. It opened with a telephone call from John Stillingfleet, M.D.

He said, with a lack of medical decorum, "That you, Poirot, old horse? Stillingfleet here."

"Ah, yes, my friend. What is it?"

"I'm speaking from Northway House—Benedict Farley's."

"Ah, yes?" Poirot's voice quickened with interest. "What of Mr. Farley?"

"Farley's dead. Shot himself this afternoon."

There was a pause, then Poirot said, "Yes."

"I notice you're not overcome with surprise. Know something about it, old horse?"

"Why should you think that?"

"Well, it isn't brilliant deduction or telepathy or anything like that. We found a note from Farley to you, making an appointment about a week ago. Perhaps you'd come round?"

"I will come immediately."

"Good for you, old boy. Some dirty work at the crossroads, eh?"

Poirot merely repeated that he would set forth immediately.

"Don't want to spill the beans over the telephone? Quite right. So long."

A quarter of an hour later, Poirot was sitting in the library, a low long room at the back of Northway House, on the ground floor. There were five other persons in the room: Inspector Barnett, Doctor Stillingfleet, Mrs. Farley, the widow of the millionaire, Joanna Farley, his only daughter, and Hugo Cornworthy, his private secretary.

Doctor Stillingfleet, whose professional manner was entirely different from his telephonic style, was a tall, long-faced young man of thirty. Mrs. Farley was obviously much younger than her husband. She was a handsome dark-haired woman. Her mouth was hard and her black eyes gave no clue to her emotions. She appeared perfectly self-possessed.

Joanna Farley had fair hair and a freckled face. The prominence of her nose and chin was clearly inherited from her father. Her eyes were intelligent and shrewd.

Hugo Cornworthy was a somewhat colorless young man, very correctly dressed. He seemed intelligent and efficient.

Poirot narrated simply the circumstances of his visit and the story told to him by Benedict Farley. He could not complain of any lack of interest.

"Most extraordinary story I've ever heard!" said the Inspector. "A dream, eh? . . . Did you know anything about this, Mrs. Farley?"

She bowed her head. "My husband mentioned it to me. It upset him very much I—I told him it was indigestion—his diet, you know, was very peculiar—and suggested his calling in Doctor Stillingfleet."

That young man shook his head. "He didn't consult me. From M. Poirot's story, I gather he went to Harley Street."

"I would like your advice on that point, Doctor," said Poirot. "Mr. Farley told me that he consulted three specialists. What do you think of the theories they advanced?"

Stillingfleet frowned. "It's difficult to say. You've got to take into account that what he passed on to you wasn't exactly what had been said to him. It was a layman's interpretation."

"You mean he had got the phraseology wrong?"

"Not exactly. I mean they would put a thing to him in professional terms, he'd get the meaning a little distorted, and then he'd recast it in his own language."

"So that what he told me was not really what the doctors said."

"He's just got it all a little wrong, if you know what I mean."

"Is it known whom he consulted?" Poirot asked.

Mrs. Farley shook her head.

Joanna Farley spoke up, "None of us had any idea he had consulted anyone."

Poirot said, "Did he speak to you about his dream?"

The girl shook her head.

"And you, Mr. Cornworthy?"

"No, he said nothing at all. I took down the letter to you at his dictation, but I had no idea as to why he wished to consult you. I thought it might possibly have something to do with some business irregularity."

40

Poirot asked, "And now as to the actual facts of Mr. Farley's death?"

When no one spoke, Inspector Barnett took upon himself the role of spokesman.

"Mr. Farley was in the habit of working in his own room on the first floor every afternoon. I understand that there was a big merger of businesses in prospect—"

He looked at Hugo Cornworthy, who said, "Consolidated Coach Lines."

"In connection with that," continued Barnett, "Mr. Farley had agreed to give an interview to two members of the press. He seldom did anything of the kind, I understand. Accordingly, two reporters arrived at a quarter past three by appointment. They waited ouside Mr. Farley's door—which was the customary place for people to wait who had an appointment with Mr. Farley. At twenty past three, a messenger arrived from the office of Consolidated Coach Lines with some urgent papers. On his leaving, Mr. Farley accompanied him to the door of the room, and from there spoke to the two members of the press.

"He said, 'I am sorry, gentlemen, to have to keep you waiting, but I have some urgent business to attend to. I will be as quick as I can.'

"The two gentlemen, Mr. Adams and Mr. Stoddart, assured Mr. Farley that they would await his convenience. He went back into his room, shut the door, and was never seen alive again."

"Continue," said Poirot.

"At a little after four o'clock," went on the Inspector, "Mr. Cornworthy here came out of his room, which is next door to Mr. Farley's, and was surprised to see the two reporters still waiting. He wanted Mr. Farley's signature on some letters and thought he had also better remind him that these two gentlemen were waiting. He accordingly went into Mr. Farley's room. To his surprise, he at first thought the room was empty. Then he caught sight of a boot sticking out behind the desk, which is placed in front of the window. He found Mr. Farley lying there dead, a revolver beside him.

"Mr. Cornworthy hurried out of the room and directed the butler to ring up Doctor Stillingfleet. By the latter's advice, Mr. Cornworthy also informed the police."

Poirot asked, "Was the shot heard by anyone?"

"No. The traffic is very noisy here and the landing window was open. It would be most unlikely if it had been noticed."

41

Poirot nodded thoughtfully. "What time is it supposed he died?" he asked.

Stillingfleet said, "I examined the body as soon as I got here—that is, at thirty-two minutes past four. Mr. Farley had been dead at least an hour."

Poirot's face was very grave. "So then, it seems possible that his death could have occurred at twenty-eight minutes past three."

"Exactly," said Stillingfleet.

"Any finger marks on the revolver?"

"Yes, his own."

"And the revolver itself?"

The Inspector took up the tale. "Was one which he kept in the drawer of his desk, just as he told you. Mrs. Farley has identified it positively. Moreover, you understand, there is only one entrance to the room—the door giving onto the landing. The two reporters were sitting exactly opposite that door, and they swear that no one entered the room from the time Mr. Farley spoke to them until Mr. Cornworthy went in at a little after four o'clock."

"So that there is every reason to suppose that Mr. Farley committed suicide?"

Inspector Barnett smiled a little. "There would have been no doubt at all, but for one point."

"And that?"

"The letter written to you."

Poirot smiled too. "I see! Where Hercule Poirot is concerned, immediately the suspicion of murder arises!"

"Precisely," said the Inspector dryly. "However, after your clearing up of the situation—"

Poirot interrupted him, "One little minute." He turned to Mrs. Farley. "Had your husband ever been hypnotized?"

"Never."

"Had he studied the question of hypnotism? Was he interested in the subject?"

She shook her head. "I don't think so." Suddenly her self-control seemed to break down. "That horrible dream! It's uncanny! That he should have dreamed that, night after night, and then—and then—it's as though he were—hounded to death!"

Poirot remembered Benedict Farley saying, *I proceed to do that which I really wish to do. I put an end to myself.*

He said, "Had it ever occurred to you that your husband might be tempted to do away with himself?"

"No—at least—sometimes he was very queer."

Joanna Farley's voice broke in, clear and scornful. "Father

42

would never have killed himself. He was far too careful of himself."

Doctor Stillingfleet said, "It isn't the people who threaten to commit suicide who usually do it, you know, Miss Farley. That's why suicides sometimes seem unaccountable."

Poirot rose to his feet. "Is it permitted," he asked, "that I see the room where the tragedy occurred?"

The doctor accompanied Poirot upstairs.

Benedict Farley's room was a much larger one than the secretary's next door. It was luxuriously furnished with deep leather-covered armchairs, a thick pile carpet, and a superb outsize writing desk.

Poirot passed behind the desk to where a dark stain on the carpet showed just before the window. He remembered the millionaire saying; *At twenty-eight minutes past three I open the second drawer down on the right of my desk, take out the revolver that I keep there, load it, and walk over to the window. And then—and then I shoot myself.*

He nodded slowly. Then he said, "The window was open like this?"

"Yes. But nobody could have got in that way."

Poirot put his head out. There was no sill or parapet and no pipes near. Not even a cat could have gained access that way. Opposite rose the blank wall of the factory, a dead wall with no windows in it.

Stillingfleet said, "Funny room for a rich man. It's like looking out onto a prison wall."

"Yes," said Poirot. He drew his head in and stared at the expanse of solid brick. "I think," he said "that wall is important."

Stillingfleet looked at him curiously.

"You mean, psychologically?"

Poirot had moved to the desk. Idly, or so it seemed, he picked up a pair of what are usually called lazy tongs. He pressed the handles; the tongs shot out to their full length. Delicately, Poirot picked up a burned match stump with them from beside a chair some feet away and conveyed it carefully to the wastepaper basket.

He murmured, "An ingenious invention"—and replaced the tongs neatly on the writing table. Then he asked, "Where were Mrs. Farley and Miss Farley at the time of the—death?"

"Mrs. Farley was resting in her room on the floor above this. Miss Farley was painting in her studio at the top of the house."

Hercule Poirot drummed idly with his fingers on the table. Then he said, "I should like to see Miss Farley."

Stillingfleet glanced at him curiously, then left the room. In another minute or two the door opened and Joanna Farley came in.

"You do not mind, mademoiselle, if I ask you a few questions?"

She returned his glance coolly. "Please ask anything you choose."

"Did you know that your father kept a revolver in his desk?"

"No."

"Where were you and your mother—that is to say, your stepmother—that is right?"

"Yes, Louise is my father's second wife. She is only eight years older than I am. You were about to say—?"

"Where were you and she on Thursday of last week? That is to say, on Thursday night."

"Thursday? Let me see. Oh, yes, we had gone to the theater. To see *The Little Dog Laughed*."

"Your father did not suggest accompanying you?"

"He never went out to theaters."

"He was not a very sociable man?"

The girl looked at him directly.

"My father," she said, "had a singularly unpleasant personality. No one who lived in close association with him could possibly have been fond of him."

"That, mademoiselle, is a very candid statement."

"I am saving you time, M. Poirot. I realize quite well what you are getting at. My stepmother married my father for his money. I lived here because I had no money to live elsewhere. There is a man I wish to marry—a poor man—my father saw to it that he lost his job. He wanted me, you see, to marry well—an easy matter, since I was to be his heiress!"

"Your father's fortune passes to you?"

"Yes. That is, he left Louise, my stepmother, a quarter of a million free of tax, and there are other legacies, but the residue goes to me." She smiled suddenly. "So, you see, M. Poirot, I had every reason to desire my father's death!"

"I see, mademoiselle, that you have inherited your father's intelligence."

She said thoughtfully, "Father was clever. One felt that with him—that he had force, driving power, but it had all turned sour—bitter. There was no humanity left."

Hercule Poirot said softly, "*Grand Dieu*, but what an imbecile I am."

Joanna Farley turned toward the door. "Is there anything more?"

"Two little questions. These tongs here"—he picked up the lazy tongs—"were they always on the table?"

"Yes. Father used them for picking up things. He didn't like stooping."

"One other question: Was your father's eyesight good?"

She stared at him. "Oh, no, he couldn't see at all. I mean, he couldn't see without his glasses. His sight had always been bad from a boy."

"But with his glasses?"

"Oh, he could see all right then, of course."

"He could read newspapers and fine print?"

"Oh, yes."

"That is all, mademoiselle." As she went out of the room, Poirot murmured, "I was stupid. It was there all the time, under my nose. And because it was so near I could not see it."

He leaned out of the window once more.

Below, in the narrow way between house and factory, he saw a small dark object.

Hercule Poirot nodded, satisfied. He went downstairs again. The others were still in the library.

Poirot addressed himself to the secretary. "I want you, Mr. Cornworthy, to recount to me in detail the exact circumstances of Mr. Farley's summons to me. When, for instance, did Mr. Farley dictate that letter?"

"On Wednesday afternoon about five thirty."

"Were there any special directions about posting it?"

"He told me to post it myself, and I did."

"Did he give any special instructions to the butler about admitting me?"

"Yes. He told me to tell Holmes—Holmes is the butler—that a gentleman would be calling at nine thirty. He was to ask the gentleman's name. He was also to ask to see the letter."

"Rather peculiar precautions, don't you think?"

Cornworthy shrugged. "Mr. Farley," he said carefully, "was rather a peculiar man."

"Any other instructions?"

"Yes. He told me to take the evening off, and immediately after dinner I went to the cinema."

"When did you return?"

45

"I let myself in about a quarter past eleven."

"Did you see Mr. Farley again that evening?"

"No."

"And he did not mention the matter the next morning?"

"No."

Poirot paused a moment, then resumed, "When I arrived, I was not shown into Mr. Farley's own room."

"No. He told me that I was to tell Holmes to show you into my room."

"Why was that? Do you know?"

Cornworthy shook his head. "I never questioned any of Mr. Farley's orders," he said dryly. "He would have resented it if I had."

"Did he usually receive visitors in his own room?"

"Usually, but not always. Sometimes he saw them in my room."

"Was there any reason for that?"

Hugo Cornworthy considered. "No, I hardly think so. I've never really thought about it."

Turning to Mrs. Farley, Poirot asked, "You permit that I ring for your butler?"

"Certainly, M. Poirot."

Very correct, very urbane, Holmes answered the bell. Mrs. Farley indicated Poirot with a gesture.

"What were your instructions, Holmes, on the Thursday night when I came here?"

Holmes cleared his throat, then said, "After dinner, Mr. Cornworthy told me that Mr. Farley expected a Mr. Hercule Poirot at nine thirty. I was to ascertain the gentleman's name, and I was to verify the information by glancing at a letter. Then I was to show him up to Mr. Cornworthy's room."

"Were you also told to knock on the door?"

An expression of distaste crossed the butler's countenance.

"That was one of Mr. Farley's orders. I was always to knock when introducing visitors—business visitors, that is," he added.

"Ah, that puzzled me! Were you given any other instructions concerning me?"

"No, sir. When Mr. Cornworthy had told me what I have just repeated to you, he went out."

"What time was that?"

"Ten minutes to nine, sir."

"Did you see Mr. Farley after that?"

"Yes sir, I took him up a glass of hot water as usual at nine o'clock."

"Was he then in his own room or in Mr. Cornworthy's?"

"He was in his own room, sir."

"You noticed nothing unusual about that room?"

"Unusual? No, sir."

"Where were Mrs. Farley and Miss Farley?"

"They had gone to the theater, sir."

"Thank you, Holmes."

Holmes bowed and left the room.

Poirot turned to the millionaire's widow.

"One more question, Mrs. Farley. Had your husband good sight?"

"No. Not without his glasses."

"He was very shortsighted?"

"Oh, yes, he was quite helpless without his spectacles."

"He had several pairs of glasses?"

"Yes."

"Ah," said Poirot. He leaned back. "I think that concludes the case."

There was silence in the room. They were all looking at the little man who sat there complacently stroking his mustache. On the Inspector's face was perplexity; John Stillingfleet was frowning; Cornworthy merely stared uncomprehending; Mrs. Farley gazed in blank astonishment; Joanna Farley looked eager.

Mrs. Farley broke the silence, "I don't understand, M. Poirot." Her voice was fretful. "The dream—"

"Yes," said Poirot. "That dream was very important."

Mrs. Farley shivered. She said, "I've never believed in anything supernatural before, but now—to dream it night after night beforehand—"

"It's extraordinary," said Stillingfleet. "Extraordinary! If Mr. Farley himself hadn't told that story—"

"Exactly," said Poirot. His eyes, which had been half closed, opened suddenly. They were very green. "If Benedict Farley hadn't told me—"

He paused a minute, looking round at a circle of blank faces.

"There are three things, you comprehend, that happened that evening which I was quite at a loss to explain. First, why make such a point of my bringing that letter with me?"

"Identification," suggested Cornworthy.

"No, no, my dear young man. Really, that idea is too ridiculous. There must be some much more valid reason. For not only did Mr. Farley require to see that letter produced but he definitely demanded that I should leave it behind. And,

47

moreover, even then he did not destroy it! It was found among his papers this afternoon. Why did he keep it?"

Joanna Farley's voice broke in, "He wanted, in case anything happened to him, that the facts of his strange dream should be made known."

Poirot nodded approvingly.

"You are astute, mademoiselle. That must—that can only be the point of the keeping of the letter. When Mr. Farley was dead, the story of that strange dream was to be told! That dream was very important. That dream, mademoiselle, was vital!"

He went on, "I will come now to the second strange point. After hearing his story, I asked Mr. Farley to show me the desk and the revolver. He seemed about to get up to do so, then suddenly refused. Why did he refuse?"

This time no one advanced an answer.

"I will put that question differently. What was there in that next room that Mr. Farley did not want me to see?"

There was still silence.

"Yes," said Poirot, "it is difficult, that. And yet there was some reason—some urgent reason. There was something in that room he could not afford to have me see.

"And now I come to the third inexplicable thing. Mr. Farley, as I was leaving, requested me to hand him the letter I had received. By inadvertence I handed him a communication from my laundress. He glanced at it and laid it down beside him. Just before I left the room, I discovered my error, and rectified it."

He looked round from one to the other. "You do not see?"

Stillingfleet said, "I don't really see how your laundress comes into it, Poirot."

"My laundress," said Poirot, "was very important. That miserable woman who ruins my collars was, for the first time in her life, useful to somebody. Surely, you see. Mr. Farley glanced at that communication—one glance would have told him that it was the wrong letter—and yet he knew nothing. Why? Because he could not see it properly!"

Inspector Barnett said sharply, "Didn't he have his glasses on?"

Hercule Poirot smiled. "Yes," he said. "He had his glasses on. That is what makes it so very interesting." He leaned forward. "Mr. Farley's dream was very important. He dreamed, you see, that he committed suicide. And a little later on, he did commit suicide. That is to say, he was alone in a room and was found there with a revolver by him, and no one entered or left the room

48

at the time that he was shot. It means, does it not, that it must be suicide?"

"Yes," said Stillingfleet.

Hercule Poirot shook his head. "On the contrary," he said. "It was murder. An unusual and a very cleverly planned murder."

Again he leaned forward, tapping the table, his eyes green and shining.

"Why did Mr. Farley not allow me to go into his own room that evening? What was there in there that I must not be allowed to see? I think, my friends, that there was Benedict Farley himself!"

He smiled at the blank faces.

"Yes, yes, it is not nonsense, what I say. Why could the Mr. Farley to whom I had been talking not realize the difference between two totally dissimilar letters? Because, *mes amis*, he was a man of normal sight, wearing a pair of very powerful glasses. Those glasses would render a man of normal eyesight practically blind . . . Isn't that so, Doctor?"

Stillingfleet murmured, "That's so, of course."

"Why did I feel that in talking to Mr. Farley I was talking to a mountebank, to an actor playing a part? Because he was playing a part!

"Consider the setting. The dim room, the green-shaded light turned blindingly away from the figure in the chair. What did I see—the famous patchwork dressing gown, the beaked nose—faked with that useful substance, nose putty—the white crest of hair, the powerful lenses concealing the eyes.

"What evidence is there that Mr. Farley ever had a dream? Only the evidence of Mrs. Farley. What evidence is there that Benedict Farley kept a revolver in his desk? Only the word of Mrs. Farley.

"Two people carried this fraud through—Mrs. Farley and Hugo Cornworthy. Cornworthy wrote the letter to me, gave instructions to the butler, went out, ostensibly to the cinema, but let himself in again immediately with a key, went to his room, made himself up, and played the part of Benedict Farley.

"And so we come to this afternoon. The opportunity for which Mr. Cornworthy has been waiting arrives. There are two witnesses on the landing to swear that no one goes in or out of Benedict Farley's room. Cornworthy waits until a particularly heavy batch of traffic is about to pass. Then he leans out of his window, and with the lazy tongs which he has purloined from the desk next door, he holds an object against the window of that room.

"Benedict Farley comes to the window. Cornworthy snatches

back the tongs, and as Farley leans out and the lorries are passing outside, Cornworthy shoots him with the revolver that he has ready. There is a blank wall opposite, remember. There can be no witness of the crime.

"Cornworthy waits for over half an hour, then gathers up some papers, conceals the lazy tongs and the revolver between them, goes out onto the landing and into the next room. He replaces the tongs on the desk, lays down the revolver after pressing the dead man's fingers on it, and hurries out with the news of Mr. Farley's 'suicide.'

"He arranges that the letter to me shall be found and that I shall arrive with my story—the story I heard from Mr. Farley's own lips—of his extraordinary dream—the strange compulsion he felt to kill himself! A few credulous people will discuss the hypnotism theory, but the main result will be to confirm without a doubt that the actual hand that held the revolver was Benedict's Farley's own."

Hercule Poirot's eyes went to the widow's face—dismay, the ashy pallor, the blind fear.

"And in due course," he finished gently, "the happy ending would have been achieved. A quarter of a million and two hearts that beat as one."

Stillingfleet and Poirot walked along the side of Northway House. On their right was the towering wall of the factory. Above them, on their left, were the windows of Benedict Farley's and Hugo Cornworthy's rooms. Hercule Poirot stooped and picked up a small object—a black stuffed cat.

"*Voila*," he said. "That is what Cornworthy held in the lazy tongs against Farley's window. You remember, he hated cats? Naturally, he rushed to the window."

"Why on earth didn't Cornworthy come out and pick it up after he'd dropped it?"

"How could he? To do so would have been definitely suspicious. After all, if this object were found, what would anyone think? Only that some child had wandered round here and dropped it."

"Yes," said Stillingfleet with a sigh. "D'you know, old horse, up to the very last minute I thought you were leading up to some subtle theory of highfalutin' psychological suggested murder? I bet those two thought so too! Nasty bit of goods, the Farley. Goodness, how she cracked! I rather like the girl. Grit, you know, and brains. I suppose I'd be thought a fortune hunter if I had a shot at her."

"You are too late, my friend. There is already someone *sur le tapis*. Her father's death has opened the way to happiness."

"Take it all round, she had a pretty good motive for bumping off the unpleasant parent."

"Motive and opportunity are not enough, Doctor," said Hercule Poirot. "There must also be the criminal temperament."

"I wonder if you'll ever commit a crime, Poirot," said Stillingfleet. "I bet you could get away with it all right. As a matter of fact, it would be too easy for you. I mean the thing would be definitely too unsporting."

"That," said Poirot, "is a typically English idea."

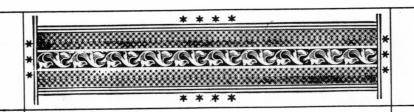

THE CASE AGAINST CARROLL

BY ELLERY QUEEN

Frederic Dannay (b. October 20, 1905) and Manfred B. Lee (b. January 11, 1905; d. April 3, 1971) are Brooklyn-born cousins who became known the world over as Ellery Queen, author of the series of mystery novels and stories featuring the detective Ellery Queen and his father, N.Y. police inspector Richard Queen. Under a second pseudonym, Barnaby Ross, they created detective Drury Lane. Since their first novel, *The Roman Hat Mystery*, in 1929 they have been responsible for the publication of nearly a hundred books. *Ellery Queen's Mystery Magazine*, which they launched in 1941, has long been acknowledged as the world's leading mystery magazine.

CARROLL FELT THE HEAT THROUGH his shoes as he got out of the taxi. In the swollen twilight even the Park across Fifth Avenue had a look of suffering. It made him worry again about how Helena was taking the humidity.

"What?" Carroll said, reaching for his wallet. It was a thirty-sixth birthday present from Helena, and he usually challenged taxi drivers to identify the leather, which was elephant hide. But tonight's hackie was glowering at the slender graystone building with its fineboned black balconies.

"I said," the driver said, "that's your house?"

"Yes." Carroll immediately felt angry. The lie of convenience had its uses, but on days like this it stung. The graystone had been erected in the Seventies by Helena's great-grandfather, and it belonged to her.

"Air conditioned, no doubt," the man said, wiping out his ear. "How would you like to live in one of them de luxe East Side hotboxes on a night like this?"

"No, thank you," Carroll said, remembering.

"I got four kids down there, not to mention my old lady. What do you think of that?"

Carroll overtipped him.

He used his key on the bronze street door with a sense of sanctuary. The day had been bad all around, especially at Hunt, West & Carroll, Attorneys-at-Law. Miss Mallowan, his secretary, had chosen this day to throw her monthly fainting spell; the new clerk had wasted three hours conscientiously looking up the wrong citations; Meredith Hunt, playing the senior partner with a heavy hand, had been at his foulest; and Tully West, ordinarily the most urbane of men, had been positively short-tempered at finding himself with only one change of shirt in the office.

And trickling through the day, acid-like, had been Carroll's worry about Helena. He had telephoned twice, and she had been extra-cheery both times. When Helena sounded extra-cheery, she was covering up something.

Had she found out?

But that wasn't possible.

Unless Tully . . . But Carroll shook his head, wincing. Tully

53

West couldn't know. His code coupled snooping with using the wrong fork and other major crimes.

It's the weather, Carroll decided fatuously; and he stepped into his wife's house.

Indoors, he felt a little better. The house with its crystal chandeliers, Italian marble, and shimmering floors was as cameo-cool as Helena herself—as all the Vanowens must have been, judging from the Sargents lording it over the walls. He had never stopped feeling grateful that they were all defunct except Helena. The Vanowens went back to the patroons, while he was the son of a track walker for the New York transit system who had been killed by a subway train while tilting a bottle on the job. Breeding had been the Vanowens' catchword; they would not have cared for Helena's choice of husband.

John Carroll deposited his hat and brief case in the foyer closet and trudged upstairs, letting his wet palm squeak along the satiny rail.

Helena was in the upstairs sitting room, reading *Winnie the Pooh* for the umpteenth time to Breckie and Louanne.

And she was in the wheelchair again.

Carroll watched his wife's face from the archway as she made the absurd Eeyore sounds the children never tired of. Through the stab of angry helplessness he felt the old wonder. Her slender body was bunched, tight in defense, against the agony of her arthritis-racked legs, but that delicate face under its coif of auburn was as serene as a nun's. Only he knew what a price she paid for that serenity.

"Daddy. It's Daddy!"

Two rockets flew at him. Laden down with sleepered arms and legs, Carroll went to his wife and kissed her.

"Now, darling," Helena said.

"How bad is it?" he growled.

"Not bad. John, you're soaked. Did you have to work so late in this swelter?"

"I suppose that's why you're in the wheelchair."

"I've had Mrs. Poole keep dinner hot for you."

"Mommy let us stay up because we were so *good*," Louanne said. "Now can we have the choc-o-late, Daddy?"

"We weren't so *very* good," Breckie said. "See, see, Louanne, I told you Daddy wouldn't forget!"

"We'll help you take your shower." Helena strained forward in the wheelchair. "Breckie angel, your bottom's sticking out.

54

John, really. Couldn't you have made it Life Savers today?"

"It's bad, isn't it?"

"A little," Helena admitted, smiling.

A little! Carroll thought as they all went upstairs in the elevator he had had installed two years before, when Helena's condition had become chronic. A little—when even at the best of times she had to drag about like an old woman.

He showered in full view of his admiring family, impotently aware of the health in his long, dark body.

When he pattered back to the bedroom he found a shaker of martinis and, on his bed, fresh linen and his favorite slacks and jacket.

"What's the matter, John?"

"I didn't think it showed," Carroll said tenderly.

He kissed her on the chocolate smudge left by Breckie's fingers.

Like a character in a bad TV drama, Hunt came with the thunder and the rain.

Carroll was surprised. He was also embarrassed by the abrupt way the children stopped chattering as the lawyer's thickset figure appeared in the dining-room doorway.

"Meredith." Carroll half rose. "I thought you were on your way to Chicago."

"I'm headed for La Guardia now," Hunt said. "Legs again, Helena?"

"Yes. Isn't it a bore?" Helena glanced at her housekeeper, who was in the foyer holding Hunt's wet things at arm's length. "Mr. Hunt will take coffee with us, Mrs. Poole."

"Yes, Ma'am."

"No, Ma'am," Meredith Hunt said. "But I thank you. *And* the Carroll small-fry. Up kind of late, aren't you?"

Breckie and Louanne edged stealthily toward their mother's chair.

"We like to wait up for our daddy," Helena smiled, drawing them to her. "How's Felicia, Meredith? I must call her as soon as this lets up a bit."

"Don't. My wife is being very Latin American these days."

Something was terribly wrong. Looking back on the day, John Carroll felt another thrill of alarm.

Helena said extra-cheerily, "Way past your bedtime, bunny rabbits! Kiss your father and say good night to Mr. Hunt."

She herded them out with her wheelchair. As she turned the

chair into the foyer, she glanced swiftly at her husband. Then she said something crisp to Mrs. Poole and they all disappeared behind the clang of the elevator door.

Carroll said, "Life's little surprises. You wanted to talk to me, Meredith?"

"Definitely." Hunt's large teeth glistened.

"Let's go up to my study."

"I can talk here."

Carroll looked at him. "What's on your mind?"

"You're a crook," Hunt said.

Carroll sat down. He reached with concentration for the crystal cigarette box on the table.

"When did you find out, Meredith?"

"I knew I was making a mistake the day I let Tully West pull that *noblesse oblige* act for Helena and sweet-talk me into taking you into the firm." The burly lawyer sauntered about the dining room, eying the marble fireplace, the paintings, the crystal cabinets, the heirloom silver. "You can't make a blue ribbon entry out of an alley accident, I always say. The trouble with Tully and Helena, John, is that they're sentimental idiots. They really believe in democracy."

The flame of the lighter danced very red. Carroll put the cigarette down, unlit.

"I wish you'd let me explain, Meredith."

"So I've kept an eye on you," Hunt said, not pausing in his stroll. "And especially on the Eakins Trust. It's going to give me a lot of satisfaction to show my blue-blood partner just how and when his mongrel protégé misappropriated twenty thousand dollars' worth of trust securities."

"Will you let me explain?"

"Explain away. Horses? The market?" Hunt swung about. A nerve in the heavy flesh beneath his right eye was jumping. "A woman?"

"Keep your voice down, Meredith."

"A woman. Sure. When a man like you is married to a—"

"Don't!" Carroll said. Then he said, "Does Tully know?"

"Not yet."

"It was my brother Harry. He got into a dangerous mess involving some hard character and he had to get out in a hurry. He needed twenty thousand dollars to square himself, and he came to me for it."

"And you stole it for him."

"I told him I didn't have it. I don't have it. My take from the

56

firm just about keeps our heads above water. It's my income that runs this house, Meredith. Or did you think I let Helena's money feed me, too? Anyway, Harry threatened to go to Helena for it."

"And, of course," Hunt said, showing his teeth again, "you couldn't let him do that."

"No," Carroll said. "No, Meredith, I couldn't. I don't expect you to understand why. Helena wouldn't hesitate to give me any amount I asked for, but . . . Well, I had no way of borrowing a wad like that overnight except to go to you or to Tully. Tully was somewhere in northern Canada hunting, and to go to you . . ." Carroll paused. When he looked up he said, "So I took it from the Eakins Trust, proving your point."

Meredith Hunt nodded with enjoyment.

Carroll pushed himself erect on his fists. "I've got to ask you to give me time. I'll replace the funds by the first of the year. It won't happen again, Meredith. Harry's in Mexico, and he won't be back. It won't happen again. The first of the year." He swallowed. "Please."

"Monday," Hunt said.

"What?"

"This is Friday. I'll give you till Monday morning to make up the defalcation. You have sixty hours to keep from arrest, prison, and disbarment. If you replace the money I'll drop the matter to protect the firm. In any event, of course, you're through at the office."

"Monday." Carroll laughed. "Why not tonight? It would be just as merciful."

"You can get the money from your wife. Or from Tully, if he's stupid enough to give it to you."

"I won't drag Helena into this!" Carroll heard his voice rising, and he pulled it down with an effort. "Or Tully—I value his friendship too much. I got myself into this jam, and all I'm asking is the chance to get myself out."

"That's your problem. I'm being very generous, under the circumstances." All the lines of Hunt's well-preserved face sagged as his cold eyes flamed with sudden heat. "Especially since the Eakins Trust isn't the only property you haven't been able to keep your hands off."

"What's that supposed to mean?"

"Your sex life is your own business as long as you don't poach on mine. Stay away from my wife."

Carroll's fist caught Hunt's big chin. Hunt staggered. Then he lowered his head and came around the table like a bull. They wrestled against the table, knocking a Sèvres cup to the floor.

"That's a lie," Carroll whispered. "I've never laid a finger on Felicia . . . on any woman but Helena."

"I've seen Felicia look at you," Hunt panted. His head came up, butting. Carroll fell down.

"*John. Meredith.*"

The wheelchair was in the doorway. Helena was as pale as her husband.

Carroll got to his feet. "Go back, Helena. Go upstairs."

"Meredith. Please leave."

The big lawyer straightened, fumbling with his expensive silk tie. He was glaring in a sort of victory. Then he went into the foyer, took his hat and topcoat from the chair in which Mrs. Poole had deposited them, and quietly left.

"John, what did he say to you?" Helena was as close to fear as she ever got. "What happened?"

Carroll began to pick up the fragments of the shattered cup. But his hands were shaking so uncontrollably that he stopped.

"Oh, darling, you promised never to lose your temper again this way—"

Carroll said nothing.

"It's not good for you." She reached over and pulled his head down to her breast. "Whatever he said, dearest, it's not worth . . ."

He patted her, trying to pull away.

"John, come to bed?"

"No. I've got to cool off."

"Darling—"

"I'll walk it off."

"But it's pouring!"

Carroll snatched his hat and topcoat from the foyer closet and plunged out of the house. He sloshed down Fifth Avenue in the rain and fog, almost running.

The next morning John Carroll got out of the taxi before the Hunt house on East 61st Street like a man dreaming. The streets had been washed clean by the downpour of the night before, and the sun was already hot, but he felt dirty and cold. He pressed the Hunt bell with a sense of doom, a vague warning of things he tried not to imagine. He shivered and jabbed at the bell again, irritably this time.

A maid with a broad Indian face finally opened the door. She led him in silence up to Felicia Hunt's rooms on the second floor. Tully West was already there, thoughtfully contemplating the postage-stamp rear garden from Felicia's picture window. West was as tall and fleshless as a Franciscan monk—an easy man with an iron-gray crewcut and unnoticeable clothes.

Carroll nodded to his partner and dropped into one of the capacious Spanish chairs Felicia surrounded herself with. "Crosstown traffic held me up. Felicia, what's this all about?"

Felicia de los Santos was in her dramatic mood this morning. She had clothed her dark plump beauty in a violently gay gown; she was already at work fingering her talisman, a ruby-and-emerald-crusted locket that had belonged to a Bourbon queen. She was the daughter of a Latin-American diplomat of Castilian blood, she had been educated in Europe after a high-walled childhood, and she was hopelessly torn between the Spanish tradition of the submissive wife and the feminism she had found in the United States. What Felicia de los Santos had seen in Meredith Hunt, an American primitive twice her age, Carroll had never fathomed.

"Meredith is missing." She had a charming accent.

"Missing? Isn't he in Chicago?"

"The Michaelson people say no." Tully West's witty, rather glacial voice was not amused today. "They phoned Felicia this morning after trying to reach our office. Meredith never got there."

"I don't understand that." Carroll felt his forehead; he had a pounding headache."He stopped by last night about half-past nine and said he was on his way to the airport."

"He wasn't on the plane, John." Hunt's wife seemed more nervous than alarmed. "Tully just telephoned La Guardia."

"All planes were grounded from about eight p.m. yesterday until three in the morning by the fog. Meredith checked in at the field all right, found his flight delayed, and left word at the desk that he'd wait around the airport. But when the fog cleared they couldn't find him." West sat Felicia Hunt down on her silk divan, gingerly. She appealed to him with her moist black eyes as if for understanding, but he turned to Carroll. "You say, John, he stopped by last night?"

"For just a few minutes. He didn't mention anything that would explain this." Carroll shut his eyes.

Felicia Hunt twisted her locket. "He's left me—deserted me."

Tully West looked shocked. "Meredith would as soon leave his wallet. My dear girl!"

59

The maid said from the doorway, "Señora. The police."

Carroll turned sharply.

Three men were in the doorway behind the Indian maid. One was broad and powerful; another was small, gray, and wiry; and the third was tall and young.

The broad man said, "Mrs. Hunt? Sergeant Velie. This is Inspector Queen." He did not bother to introduce the tall young man. "We've got bad news for you."

"My husband—"

"An officer found him around six thirty this morning over on East 58th, near the Queensboro Bridge, in a parked Thunderbird. He was spread across the wheel with a slug in his brain."

She got to her feet, clutching the pendant. Then her eyes turned over and she pitched forward.

West and Carroll both caught her before their mouths could close. They hauled her onto the divan and Carroll began to chafe her hands. The maid ran to the bathroom.

"Ever the delicate touch, Velie," the tall young man remarked from the doorway. "Couldn't you have hit her over the head?"

Sergeant Velie ignored him. "I forgot to mention he's dead. Who are you?"

"I'm Tully West, that's John Carroll." West was very pale. "We're Hunt's law partners. Mrs. Hunt phoned us this morning when her husband failed to show up in Chicago for a business appointment. He was to have taken the eleven p.m. plane—"

"That's already been checked." The small gray man was watching the maid wave a bottle of smelling salts under Felicia Hunt's little nose. "Hunt didn't come back home last night? Phone or anything?"

"Mrs. Hunt says not."

"Was he supposed to be traveling alone?"

"Yes."

"Make such trips often?"

"Yes. Hunt was outside man for the firm."

"Was he in the habit of driving his car to airports?"

"Yes. He'd park it and pick it up on his return."

"Carrying any valuables last night?"

"Just cash for the trip, as far as I know. And a dispatch case containing some papers and a change of linen."

Felicia Hunt shuddered and opened her eyes. The maid eased her expertly back on the divan and slipped a pillow under her head. The young widow lay there like Goya's Duchess, fingering her locket. Carrol straightened.

60

"Suicide," Tully West said, and he cleared his throat. "It was suicide?"

"Not on your tintype," Inspector Queen said. "Hunt was murdered, and when we identify the Colt Woodsman we found in the car, we'll know who murdered him. Until we do, any suggestions?"

Carroll glared around helplessly. Then he clapped his hand over his mouth and ran into the bathroom. They heard him gagging.

"Was Mr. Carroll unusually fond of Mr. Hunt?" asked the tall young man politely.

"No," Tully West said. "I mean—oh, damn it all!"

"Detectives will be talking to you people later in the day." The Inspector nodded at his sergeant, said, "Come along, Ellery" to the tall young man, and then he marched out with his old man's stiff-kneed bounce . . .

"Come in, please." Inspector Queen did not look up from the report he was reading.

John Carroll came into the office between Tully West and a detective. The partners' faces were gray.

"Have a seat."

The detective left. In a rivuleted leather chair at one corner of his father's office Ellery sprawled over a cigarette. A small fan was going behind the old man, ruffling his white hair. It made the only noise in the room.

"See here," Tully West said frigidly. "Mr. Carroll's been interrogated from hell to breakfast by precinct detectives, Homicide Squad men, the Deputy Chief Inspector in charge of Manhattan East, and detectives of the Homicide Bureau. He's submitted without a murmur to fingerprinting. He's spent a whole morning in the Criminal Courts Building being taken apart piece by piece by an Assistant District Attorney who apparently thinks he can parlay this case into a seat in Congress. May I suggest that you people either fish or cut bait?"

The Inspector laid aside the report. He settled back in his swivel chair, regarding the Ivy League lawyer in a friendly way. "Any special reason, Mr. West, why you insisted on coming along this morning?"

"Why?" West's lips were jammed together. "Is there an objection to my being here?"

"No." The old man looked at Carroll. "Mr. Carroll I'm throwing away the book on this one. You'll notice there's not even a

61

stenographer present. Maybe if we're frank with each other we can cut corners and save everybody a lot of grief. We've been on this homicide for five days now, and I'm going to tell you what we've come up with."

"But why me?" John Carroll's voice came out all cracked.

West touched his partner's arm. "You'll have to forgive Mr. Carroll, Inspector. He's never learned not to look a gift horse in the mouth. Shut up, John, and listen."

The old man swiveled creakily to look out his dusty window. "As far as we can reconstruct the crime, Hunt's killer must have followed him to La Guardia last Friday night. A bit past midnight Hunt reclaimed his car at the parking lot and drove off, in spite of the fact that he'd told the airline clerk at ten-thirty that he'd wait around for the fog to lift. It's our theory that the killer met him at La Guardia and talked him into taking a ride, maybe on a plea of privacy. That would mean that after reclaiming his car Hunt picked the killer up and they drove off together.

"We have no way of knowing how long they cruised around before crossing the Queensboro Bridge into Manhattan, but at about one forty-five a.m. a patrol car passed the Thunderbird on East 58th, parked where it was later found with Hunt's body in it. The Assistant Medical Examiner says Hunt was killed between two and four a.m. Saturday, so when the patrol car passed at a quarter to two, Hunt and his killer must have been sitting in it, still talking.

"Now." Inspector Queen swiveled back to eye Carroll. "Item one: Hunt was shot to death with a bullet from the Colt Woodsman .22 automatic found beside the body. That pistol, Mr. Carroll, is registered in your name."

Carroll's face went grayer. He made an instinctive movement, but West touched his arm again.

"Item two: motive. There's nothing to indicate it could have had anything to do with Hunt's trip, or any client. Your firm doesn't practise criminal law, your clients are conservative corporations, and the Chicago people had every reason to want Hunt to stay healthy—he was going to save them a couple of million dollars in a tax-refund suit against the government. Mr. West himself has gone over the contents of Hunt's dispatch case, and he says nothing is missing. Robbery? Hunt's secretary got him three hundred dollars from the bank Friday for his trip, and well over that amount was found in his wallet. Hunt's Movado wrist watch and jade ring were found on him.

"That's the way it stood till Monday morning. Then Hunt

62

himself tipped us off to the motive. He wrote us a letter."

"Hunt *what?*" Carroll cried.

"By way of Miss Connor, his secretary. She found it in the office mail on Monday morning. Hunt wrote it on airline stationery from La Guardia on Friday night and dropped it into a mailbox there, probably before his killer showed up.

"It was a note to his secretary," the Inspector went on, "instructing her that if anything should happen to him over the week-end she was to deliver the enclosure, a sealed envelope, to the police. Miss Connor brought it right in."

West said, "Good old Meredith." He looked disgusted.

"Hunt's letter to us, Mr. Carroll, says that he visited your home on Fifth Avenue before going to the airport Friday evening—tells us why, tells us about your fight . . . incidentally clearing up the reason for the bruise on his mouth. So, you see, we know all about that trust fund, and Hunt's ultimatum to you a few hours before he was knocked off. He even mentioned his suspicions about you and Mrs. Hunt." The Inspector added mildly, "That's two pretty good motives, Mr. Carroll. Care to change your statement?"

Carroll's mouth was open. Then he jumped up. "It's all a horrible misunderstanding," he stammered. "There's never been a thing between Felicia Hunt and me—"

"John." West pulled him down. "Inspector, Meredith Hunt was stupidly jealous of his wife. He even accused me on occasion of making passes at her. I can't speak about Mrs. Hunt's feelings, but John Carroll is the most devoted married man I know. He's crazy about his wife and children."

"And the defalcation?" the Inspector murmured.

"John's told me all about that. His no-good brother was in serious trouble and John foolishly borrowed the money from one of the trusts our firm administers to get the brute out of it. I've already replaced it from my personal funds. Any talk of theft or prosecution is ridiculous. If I'd known about Meredith's ultimatum I'd have been tempted to pop him one myself. We all have our weak moments under stress. I've known John Carroll intimately for almost ten years. I can and do vouch for his fundamental honesty."

Ellery's voice said from his corner, "And when exactly did Mr. Carroll tell you about his weak moment, Mr. West?"

The lawyer was startled. Then he turned around and said with a smile, "I don't believe I'll answer that."

"The gun," Inspector Queen prompted.

63

"It's John's, Inspector, of course. He's a Reserve officer, and he likes to keep up his marksmanship. We both do a bit of target shooting now and then at a gun club we belong to downtown, and John keeps the target pistol in his desk at the office. Anyone could have lifted that Woodsman and walked off with it. The fact that John keeps it in the office is known to dozens of people."

"I see." The old man's tone specified nothing. "Now let's get to last Friday night. We'll play it as if you've never been questioned, Mr. Carroll. I suppose you can establish just where you were between two and four a.m. last Saturday?"

Carroll put his head between his hands and laughed.

"Well, can you?"

"I'll try to explain again, Inspector," Carroll said, straightening up. "When I lose my temper, as I did with Meredith on Friday night, I get a violent physical reaction. It takes me hours sometimes to calm down. My wife knows this, and after Meredith left for La Guardia she tried to get me to go to bed. I'm sorry now I didn't take her advice! I decided instead to walk it off, and that's just what I did. I must have walked around half the night."

"Meet anyone you know?"

"I've told you. No."

"What time was it when you got back home?"

"I don't remember. All I know is, it was still dark."

"Was it also still foggy?" the voice from the corner said.

Carroll jumped. "No, it wasn't."

Ellery said, "The fog lifted about two a.m., Mr. Carroll."

"You're sure you can't recall the time even approximately?" Inspector Queen's tone was patience itself. "I mean the time you got home?"

Carroll began to look stubborn. "I just didn't notice."

"Maybe Mrs. Carroll did?"

"My wife was asleep. I didn't wake her."

"Item three," the Inspector remarked. "No alibi. And item four: fingerprints."

"Fingerprints?" Carroll said feebly.

"John's? Where, Inspector?' Tully West asked in a sharp tone. "You realize they wouldn't mean anything if you found them on the pistol."

"We hardly ever find fingerprints on automatics, Mr. West. No, in Hunt's car."

Through the roaring in his ears John Carroll thought: So that's why they fingerprinted me Monday . . . He blinked as he heard the old amusement in his partner's voice.

"Surely you found other prints in the car besides John's and, I assume, Hunt's?"

The old man looked interested. "Whose, for instance?"

"Well, there must be at least a set traceable to the attendant in the public garage where Hunt parked his car."

"Well?"

"And, of course," West said with a smile, "a few of mine."

"Yours, Mr. West?"

"Certainly. Hunt drove John and me home from the office in the Thunderbird on Thursday night—the night before the murder. So I'm going to have to insist that you fingerprint me, too."

Inspector Queen snapped, "Of course, Mr. West. We'll be glad to oblige," and glanced over at the leather chair.

"I have a naive question for you, Carroll." Ellery was studying the smoke-curl of his cigarette. "Did you kill Meredith Hunt?"

"Hell, no," John Carroll said. "I haven't killed anybody since Leyte."

"I think I'm going to advise you not to say any more, John!" Tully West rose. "Is that all, Inspector?"

"For now. And Mr. Carroll."

"Yes?"

"The usual—you're not to leave town. Understand?"

John Carroll nodded slowly. "I guess I do."

Through the lobby of Police Headquarters, down the worn steps to the sidewalk, neither partner said anything. But when they were in a taxi speeding uptown, Carroll kicked the jump-seat and muttered, "Tully, there's something I've got to know."

"What's that?"

"Do *you* think I murdered Meredith?"

"Not a chance."

"Do you really mean that?"

West's monkish face crinkled. "We Wests haven't stuck our necks out since Greatgrandfather West had his head blown off at Chancellorsville."

Carroll sank back. The older man glanced out the cab window at Fourth Avenue.

"On the other hand, you don't lean your weight on a lily pad when a nice big rock is handy. My knowledge of corporation and tax law—or yours, John—isn't going to do much good if that old coot decides to jump. You may need a topflight criminal lawyer soon. To tell the truth, I've been thinking of Sam Rayfield."

"I see. All right, Tully, whatever you say." Carroll studied an

65

inflamed carbuncle on their driver's neck. "Tully, what's the effect of this thing going to be on Helena? And on Breckie, Louanne? My God."

He turned to the other window, lips trembling.

A detective from the 17th Precinct made the arrest that afternoon. He and his partner appeared at the Madison Avenue offices of Hunt, West & Carroll just before five o'clock. Carroll recognized them as the men who had questioned him the previous Saturday afternoon; they were apparently the local detectives "carrying" the case.

Miss Mallowan fainted out of season. Tully West's secretary dragged her away.

"I'd like to call my wife," Carroll said.

"Sure, but make it snappy."

"Listen, sweetheart," Carroll said into the phone. He was amazed at the steadiness of his voice. "I'm being arrested. You're not to come running down to the Tombs, do you hear? I want you to stay home and take care of the kids. Understand, Helena?"

"You listen to me." Helena's voice was as steady as his. "You're to let Tully handle everything. I'll tell the children you've had to go off on business. And I'll see you as soon as they'll let me. Do *you* understand, darling?"

Carroll licked his lips. "Yes."

Tully West came running out as they waited for the elevator. "I'm getting Rayfield on this right away. And I'll keep an eye on Helena and the kids. You all right, John?"

"Oh, wonderful," Carroll said wryly.

West gripped his hand and dashed off.

The hard gray-and-green face of the Criminal Courts Building, the night in the cell, the march across the bridge from the prison wing the next morning, his arraignment in one of the chill two-story courtrooms, Helena's strained face as she labored up to kiss him, Tully West's droopy look, the soft impressive voice of Samuel Rayfield, the trap of the judge's gray mouth as he fixed bail at fifty thousand dollars . . . to John Carroll, all of it jumbled into an indigestible mass. He was relieved to find himself back in the cell, and he dozed off at once.

Friday morning the pain caught up with him. Everything hurt

66

sharply. When he was taken into the office of the court clerk, he could not bear to look at the two lawyers, or at his wife. He felt as if his clothing had been taken away.

He heard only dimly the colloquy with the clerk. It had something to do with the bail . . . Suddenly Carroll realized that it was his wife who was putting up the bail bond, paying the ransom for his freedom out of the Vanowen money.

"Helena, no!"

But he voiced the cry only in his head. The next thing he knew they were marching out of the court clerk's office.

"Am I free?" Carroll asked foolishly.

"You're free, darling," Helena whispered.

"But fifty thousand dollars," he muttered. "Your money . . ."

"Oh, for heaven's sake, John," West said. "The bail is returnable on the first day of the trial, when you resubmit to the custody of the court. You know that."

"John, dear, it's only money."

"Helena, I didn't do it . . ."

"I know, darling."

Rayfield interposed his genial bulk between them and the lurking photographers and reporters. Somehow, he got them through the barrage of flashbulbs.

As the elevator doors closed, Carroll suddenly noticed a tall man lounging in the corridor, a youngish man with bright eyes. A shock of recognition, rather unpleasant, ran through him. It was that Inspector's son, Ellery Queen. What was he doing here?

The question needled him all the way home.

Then he was safe behind the grayfront of Fifth Avenue. In the Tombs, Carroll had coddled the thought of that safety, wrapping himself in it against the cold steel and antiseptic smell. But they were still with him. When Mrs. Poole took the children tactfully off to the Park, Carroll shivered and gave himself up to the martini that West handed him.

"What was it Meredith used to say about your martinis, Tully? Something about having to be a fifth-generation American to know how to mix one properly?"

"Meredith was a middle-class snob." West raised his glass. "Here's to him. May he never know what hit him."

They sipped in silence.

Then Helena set her glass down. "Tully. Just what does Mr. Rayfield think?"

"The trial won't come up until October."

"That's not what I asked."

"Translation," Carroll murmured. "What are defendant's chances?"

"Rayfield hasn't said." West downed the rest of his drink in a gulp, something he never did.

Helena's silky brows drew the slightest bit toward each other. She said suddenly, "John, you have some enemy you don't know about. Someone who hates you enough to commit murder with your gun. Who is it? Think, darling!"

Carroll shook his head.

"I don't believe it's that at all, Helena," West said, pouring a refill. "Taking John's pistol might have been an act of sheer opportunism. Whoever it was might have lifted mine if I'd left it around. Seems to me the question properly is, Who had it in for Meredith?"

Carroll said, "Ask the police. Ask that lip-smacking little Assistant District Attorney."

They were all quiet again.

"But it's true," John Carroll mumbled at last. "It's true I've got to do something . . ."

Tully West's eyes met Helena Carroll's briefly.

"Here, John. Have another martini."

Carroll spent the weekend in seclusion. The telephone kept ringing, but Helena refused to let him be disturbed.

By Sunday night he had made up his mind. Helena heard him typing away on the portable, but when she tried to go in to him, she found the bedroom door locked.

"John! Are you all right?"

"I'll be out in a minute."

When he unlocked the door he was tucking an envelope into his inside breast pocket. He looked calmer, as if he had won a battle.

He helped her over to the chaise. "There's something I've never told anyone, Helena, not even you. I gave my word not to."

"What are you talking about, darling?"

"I've had a big decision to make. Helena, I'm going to come out of this all right. All I ask you to do is stop worrying and trust me. No matter what happens, will you trust me?"

"Oh, John!"

He stooped to kiss her. "I'll be back in a few minutes."

He walked over to Madison Avenue and went into a deserted delicatessen store. In the telephone booth he dialed Meredith Hunt's number.

"Serafina? Mr. Carroll. Let me talk to Mrs. Hunt."

Felicia Hunt's accent vibrated in his ear without its usual charm. "John, are you mad? Suppose they have my telephone tapped? You know what Meredith wrote to them!"

"I also know he got it all cross-eyed," Carroll said. "Felicia, I want to see you. Tomorrow I'm going into the office to start helping Tully salvage something from the wreckage, but on my way home I'm stopping in at your place with somebody about six-thirty. Will you be there?"

She sounded exasperated. "I can't go anywhere so soon after the funeral, you know that. Whom are you bringing?"

"No one you know."

"John, I wish you wouldn't—" He hung up.

When the maid with the Indian face opened the door Carroll said, "After you, Gunder," and the man with him stepped nervously into the Hunt house. He was a chubby citizen with a wet pink scalp and rimless eyeglasses. He carried a small leather case.

"The Señora waits upstairs," Serafina said sullenly.

"Get Mr. Gunder a magazine or something," Carroll said. "This won't take long, Gunder."

The man seated himself on the edge of a foyer chair. Carroll hurried up the stairs, taking his brief case with him.

Felicia Hunt was all in black. Even her stockings were black. She gave Carroll a turn; it was rather like walking in on a character drawn by Charles Addams. She wore no make-up and, for the first time since Carroll had known her, no jewelry, not even her pendant. The brilliant fingernails she usually affected were now colorless. Her fingers kept exploring her bosom petulantly.

"Meaning no disrespect to an old Spanish custom," Carroll said, "is this mourning-in-death absolutely necessary, Felicia? You look like a ghost."

"Thank you," Felicia said spitefully. "Always the *caballero*. Where I come from, John, you do certain things in certain ways. Not that I would dare show my face in the street! Reporters . . . may they all *rot*. What do you want?"

Carroll set his brief case down by the escritoire, went to the door, and carefully closed it. She watched him with sudden interest. He glanced about, nodded at the drawn drapes.

"How mysterious," the widow said in a new tone. "Are you going to kill me or kiss me?"

Carroll laughed. "You're a nourishing dish, Felicia, but if I didn't have an appetite for you a year ago I'd hardly be likely to drool now."

She flung herself on the divan. "Go away," she said sulkily. "I loathe you."

"Why? Because it took you too long to realize what it would mean to Señor the Ambassador, your father, if your passes at me ever got into the newspapers? You didn't loathe me when you were throwing yourself at me all over town, waylaying me in restaurants, making Meredith suspect I was fouling his nest. Have you forgotten those steaming *billets-doux* you kept sending me, Felicia?"

"And you protected me by saying nothing about them. Very noble, John. Now get out."

"Yes, I protected you," Carroll said slowly, "but it begins to look as if I can't protect you any longer. I've told everyone—the police, the D.A., Helena, Tully, Rayfield—that I walked the streets in the rain most of the night that Meredith was shot. As far as they're concerned, right now I have no alibi for the two-hour stretch between two and four a.m., when they say he was murdered."

She was beginning to look apprehensive.

"But now I'm afraid I'm going to have to tell them that between one o'clock and four-thirty that morning you and I were alone in this room, Felicia. That the fact is, I've had an alibi all along—you—and I kept my mouth shut about it because of how it would look if the story came out."

She said hoarsely, "You wouldn't."

"Not if I can help it." Carroll shrugged. "For one thing, I'm quite aware that nobody, not even Helena, would believe I spent three and a half hours alone with you that night just trying to get you to talk Meredith out of ruining my life. Especially if it also came out, as might very well happen, how you'd run after me, written me those uninhibited love letters."

Her white skin turned ghastly.

"They'd jump to the worst possible conclusion about that night. I don't want that any more than you do, Felicia, although for a different reason. A woman in Helena's physical condition never feels very secure about her husband, no matter how faithful he is to her. A yarn like this . . ." Carroll set his jaw. "I love Helena, but I may have no choice. I'm no storybook hero, Felicia. I'm facing the possibility of the electric chair. That alibi is my life insurance policy. I wouldn't be any good to Helena and the children dead."

"Crucified," Felicia Hunt said bitterly. "I'd be crucified! I won't do it."

"You've got to."

"I won't! You can't make me!"

"If I have to, I will."

Murder glittered from her black eyes. But Carroll did not flinch, and after a moment the glitter flickered and she turned away.

"What do you want me to do?"

"I've typed out a statement. At the moment, all you have to do is sign it. I've brought a man with me to notarize your signature; he's downstairs. He has no idea what kind of document it is. I'll lock it in my safe at the office. Don't look at me that way, Felicia. I've got to protect myself now. You ought to be able to understand that."

She said venomously, "Go call your damned notary," and jumped off the divan.

"You'd better read the statement first."

Carroll took a long manila envelope from his brief case. It was unsealed, bound with a red rubber band. He removed the rubber band, opened the envelope, and took from it a folded sheet of typewriter paper. He unfolded it and handed it to her.

She read it carefully, twice. Then she laughed and handed it back.

"Pig."

Carroll went to the door, paper in hand, and opened it. "Mr. Gunder? Would you come up now, please?"

The notary appeared, mopping his pink scalp. In the other hand he clutched the leather case. He sneaked a glance at Felicia's figure and immediately looked away.

"This is Mrs. Felicia de los Santos Hunt, widow of the late Meredith Hunt," Carroll said. "Do you need proof of her identity?"

"I've seen Mrs. Hunt's picture in the papers." Gunder had a pink sort of voice, too. He opened his case and spread out on the escritoire an ink pad, several rubber stamps, and a notary's seal. From his breast pocket he produced a fountain pen as big as a cigar. "Now," he said. "We're all set."

Carroll laid the statement, folded except for the bottom section, on the escritoire. He kept his hand on the fold. Felicia snatched the pen from the notary and signed her name in a vicious scrawl.

When the notary was finished, Carroll slipped the paper into the manila envelope, put the red rubber band around it, and stowed the envelope in his brief case. He rezipped the case.

"I'll see you out, Gunder."

They passed Serafina on the stairs; she was wiping the banister with a damp cloth and did not look around.

In the foyer Carroll gave the little man a ten dollar bill, relocked the street door behind him, and returned upstairs. Serafina would not give an inch; he had to walk around her.

Her mistress was lying on the divan, also turned away from him. Goya's Duchess, Carroll thought, rear view. He could hear the Indian maid slamming things around in the bathroom.

"Thanks, Felicia. You've saved my life."

She did not reply.

"I promise I won't use the statement except as a last resort."

When she continued to ignore him, Carroll picked up his brief case and left.

Carroll surrendered himself to the Court on the morning of the second Monday in October. In the battlefield of the photographers' flashbulbs, through the crowded corridor, in the courtroom, the only thing he could think of was where the summer had gone. July, August, September seemed never to have existed. Certainly they did not occupy the same space-time as the nightmare he was walking into.

The nightmare shuttled fast, a disconnected sequence of pictures like random frames from a film. The group face of the panel, one compound jury eye and mouth, the shuffling of shoes, mysterious palavers before the bench of the black-robed man suspended in midair—opening statements, questions, answers, gavels, objections . . . Suddenly it was Wednesday evening and Carroll was back in his cell.

He felt a childish impulse to laugh aloud, but he choked it off.

He must have dozed, for the next thing he knew Tully West was peering down at him as from a great height, and behind him peered a familiar figure. Carroll could not remember the cell door's opening or closing.

He sat up quickly.

"John, you remember Ellery Queen."

Carroll nodded. "You gents are doing quite a job on me, Queen."

"Not me," Ellery said. "I'm strictly ground observer corps."

"Then what do you want?"

"Satisfaction," Ellery said. "I'm not getting it."

72

Carroll glanced at his partner. "What's this, Tully?"

"Queen came to me after the session today and expressed interest in your case." West managed a smile. "It struck me, John, this might be a nice time to encourage him."

Carroll rested his head against the cell wall. For days, part of his mind had been projecting itself into the execution chamber at Sing Sing, and another part had counterattacked with thoughts of Helena and Breckie and Louanne. He took Helena and the children to sleep with him for sheer self-preservation.

"What is it you're not satisfied about?"

"That you shot Hunt."

"Thanks," Carroll laughed. "Too bad you're not on the jury."

"Yes," Ellery said. "But then I don't have the respectful jury mind. I'm not saying you didn't shoot Hunt; I'm just not convinced. Something about this case has bothered me from the start. Something about you, in fact. I wish you'd clear it up, if not for my sake then for yours. It's later than you apparently think."

Carroll said very carefully, "How bad is it?"

"As bad as it can be."

"I've told Queen the whole story, John." West's urbanity was gone; he even did a little semaphore work with his long arms. "And I may as well tell you that Rayfield holds out damned little hope. He says today's testimony of the night man at the office building was very damaging."

"How could it be?" Carroll cried. "He admitted himself he couldn't positively identify as me whoever it was he let into the building that night. It wasn't me, Tully. It was somebody who deliberately tried to look like me—coat and hat like mine, my stumpy walk from that leg wound on Leyte, easily imitated things like that. And then the guy lets himself into our office and swipes my gun. I should think even a child would see I'm being had!"

"Where would a stranger get a key to your office?" Ellery asked.

"How do I know? How do I know he was even a stranger?"

After a while Carroll became conscious of the silence. He looked up angrily.

"You don't believe me. Actually, neither of you believes me."

West said, "It's not that, John," and began to pace off the cell.

"Look," Ellery said. "West tells me you've hinted at certain important information that for some unimaginable reason you've been holding back. If it can do anything to clear you, Carroll, I'd advise you to toss it into the pot right now."

A prisoner shouted somewhere. West stopped in his tracks. Carroll put his head between his hands.

"I did something that Friday night that can clear me, yes."

"What!" West cried.

"But it's open to all sorts of misinterpretation, chiefly nasty."

"Nastier than the execution chamber at Sing Sing?"

West said, "A woman," with a remote distaste.

"That's right, Tully." Carroll did not look at Ellery, feeling vaguely offended at his indelicacy. "And I promised her I wouldn't use this except as a last resort. It wasn't for her sake, God knows. I've kept my mouth shut because of Helena. Helena loves me, but she's a woman, and a sick woman at that. If she shouldn't believe me . . ."

"Let me get this straight," Ellery said. "You were with this other woman during the murder period? You can actually prove an alibi?"

"Yes."

"And he keeps quiet about it!" West dropped to the steel bunk beside his friend. "John, how many kinds of idiot are you? Don't you have any faith in Helena at all? What happened? Who's the woman?"

"Felicia."

West said, "Oh."

"Mrs. Hunt?" Ellery said sharply.

"That's right. I wandered around in the rain that night trying to figure out how I was going to stop Meredith from disclosing that twenty thousand dollar lunacy and having me arrested. That's when I thought of Felicia. She'd always been able to get anything out of Meredith that she wanted. I phoned her from a pay station and asked if I couldn't come right over." Carroll muttered, "I was pretty panicky, I guess . . ." His voice petered out.

"Well, well?" West said impatiently.

"She was still up, reading in bed. When I told her what it was about, she said to come over. She let me in herself. The maid was asleep, I suppose—anyway, I didn't see Serafina."

"And the time?" Ellery demanded.

"It was just about one a.m. when I got there. I left at four-thirty." Carroll laughed. "Now you know why I've kept quiet about this. Can I expect my wife to believe that I spent three and a half hours in the middle of the night alone with Felicia in her bedroom—and she in a sheer nightgown and peekaboo neg-

74

ligee, by God!—just talking? And not getting anywhere, I might add."

"Three and a half hours?" Ellery's brows went up.

"Felicia didn't see any reason why she should save my neck. Charming character." Carroll's shoulders sloped. "Well, I told you what it would sound like. I'm sure I'd doubt the story myself."

"How much of the time did you have to fight for your honor?" West murmured. "If I didn't know John so well, Queen, I'd be skeptical, too. Felicia's had a mad thing for him. But he's always been allergic to her. I suppose, John, she was willing to make a deal?"

"Something like that."

"One night of amour in return for her influence on dear Meredith in your behalf. Yes, that would be Felicia's little libido at work. But Helena . . ." West frowned. "Quite a situation at that."

Ellery said, "It will have to be risked. Carroll, will Mrs. Hunt support your alibi in court?"

"She'd find it pretty tough to deny her own signature. I had her sign a full statement before a notary."

"Good. Where is the statement?"

"In my safe at the office. It's in a plain manila envelope marked 'Confidential' and bound around with a red rubber band."

"I suggest you give West permission to open your safe, and I'd like to go along as security. Right now."

Carroll bit his lip. Then, abruptly, he nodded.

"Do you know the combination, West?"

"Unless John's changed it. It's one of those letter combination safes in which you can make the combination any word you want. John, is the combination word still 'Helena'?"

"No. I've changed the damn thing four times this summer. The word now is 'rescue'."

"And that," West said solemnly, "is sheer poetry. Well, John, if the open-sesame that Queen lugs around in his wallet should work again in this Bastille, we'll be back with you shortly."

They were as good as West's word. Less than ninety minutes later the guard admitted them once more to Carroll's cell. Ellery had the manila envelope in his hand. He tossed the envelope to the bunk.

"All right, Carroll, let's hear it."

"You haven't opened it?"

"I'd rather you did that yourself."

Carroll picked up the envelope. He slipped the red rubber band off and around his wrist and, with an effort, inserted his fingers into the envelope.

West said, "John. What's the matter?"

"Is this a gag?" Carroll was frantic. His fingers kept clawing around inside the envelope.

"Gag?"

"It's empty! The statement's not here!"

Ellery took the envelope from Carroll's shaking hand, squeezed it open, and peered inside. "When did you see the contents last?"

"I opened the safe several times this summer to make sure the envelope was still there, but I never thought to examine it. I just took it for granted . . ." Carroll sprang from the bunk. "Nobody could have got into that safe—nobody! Not even my secretary. Nobody knew the combination words!"

"John, John." West was shaking him.

"But how in God's nane . . . Unless the safe was broken into! Was it broken into, Queen?"

"No sign of it."

"Then I don't understand!"

"One thing at a time." Ellery took Carroll's other arm and they got him back on the bunk. "The loss isn't necessarily fatal. All you have to do is make sure Mrs. Hunt takes the stand and repeats her statement under oath. She'd have been called to testify, anyway, once the written statement had been placed in evidence. Isn't that right, West?"

"Yes. I'll get hold of Felicia right off."

Carroll was gnawing his fingernails. "Maybe she won't agree, Tully. Maybe . . ."

"She'll agree." West was grim. "Queen, would you come with me? This is one interview I prefer an unbiased witness for. Keep your shirt on, John."

They were back in Carroll's cell with the first grays of dawn. Carroll, who had dropped off to sleep, sat up stupidly. Then he jerked wide-awake. His partner's monkish flesh had acquired a flabbiness he had never seen before.

Carroll's glance darted to the tall shadow in the corner of the cell.

"What's wrong now?" Carroll chattered. "What's happened?"

"I'm afraid . . . the absolute worst." Ellery's voice was full of trouble. "The Hunt house is closed down, Carroll. I'm sorry. Felicia Hunt seems to have disappeared."

That was a bad time for John Carroll. Ellery and West had to do some hard and fast talking to keep him from going to pieces altogether. They talked and talked through the brightening gloom and the tinny sounds of the prison coming to life.

"Hopeless. It's hopeless," Carroll kept muttering.

"No," Ellery said. "It only looks hopeless, Carroll. The Fancy Dan who weaves an elaborate shroud for somebody else more often than not winds up occupying it himself. The clever boys trip over their own cleverness. There's a complex pattern here, and it's getting more tangled by the hour. That's good, Carroll. It's not hopeless at all."

But Carroll only shook his head.

West was circling the cell like a frustrated hawk. "On the other hand, Queen, let's face the facts. John has lost his alibi—the only thing that could surely save him."

"Only temporarily."

"We've got to get that alibi back!"

"We will. Stop running around in circles, West. You're making me nervous. The obvious step is to find that woman."

West looked helpless. "But where do I start? Will you help, Queen?"

Ellery grinned. "I've been hoping you'd ask me that. If Carroll's agreeable, I'd be glad to. Want me to help, Carroll?"

The man on the bunk roused himself. "Want you? I'd take the devil himself! The question is, What can you do?"

"This and that. Here, have a smoke." Ellery jabbed a cigarette between Carroll's swollen lips. "West, you look beat. How about going home and catching some sleep? Oh, and give my father a ring, will you? Tell him about this Felicia Hunt development and ask him for me to hop right on it."

When West had gone, Ellery seated himself on the bunk. For a moment he watched Carroll smoke. Then he said, "Carroll."

"What?"

"Stop feeling sorry for yourself and listen to me. First, let's try to track down that business of the missing alibi statement. Go back to the time when you approached Felicia to sign it. Where did the meeting take place? When? Give me every fact you can remember, and then dig for some you've forgotten."

He listened closely. When Carroll was finished, Ellery nodded.

"It's about as I figured. After Mrs. Hunt signed the statement and Gunder notarized her signature and went away, you left with the envelope in your brief case and instead of going home you returned to your office. You never once, you say, let go of the brief case. In the office you placed the envelope in your safe without checking its contents, locked the safe, and adjusted the dial to a new combination word. And on the three or four subsequent occasions when you checked on the envelope, you claim nobody could have removed the statement from it while you had the safe open, or discovered the new combination you kept setting.

"When the envelope finally was taken from the safe, the only hands not your own to touch it were mine, last night. And I'll vouch for the fact that the statement couldn't have been stolen from me or lost from the envelope on the way over here." Ellery tapped the manila envelope still in Carroll's hand. "So this was empty when I took it from the safe. Carroll, it's been empty for months. It was empty before you ever put it in the safe."

Carroll looked at it, dazed.

"Only one conclusion possible." Ellery lit another cigarette for him, and one for himself. "The only time the envelope was not actually in your physical possession, or in the safe, or in my hands, was for a couple of minutes in the Hunt house the night Felicia signed the statement. You say that after she signed and Gunder notarized her signature, you slipped the statement into the envelope and the envelope into your brief case, that you then took Gunder downstairs to pay him off and see him out. During that couple of minutes the brief case and its contents were out of your sight and control. Therefore that's when the great disappearance took place. And since Mrs. Hunt was the only one in the room with the brief case . . ."

"*Felicia?*"

"Nobody else. Why should she have taken the statement she had just signed, Carroll? Any idea?"

"She double-crossed me, damn her," Carroll said in a thick voice. "And now she's ducked out to avoid having to tell the story under oath."

"We'll get her to duck right back in if we have to extradite her from Little America." Ellery rose and squeezed Carroll's shoulder. "Hang on, Johnny."

Felicia Hunt's whereabouts remained a mystery for as long as it took Ellery to go from the Tombs to Police Headquarters. His father had just come into the office and he was elbow-deep in reports.

"Yes, West phoned me," the Inspector said, without looking up. "If he'd hung on, I'd have been able to tell him in three minutes where Felicia Hunt is. Blast it all, where's that Grierson affidavit!"

Ellery waited patiently.

"Well?" he said at last. "I'm still hanging."

"What? Oh!" Inspector Queen leaned back. "All I did was phone Smallhauser at the D.A.'s office. It seems a couple of days before Carroll's trial started—last Saturday morning—Hunt's widow showed up at the D.A.'s all tricked out in that ghastly mourning she wears, with her doctor in tow. The doctor told Smallhauser Mrs. Hunt was in a dangerously nervous state and couldn't face the ordeal of the trial. He wanted her to get away from the city. Seems she'd bought a cottage up in northern Westchester this summer and a few days up there by herself were just what the M.D. ordered, and was it all right with the D.A.? Well, Smallhauser didn't like it, but he figured that with the cottage having a phone he could always get her back to town in a couple of hours. So he said okay, and she gave her maid a week off and went up there Saturday afternoon. What's the hassle?"

Ellery told him. His father listened suspiciously.

"So that's what West was being so mysterious about," he exclaimed. "An alibi! The D.A.'s going to love this."

"So will Rayfield. He doesn't know about it yet either."

The Inspector cocked a sharpening eye. "What's your stake in this pot?"

"The right," Ellery said piously. "And seeing that it prevails."

His father grunted and reached for the telephone. When he set it down, he had a Mt. Kisco number scribbled on his pad.

"Here, you call her," he said. "I'm working the other side of the street. And don't use a city phone for a toll call! You know where to find a booth."

Ellery was back in front of his father's desk in forty-five minutes.

"What now?" Inspector Queen said. "I was just on my way to the Bullpen."

"She doesn't answer."

"Who doesn't answer?"

"The Hunt lady," Ellery said. "Remember the case? I've phoned at five-minute intervals for almost an hour. Either she's gone into an early hibernation, or she's back in Central America charming the hidalgos."

"Or she just isn't answering her phone. Look, son, I'm up to my lowers this morning. The case is out of my hands, anyway. Keep calling. She'll answer sooner or later."

Ellery tried all day, slipping in and out of the courtroom every half hour. At a little past three the Assistant District Attorney rested his case, and on the request of the defense, Judge Joseph H. Holloway adjourned the trial until the next morning.

Ellery managed to be looking elsewhere when John Carroll was taken from the courtroom. Carroll walked as if his knees were giving way. But as the room cleared, Ellery caught Tully West's eye. West, who was stooping over Helena Carroll in distress, nodded and after a moment came over.

"What about Felicia? She'll testify, won't she?" West sounded urgent.

Ellery glanced over at the reporters surrounding the portly figure of Rayfield. Some were glancing back, noses in the wind.

"We can't talk here, West. Can you get away?"

"I'll have to take Helena home first." West was braced, like a man set for a blow. "Where?"

"My father's office as soon as you can make it."

"What about Rayfield?"

"Better not say anything to him those newsmen can overhear. We can get in touch with him tonight."

It was nearly five o'clock before the tall lawyer hurried into the Inspector's office. He looked haunted.

"Sorry, Helena went to pieces on me. I had to tell her all about John's alibi. Now she's more confused than ever. Damn it, why didn't John trust her in the first place?" West wiped his face. He said slowly, "And now I suppose you'll tell me Felicia refuses to cooperate."

"I almost wish that were it." Ellery was looking haggard himself. "West, I've been phoning since eight-thirty this morning. I tried again only ten minutes ago. She doesn't answer."

"She isn't there?"

"Maybe." Inspector Queen was looking annoyed. "Ellery, why the devil won't you ask the help of the state police? We could have a report on her in an hour."

"No." Ellery got up. "West, do you have your car?"

"I cabbed down."

80

Ellery glanced at his father. The old man threw up his hands and stamped out.

"I ought to have my head examined! Velie, get me a car."

They drove out of the city on Saw Mill River Parkway, Sergeant Velie at the wheel and Inspector Queen beside him nursing his grouch. Behind them, from opposite windows, Ellery and West studied the scenery. They were studying it long after darkness fell.

The sergeant turned the unmarked squad car off the Parkway near Mt. Kisco.

"Pull up at that gas station." They were the first words the Inspector had uttered since leaving the city.

"Stony Ride Road?" the attendant said. "That's up between here and Bedford Hills. Dirt road that goes way off to hell and gone. Who you looking for?"

"The Hunt place.

"Hunt? Never heard."

Ellery stuck his head out. "How about Santos?"

"Santos. Yeah, dame of that name bought the old Meeker place this summer. You follow along here about a mile and a half . . ."

"Using her maiden name," West said as they drove away. "Meredith would have loved that."

The Queens said nothing.

Stony Ride Road climbed and twisted and swooped back, jolting their teeth. The darkness was impressive. They saw only two houses in three miles. A mile beyond the second, they found Felicia Hunt's cottage. Sergeant Velie very nearly drove past it. Its windows were as black as the night itself.

Velie swung the car between two mossy pillars into a crushed-stone driveway.

"No, Velie, stop here and shine your brights dead on the house." The Inspector sounded troubled.

"She's gone," West growled. "She's gone or she never came here at all! What am I going to tell John?"

Ellery borrowed the sergeant's flash and got out. The Inspector put his small hand on Tully West's arm.

"No, Mr. West, we'll wait here." Trouble was in his look, too.

It was a verdigrised fieldstone cottage with rusty wood trim and a darkly shingled roof, cuddled against wild woods. Ellery played his flash on the door. They saw him extend his foot and toe in the door, and they saw it swing back.

81

He went into the house, flash first. A moment later the hall lit up.

He was in the house exactly two minutes.

At the sight of his face Inspector Queen and Sergeant Velie jumped from the car and ran past him and into the cottage.

Ellery said, "You can tell John to forget his alibi, West. She's in there—dead."

Felicia Hunt was lying on the bedroom floor face down, which was unfortunate. The back of her head had been crushed, and the bloody shards of the heavy stoneware vase that had crushed it strewed the floor around her. In the debris were some stiff chrysanthemums, looking like big dead insects. One of them had fallen on her open right palm.

West swallowed and retreated rapidly to the hall.

She had been dressed in a rainbow-striped frock of some iridescent material when death caught her. Jewels glittered on her hands and arms and neck. There were pomponned scuffs on her feet, her legs were bare, and the dead lips and cheeks and eyes showed no trace of make-up.

"She's been dead at least four days, maybe five," Inspector Queen said. "What do you make it, Velie?"

"Nearer four," the big sergeant said. "Last Sunday some time, I'd say, Inspector." He glanced with longing at the tightly closed windows.

"Better not, Velie."

The two men rose. They had touched nothing but the body, and that with profound care.

Ellery stood watching them morosely.

"Find anything, son?"

"No. That rain the other night wiped out any tire tracks or footprints that might have been left. Some spoiling food in the refrigerator, and her car is in the garage behind the house. No sign of robbery." Ellery added suddenly, "Doesn't something about her strike you as queer?"

"Yeah," Sergeant Velie said. "That posy in her hand ought to be a lily."

"Spare us, Velie! What, Ellery?"

"The way she's dressed."

They stared down at her. Tully West came back to the doorway, still swallowing.

The sergeant said, "Looks like she was expecting somebody, the way she's all dolled up."

"That's just what it doesn't look like," Inspector Queen snapped. "A woman as formally brought up as this one, who's expecting somebody, puts on shoes and stockings, Velie—doesn't go around barelegged and wearing bedroom slippers. She hadn't even made up her face or polished her nails. She was expecting nobody. What about the way she's dressed, Ellery?"

"Why isn't she still in mourning?"

"Huh?"

"She drives up here alone Saturday after wearing nothing but unrelieved black in town, and within twenty-four hours or less she's in a color-happy dress, back wearing her favorite jewelry, and having a ball for herself. It tells a great deal about Felicia de Los Santos Hunt."

"It doesn't tell me a thing," his father retorted. "What I want to know is why she was knocked off. It wasn't robbery. And there's nothing to indicate rape, although it's true a would-be rapist might have panicked—"

"Isn't it obvious that this is part and parcel of Hunt's murder and the frame-up of John Carroll?" West broke in with bitterness. "Rape! Felicia was murdered to keep her from giving John the alibi that would get him off the hook."

The Inspector nibbled his mustache.

"What does it take to convince you people that somebody is after Carroll's hide?"

"That sounds like sense, Dad."

"Maybe."

"At the least, the Hunt woman's murder is bound to give the case against Carroll a different look.—Dad, before Velie phones the state police."

"Well?"

"Let's you and Velie and I really give this place a going over."

"What for, Ellery?"

"For that alibi statement Felicia signed and then took back when Carroll wasn't looking. It's a long shot, but . . . who knows?"

Their session with the state police took the rest of the night. It was sunrise before they got back to the city.

West asked to be dropped off at Beekman Place.

"Sam Rayfield won't thank me for waking him up, but then I haven't had any sleep at all. Who's going to tell John?"

"I will," Ellery said.

West turned away with a grateful wave.

"So far so bad," the Inspector said as they sped downtown. "Now all I have to do is talk the D.A.'s office into joining Rayfield in a plea to Judge Holloway, and why I should have to do it is beyond me!"

"You going home, Inspector?"

"Sure I'm going home, Velie! I can take Smallhauser's abuse over my own phone as well as at Headquarters. And maybe get some sleep, too. How about you, son?"

"The Tombs," Ellery said.

He parted with Sergeant Velie at the Headquarters garage and walked over to the Criminal Courts Building. His head was muddy, and he wanted to cleanse it. He tried not to think of John Carroll.

Carroll woke up instantly at the sound of the cell door.

"Queen! How did you make out with Felicia?"

Ellery said, "We didn't."

"She won't testify?"

"She can't testify. John, she's dead."

It was brutal, but he knew no kinder formula. Carroll was half sitting up, leaning on an elbow, and he remained that way. His eyes kept blinking in a monotonous rhythm.

"Dead . . ."

"Murdered. We found her on the bedroom floor of her cottage with her head smashed in. She'd been dead for days."

"Murdered." Carroll blinked and blinked. "But who—?"

"There's not a clue. So far, anyway." Ellery lit a cigarette and held it out. Carroll took it. But then he dropped it and covered his face with both hands. "I'm sorry, John," Ellery said.

Carroll's hands came down. He had his lower lip in his teeth.

"I'm no coward, Queen. I faced death a hundred times in the Pacific and didn't chicken out. But a man likes to die for some purpose . . . I'm scared."

Ellery looked away.

"There's got to be some way out of this!" Carroll dropped off the bunk and ran in his bare feet to the bars of the cell, to grasp them with both hands. But then he whirled and sprang at Ellery, seizing him by the arms. "That statement—that's my out, Queen! Maybe she didn't destroy it. Maybe she took it up there with her. If you can find it for me—"

"I've looked," Ellery said gently. "And my father looked, and Sergeant Velie, too. We covered the cottage inside and out. It took us over two hours. We didn't call the local police until we were satisfied it wasn't there."

"But it's got to be there! My life depends on it! Don't you see?" He shook Ellery.

"Yes, John."

"You missed it. Maybe she put it in an obvious place, like in that story of Poe's. Did you look in her purse? Her luggage?"

"Yes, John."

"Her suits—coats—the linings—"

"Yes, John."

"Her car—?"

"And her car."

"Then maybe it was on her," Carroll said feverishly. "On her person. Did you . . .? No, I suppose you wouldn't."

"We would and we did." Ellery's arms ached. He wished Carroll would let go.

"How about that big ruby-and-emerald locket she was so hipped on? The alibi statement was only a single sheet of paper. She might have wadded it up and hidden it in the locket. Did you look there while you were searching the body?"

"Yes, John. All we found in the locket were two photos, Spanish-looking elderly people. Her parents, I suppose."

Carroll released him. Ellery rubbed his arms.

"How about books?" Carroll mumbled. "Felicia was always reading some trashy novel or other. She might have slipped it between two pages—"

"There were eleven books in the house, seven magazines. I went through them myself."

In the cold cell Carroll wiped the perspiration from his cheeks.

"Desk with a false compartment? . . . Cellar? . . .Is there an attic? . . .Did you search the garage?"

He went on and on. Ellery waited for him to run down.

When Carroll was finally quiet, Ellery called the guard. His last glimpse of the young lawyer was of a spreadeagled figure, motionless on the bunk, eyes shut. All Ellery could think of was a corpse.

Judge Joseph H. Holloway shook his head. He was a gray-skinned, frozen-eyed old-timer of the criminal courts, known to practising members of the New York bar as Old Steelguts.

"I didn't come down to my chambers an hour early on a Monday morning, Counselor Rayfield, for the pleasure of listening to your mellifluous voice. That pleasure palled on me a long time ago. I granted an adjournment Friday morning because of the Hunt woman's murder, but do you have any evidence to warrant a further postponement? So far I've heard nothing but a lot of booshwah."

Assistant District Attorney Smallhauser nodded admiringly. Judge Holloway's fondness for the slang of his youth—indulged in only *in camera*, of course—was trifled with at the peril of the trifler. "Booshwah is *le mot juste* for it, Your Honor. I apologize for being a party to this frivolous waste of your time."

Samuel Rayfield favored the murderous little assistant D.A. with a head-shrinking glance and clamped his teeth more firmly about his cold cigar. "Come off it, Joe," he said to Judge Holloway. "This is a man's life we're playing with. We're not privileged to kick him to death simply because he acted like a damn fool in holding back his alibi. All I want this adjournment for is time to look for that alibi statement the Hunt woman signed when she was alive enough to write."

Judge Holloway's dentures gleamed toward Smallhauser.

"The alibi statement your client *says* the Hunt woman signed," the little D.A. said with his prim smile.

The Judge's dentures promptly turned to Rayfield.

"I've got the notary, Gunder, to attest to the fact that she signed it," the portly lawyer snapped.

"That she signed some paper, yes. But you people admit yourselves that Carroll concealed the text of the paper from Gunder. For all Gunder knows he might have been notarizing the woman's signature to the lease of a new dog house." The little D.A. turned his smile on the Judge. "I'm bound to say, Your Honor, this whole thing smells more and more to me like a stall."

"Come around some time when you've put on long pants and I'll show you what a real stall smells like, Smallhauser!" the famous lawyer said. "Joe, I'm not stalling. There's a chance she didn't destroy the statement. Not much of one, I admit, but I wouldn't sleep nights if I thought I hadn't exhausted every avenue of investigation in Carroll's behalf."

"You wouldn't lose half of a strangled snore," the Judge said with enjoyment. "Look, Sam, it's all conjecture, and you know it. You can't even show that Mrs. Hunt stole that alleged statement of hers from Carroll in the first place."

"Ellery Queen showed—"

"I know what Ellery Queen showed. He showed his usual talent for making something out of nothing. Ellery's idea of proof!" The old jurist snorted. "And even if the Hunt woman did steal an alibi statement from Carroll, what did she steal it for if not to burn it or flush it down a toilet? And even if she held on to it, where is it? The Queens didn't find it in her Westchester cottage. You yourself ransacked her New York house over the week-end. You got a court order to examine her safe deposit box. You questioned her maid and the people in Carroll's office and God knows who else—all without result. Be reasonable, Sam! That alibi statement either never existed or, if it did, it doesn't exist any more. I can't predicate a postponement on the defendant's unsupported allegation of alibi. You know I can't."

"Of course, if you'd like to put Carroll on the stand," Smallhauser said with a grin, "so I can cross-examine him—"

Rayfield ignored him. "All right, Joe. But you can't deny that Hunt's wife has also been murdered. That's a fact, and in evidence of it we can produce a corpse.And I don't believe in coincidences. When a man's murder is followed by his wife's murder, I say the two are connected. The connection in this case is obvious. The murder of Felicia Hunt was committed in order to blow up Carroll's alibi for the murder of Meredith Hunt and to cement Carroll's conviction. How can his trial proceed with this area unexplained? I tell you, Joe, this man is being framed by somebody who's committed two murders in order to pull the frame off! Give us time to explore."

"I remember once sitting here listening to Ellery Queen," Judge Holloway said grimly. "You're beginning to sound like his echo. Sam, evidence is what trials are ruled by, and evidence is what you ain't got. Motion denied. My courtroom, gentlemen, ten o'clock on the nose."

Ellery got the answer that Thursday afternoon in the half-empty courtroom while the jury was out deliberating John Carroll's fate.

It came to him after an agonizing reappraisal of the facts as he knew them. He had gone over them countless times before. This time—in the lightning flash he had begun to think would never strike again—he saw it.

By good luck, at the time it came, he was alone. Carroll had been taken back to the Tombs, and his wife and the two lawyers had gone with him so that he would not have to sweat the waiting out alone.

A sickish feeling invaded Ellery's stomach. He got up and went out and found the nearest men's room.

When he returned to the courtroom, Tully West was waiting for him.

87

"Helena wants to talk to you." West's face was green, too.

"No."

"I beg your pardon?"

Ellery shook his head clear. "I mean—yes, of course."

West misunderstood. "I don't blame you. I wish I were anywhere else myself. Rayfield was smart—he bowed out for 'coffee'."

Carroll was being held in a detention room under guard. Ellery was surprised at his calm, even gentle, look. It was Helena Carroll's eyes that were wild. He was holding her hands, trying to console her.

"Honey, honey, it's going to come out all right. They won't convict an innocent man."

"Why are they taking so *long*? They've been out five hours!"

"That's a good sign, Helena," West said. "The longer they take, the better John's chances are."

She saw Ellery then, and she struggled to her feet and was at him so swiftly that he almost stepped back.

"I thought you were supposed to be so marvelous at these things! You haven't done anything for John—anything."

Carroll tried to draw her back, but she shook him off. Her painetched face was livid.

"I don't care, John! You should have hired a real detective while there was still time. I wanted you to— I *begged* you and Tully not to rely on somebody so close to the police!"

"Helena, really." West was embarrassed.

Ellery said stonily, "No, Mrs. Carroll is quite right. I wish I had never got mixed up in it."

She was staring at him intently. "That almost sounds as if . . ."

"As if what, Helena?" West was trying to humor her, get her away.

"As if he knows. *Tully, he does*. Look at his face!" She clawed at Ellery. "You know, and you won't say anything! You talk, do you hear? Tell me! *Who's behind this?*"

West was flabbergasted. With surprise John Carroll studied Ellery's face for a moment, then he went to the barred window and stood there rigidly.

"Who?" His wife was weeping now. "*Who?*" .

But Ellery was as rigid as Carroll. "I'm sorry, Mrs. Carroll. I can't save your husband. It's too late."

"Too late," she said hysterically. "How can you say it's too late when—"

"Helena." West took the little woman by the arms and forcibly

88

sat her down. Then he turned to Ellery, his lean face dark. "What's this all about, Queen? You sound as if you're covering up for someone. Are you?"

Ellery glanced past the angry lawyer to the motionless man at the window.

"I'll leave it up to John," he said. "Shall I answer him, John?"

For a moment it seemed as if Carroll had not heard. But then he turned, and there was something about him—a dignity, a finality—that quieted Tully West and Helena Carroll and sent their glances seeking each other.

Carroll replied clearly, "*No.*"

Looking out over the prison yard from the Warden's office, Ellery thought he had never seen a lovelier spring night sky, or a sadder one. A man should die on a stormy night, with all Nature protesting. This, he thought, this is cruel and unusual punishment.

He sought the Warden's clock.

Carroll had fourteen minutes of time left.

The Warden's door opened and closed behind him. Ellery did not turn around. He thought he knew who it was. He had been half expecting his father for an hour.

"Ellery. I looked for you at the Death House."

"I was down there before, Dad. Had a long talk with Carroll. I thought you'd be here long ago."

"I wasn't intending to come at all. It isn't my business. I did my part of it. Or maybe that's why I'm here. After a lifetime of this sort of thing, I'm still not hardened to it . . . Ellery."

"Yes, Dad."

"It's Helena Carroll. She's hounded and haunted me. She's waiting in an Ossining bar right now with West. I drove them up. Mrs. Carroll thinks I have some drag with you. Do I?"

Ellery said from the window, "In practically everything, Dad. But not in this."

"I don't understand you," the Inspector said heavily. "If you have information that would save Carroll, how can you keep buttoned up now?—here? All right, you saw something we didn't. It is my job you're worried about, because I helped put Carroll on this spot? If you know something that proves his innocence, the hell with me."

"I'm not thinking of you."

"Then you can only be thinking of Carroll. He's protecting somebody, he's willing to go to the Chair for it, and you're helping him do it. Ellery, you can't do that." The old man clutched his arm. "There's still a few minutes. The Warden's got an open line to the Governor's office."

But Ellery shook his head.

Inspector Queen stared at his son's set profile for a moment. Then he went over to a chair and sat down, and father and son waited.

At 11:04 the lights suddenly dimmed.
Both men stiffened.
The office brightened.
At 11:07 it happened again.
And again at 11:12.

After that there was no change. Ellery turned away from the window, fumbling for his cigarettes.

"Do you have a light, Dad?"

The old man struck a match for him. Ellery nodded and sat down beside him.

"Who's going to tell her?" his father said suddenly.

"You are," Ellery said. "I can't."

Inspector Queen rose. "Live and learn," he said.

"Dad—"

The opening of the door interrupted them. Ellery got to his feet. The Warden's face was as haggard as theirs. He was wiping it with a damp handkerchief.

"I never get used to it," he said, "never . . . He went very peacefully. No trouble at all."

Ellery said, "Yes, he would."

"He gave me a message for you, by the way."

"Thanking him, I suppose," Inspector Queen said bitterly.

"Why, yes, Inspector," the Warden said. "He said to tell your son how grateful he was. What on earth did he mean?"

"Don't ask *him*," the Inspector said. "My son's constituted himself a one-man subcommittee of the Almighty. Where you going to wait for me, Ellery?" he demanded as they left the Warden's office. "I mean while I do the dirty work?"

Ellery said stiffly, "Take Helena Carroll and Tully West back to the city first."

"Just tell me one thing. What was Carroll grateful to you for? Who'd you help him cover up?"

Ellery shook his head. "I'll see you at home afterward."

90

"Well?" the old man said. He had got into his frayed bathrobe and slippers, and he was nursing a cup of stale coffee with his puffy hands. He looked exhausted. "And it had better be good."

"Oh, it's good," Ellery said. "If good is the word." He had not undressed, had not even removed his topcoat. He sat there as he had come in from the long drive to wait for his father. He stared at the blank Queen wall. "It was a slip of the tongue. I remembered it. After a long time of not remembering, I remembered it. It wouldn't have made any difference if the slip had never been made, or if I'd forgotten it altogether. Any difference to Carroll, I mean. He was sunk from the start. I couldn't save him, Dad, He'd had it."

"What slip?" the old man demanded. "Of whose tongue? or was I deaf as well as blind?"

"I was the only one who heard it. It had to do with Felicia Hunt. Her husband dies and she goes into Spanish mourning, total and unadorned. But when she gets off by herself in that hillside cottage, back on go the gay clothes, her favorite jewelry. By herself, mind you—alone. Safe from all eyes, even her maid's."

Ellery stared harder at the blank wall. "When we got back to town after finding her body, I went directly to the Tombs to tell Carroll about the murder in Westchester of the only human being who could give him an alibi. Carroll was frantic. His mind went back to the alibi statement she had signed and then taken from his brief case unknown to him at the time. It was all he could think of, naturally. If that piece of paper existed, if she had hidden it instead of destroying it, he could still be saved. He kept pounding at me. Maybe she'd hidden it in her luggage, her car, a secret drawer. He went on and on. And one of the places he mentioned as a possible hiding place of the statement was the locket of the ruby-and-emerald pendant Felicia Hunt was so fond of. 'Did you look there?' he asked me. *While you were searching the body?*'"

Ellery flung aside a cigarette he had never lit. "That question of his was what I finally remembered."

"He knew she was wearing the pendant . . ."

"Exactly, when no one could have known except ourselves when we found her—and the one who had murdered her there five days earlier."

He sank deeper into his coat. "It was a blow, but there it was—John Carroll had murdered Felicia Hunt. He'd had the opportunity, of course. You and Velie agreed that the latest she

91

could have been murdered was the preceding Sunday. And on that Sunday Carroll was still free on bail. It wasn't until the next morning, Monday, that he had to resubmit to the custody of the court for the commencement of his trial."

"But it doesn't add up," Inspector Queen spluttered. "The Hunt woman's testimony would get him an acquittal. Why should Carroll have knocked off the only witness who could give him his alibi?"

"Just what I asked myself. And the only answer that made sense was: Carroll must have had reason to believe that when Felicia took the stand in court, she was going to tell the truth."

"Truth? The truth about what?"

"About Carroll's alibi being false."

"False?"

"Yes. And from his standpoint, of course, that would compel him to kill her. To protect the alibi."

"But without her he had no alibi, true *or* false!"

"Correct," Ellery said softly, *"but when Carroll drove up to Westchester he didn't know that.* At that time he thought he had her signed statement locked in his office safe. He didn't learn until days after he had killed her—when West and I opened the safe and found the envelope empty—that he no longer had possession of the alibi statement, hadn't had possession for months, in fact—that, as I pointed out to him, Felicia Hunt must have taken it from his brief case while he was downstairs showing the notary out. No wonder he almost collapsed."

"I'll be damned," the Inspector said. "I'll be double-damned."

Ellery shrugged. "If Carroll's alibi for Meredith Hunt's murder was a phony, then the case against him stood as charged. The alibi was the only thing that gave him the appearance of innocence. If in fact he had no alibi, everything pointed to his guilt of Hunt's murder, as the jury rightfully decided.

"Carroll filled in the details for me earlier tonight in the Death House." Ellery's glance went back to the wall. "He said that when he left his house that rainy night after Hunt's ultimatum, to walk off his anger, the fog gave him a slight lease on hope. Maybe Hunt's plane was grounded and Hunt was still within reach. He phoned La Guardia and found that all flights had been delayed for a few hours. On the chance that Hunt was hanging around the airport, Carroll stopped in at his office and got his target pistol. He had some vague idea, he said, of threatening Hunt into a change of heart.

"He took a cab to La Guardia, found Hunt waiting for the fog to clear, and persuaded him to get his car from the parking lot so that they could talk in privacy. Eventually Hunt meandered back to Manhattan and parked on East 58th Street. The talk in the car became a violent quarrel. Carroll's hair-trigger temper went off, and he shot Hunt. He left Hunt in the Thunderbird and stumbled back home in the rain.

"The next morning, when we called on Mrs. Hunt to announce her husband's killing and found Carroll and West there, and you mentioned that the killer had left his gun in Hunt's car, Carroll was sick. Remember he ran into the bathroom? He wasn't acting that time. For the first time he realized that, in his fury and panic, he'd completely forgotten about the gun.

"As a lawyer," Ellery went on, "he knew what a powerful circumstantial case loomed against him, and that the only thing that could save him was an equally powerful alibi. He saw only one possible way to get it. He had never destroyed the love letters Felicia Hunt had written him during her infatuation. And he knew her dread of scandal. So he fabricated a statement out of the whole cloth about having spent the murder period in her bedroom 'pleading' with her to intercede with her husband, and he took the statement to her. He didn't have to spell out his threat. Felicia understood clearly enough the implication of his proposal . . . that if she didn't give him the phony alibi he needed, he would publish her love letters and ruin her with her straitlaced Latin-American family and compatriots. She signed."

"But why didn't Carroll produce the alibi right away, Ellery? What was his point in holding it back?"

The legal mind again. If he produced it during the investigation, even if it served to clear him, the case would still be open on the books and later he might find himself back in it up to his ears. But if he stood trial for Hunt's murder and *then* produced the fake alibi and was acquitted—he was safe from the law forever by the rule of double jeopardy. He couldn't be tried again for Hunt's killing after that even if the alibi should at some future date be exposed as a fake.

"He knew from the beginning," Ellery continued, "that Felicia Hunt was the weak spot in his plan. She was neurotic and he was terribly afraid she might wilt under pressure when he needed her most. As the trial approached, Carroll told me, he got more and more nervous about her. So the day before it was scheduled to start, he decided to talk to her again. Learning that she'd gone into retreat up in Westchester, he found an excuse to get away from his family and drove up to the cottage. His worst fears were realized. She told him that she had changed her mind. Scandal or no scandal, she wasn't going to testify falsely under oath and lay herself open to perjury. What she didn't tell him—it might possibly have saved her life if she had—was that she'd stolen and destroyed the alibi statement he had forced her to sign months before.

"Carroll grabbed the nearest heavy object and hit her over the head with it. Now at least, he consoled himself, she wouldn't be able to repudiate her signed statement, which he thought was in his office safe."

"And you've kept all this to yourself," his father muttered. "Why, Ellery? You certainly didn't owe Carroll anything."

Ellery turned from the wall. He looked desperately tired.

"No, I didn't owe Carroll anything . . . a man with a completely cockeyed moral sense . . . too proud to live on his wife's money, yet capable of stealing twenty thousand dollars . . . a faithful husband who nevertheless kept the love letters of a woman he despised for their possible future value to him . . . a man with a strange streak of honesty who was capable of playing a scene like an accomplished actor . . . a loving father who permitted himself to murder two people.

"No, I didn't owe him anything," Ellery said, "but he wasn't the only one involved. And no one knew that better than Carroll. The afternoon that the answer came to me, while we were waiting for the jury to come in, I told Mrs. Carroll I couldn't save her husband, that it was too late. Carroll was the only one present who knew what I meant. He knew I meant it was too late for *him*, that I couldn't save him because I knew he was guilty. And when I put it up to him, he gave me to understand that I wasn't to give him away. It wasn't for his own sake—he knew the verdict the jury was going to bring in. He knew he was already a dead man.

"And so I respected his last request. I couldn't save him, but I could save his family's memories of him. This way Helena Carroll and little Breck and Louanne will always think John Carroll died the victim of a miscarriage of justice." Ellery shucked his topcoat and headed for his bedroom. "How could I deny them that comfort?"

THE ZERO CLUE

BY REX STOUT

Rex Stout was born in Noblesville, Indiana, on December 1, 1886, the sixth of nine children of John and Lucetta Stout. Always precocious in arithmetic, he invented as a young man a school savings bank system he sold to 400 schools. He retired from its management with $400,000 in 1927 and turned to serious writing. In 1934 his 286-pound sleuth Nero Wolfe was born. Mr. Stout was active in writers' organizations and shared with Wolfe a love of gardening and good food. He died on October 27, 1975.

IT BEGAN WITH A COMBINATION OF circumstances, but what doesn't? To mention just one, if there hadn't been a couple of checks to deposit that morning I might not have been in that neighborhood at all.

But I was, and, approving of the bright sun and the sharp, clear air, I turned east off of Lexington Avenue into 37th Street and walked some forty paces to the number. It was a five-story yellow brick. The lobby, not much bigger than my bedroom, had a fancy rug, a fireplace without a fire, some greenery, and a watchdog in uniform who looked at me suspiciously.

As I opened my mouth to meet his challenge, circumstances combined. A big guy in a dark-blue top-coat and a gray Homburg, entering from the street, breezed past me, heading for the elevator, and as he did so the elevator door opened and a dark-haired girl with a fur jacket over her arm emerged.

Four of us in that undersized lobby made a crowd, and we had to maneuver. Meanwhile, I was speaking to the watchdog, "My name's Goodwin and I'm calling on Leo Heller."

His expression changing, he blurted at me, "You the Archie Goodwin who works for Nero Wolfe?"

The girl stopped short and turned, and the big guy, inside the elevator, blocked the door from closing and stuck his head out, while the watchdog was going on, "I've saw your picture in the paper, and, look, I want Nero Wolfe's autograph."

It would have been more to the point if he had wanted mine, but I'm not petty. The man in the elevator, which was self-service, was letting the door close, but the girl was standing by, and I hated to disappoint her by denying I was me, as of course I would have had to do if I had been there on an operation that needed cover.

I was actually not on an operation at all. Chiefly, I was satisfying my curiosity. At five in the afternoon the day before, in Nero Wolfe's office on the ground floor of his old brownstone house on West 35th Street, there had been a phone call. After taking it I had gone to the kitchen to get a glass of water. Fritz Brenner, the chef and housekeeper, was boning a pig's head for what he calls *fromage de cochon*. I told him I was going upstairs to do a little yapping.

"He is so happy up there," Fritz protested, but there was a gleam in his eye. He knows darned well that if I quit yapping, the day would come when there would be no money in the bank to meet the payroll, including him.

I went up three flights to the roof, where ten thousand square feet of glass in aluminum frames make a home for ten thousand orchid plants. The riot of color doesn't take my breath any more, but it is unquestionably a show, and as I went through that day, I kept my eyes straight ahead to preserve my mood for yapping intact. However, it was wasted. In the intermediate room Wolfe was glaring at a box of *Odontoglossum* seedlings in his hand, while Theodore Horstmann, the orchid nurse, stood nearby with his lips tightened to a thin line.

As I approached, Wolfe transferred the glare to me and barked savagely, "Thrips!"

I did some fast mood-shifting. There's a time to yap and a time not to yap. But I walked up to him.

"What do you want?" he rasped.

"I realize," I said politely but firmly, "that this is ill-timed, but I told Mr. Heller I would speak to you. He phoned—"

"Speak to me later! If at all!"

"I'm to call him back. It's Leo Heller, the probability wizard. He says that calculations have led him to suspect that a client of his may have committed a serious crime, but it's only a suspicion. He doesn't want to tell the police until it has been investigated, and he wants us to investigate. I asked for details but he wouldn't give them on the phone. I thought I might as well run over there now—it's over on East Thirty-seventh Street—and find out if it looks like a job. He wouldn't—"

"No!"

"My eardrums are not insured. No what?"

"Get out!" He shook the thrips-infested seedlings at me. "That man couldn't hire me for any conceivable job on any imaginable terms! Get out!"

I turned, prompt but dignified, and went. But on my way back down to the office I was wearing a grin. Even without the thrips, Wolfe's reaction to my message would have been substantially the same, which was why I had been prepared to yap. The thrips had merely keyed it up.

Leo Heller had been tagged by fame, with articles about him in magazines and Sunday newspapers. While making a living as a professor of mathematics at Underhill College, he had begun, for amusement, to apply the laws of probability, through highly

97

complicated mathematical formulas, to various current events, ranging from ball games and horse races to farm crops and elections. Checking back on his records after a couple of years, he had been startled and pleased to find that the answers he had got from his formulas had been 86.3 per cent correct, and he had written a piece about it for a magazine.

Naturally, requests had started coming, from all kinds of people for all kinds of calculations. Heller had granted some of them, to be obliging, but when he had tried telling a woman in Yonkers where to look for $31,000 in currency she had lost, and she had followed instructions and found it, and had insisted on giving him two grand, he resigned his professorship.

That had been three years ago, and now he was sitting pretty. It was said that his annual take was in six figures, that he returned all his mail unanswered, accepting only clients who called in person, and that there was nothing on earth he wouldn't try to dope a formula for, provided he was furnished with enough factors to make it feasible.

It had been suggested that he should be hauled in for fortunetelling, but the cops and the D.A.'s office let it lay, as well they might, since he had a college degree and there were at least a thousand fortunetellers operating in New York who had never made it through high school.

It wasn't known whether Heller was keeping his percentage up to 86.3, but I happened to know it wasn't goose eggs. Some months earlier a president of a big corporation had hired Wolfe to find out which member of his staff was giving trade secrets to a competitor. I had been busy on another case at the time, and Wolfe had put Orrie Cather on the collection of details.

Orrie had made a long job of it, and the first we knew we were told by the corporation president that he had got impatient and gone to Leo Heller with the problem. Heller cooked up a formula and came out with an answer: the name of one of the junior vice-presidents, and the junior VP had confessed!

Our client freely admitted that most of the facts he had given Heller for the ingredients of his formula had been supplied by us, gathered by Orrie Cather. He offered no objection to paying our bill, but Wolfe was so sore he actually told me to send no bill—an instruction I disregarded, knowing how he would regret it after he had cooled off. However, he still had it in for Leo Heller. Taking on any kind of job for him would have been absolutely off the program that day or any other day, even if there had been no thrips within a mile of 35th Street.

Back downstairs in the office, I phoned Heller and told him nothing doing. "He's extremely sensitive," I explained, "and this is an insult. As you know, he's the greatest detective that ever lived, and—do you know that?"

"I'm willing to postulate it," Heller conceded, in a thin voice that tended to squeak. "Why an insult?"

"Because you want to hire Nero Wolfe, meaning me really, to collect facts on which you can base a decision whether your suspicion about your client is justified. You might as well try to hire Stan Musial as bat boy for a rookie outfielder. Mr. Wolfe doesn't sell the raw material for answers, he sells answers."

"I'm quite willing to pay him for an answer—any amount short of exorbitance, and in cash. I'm gravely concerned about this situation, and my data are insufficient. I shall be delighted if, with the data, I get an answer from Mr. Wolfe, and—"

"And," I put in, "if his answer is that your client has committed a serious crime, as you suspect, he decides whether and when to call a cop, not you. Yes?"

"Certainly." Heller was eager to oblige. "I do not intend or desire to shield a criminal—on the contrary."

"Okay. Then it's like this: It wouldn't do any good for me to take it up with Mr. Wolfe again today, because his feelings have been hurt. But tomorrow morning I have to go to our bank on Lexington Avenue, not far from your place, and I could drop in to see you. Frankly, I doubt if Mr. Wolfe will take this case on, but we can always use money and I'll try to sell him. Shall I come?"

"What time?"

"Say a quarter past ten."

"Come ahead. My business begins at eleven. Take the elevator to the fifth floor. An arrow points right, to the waiting room, but go left, to the door at the end of the hall and push the button, and I'll let you in. If you're on time we'll have more than half and hour."

"I'm always on time."

That morning I was a little early. It was nine minutes past ten when I entered the lobby on 37th Street and gave the watchdog my name.

I told the watchdog I would try to get Nero Wolfe's autograph for him, and wrote his name in my notebook: Nils Lamm. Meanwhile, the girl stood there, frowning at us. She was twenty-three or four, and without the deep frown her face would probably have deserved attention. Since she showed no trace of embarrassment at staring fixedly at a stranger, I saw no reason why I should, but something had to be said, so I asked her, "Do you want one?"

She cocked her head. "One what?"

"Autograph. Either Mr. Wolfe's or mine, take your pick."

"Oh. You are Archie Goodwin, aren't you? I've seen your picture, too."

"Then I'm it."

"I . . . " She hesitated, then made up her mind. "I want to ask you something."

"Shoot."

Someone trotted in from the street, a brisk female in mink, executive type, between twenty and sixty, and the girl and I moved aside to clear the lane to the elevator. The newcomer told Nils Lamm she was seeing Leo Heller and refused to give her name, but when Lamm insisted, she coughed it up: Agatha Abbey, she said, and he let her take the elevator.

The girl told me she had been working all night and was tired, so we went to a bench by the fireplace. Close up, I would still have said twenty-three or -four, but someone or something had certainly been harrassing her. Naturally, there was a question in my mind about the night work.

She answered it: "My name's Susan Maturo, registered nurse."

"Thanks. You know mine and I'm a registered detective."

She nodded. "That's why I want to ask you something. If I hired Nero Wolfe to investigate a—a matter, how much would it cost?"

I raised my shoulders half an inch and let them down. "It all depends. The kind of matter, the amount of time taken, the wear and tear on his brain, the state of your finances."

I paused, letting it hang, to return a rude stare that was being aimed at us by another arrival, a thin, tall, bony specimen in a brown suit that badly needed pressing, with a bulging brief case under his arm. When my gaze met his he called it off and strode to the elevator, without any exchange with Nils Lamm.

I resumed to Susan Maturo: "Have you got a matter, or are you just researching?"

"Oh, I've got a matter." She set her teeth on her lip, nice teeth and not a bad lip, and kept them that way a while, regarding me. Then she went on, "It hit me hard, and it's been getting worse instead of better. I decided to come to this Leo Heller and see what he could do, so I came this morning. I was sitting up there in his waiting room—two people were already there, a man and a woman—and I felt suddenly that I was just being bitter and vindictive, and I don't think I'm like that."

Apparently, she needed some cooperation, so I assured her, "You don't look vindictive."

She touched my sleeve with her fingertips to thank me. "So I got up and left. Then, as I was leaving the elevator, I heard that man saying your name and who you are, and it popped into my head to ask you. I asked how much it would cost to have Nero Wolfe investigate, but that was premature, because what I really want is to tell him about it and to get his advice about investigating."

She was dead-serious, so I arranged my face and voice to fit. "It's like this," I told her. "For that kind of approach to Mr. Wolfe, with no big fee in prospect, some expert preparation is required, and I'm the only expert in the field." I glanced at my wrist and saw 10:19. "I've got a date, but I can spare five minutes if you want to brief me on the essentials, and then I'll tell you how it strikes me. What was it that hit you?"

She looked at me, shot a glance at Nils Lamm, who couldn't have moved out of earshot in that lobby if he had wanted to, and came back to me. "When I start to talk about it," she said, "it sticks in my throat and chokes me, and five minutes wouldn't be enough. Anyway, I need someone old and wise like Nero Wolfe. Won't you let me see him?"

I promised to try, but I told her it would be a waste of time and effort for me to take her in to Wolfe cold. Though I was neither old nor wise she would have to give me at least a full outline before I could furnish either an opinion or help.

She agreed that that was reasonable and gave me her address and phone number, and we arranged to communicate later in the day. She slipped into her jacket and I went and opened the door for her, and she departed.

On the way up in the elevator my watch said 10:28, so I wasn't on time, after all, but we would still have half an hour before Heller's business day began. On the fifth floor a plaque on the wall facing the elevator was lettered LEO HELLER, WAITING ROOM, with an arrow pointing right, and at the end of the narrow hall a door bore the invitation, WALK IN.

I turned left, toward the other end, where I pushed a button beside a door, noticing as I did so that the door was ajar a scanty inch. When my ring brought no response, and a second one, more prolonged, didn't, either, I shoved the door open, crossed the sill, and called Heller's name.

101

No reply. There was no one in sight.

Thinking that he had probably stepped into the waiting room and would soon return, I glanced around to see what the lair of a probability wizard looked like, and was impressed by some outstanding features. The door, of metal, was a good three inches thick, either for security or for sound-proofing, or maybe both. If there were any windows they were behind the heavy draperies; the artificial light came indirectly from channels in the walls just beneath the ceiling. The room was air-conditioned. There were locks on all the units of a vast assembly of filing cabinets that lined the rear wall. The floor, with no rugs, was tiled with some velvety material on which a footfall was barely audible.

The thick door was for sound-proofing. I had closed it, nearly, on entering, and the silence was complete. Not a sound of the city could be heard, though the clang and clatter of Lexington Avenue was almost next door one way and of Third Avenue the other.

I crossed for a look at the desk, but there was nothing remarkable about it except that it was twice the usual size. Among other items it held a vase of flowers, a rack of books with titles that were not tempting, an abacus of ivory or a good imitation, and a stack of legal-size working pads. Stray sheets of paper were scattered about, and a single pad had on its top sheet some scribbled formulas that looked like doodles by Einstein. Also, a jar of sharpened lead pencils had been overturned, and some of them were in a sort of pattern near the edge of the desk.

I had been in there ten minutes and no Heller, and when, at eleven o'clock by schedule, Wolfe came down to the office from his morning session with the orchids, it was desirable that I should be present. So I went, leaving the door ajar as I had found it, walked down the hall to the door of the waiting room at the other end, and entered.

This room was neither air-conditioned nor sound-proofed. Someone had opened a window a couple of inches and the din was jangling in. Five people were here and there on chairs, three of whom I had seen before: the big guy in the dark-blue topcoat and Homburg, the brisk female in mink who called herself Agatha Abbey, and the tall, thin specimen with a brief case.

Neither of the other two was Leo Heller. One was a swarthy little article, slick and sly, with his hair pasted to his scalp, and the other was a big blob of an overfed matron with a spare chin.

I addressed the gathering: "Has Mr. Heller been in here?"

A couple of them shook their heads, and the swarthy article

said hoarsely, "Not visible till eleven o'clock, and you take your turn."

I thanked him, left, and went back to the other room. Still no Heller. I didn't bother to call his name again, since even if it had flushed him I would have had to leave immediately. So I departed.

Down in the lobby I told Nils Lamm I'd see what I could do about an autograph. Outside, deciding there wasn't time to walk it, I flagged a taxi. Home again, I hadn't been in the office more than twenty seconds when the sound came of Wolfe's elevator descending.

That was a funny thing. I'm strong on hunches, and I've had some beauts during the years I've been with Wolfe; but that day there wasn't the slightest glimmer of something impending.

I was absolutely blithe as I asked Wolfe how the anti-thrips campaign was doing, and later, after lunch, as I dialed the number Susan Maturo had given me. I admit I was a little dampened when I got no answer, since I had the idea of finding out some day how she would look with the frown gone.

But still later, shortly after six o'clock, I went to answer the doorbell, and through the one-way glass panel, saw Inspector Cramer of Manhattan Homicide there on the stoop. There was an instant reaction on the lower third of my spine, but I claim no credit for a hunch, since, after all, a homicide Inspector does not go around ringing doorbells to sell tickets to the policemen's annual ball.

I took him to the office, where Wolfe was scowling at the three United States senators on television.

Cramer, bulky and burly, with a big red face and sharp gray eyes, sat in the red-leather chair near the end of Wolfe's desk. "I dropped in on the way down and I haven't got long." He was gruff, which was normal. "I'd appreciate some quick information. What are you doing for Leo Heller?"

"Nothing." Wolfe was brusque, which was also normal.

"You're not working for him?"

"No."

"Then why did Goodwin go to see him this morning?"

"He didn't."

"Hold it," I put in. "I went on my own, just exploring. Mr. Wolfe didn't know I was going. This is the first he's heard of it."

There were two simultaneous looks of exasperation— Cramer's at Wolfe, and Wolfe's at me.

Cramer backed his up with words: "For Pete's sake! This is the rawest one you ever tried to pull! Been rehearsing it all afternoon?"

Wolfe let me go temporarily, to cope with Cramer. "Pfui! Suppose we have. Justify your marching into my house to demand an accounting of Mr. Goodwin's movements. What if he did call on Mr. Heller? Has Mr. Heller been found dead?"

"Yes."

"Indeed." Wolfe's brows went up a little. "Violence?"

"Murdered. Shot through the heart."

"On his premises?"

"Yeah. I'd like to hear from Goodwin."

Wolfe's eyes darted to me. "Did you kill Mr. Heller, Archie?"

"No, sir."

"Then oblige Mr. Cramer, please. He's in a hurry."

I obliged. First telling about the phone call the day before, and Wolfe's refusal to take on anything for Heller, and my calling Heller back. I then reported on my morning visit at 37th Street, supplying all details. I did soft-pedal Susan Maturo's state of harassment, putting it merely that she asked me to arrange for her to see Wolfe and didn't tell me what about.

When I had finished, Cramer had a few questions. Among them: "So you didn't see Heller at all?"

"Nope."

He grunted. "I know only too well how nosy you are, Goodwin. There were three doors in the walls of that room besides the one you entered by. You didn't open any of them?"

"Nope."

"One of them is the door to the closet in which Heller's body was found by a caller, a friend, at three o'clock this afternoon. The Medical Examiner says that the breakfast Heller ate at nine thirty hadn't been in him more than an hour when he died, so it's practically certain that the body was in the closet while you were there in the room. As nosy as you are, you're telling me that you didn't open the door and see the body?"

"Yep. I apologize. Next time I'll open every door in sight."

"A gun had been fired. You didn't smell it?"

"No. The room is air-conditioned."

"You didn't look through the desk drawers?"

"No. I apologize again."

"We did." Cramer took something from his breast pocket. "In one drawer we found this envelope, sealed. On it was written in pencil, in Heller's hand, *Mr. Nero Wolfe*. In it were five one-hundred-dollar bills."

104

"I'm sorry I missed that," I said with feeling.

Wolfe stirred. "I assume that has been examined for fingerprints."

"Certainly."

"May I see it, please?"

Wolfe extended a hand. Cramer hesitated a moment, then tossed it across to the desk, and Wolfe picked it up. He took out the bills, crisp new ones, counted them, and looked inside the envelope.

"This was sealed," he observed dryly, "with my name written on it, and you opened it."

"We sure did." Cramer came forward in his chair with a hand stretched. "Let me have it."

It was a demand, not a request, and Wolfe reacted impulsively. If he had taken a second to think he would have realized that if he claimed it he would have to earn it, or at least pretend to, but Cramer's tone of voice was the kind of provocation he would not take.

He returned the bills to the envelope and put it in his pocket. "It's mine," he stated.

"It's evidence," Cramer growled, "and I want it."

Wolfe shook his head. "Evidence of what?" He tapped his pocket with a fingertip. "My property. Connect it, or connect me, with a crime."

Cramer was controlling himself, which wasn't easy in the circumstances. "I might have known," he said bitterly. "You want to be connected with a crime? Okay. I don't know how many times I've sat in this chair and listened to you making assumptions. Now I've got some of my own to offer, but first here are a few facts: In that building on Thirty-seventh Street, Heller lived on the fourth floor and worked on the fifth, the top floor. At five minutes to ten this morning, on good evidence, he left his living quarters to go up to his office. Goodwin says he entered that office at ten twenty-eight, so if the body was in the closet when Goodwin was there, and it almost certainly was, Heller was killed between nine fifty-five and ten twenty-eight. We can't find anyone who heard the shot, and the way that room is sound-proofed we probably never will. We've tested it."

Cramer squeezed his eyes shut and opened them again, a trick of his. "Very well. The doorman always demanded the name of anyone he didn't recognize. We've got a list from him of everyone who entered the place during that period. Most of these callers have been collected and we're getting the others.

There were six of them. The nurse, Susan Maturo, left before Goodwin went up, and the other five left later, at intervals, when they got tired waiting for Heller to show up—according to them. As it stands now, and I don't see what could change it, one of them killed Heller. Any of them, on leaving the elevator at the fifth floor, could have gone to Heller's office and shot him, and then gone on to the waiting room."

Wolfe muttered, "Putting the body in the closet?"

"Of course, to postpone its discovery. If someone happened to see the murderer leaving the office, he had to be able to say he had gone in to look for Heller and Heller wasn't there. He couldn't say that if the body was there in sight. There are marks on the floor where the body—and Heller was a featherweight—was dragged to the closet. In leaving, the murderer left the door ajar, to make it more plausible, if someone saw him, that he had found it that way. Also—"

"Fallacy."

"I'll tell him you said so the first chance I get. Also, of course he couldn't leave the building. Knowing that Heller started to see callers at eleven o'clock, those people had all come early so as not to have a long wait. Including the murderer. He had to go to the waiting room and wait with the others. One of them did leave, the nurse, and she made a point of telling Goodwin why she was going. It's up to her to make it stick under questioning."

"You were going to connect me with a crime."

"Right." Cramer was positive. "First, one more fact. The gun was in the closet with the body, under it on the floor. It's a nasty little short-nose revolver, and there's not a chance in a thousand of tracing it, though we're trying. Now, here are my assumptions: The murderer went armed to kill, pushed the button at the door of Heller's office, and was admitted. Since Heller went to his desk and sat, he couldn't—"

"Established?"

"Yes. He couldn't have been in fear of a mortal attack. But after some conversation, which couldn't have been more than a few minutes on account of the timetable as verified, he was not only in fear, he felt that death was upon him, and in that super-sound-proofed room he was helpless. The gun had been drawn and was aimed at him. He talked, trying to stall, not because he had any hope of living, but because he wanted to leave a message to be read after he was dead.

"Shaking with nervousness, with a trembling hand, perhaps a pleading one, he upset the jar of pencils on his desk, and then he

106

nervously fumbled with them, moving them around on the desk in front of him, all the while talking. Then the gun went off and he wasn't nervous any more. The murderer circled the desk, made sure his victim was dead, and dragged the body to the closet. It didn't occur to him that the scattered pencils had been arranged to convey a dying message. If it had, one sweep of the hand would have taken care of it."

Cramer stood up. "If you'll let me have eight pencils I'll show you how they were."

Wolfe opened his desk drawer, but I got there first, with a handful taken from my tray. Inspector Cramer moved around to Wolfe's side, and Wolfe, making a face, moved his chair over to make room.

"I'm in Heller's place at his desk," Cramer said, "and I'm putting them as he did from where he sat. Getting the eight pencils arranged to his satisfaction, he stepped aside. "There it is; take a look."

Wolfe inspected it from his side, and I from mine. It was like this from Wolfe's side.

"You say," Wolfe inquired, "that was a message?"

"Yes," Cramer asserted. "It has to be."

"By mandate? Yours?"

"Blah. You know there's not one chance in a million those pencils took that pattern by accident. Goodwin, you saw them. Were they like that?"

"Approximately," I conceded. "I didn't know there was a corpse in the closet at the time, so I wasn't as interested in it as you were. But since you ask me, the pencil points were all in the same direction, and an eraser from one of them was there in the middle." I put a fingertip on the spot. "Right there."

"Fix it as you saw it."

I went around to Wolfe's side of the desk and did as requested, removing an eraser from one of the pencils and placing it as I had indicated. Then it was like this:

"Of course," I said, "you had the photographer shoot it. I don't say that's exact, but they were pointing in the same direction, and the eraser was there."

"Didn't you realize it was a message?"

"Sure I thought it was Heller's way of telling me he had gone to the bathroom and would be back in eight minutes. Eight pencils, see? Pretty clever. Isn't that how you read it?"

"It is not." Cramer was emphatic. "I think Heller turned it sideways to make it less likely that his attacker would see what it was. Move around here, please? Both of you. Look at it from here."

Wolfe and I joined him at the left end of the desk and looked as requested. One glance was enough. You can see what we saw by turning the page a quarter-turn counter-clockwise.

Cramer spoke: "Could you ask for a plainer NW?"

"I could," I objected. "Why the extra pencil on the left of the W?"

"He put it there deliberately, for camouflage, to make it less obvious, or it rolled there accidentally. I don't care which. It is unmistakably NW." He focused on Wolfe. "I promised to connect you with a crime."

Wolfe, back in his chair, interlaced his fingers. "You're not serious."

"Who says I'm not." Cramer returned to the red-leather chair. "That's why I came here, and came alone. You deny you sent Goodwin there, but I don't believe you. He admits he was in Heller's office ten minutes. He has to admit it, since the doorman saw him go up and five people saw him enter the waiting room. In a drawer in Heller's desk is an envelope addressed to you, containing five hundred dollars in cash.

"But the clincher is that message. Heller, seated at his desk, sure that he is going to be killed in a matter of seconds, uses those seconds to leave a message. Can there be any question what the message was about? Not for me. It was about the person or

108

persons responsible for his death. I am assuming that its purpose was to identify that person or persons. Do you reject that assumption?"

"No. I think it quite likely. Highly probable."

"You admit it?"

"I don't admit it, I state it."

"Then I ask you to suggest any person or persons other than you whom the initials NW might identify. Unless you can do that here and now I'm going to take you and Goodwin downtown as material witnesses. I've got men in cars outside. If I didn't do it the D.A. would."

Wolfe straightened up and sighed. "You are being uncommonly obnoxious, Mr. Cramer." He got to his feet. "Excuse me a moment."

Detouring around Cramer's feet, he crossed to the other side of the room, to the bookshelves back of the big globe, and took a book down. He was too far away for me to see what it was. He turned first to the back of the book, where the index would be if it had one, and then to a page near the middle of it.

He went on to another page, and another, while Cramer, containing his emotions under pressure, got a cigar from a pocket, stuck it in his mouth, and sank his teeth in it. He never lit one.

Finally Wolfe returned to his desk, opened a drawer and put the book in it, and closed and locked the drawer.

Cramer was speaking: "I'm not being fantastic. You didn't kill him; you weren't there. I'm not even assuming Goodwin killed him, though he could have. I'm saying that Heller left a message that would give a lead to the killer. The message says NW, and that stands for Nero Wolfe. Therefore, you know something, and I want to know what. I want a yes or no to this: Do you or do you not know something that may indicate who murdered Leo Heller?"

Wolfe, settled in his chair again, nodded. "Yes."

"Ah. You do. What?"

"The message he left."

"The message only says NW. Go on from there."

"I need more information. I need to know—are the pencils still there on his desk as you found them?"

"Yes. They haven't been disturbed."

"You have a man there, of course. Get him on the phone and let me talk to him. You will hear us."

Cramer hesitated; then, deciding he might as well string

along, he came to my desk, dialed a number, got his man, and told him Wolfe would speak to him. Wolfe took it with his phone while Cramer stayed at mine. I picked up the third phone on the table.

Wolfe was courteous but crisp: "I understand those pencils are there on the desk as they were found, that all but one of them have erasers in their ends, and that an eraser is there on the desk, between the two groups of pencils. Is that correct?"

"Right." The dick sounded bored.

"Take the eraser and insert it in the end of the pencil that hasn't one in it. I want to know if the eraser was loose enough to slip out accidentally."

"Inspector, are you on? You said not to disturb—"

"Go ahead," Cramer growled. "I'm right here."

"Yes, sir. Hold it, please."

There was a long wait, and then he was back on: "The eraser couldn't have slipped out accidentally. Part of it is still clamped in the pencil. It had to be torn out, and the torn surfaces are bright and fresh. I can pull one out of another pencil and tell you how much force it takes."

"No thank you, that's all I need. But, for the record, I suggest that you send the pencil and eraser to the laboratory to check that the torn surfaces fit."

"Do I do that, Inspector?"

"Yeah, you might as well. Mark them properly."

"Yes, sir."

Cramer returned to the red-leather chair, and I went to mine. He tilted the cigar upward from the corner of his mouth and demanded, "So what?"

"You know quite well what," Wolfe declared. "The eraser was yanked out and placed purposely. It was a part of the message. No doubt as a dot after the N to show it was an initial? And he was interrupted, permanently, before he could put one after the W?"

"Sarcasm don't change it any. It's still NW."

"No. It isn't. It never was."

"For me and the District Attorney it is. I guess we'd better get on down to his office."

Wolfe upturned a palm. "There you are. You're not hare-brained, but you are pigheaded. I warn you, sir, that if you proceed on the assumption that Mr. Heller's message says NW you are doomed; the best you can expect is to be tagged a jackass."

"I suppose you know what it does say."

"Yes."

"I'm waiting."

"You'll continue to wait. If I thought I could earn this money"—Nero Wolfe tapped his pocket—"by deciphering that message for you, that would be simple, but in your present state of mind you would only think I was contriving a humbug."

"Try me."

"No, sir." Wolfe half closed his eyes. "An alternative. You can go on as you have started and see where it lands you, understanding that Mr. Goodwin and I will persistently deny any knowledge of the affair or those concerned in it except what has been given you, and I'll pursue my own course; or you can bring the murderer here and let me at him—with you present."

"I'll be glad to. Name him."

"When I find him. I need all six of them, to learn which one Heller's message identifies. Since I can translate the message and you can't, you need me more than I need you, but you can save me much time and trouble and expense."

Cramer's level gaze had no trace whatever of sympathy. "If you can translate that message and refuse to disclose it, you're withholding evidence."

"Nonsense. A conjecture is not evidence. Heaven knows your conjecture that it says NW isn't. Nor is mine, but it should lead to some if I do the leading." Wolfe flung a hand impatiently and his voice rose: "Confound it, do you think I welcome an invasion of my premises by platoons of policemen herding a drove of scared citizens?"

Cramer took the cigar from his mouth and regarded it as if trying to decide exactly what it was. That accomplished, he glanced at Wolfe and then looked at me, by no means as a bosom friend.

"I'll use the phone," he said, and got up and came to my desk . . . With three of the six scared citizens, it was a good thing that Wolfe didn't have to start from scratch. They had been absolutely determined not to tell why they had gone to see Leo Heller, and, as we learned from the transcripts of interviews and copies of statements they had signed, the cops had had a time dragging it out of them.

By the time the first one was brought to us in the office, a little after eight o'clock, Wolfe had sort of resigned himself to personal misery. Not only had he had to devour his dinner in one-fourth the usual time, also, he had been compelled to break

111

one of his strictest rules and read documents while eating—and all that in the company of Inspector Cramer, who had accepted an invitation to have a bite.

Of course, Cramer returned to the office with us, and called in, from the assemblage in the front room, a police stenographer, who settled himself in a chair at the end of my desk. Sergeant Purley Stebbins, who once in a spasm of generosity admitted that he couldn't prove I was a hoodlum, after bringing the citizen in and seating him facing Wolfe and Cramer, took a chair against the wall.

The citizen, whose name was John R. Winslow as furnished by the documents, was the big guy in a dark-blue topcoat and Homburg who had stuck his head out of the elevator for a look at Archie Goodwin. He was one of the three who had tried to refuse to tell what he had gone to Heller for; and considering what it was I couldn't blame him much.

He started in complaining: "This is unconstitutional! Nero Wolfe is a private detective and I don't have to submit to questioning by him."

"I'm here," Cramer said. "I can repeat Wolfe's questions if you insist, but it will take more time."

"Suppose," Wolfe suggested, "we start and see how it goes. I've read your statement, Mr. John Winslow, and I—"

"They had no right to let you! They promised me it would be confidential unless it had to be used as evidence!"

"Please, Mr. Winslow, don't bounce up like that. A hysterical woman is bad enough, but a hysterical man is insufferable. I assure you I am as discreet as any policeman. According to your statement, today was your third visit to Mr. Heller's office. You were trying to supply him with enough information for him to devise a formula for determining how much longer your aunt will live. You expect to inherit a considerable fortune from her, and you wanted to make plans intelligently based on expectations. So you say, but reports are being received which indicate that you are deeply in debt and are hard pressed. Do you deny that?"

"No." Winslow's jaw worked. "I don't deny it."

"Are your debts, or any part of them, connected with any violation of the law? Any criminal act?"

"No!"

"Granted that Mr. Heller could furnish a valid calculation on your aunt's life, how would that help you any?"

Winslow looked at Cramer, and met only a stony stare. He

went back to Wolfe: "I was negotiating to borrow a very large sum against my—expectations. There was to be a certain percentage added for each month that passed before repayment was made, and I had to know what my chances were. It was a question of probabilities, and I went to an expert."

"What data had you given Heller as a basis for his calculations?"

"I couldn't . . . all kinds of things."

"For instance?" Wolfe insisted.

Winslow looked at the police stenographer and me, but we couldn't help. He returned to Wolfe. "Hundreds of things. My aunt's age, her habits—eating, sleeping—the ages of her parents and grandparents when they died, her weight and build—I gave him photographs—her activities and interests, her temperament, her attitude to doctors, her politics—"

"Politics?"

"Yes. Heller said her pleasure or pain at the election of Eisenhower was a longevity factor."

Wolfe grunted. "The claptrap of the charlatan. Did he also consider as a longevity factor the possibility that you might intervene by dispatching your aunt?"

That struck Winslow as funny. He did not guffaw, but he tittered, and it did not suit his build.

Wolfe insisted, "Did he?"

"I really don't know, really," Winslow tittered again.

"From whom did your aunt inherit her fortune?"

"Her husband, my uncle Norton."

"When did he die?"

"Six years ago. He was shot accidentally while hunting. Hunting deer."

"Were you present?"

"Not present, no. I was more than a mile away at the time."

"Did you get a legacy from him?"

"No." Some emotion was mobilizing Winslow's blood and turning his face pink. "He left me six cents in his will. He didn't like me."

Wolfe turned to speak to Cramer, but the Inspector forestalled him: "Two men are already on it. The shooting accident was up in Maine."

"There was no mystery about my uncle's death," Winslow said. "My aunt would be amused, as I am, at the idea of my having killed him, and she would be amused at the idea that I might try to kill her. As a matter of fact, I wouldn't mind a bit having her know **about** that, but if she finds out what I went to Leo Heller for—**heaven** help me." He gestured in appeal. "I was promised, absolutely **promised**."

"We **disclose** people's private affairs," Cramer rumbled, "only when **it is** unavoidable."

Wolfe **was** pouring beer. When the foam was at the rim he put the **bottle down** and resumed: "I have promised nothing, Mr. Winslow, **but** I have no time for tattle. Here's a suggestion: You're **in this** pickle only because of your association with Mr. Heller, **and** the question is, was there anything in that association to **justify this** badgering? Suppose you tell us. Start at the beginning, and **recall** as well as you can every word that passed between you. Go **right through it. I'll interrupt** as little as possible."

"You've **already** seen it," Cramer objected. "The transcript, the statement. Why, have you got a lead or haven't you?"

Wolfe **nodded.** "We have a night for it," he said, not happily. "Mr. **Winslow** doesn't know what the lead is, and it's Greek to you." **He** went to Winslow, "Go ahead, sir. Everything that you said to **Mr.** Heller, and everything he said to you."

It took **more** than an hour, including interruptions. The interruptions came from various city employees who were scattered around the house working on other scared citizens, and from the **tele**phone. Two of the phone calls were from homicide dicks **who were** trying to locate a citizen who had got mislaid— one named Henrietta Tillotson, Mrs. Albert Tillotson, the overfed matron whom I had seen in Heller's waiting room.

When **Purley** Stebbins got up to escort Winslow from the room, **Wolfe's** lead was still apparently Greek to Cramer, as it was to me. As the door closed behind them Cramer spoke emphatically, "It's a farce. I think that message was NW, meaning you, and you're stalling for some kind of a play."

"And **if so?**" Wolfe was testy. "Why are you tolerating this? Because if the message did mean me I'm the crux, and your only alternative is to cart me downtown, and that would merely make me mum and you know it."

He drank beer and put the glass down. "However, maybe we can expedite it without too great a risk. Tell your men who are now interviewing these people to be alert for something connected with the figure six. They must give no hint of it, they must themselves not mention it, but if the figure six appears in any segment of the interview they should concentrate on that segment until it is exhausted. They all know, I presume, of Heller's suspicion that one of his clients had committed a serious crime?"

"They know that Goodwin says so. What's this about six?"

Wolfe shook his head. "That will have to do. Even that may be foolhardy, since they're your men, not mine."

"Winslow's uncle died six years ago and left him six cents."

"I'm quite aware of it. You say that is being investigated. Do you want Mr. Goodwin to pass this word?"

Cramer said no thanks, he would, and left the room.

By the time he returned, citizen number two had been brought in by Stebbins, introduced to Wolfe, and seated where Winslow had been. It was Susan Maturo. She looked fully as harassed as she had that morning, but I wouldn't say much more so. There was now, of course, a new aspect to the matter: Did she look harassed, or guilty?

If Heller had been killed by the client whom he suspected of having committed a crime, it must have been a client he had seen previously at least once, or how could he have got ground for suspicion? According to Susan Maturo, she had never called on Heller before and had never seen him.

Actually, that eliminated neither her nor Agatha Abbey, who also claimed that that morning had been her first visit. It was known that Heller had sometimes made engagements by telephone to meet prospective clients elsewhere, and Miss Maturo and Miss Abbey might well have been among that number.

Opening up on her, Wolfe was not too belligerent, probably because she had accepted an offer of beer and, after drinking some, had licked her lips. It pleases him when people share his joys.

"You are aware, Miss Maturo," he told her, "that you are in a class by yourself. The evidence indicates that Mr. Heller was killed by one of the six people who entered that building this morning to call on him, and you are the only one of the six who departed before eleven o'clock, Mr. Heller's appointment hour. Your explanation of your departure as given in your statement is close to incoherent. Can't you improve on it?"

She looked at me. "I've reported what you told me," I assured her. "Exactly as you said it."

She nodded at me vaguely and turned to Wolfe: "Do I have to go through it again?"

"You will probably," Wolfe advised her, "have to go through it again a dozen times. Why did you leave?"

She gulped, started to speak, found no sound was coming out, and had to start over again. "You know about the explosion and fire at the Montrose Hospital a month ago?"

"Certainly. I read newspapers."

"You know that three hundred and two people died there that night. I was there working, in Ward G on the sixth floor. In addition to those who died many were injured, but I went all through it and I didn't get a scratch or a burn. My dearest friend was killed, burned to death trying to save the patients. Another dear friend is crippled for life, and a young doctor I was engaged to marry—he was killed in the explosion. I don't know how I came out of it without a mark, because I tried to help, I'm positively sure of that—but I did. That's one trouble, I guess, because I couldn't be glad about it—how could I?"

She seemed to expect an answer, so Wolfe muttered, "No. Not to be expected."

"I am not," she said, "the kind of person who hates people."

She stopped, so Wolfe said, "No?"

"No, I'm not. I never have been. But I began to hate the man, or the woman, who put the bomb there. I can't say I went out of my mind, because I don't think I did, but I felt as if I had. After two weeks I tried to go back to work at another hospital, but I couldn't. I read all there was in the newspapers, hoping they would catch him. I couldn't think of anything else. I even dreamed about it every night. I went to the police and wanted to help, but of course they had already questioned me and I had told them everything I knew. The days went by and it looked as if they never would catch him. I had read about that Leo Heller, and I decided to go to him and get him to do it."

Wolfe made a noise, and her head jerked up. "I said I hated him!"

Wolfe nodded. "So you did. Go on."

"And I went, that's all. I had some money saved and I could borrow some, to pay him. But while I was sitting there in the waiting room, with that man and woman there, I suddenly thought I must be crazy. I must have got so bitter and vindictive I didn't realize what I was doing. I wanted to think about it, so I got up and left.

"Going down in the elevator I felt as if a crisis had passed—that's a feeling a nurse often has about other people—and then as I left the elevator I heard the names Archie Goodwin and Nero Wolfe. The idea came to me—why not get them to find the person who planted the bomb? So I spoke to Mr. Goodwin, but I couldn't make myself tell him about it. I just told him I wanted to

116

see Nero Wolfe to ask his advice. Mr. Goodwin said he would try to arrange it, and he would phone me or I could phone him."

She fluttered a hand. "That's how it was."

Wolfe regarded her. "It's not incoherent, but neither is it sapient. Do you consider yourself intelligent?"

"Why—yes. Enough to get along. I'm a good nurse, and a good nurse has to be intelligent."

"Yet you thought that by some hocus-pocus that quack could expose the man who planted the bomb in the hospital?"

"I thought he did it scientifically. I knew he had a great reputation, just as you have."

"Good heavens!" Wolfe opened his eyes wide at her. "Well, what were you going to ask my advice about?"

"Whether you thought there was any chance—whether you thought the police were going to find him."

Wolfe's eyes were back to normal, half shut again. "This performance I'm engaged in, Miss Maturo—this inquisition of a person involved by circumstance in a murder—is a hubbub in a jungle; at least, in its preliminary stage. Blind, I grope, and proceed by feel. You say you never saw Mr. Heller, but you can't prove it. I am free to assume that you had seen him, not at his office, and talked with him; that you were convinced, no matter how, that *he* had planted the bomb in the hospital and caused the holocaust; and that, moved by an obsessive rancor, you went to his place and killed him. One ad—"

She broke in: "Why on earth would I think he had planted the bomb?"

"I have no idea. As I said, I'm groping. One advantage of that assumption would be that you have confessed to a hatred so overpowering that surely it might have impelled you to kill if and when you identified its object. It is Mr. Cramer, not I, who is deploying the hosts of justice in this enterprise, but no doubt two or three men are calling on your friends and acquaintances to learn if you have ever hinted a suspicion of Leo Heller in connection with the hospital disaster. Also, they are probably asking whether you had any grudge against the hospital that might have provoked you to plant the bomb yourself."

A muscle at the side of her neck was twitching. "Me? Is that what it's like?"

"It is, indeed. That wouldn't be incongruous. Your proclaimed abhorrence of the perpetrator could be simply the screeching of your remorse."

"Well, it isn't." Suddenly she was out of her chair, and a bound

117

"I wish to speak with you privately," she told Inspector Cramer.

She was one of those. Her husband was president of something, and therefore it was absurd to suppose that she was not to expect privileges. It took Cramer a good five minutes to get it into her head that she was just one of the girls. It was a shock that she had to take time out to decide how to react to it.

She decided on a barefaced lie. She demanded to know if the man who had brought her there was a member of the police force. Cramer replied that he was.

"Well," she declared, "he shouldn't be. You may know that late this afternoon a police officer called at my residence to see me. He told me that Leo Heller had been murdered, and wanted to know for what purpose I had gone to his office this morning. Naturally, I didn't want to be involved in an ugly thing like that, so I told him I hadn't gone to see Leo Heller, but he convinced me that that wouldn't do, so I said I had gone to see him, but on an intimate personal matter that I wouldn't tell . . . Is that man putting down what I'm saying?"

"Yes. That's his job."

"I wouldn't want it. Nor yours, either . . . The officer insisted that I must tell why I had gone to see Heller, and I refused. When he said he would have to take me to the District Attorney's office, under arrest if necessary, and I saw that he meant it, I told him. I told him that my husband and I have been having some difficulty with our son, especially his schooling, and I went to Heller to ask what college would be best for him. I answered the officer's questions within reason, and finally he left. Perhaps you knew all this."

Cramer nodded. "Yes."

"Well, after the officer had gone I began to worry, and I went to see a friend and ask her advice. The trouble was that I had given Heller many details about my son, some of them very intimate and confidential, and since he had been murdered, the police would probably go through all his papers. Those details were private and I wanted to keep them private. I knew that Heller had made all his notes in a personal shorthand that no one else could read; anyhow, he had said so, but I couldn't be sure. After I had discussed it with my friend a long time, I decided to go to Heller's place and ask whoever was in charge to let me have any papers relating to my family affair, since they were not connected with the murder."

"I see," Cramer assured her.

"And that's what I did. The officer there pretended to listen to me, he pretended to be agreeing with me, and then suddenly he arrested me for trying to bribe an officer. When I indignantly denied it, as of course I did, and started to leave, he detained me by force. He actually was going to put handcuffs on me! So I came with him, and here I am. I hope you realize I have a complaint to make and I am making it!"

Cramer was eyeing her. "Did you try to bribe him?"

"No, I didn't!"

"You didn't offer him money?"

"No!"

Purley Stebbins permitted a low sound, half growl and half snort, to escape him. Cramer, ignoring that impertinence from a subordinate, took a deep breath and let it out again.

"Shall I take it?" Wolfe inquired.

"No, thank you," Cramer said acidly. He was keeping his eyes on Mrs. Tillotson. "You're making a mistake, madam," he told her. "All these lies don't do you any good. They just made it harder for you. Try telling the truth for a change."

She drew herself up, but it wasn't very impressive because she was pretty well fagged after her hard day. "You're calling me a liar," she accused Cramer, "and in front of witnesses." She pointed a finger at the police stenographer. "You get that down just the way he said it!"

"He will," Cramer assured her. "Look, Mrs. Tillotson. You admit you lied about going to see Heller until you realized that the doorman would swear that you were there not only this morning but also previously. Now, about your trying to bribe an officer. That's a felony. If we charge you with it, and you go to trial, I can't say who the jury will believe, you or the officer, but I know who I believe. I believe him, and you're lying about it."

"Get him in here," she challenged. "I want to face him."

"He wants to face you, too, but that wouldn't help any. I'm satisfied that you're lying, and also that you're lying about what you wanted to get from Heller's files. He made his notes in a private code that it will take a squad of experts to decipher, and you knew that. I do not believe that you took the risk of going there and trying to bribe an officer just to get his notes about you and your family.

"I believe there is something in his files that can easily be recognized as pertaining to you or your family, and that's what you were after. In the morning we'll have men going through the contents of the files, item by item, and if anything like that is there they'll spot it. Meanwhile, I'm holding you for further questioning about your attempt to bribe an officer. If you want to telephone a lawyer, you may. One phone call, with an officer present."

Cramer's head swiveled. "Stebbins, take her to Lieutenant Rowcliff, and tell him how it stands."

Purley arose. Mrs. Tillotson was shrinking, looking less over-fed every second. "Will you wait a minute?" she demanded.

"Two minutes, madam. But don't try cooking up any more lies. You're no good at it."

"That man misunderstood me. I wasn't trying to bribe him."

"I said you may phone a lawyer—"

"I don't want a lawyer." She was sure about that. "If they go through those files they'll find what I was after, so I might as well tell you. It's some letters in envelopes addressed to me. They're not signed, they're anonymous, and I wanted that Heller to find out who sent them."

"Are they about your son?"

"No. They're about me. They threatened me with something, and I was sure it was leading up to blackmail."

"How many letters?"

"Six."

"What do they threaten you with?"

"They—they don't exactly threaten. They're quotations from things. One of them says, 'He that cannot pay let him pray.' Another one says, 'So comes a reckoning when the banquet's o'er.' The others are longer, but that's what they're like."

"What made you think they were leading up to blackmail?"

"Wouldn't you?" 'He that cannot pay let him pray.' "

"And you wanted Heller to identify the sender. How many times had you seen him?"

"Twice."

"Of course you had given him all the information you could. We'll get the letters in the morning, but you can tell us now what you told Heller. As far as possible, everything that was said by both of you."

I permitted myself to grin, and glanced at Wolfe to see if he was properly appreciative of Cramer's adopting his approach, but he was just sitting there looking patient.

It was hard to tell, for me at least, how much Mrs. Tillotson was giving and how much she was covering. If there was something in her past that someone might have felt she should pay for or give a reckoning of, either she didn't know what it was, or she

122

had kept it from Heller. Or if she had told him she certainly didn't intend to let us in on it.

Cramer played her back and forth until she was so tied up in contradictions that it would have taken a dozen mathematical wizards to make head or tail of it.

Wolfe finally intervened. He glanced up at the wall clock and announced, "It's after midnight. Thank heaven, you have an army to start sorting this out and checking it. If Lieutenant Rowcliff is still here, let him have her and let's have some cheese. I'm hungry."

Cramer, as ready for a recess as anybody, had no objection. Purley Stebbins removed Mrs. Tillotson and I went to the kitchen to give Fritz a hand, knowing that he was running himself ragged furnishing trays of sandwiches to flocks of homicide personnel distributed all over the premises.

When I returned to the office with a supply of provender, Cramer was riding Wolfe, pouring it on, and Wolfe was leaning back in his chair with his eyes shut. I passed around plates of Fritz's *il pesto* and crackers, with beer for Wolfe and the stenographer, coffee for Cramer and Stebbins, and milk for me.

In four minutes Cramer inquired, "What is this stuff?"

Wolfe told him. *"Il pesto."*

"What's in it?"

"Canestrato cheese, anchovies, pig liver, black walnuts, chives, sweet basil, garlic, and olive oil."

"For Pete's sake!"

In another four minutes Cramer addressed me in the tone of one doing a gracious favor. "I'll take some more of that, Goodwin."

But while I was gathering the empty plates he started in on Wolfe again. Wolfe didn't bother to counter. He waited until Inspector Cramer halted for breath and then growled, "It's now nearly one o'clock and we have three more."

Cramer sent Purley for another scared citizen. This time it was the thin, tall, bony specimen who, entering the lobby on 37th Street that morning, had stopped to aim a rude stare at Susan Maturo and me. Having read his statement, I now knew that his name was Jack Ennis, that he was an expert diemaker, at present unemployed, that he was unmarried, that he lived in Queens, and that he was a born inventor who had not yet cashed in. His brown suit had not been pressed.

When Cramer told him that questions from Wolfe were to be considered a part of the official inquiry into Leo Heller's death,

Ennis cocked his head to appraise Wolfe as if deciding whether or not such a procedure deserved his okay.

"You're a self-made man," he told Wolfe. "I've read about you. How old are you?"

Wolfe returned his gaze. "Some other time, Mr. Ennis. To-night you're the target, not me. You're thirty-eight, aren't you?"

Ennis smiled. He had a wide mouth with thin, colorless lips, and his smile wasn't especially attractive. "Excuse me if you thought I was being fresh asking how old you are. I know you're right at the top of your racket, and I wondered how long it took you to get started up. I'm going to the top too, before I'm through, but it's taking me a long time to get a start. How old were you when you first got your name in the paper?"

"Two days. A notice of my birth . . . I understand that your call on Leo Heller was connected with your determination to get a start as an inventor?"

"That's right." Ennis smiled again. "Look. The cops have been at me now for seven hours, and where are they? What's the sense in going on with it? Why would I want to kill that guy?"

"That's what I'd like to know."

"Well, search me. I've got patents on six inventions, and none of them is on the market. One of them is not perfect—I know it's not, but it needs only one more trick to make it an absolute whiz. I can't find the trick. I've read about this Heller, and it seemed to me that if I gave him all the dope, all the stuff he needed for one of his formulas, there was a good chance he would come up with the answer.

"So I went to him. I spent three long sessions with him. He finally thought he had enough to try to work up a formula, and he was taking a crack at it. I had a date to see him this morning and find out how it was going."

Ennis stopped for emphasis. "So I'm hoping. After all the sweating I've done and the dough I've spent, maybe I'm going to get it at last. So I go. I go upstairs to his office and shoot him dead, and then go to the waiting room and sit down and wait." He smiled. "Listen. If you want to say there are smarter men than me, I won't argue. Maybe you're smarter, yourself. But I'm not a lunatic, am I?"

Wolfe's lips were pursed. "I won't commit myself on that, Mr. Ennis. But you have by no means demonstrated that it is fatuous to suppose you might have killed Heller. What if he devised a formula from the data you supplied, discovered the trick that would transform your faulty contraption into a whiz, as you

124

expressed it, and refused to divulge it except on intolerable terms? That would be a motive for murder."

"It sure would," Ennis agreed without reservation. "I would have killed him with pleasure." He leaned forward and was suddenly intense. "Look. I'm headed for the top. I've got what I need in here"—he tapped his forehead—"and nothing and nobody is going to stop me. If Heller had done what you said I might have killed him, I don't deny it, but he didn't."

He jerked to Cramer: "And I'm glad of a chance to tell you what I've told those bozos that have been grilling me: I want to go through Heller's papers to see if I can find the formula he worked up for me. Maybe I can't recognize it, and if I do I doubt if I can figure it out, but I want to look for it, and not next year, either."

"We're doing the looking," Cramer said dryly. "If we find anything that can be identified as relating to you, you'll see it, and eventually you may get it."

"I don't want it eventually, I want it now. Do you know how long I've been working on that thing? Four years! It's mine, you understand that; it's mine!" He was getting upset.

"Calm down, bud," Cramer advised him. "We're right with you in seeing to it that you get what's yours."

"Meanwhile," Wolfe said, "There's a point or two: When you entered that building this morning, why did you stop and gape at Mr. Goodwin and Miss Maturo?"

Ennis' chin went up. "Who says I did?"

"I do, on information . . . Archie. Did he?"

"Yes," I stated. "Rudely."

"Well," Ennis told Wolfe, "He's bigger than I am. Maybe I did, at that."

"Why? Any special reason?"

"It depends on what you call special. I thought I recognized her, a girl I knew once, and then saw I was wrong. She was much too young."

"Very well. I would like to explore my suggestions, which you reject, that Heller was trying to do you out of your invention as perfected by his calculations. I want you to describe the invention as you described it to him, particularly the flaw which you had tried to rectify."

I won't attempt to report what followed, and I couldn't anyhow, since I understood less than a tenth of it. I did gather that it was a gadget intended to supersede all existing X-ray machines, but beyond that I got lost in a wilderness of cathodes and atomicity and coulombs.

If talking like a character out of space-science fiction proves you're an inventor, that bird was certainly one. He stood up to make motions to illustrate, and grabbed a pad and pencil from Wolfe's desk to explain with drawings. After a while it began to look as if it would be impossible to stop him. They finally managed it, with Sergeant Stebbins lending a hand by marching over and taking his elbow.

On his way out he turned at the door to call back: "I want that formula, and don't you forget it!"

The female of an executive type was still in mink, or, rather, she had it with her, but she was not so brisk. As I said before, that morning I would have classified her as between twenty and sixty, but the day's experiences had worn her down closer to reality, and I would now have put her at forty-seven. However, she was game. With all she had gone through, at that late hour, she still let us know, as she deposited the mink on a chair, sat on another, crossed her legs, that she was cool and composed and in command.

My typing her as an executive had been justified by the transcripts. Her name really was Agatha Abbey, and she was executive editor of a magazine, *Mode*, which I did not read regularly.

After Cramer had explained the nature of the session, including Wolfe's status, Wolfe took aim and went for the center of the target: "Miss Abbey. I presume you'd like to get to bed—I know I would—so we won't waste time flouncing around. Three things about you."

He held up a finger. "First: You claim that you never saw Leo Heller. It is corroborated that you had not visited his place before today, but whether you had seen him elsewhere will be thoroughly investigated by men armed with pictures. They will ask people at your place of business, at your residence, and at other likely spots. If it is found that you had, in fact, met him and conferred with him, you won't like it."

He raised two fingers. "Second: You refused to tell why you went to see Heller. That does not brand you as a miscreant, since most people have private matters which they innocently and jealously guard; but you clung to your refusal beyond reason, even after it was explained that the information had to be given by all six persons who called on Heller this morning, and you were assured that it would be revealed to no one unless it proved to be an item of evidence in a murder case. You finally did give the information, but only when you perceived that if you didn't there would be a painstaking investigation into your affairs and movements."

He raised three fingers. "Third: When the information was wormed out of you, it was almost certainly flummery. You said that you wanted to engage Heller to find out who had stolen a ring from a drawer of your desk some three months ago. That was childish nonsense. I grant that even though the ring was insured, you may have been intent on disclosing the culprit, but if you have enough sense to hold a well-paid job in a highly competitive field, as you have, surely you would have known that it was stupid to suppose Heller could help you. Singling out a sneak thief from among a hundred possibilities was plainly an operation utterly unsuited to his technique, and even to his pretensions."

Wolfe moved his head an inch to the left and back again. "No, Miss Abbey, it won't do. I want to know whether you saw Leo Heller before today, and in any case what you wanted of him."

She answered in a controlled, thin, steely voice. "You make it sound overwhelming, Mr. Wolfe."

"Not I. It *is* overwhelming."

Her sharp, dark eyes went to Cramer. "You're an Inspector, in charge of this business?"

"That's right."

"Do the police share Mr. Wolfe's—skepticism?"

"You can take what he said as coming from me."

"Then, no matter what I tell you about why I went to see Heller, you'll check it?"

"Not necessarily. If it fits all right, and if we can't connect it with the murder, and if it's a private, confidential matter, we'll let it go at that. If we do check any, we'll be careful. There are enough innocent citizens sore at us already."

Her eyes darted back to Wolfe. "What about you, Mr. Wolfe? Will you have to check?"

"I sincerely hope not. Let Mr. Cramer's assurance include me."

Her eyes went around. "What about these men?"

"They are trained confidential assistants. They hold their tongues or they lose their jobs."

The tip of her tongue came out and went in. "I'm not satisfied, but what can I do? If my only choice is between this and the whole New York detective force pawing at me, I take this. I phoned Leo Heller ten days ago, and he came to my office and

127

spent two hours there. It was a business matter, not a personal one. I'm going to tell you exactly what it was, because I'm no good at ad-libbing a phony."

She was hating it, but she went on: "You said I have sense enough to hold a well-paid job in a highly competitive field, but if you only knew. It's not a field, it's a corral of wild beasts. There are six female tigers trying to get their claws on my job right now, and if they all died tonight there would be six others tomorrow. If it came out what I went to Leo Heller for, that would be the finish of me."

The top of her tongue flashed out and in. "So that's what this means to me. A magazine like *Mode* has two main functions, reporting and predicting. American women want to know what is being made and worn in Paris and New York, but even more they want to know what is going to be made and worn next season. *Mode's* reporting has been good enough, I've been all right on that, but for the past year our predictions have been utterly rotten. We've got the contacts, but something has gone haywire, and our biggest rival has made monkeys of us. Another year like that, even another season, and goodbye."

Wolfe grunted. "To the magazine?"

"No, to me. So I decided to try Leo Heller. We had carried a piece about him, and I had met him. The idea was to give him everything we had, and we had plenty, about styles and colors and trends for the past ten years, and have him figure the probabilities six months ahead. He thought it was feasible, and I don't think he was a faker. He had to come to the office to go through our stuff. Of course, I had to camouflage what he was there for, but that wasn't hard. Do you want to know what I told them he was doing?"

"I think not," Wolfe muttered.

"So he came. I phoned him the next day, and he said it would take him as least a week to determine whether he had sufficient information to make up a probability formula. Yesterday I phoned again, and he said he had something to discuss and asked me to call at his place this morning. I went. You know the rest of it."

She stopped. Wolfe and Inspector Cramer exchanged glances. "I would like," Wolfe said, "to have the names of the six female tigers who are after your job."

She turned white. I have never seen color leave a face faster. "Darn you!" she said in bitter fury. "So you're a rat, like everybody else!"

Wolfe showed her a palm. "Please, madam. I have no desire to betray you to your enemies. I merely want—"

He saved his breath because his audience was leaving. She got up and headed for the door. Stebbins looked at Wolfe, Wolfe shook his head, and Stebbins trailed after her.

As he left the room at her heels Cramer called to him, "Bring Busch!" Then he turned to Wolfe to protest: "You had her open. Why give her a breather?"

Wolfe made a face. "The miserable wretch. She was dumb with rage and it would have been futile to keep at her. But you're keeping her?"

"You're right we are. For what?" He was out of his chair, glaring down at Wolfe. "Tell me for what! Except for dragging that out of that woman, there's not one single—"

He was off again. I miss no opportunity of resenting Inspector Cramer; I enjoy it and it's good for my appetite, but I must admit that on that occasion he seemed to me to have a point. I still had seen or heard no indication whatever that Wolfe's statement that he had a lead was anything but a stall.

So as Cramer yapped at my employer, I had a private feeling that some of the sentiments he expressed were not positively preposterous. He was still at it when the door opened to admit Stebbins with the sixth customer.

The sergeant, after conducting this one to the seat the others had occupied, facing Wolfe and Cramer, did not go to the chair against the wall, which he had favored throughout the evening. Instead, he lowered his bulk onto one at Cramer's left, only two arms' lengths from the subject.

That was interesting, because it meant that he was voting for Karl Busch as his pick of the lot, and while Stebbins had often been wrong, I had known him, more than once, to be right.

Karl Busch was the slick, sly, swarthy little article with his hair pasted to his scalp. In the specifications on his transcript I had noted the key NVMS, meaning No Visible Means of Support, but that was just a nod to routine. The details of the report on him left no real doubt as to the sources he tapped for jack.

He was a Broadway smoothie, third grade. He was not in the theater, or sports, or the flicks, or any of the tough rackets, but he knew everyone who was, and as the engraved lettuce swirled around the midtown corners and got trapped in the nets of the collectors, legitimate and otherwise, he had a hundred little dodges for fastening onto a specimen for himself.

To him Cramer's tone was noticeably different. "This is Nero

Wolfe," he rasped. "Answer his questions. You hear, Busch?"

Busch said he did.

Wolfe, who was frowning, studying him, spoke, "Nothing is to be gained, Mr. Busch, by my starting the usual rigmarole with you. I've read your statement, and I doubt if it would be worthwhile to try to pester you into a contradiction. But you had three conversations with Leo Heller, and in your statement they are not reported, merely summarized. I want the details of those conversations, as completely as your memory will furnish. Start with the first one, two months ago. Exactly what was said?"

Busch slowly shook his head. "Impossible, mister."

"You won't try?"

"It's this way: If I took you to the pier and ast you to try to jump across to Brooklyn, what would you do? You'd say it was impossible and why get your feet wet. That's me."

"I told you," Cramer snapped, "to answer his questions."

Busch extended a dramatic hand in appeal. "What do you want me to do—make it up?"

"I want you to do what you were told to the best of your ability."

"Okay. This will be good. I said to him, Mr. Heller, my name's Busch and I'm a broker. He said broker of what, and I said of anything people want broken, just for a gag, but he had no sense of humor, so I dropped that and explained. I told him there was a great demand among all kinds of people to know what horse was going to win a race the day before the race was run or even an hour before. I had read about his line of work and thought that he could help to meet that demand.

"He said that he had thought several times about using his method on horse races, but he didn't care himself to use the method for personal bets because he wasn't a betting man. He said for him to make up one of his formulas for just one race would take an awful lot of research. It would cost so much it wouldn't be worth it for any one person unless that person made a high-bracket plunge."

"You're paraphrasing it," Wolfe objected. "I'd prefer the words that were used."

"This is the best of my ability, mister."

"Very well. Go on."

"I said I wasn't a high-bracket boy myself, but anyway that wasn't here or there or under the rug, because what I had in mind was a wholesale setup. I had figgers to show him. Say he did ten races a week. I could round up at least twenty customers right off the bat. All he had to do was crack a percentage of forty or better and it would start a fire you couldn't put out if you ran a river down it. We could have a million customers if we wanted 'em. We would hand-pick a hundred and no more, and each one would ante one C per week, which, if I can add at all, would make ten grand every seven days."

"Go on."

"Well, that would make half a million per year, and Heller and me would split. Out of my half I would expense the operating, and out of his half he would expense the dope. He would have to walk on his nose to cut under a hundred grand all clear, and I wouldn't do so bad. We didn't sign no papers, but he could smell it, and after two more talks he agreed to do a dry run on three races.

"The first one he worked on his answer was the favorite, a horse named White Water, and it won, but it was just exercise for that rabbit. The next one it was heads or tails between two sweethearts. Heller had the winner all right, a horse named Short Order, but on a fifty-fifty call you don't exactly panic. But get this next one."

Busch gestured dramatically for emphasis. "Now, get it. This animal was forty to one, but it might as well have been four hundred. It was a muscle-bound, sore-jointed hyena named Zero. That alone, a horse named Zero, was enough to put the curse of six saints on it, but also it was the kind of looking horse which, if you looked at it, would make you think promptly of canned dog food.

"When Heller came up with that horse, I thought, oh-oh, he's a loon after all, and watch me run. Well, you ast me to tell you the words we used, me and Heller. If I told you some I used when that Zero horse won that race, you would lock me up. Not only was Heller batting a thousand, but he had kicked through with the most—What are you doing, taking a nap?"

We all looked at Wolfe. He was leaning back with his eyes shut tight, and was motionless except for his lips, which were pushing out and in, and out and in, and again out and in. Cramer and Stebbins and I knew what that meant: something had hit his hook, and he had yanked and had a fish on.

A tingle ran up my spine. Stebbins arose and took a step to stand at Busch's elbow. Cramer just sat with his eyes on Wolfe.

Busch asked, "Is he having a fit?"

Wolfe's eyes opened and he came forward in his chair. "No, I'm not," he snapped, "but I've been having one all evening . . .

131

Mr. Cramer. Will you please have Mr. Busch removed? Temporarily."

Cramer, with no hesitation, nodded at Purley, and Purley touched Busch's shoulder and they went. The door closed behind them, but it wasn't more than five seconds before it opened again and Purley was back with us. He wanted as quick a look at the fish as his boss and me.

"Have you ever," Wolfe was asking Cramer, "called me, point-blank, a dolt and a dotard?"

"Those aren't my words, but I've certainly called you."

"You may do so now. Your opinion of me at its lowest was far above my present opinion of myself." He looked up at the clock, which said five past three. "We now need a proper setting. How many of your staff are in my house?"

"Fourteen."

"We want them all in here, for the effect of their presence. Half of them should bring chairs. Also, of course, the six persons we have interviewed. This shouldn't take too long—possibly an hour, though I doubt it. I certainly won't prolong it."

Cramer was looking contrary. "You've already prolonged it plenty. You mean you prolonged it plenty. You mean you're prepared to name him?"

"I am not. I haven't the slightest notion who it is. But I am prepared to make an attack that will expose him—or her—and if it doesn't, I'll have no opinion of myself at all." Wolfe flattened his palms on his desk, for him a violent gesture. "Confound it, don't you know me well enough to realize when I'm ready to strike?"

"I know you too darn' well." Cramer looked at his sergeant. "Okay, Purley. Collect the audience."

The office is a good-sized room, but there wasn't much unoccupied space left when that gathering was fully assembled. The biggest assortment of homicide employees I had ever gazed on extended from wall to wall in the rear of the six subjects. Cramer was planted in the red-leather chair with Stebbins on his left, and the stenographer was hanging on at the end of my desk.

The six citizens were in a row up front, and none of them looked merry.

Wolfe's eyes went from right to left and back again, taking them in. He spoke: "I'll have to make this somewhat elaborate, so that all of you will clearly understand the situation. I could not at the moment hazard even a venturesome guess as to which of you killed Leo Heller, but I now know how to find out and I propose to do so."

Wolfe interlaced his fingers in front of his middle mound. "We have from the first had a hint that has not been imparted to you. Yesterday—Tuesday, that is —Heller telephoned here to say that he suspected that one of his clients had committed a serious crime and to hire me to investigate. I declined, for reasons we needn't go into, but Mr. Goodwin took it upon himself to call on Heller this morning to discuss the matter."

He shot me a glance and I met it. Merely an incivility. He went' on to them: "He entered Heller's office but found it unoccupied. Tarrying there for some minutes, and meanwhile exercising his highly trained talent for observation, he noticed, among other details, that some pencils and an eraser from an overturned jar were arranged on the desk in a sort of pattern. Later on that same detail was, of course, noted by the police. It was a feature of that detail which led Mr. Cramer to come to see me. He assumed that Heller, seated at his desk and threatened with a gun, knowing or thinking he was about to die, had made the pencil pattern to leave a message, and that the purpose of the message was to give a clue to the identity of the murder. On that point I agreed with Mr. Cramer. Will you all approach, please, and look at this arrangement on my desk? These pencils and the eraser are placed approximately the same as those on Heller's desk. From your side you are seeing them as Heller intended them to be seen."

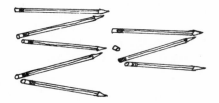

The six did as requested, and they had company. Not only did most of the homicide subordinates leave their chairs and come forward for a view, but Cramer himself got up and took a glance—maybe just curiosity, but I wouldn't put it past him to suspect Wolfe of a shenanigan. However, the pencils and eraser were properly placed, as I ascertained by arising and stretching to peer over shoulders.

When they were all seated again Wolfe resumed: "Mr. Cramer

133

had a notion about the message which I rejected and will not bother to expound. My own notion of it, conceived almost immediately, came merely as a stirring of memory. It reminded me vaguely of something I had seen somewhere. The vagueness disappeared when I reflected that Heller had been a mathematician, academically qualified and trained. The memory was old, and I checked it by going to my shelves for a book I had read some ten years ago. Its title is *Mathematics for the Million*, by Lancelot Hogben. After verifying my recollection, I locked the book in a drawer, because it seemed to me it would be a pity for Mr. Cramer to waste time leafing through it."

"Let's get on," Cramer growled.

Wolfe did so. "As told in Mr. Hogben's book, more than two thousand years ago what he calls a matchstick number script was being used in India. Three horizontal lines stood for two, and so on. That was indeed primitive, but it had greater possibilities than the clumsy devices of the Hebrews and Greeks and Romans. Around the time of the birth of Christ some brilliant Hindu improved upon it by connecting the horizontal lines with diagonals, making the units unmistakable."

He pointed to the arrangement on his desk. "These five pencils on your left form a 3 exactly as the Hindus formed a 3, and the three pencils on your right form a 2. These Hindu symbols are one of the great landmarks in the history of number language. You will note, by the way, that our own forms of the figure 3 and of the figure 2 are taken directly from these Hindu symbols."

A couple of them got up to look, and Wolfe politely waited until they were seated again. "So, since Heller had been a mathematician, and since those were famous patterns in the history of mathematics, I assumed that the message was a 3 and a 2. But evidence indicated that the eraser was also a part of the message and must be included. That was simple. It is the custom of an academic mathematician, if he wants to scribble 4 times 6, or 7 times 9, to use for the 'times' not an X, as we laymen do, but a dot. It is so well known a custom that Mr. Hogben uses it in his book without thinking it necessary to explain it, and therefore I confidently assumed that the eraser was meant for a dot, and that the message was 3 times 2, or 6."

Wolfe compressed his lips and shook his head. "That was an impetuous imbecility. During the whole seven hours that I sat here poking at you people, I was trying to find some connection with the figure 6 that would either set one of you clearly apart, or relate you to the commission of some crime, or both. Preferably both, of course, but either would serve. In the interviews the figure 6 did turn up with persistent monotony, but with no promising application, and I could only ascribe it to the mischief of coincidence.

"So at three o'clock in the morning I was precisely where I had been when I started. Without a fortuitous nudge I can't say how long it would have taken me to become aware of my egregious blunder, but I got the nudge, and I can at least say that I responded promptly and effectively. The nudge came from Mr. Busch when he mentioned the name of a horse, Zero."

He upturned a palm. "Of course. Zero! I had been a witless ass. The use of the dot as a symbol for 'times' is a strictly modern device. Since the rest of the message, the figures 3 and 2, were in Hindu number script, surely the dot was, too—provided that the Hindus had made any use of the dot. And what made my blunder so unforgivable was that the Hindus had indeed used a dot; they had used it, as explained in Hogben's book, for the most brilliant and imaginative invention in the whole history of the language of numbers. For when you have once decided how to write 3 and how to write 2, how are you going to distinguish among 32 and 302 and 3002 and 30002?

"That was the crucial problem in number language, and the Greeks and Romans, for all their intellectual eminence, never succeeded in solving it. Some Hindu genius did, twenty centuries ago. He saw that the secret was position. Today we use our zero exactly as he did, to show position, but instead of a zero he used a dot. That's what the dot was in the early Hindu number language; it was used like our zero. So Heller's message was not 3 times 2, or 6; it was 3 zero 2, or 302."

Susan Maturo started, jerking her head up. Wolfe rested his eyes on her.

"Yes, Miss Maturo. Three hundred and two people died in the explosion and fire at the Montrose Hospital a month ago. You mentioned that figure when you were talking with me, but even if you hadn't when I realized that Heller's message was the figure 302, I would certainly have eventually connected it with that disaster."

"But it's—" She was staring. "You mean it is connected?"

"I'm proceeding on that obvious assumption. I am assuming that through the information one of you six people furnished Leo Heller as factors for a formula, he formed a suspicion that one of you had committed a serious crime, and that his message,

135

the figure 302, indicates that the crime was the planting of a bomb in the Montrose Hospital which caused the deaths of three hundred and two people—or at least involvement in that crime."

It seemed as if I could see or feel muscles tightening all over the room. Most of those dicks, maybe all of them, had, of course, been working on the Montrose thing. Cramer pulled his feet back, and his hands were fists. Purley Stebbins took his gun from his holster and rested it on his knee.

"So," Wolfe continued, "Heller's message identified not the person who was about to kill him, not the criminal, but the crime. That was superbly ingenious and, considering the situation he was in, he deserves our deepest admiration. He has mine, and I retract any derogation of him. It would seem natural to concentrate on Miss Maturo, since she was certainly connected with that disaster, but first let's clarify the matter. I'm going to ask the rest of you if you have at any time visited the Montrose Hospital, or been connected with it in any way, or had dealings with any of its personnel. Take the question just as I have stated it." His eyes went to the end of the row, at the left. "Mrs. Tillotson? Answer, please. Have you?"

"No." It was barely audible.

His eyes moved. "Mr. Ennis?"

"I have not. Never."

"We'll skip you, Miss Maturo. Mr. Busch?"

"I've never been in a hospital."

"That answers only a third of the question. Answer all of it."

"The answer is no, mister."

"Miss Abbey?"

"I went there once about two years ago, to visit a patient, a friend. That was all." The tip of her tongue came out and in. "Except for that one visit I have never been connected with it in any way or dealt with any of its personnel."

"That is explicit. Mr. Winslow?"

"No to the whole question. An unqualified no."

"Well." Wolfe did not look frustrated. "That would seem to isolate Miss Maturo, but it is not conclusive." His head turned. "Mr. Cramer. If the person who not only killed Leo Heller but also bombed that hospital is among these six, I'm sure you won't want to take the slightest risk of losing him. I have a suggestion."

"I'm listening," Cramer growled.

"Take them in as material witnesses, and hold them without bail if possible. Starting immediately, collect as many as you can of the former staff of that hospital. There were scores who

136

survived, and other scores who were not on duty at the time. Get all of them if possible, spare no effort, and have them look at these people and say if they have ever seen any of them.

"Meanwhile, of course, you will be working on Miss Maturo, but you have heard the denials of the other five, and if you get reliable evidence that one of them has lied I'm sure you will need no further suggestion from me. Indeed, if one of them had lied and leaves this room, in custody, with that lie undeclared, that alone will be half the battle. I'm sorry—"

"Wait a minute."

All eyes went to one spot. It was Jack Ennis, the inventor. His thin, colorless lips were twisted, but not in a smile. The look in his eyes showed that he had no idea of smiling.

"I didn't tell an exact lie," he said.

Wolfe's eyes were slits. "Then an inexact lie, Mr. Ennis?"

"I mean I didn't visit that hospital as a hospital. And I didn't have dealings with them; I was just trying to. I wanted them to give my X-ray machine a trial. One of them was willing to, but the other two talked him down."

"When was this?"

"I was there three times, twice in December and once in January."

"I thought your X-ray machine had a flaw."

"It wasn't perfect, but it would work. It would have been better than anything they had. I was sure I was going to get it in, because he was for it—his name is Halsey—and I saw him first, and he wanted to try it. But the other two talked him out of it, and one of them was very—he—" He petered out.

Wolfe prodded him. "Very what, Mr. Ennis?"

"He didn't understand me! He hated me!"

"There are people like that. There are all kinds of people. Have you ever invented a bomb?"

"A bomb?" Ennis's lips worked, and this time I thought he actually was trying to smile. "Why would I invent a bomb?"

"I don't know. Inventors invent many things. If you have never tried your hand at a bomb, of course you have never had occasion to get hold of the necessary materials—for instance, explosives. It's only fair to tell you what I now regard as a reasonable hypothesis: that you placed the bomb in the hospital in revenge for an injury, real or fancied; that included in the data you gave Leo Heller was an item or items which led him to suspect you of that crime; that something he said led you, in turn, to suspect that he suspected; that when you went to his place this morning you went armed, prepared for action if your suspicion was verified; that when you entered the building you recognized Mr. Goodwin as my assistant; that you went up to Heller's office and asked him if Mr. Goodwin was there for an appointment with him, and his answer heightened or confirmed your suspicion and you produced the gun; that—"

"Hold it," Inspector Cramer snapped. "I'll take it from here. Purley, get him out and—"

Purley was a little slow. He was up, but Ennis was up faster and off in a flying dive for Wolfe. I dived too, and got an arm, and jerked. He tore loose, but by then a whole squad was there, swarming into him, and since I wasn't needed I backed off.

As I did so, someone dived at me, and Susan Maturo was up against me, gripping my lapels. "Tell me!" she demanded. "Tell me! Was it him?"

I told her promptly and positively, to keep her from ripping my lapels off. "Yes," I said.

Two months later a jury of eight men and four women agreed with me.

THE CASE OF
THE CRIMSON KISS

BY ERLE STANLEY GARDNER

Erle Stanley Gardner, who was born on July 17, 1889, had sales of 200 million copies of his books in America alone when he died in 1970. His total output is said to be 120 books, but it would not be surprising if this were an underestimate. His Perry Mason stories began in 1932 with *The Case of the Velvet Claws*. He achieved later success with his Donald Lam-Bertha Cool series, which he wrote under one of his many pen-names, A. A. Fair.

PREOCCUPIED WITH PROBLEMS of her own happiness, Fay Allison failed to see the surge of bitter hatred in Anita's eyes. So Fay, wrapped in the mental warmth of romantic thoughts, went babbling on to her roommate, her tongue loosened by the cocktail which Anita had prepared before their makeshift dinner.

"I'd known I loved him for a long time," she said, "but honestly, Anita, it never occurred to me that Dane was the marrying kind. He'd had that one unfortunate affair, and he'd always seemed so detached and objective about everything. Of course, underneath all that reserve he's romantic and tender. . . . Anita, I'm so lucky, I can hardly believe it's true."

Anita Bonsal, having pushed her dinner dishes to one side, toyed with the stem of her empty cocktail glass. Her eyes were pinpricks of black hatred which she was afraid to let Fay Allison see. "You've fixed a date?" she asked.

"Just as soon as Aunt Louise can get here. I want her to be with me. I—and, of course, I'll want you, too."

"When will Aunt Louise get here?"

"Tomorrow or next day, I think. I haven't heard definitely."

"You've written her?"

"Yes. She'll probably take the night plane. I mailed her my extra keys so she can come right on in whenever she gets here, even if we aren't home."

Anita Bonsal was silent, but Fay Allison wanted to talk. "You know how Dane is. He's always been sort of impersonal. He took you out at first as much as he did me, and then he began to specialize on me. Of course, you're so popular, you didn't mind. It's different with me. Anita, I was afraid to acknowledge even to myself how deeply I felt, because I thought it might lead to heartache."

"All my congratulations, dear."

"Don't you think it will work out, Anita? You don't seem terribly enthusiastic."

"Of course it will work out. It's just that I'm a selfish devil and

140

it's going to make a lot of difference in my personal life—the apartment and all that. Come on; let's get the dishes done. I'm going out tonight and I suppose you'll be having company."

"No, Dane's not coming over. He's going through a ceremony at his bachelor's club—one of those silly things that men belong to. He has to pay a forfeit or something, and there's a lot of horseplay. I'm so excited I'm just walking on air."

"Well," Anita said, "I go away for a three-day weekend and a lot seems to happen around here. I'll have to start looking for another roommate. This apartment is too big for me to carry by myself."

"You won't have any trouble. Just pick the person you want. How about one of the girls at the office?"

Anita shook her head, tight-lipped.

"Well, of course, I'll pay until the fifteenth and then—"

"Don't worry about that," Anita said lightly. "I'm something of a lone wolf at heart. I don't get along too well with most women, but I'll find someone. It'll take a little time for me to look around. Most of the girls in the office are pretty silly."

They did the dishes and straightened up the apartment, Fay Allison talking excitedly, laughing with lighthearted merriment, Anita Bonsal moving with the swift, silent efficiency of one who is skillful with her hands.

As soon as the dishes had been finished and put away, Anita slipped into a long black evening dress and put on her fur coat. She smiled at Fay and said, "You'd better take some of the sleeping pills tonight, dear. You're all wound up."

Fay said, somewhat wistfully, "I am afraid I talked you to death, Anita. I wanted someone to listen while I built air castles. I—I'll read a book. I'll be waiting up when you get back."

"Don't," Anita said. "It'll be late."

Fay said wistfully, "You're always so mysterious about things, Anita. I really know very little about your friends. Don't you ever want to get married and have a home of your own?"

"Not me. I'm too fond of having my own way, and I like life as it is," Anita said, and slipped out through the door.

She walked down the corridor to the elevator, pressed the button, and when the cage came up to the sixth floor, stepped in, pressed the button for the lobby, waited until the elevator was halfway down, then pressed the *Stop* button, then the button for the seventh floor.

The elevator rattled slowly upward and came to a stop.

Anita calmly opened her purse, took out a key, walked down

the long corridor, glanced swiftly back toward the elevator, then fitted the key to Apartment 702, and opened the door.

Carver L. Clements looked up from his newspaper and removed the cigar from his mouth. He regarded Anita Bonsal with eyes that showed his approval, but he kept his voice detached as he said, "It took you long enough to get here."

"I had to throw a little wool in the eyes of my roommate, and listen to her prattle of happiness. She's marrying Dane Grover."

Carver Clements put down the newspaper. "The hell she is!"

"It seems he went overboard in a burst of romance, and his attentions became serious and honorable," Anita said bitterly. "Fay has written her aunt, Louise Marlow, and as soon as she gets here they'll be married."

Carver Clements looked at the tall brunette. He said, "I had it figured out that you were in love with Dane Grover, yourself."

"So that's been the trouble with you lately!"

"Weren't you?"

"Heavens, no!"

"You know, my love," Clements went on, "I'd hate to lose you now."

Anita flared in her eyes. "Don't think you own me!"

"Let's call it a lease," he said.

"It's a tenancy-at-will," she flared. "And kindly get up when I come into the room. After all, you might show some manners."

Clements arose from the chair. He was a spidery man with long arms and legs, a thick, short body, a head almost bald, but he spent a small fortune on clothes that were skillfully cut to conceal the chunkiness of his body. He smiled, and said, "My little spitfire! But I like you for it. Remember, Anita, I'm playing for keeps. As soon as I can get my divorce straightened out."

"You and your divorce!" she interrupted. "You've been pulling that line—"

"It isn't a line. There are some very intricate property problems. They can't be handled abruptly. You know that."

She said, "I know that I'm tired of all this pretense. If you're playing for keeps, make me a property settlement."

"And have my wife's lawyers drag me into court for another examination of my assets after they start tracing the checks? Don't be silly."

His eyes were somber in their steady appraisal. "I like you, Anita. I can do a lot for you. I like that fire that you have. But I want it in your heart and not in your tongue. My car's in the parking lot. You go on down and wait. I'll be down in five minutes."

She said, "Why don't you take me out as though you weren't ashamed of me?"

"And give my wife the opportunity she's looking for? Then you *would* have the fat in the fire. The property settlement will be signed within five or six weeks. After that I'll be free to live my own life in my own way. Until then—until then, my darling, we have to be discreet in our indiscretions."

She started to say something, checked herself, and stalked out of the apartment.

Carver Clements's automobile was a big, luxurious sedan equipped with every convenience; but it was cold sitting there, waiting.

After ten minutes, which seemed twenty, Anita grew impatient. She flung open the car door, went to the entrance of the apartment house, and angrily pressed the button of 702.

When there was no answer, she knew that Clements must be on his way down, so she walked back out. But Clements didn't appear.

Anita used her key to enter the apartment house. The elevator was on the ground floor. She made no attempt at concealment this time, but pressed the button for the seventh floor, left the elevator, strode down the corridor, stabbed her key into the metal lock of Clements' apartment, and entered the room.

Carver L. Clements, dressed for the street, was lying sprawled on the floor.

A highball glass lay on its side, two feet from his body. It had apparently fallen from his hand, spilling its contents as it rolled along the carpet. Clements's face was a peculiar hue, and there was a sharp, bitter odor which seemed intensified as she bent toward his froth-flecked lips. Since Anita had last seen him, he had quite evidently had a caller. The print of half-parted lips flared in gaudy crimson from the front of his bald head.

With the expertness she had learned from a course in first-aid, Anita pressed her finger against the wrist, searching for a pulse. There was none.

Quite evidently, Carver L. Clements, wealthy playboy, yachtsman, broker, gambler for high stakes, was dead.

In a panic, Anita Bonsal looked through the apartment. There were all too many signs of her occupancy—nightgowns, lingerie, shoes, stockings, hats, even toothbrushes and her favorite tooth paste.

Anita Bonsal turned back toward the door and quietly left the apartment. She paused in the hallway, making certain there was no one in the corridor. This time she didn't take the elevator, but walked down the fire stairs, and returned to her own apartment. . . .

Fay Allison had been listening to the radio. She jumped up as Anita entered.

"Oh, Anita, I'm so glad! I thought you wouldn't be in until real late. What happened? It hasn't been a half-hour."

"I developed a beastly headache," Anita said. "My escort was a trifle intoxicated, so I slapped his face and came home. I'd like to sit up and have you tell me about your plans, but I do have a headache, and you must get a good night's sleep tonight. You'll need to be looking your best tomorrow."

Fay laughed. "I don't want to waste time sleeping. Not when I'm so happy."

"Nevertheless," Anita said firmly, "we're going to get to bed early. Let's put on pajamas and have some hot chocolate. Then we'll sit in front of the electric heater and talk for just exactly twenty minutes."

"Oh, I'm so glad you came back!" Fay said.

"I'll fix the drink," Anita told her. "I'm going to make your chocolate sweet tonight. You can start worrying about your figure tomorrow."

She went to the kitchen, opened her purse, took out a bottle of barbiturate tablets, emptied a good half of the pills into a cup, carefully ground them up into powder, and added hot water until they were dissolved.

When she returned to the living-room, carrying the two steaming cups of chocolate frothy with melted marshmallows floating on top, Fay Allison was in her pajamas.

Anita Bonsal raised her cup. "Here's to happiness, darling."

After they had finished the first cup of chocolate, Anita talked Fay into another cup, then let Fay discuss her plans until drowsiness made the words thick, the sentence detached.

"Anita, I'm so sleepy all of a sudden. I guess it's the reaction from having been so keyed up. I . . . darling, it's all right if I . . . You don't care if I. . . ."

"Not at all, dear," Anita said, and helped Fay into bed, tucking her in carefully. Then she gave the situation careful consideration.

The fact that Carver Clements maintained a secret apartment in that building was known only to a few of Clements's cronies. These people knew of Carver Clements's domestic difficulties and knew why he maintained this apartment. Fortunately, however, they had never seen Anita. That was a big thing in her favor. Anita was quite certain Clements's death hadn't been due to a heart attack. It had been some quick-acting, deadly poison. The police would search for the murderer.

It wouldn't do for Anita merely to remove her things from that apartment, and, besides, that wouldn't be artistic enough. Anita had been in love with Dane Grover. If it hadn't been for that dismal entanglement with Carver Clements . . . However, that was all past now, and Fay Allison, with her big blue eyes, her sweet, trusting disposition, had turned Dane Grover from a disillusioned cynic into an ardent suitor.

Well, it was a world where the smart ones got by. Anita had washed the dishes. Fay Allison had dried them. Her fingerprints would be on glasses and on dishes. The management of the apartment house very considerately furnished dishes identical in pattern, so it needed only a little careful work on her part. The police would find Fay Allison's nightgowns in Carver Clements's secret apartment. They would find glasses that had Fay's fingerprints on them. And when they went to question Fay Allison, they would find she had taken an overdose of sleeping pills.

Anita would furnish the testimony that would make it all check into a composite, sordid pattern. A girl who had been the mistress of a rich playboy, then had met a younger and more attractive man who had offered her marriage. She had gone to Carver Clements and wanted to check out, but with Carver Clements one didn't simply check out. So Fay had slipped the fatal poison into his drink, and then had realized she was trapped when Anita returned home unexpectedly and there had been no chance for Fay to make a surreptitious removal of her wearing apparel from the upstairs apartment. Anita would let the police do the figuring. Anita would be horrified, simply stunned, but, of course, cooperative.

Anita Bonsal deliberately waited three hours until things began to quiet down in the apartment house, then she took a suitcase and quietly went to work, moving with the smooth efficiency of a woman who has been accustomed to thinking out every detail.

When she had finished, she carefully polished the key to Apartment 702 so as to remove any possible fingerprints, and dropped it in Fay Allison's purse. She ground up all but six of the remaining sleeping tablets and mixed the powder with the chocolate which was left in the canister.

145

After Anita put on pajamas she took the remaining six tablets, washed off the label with hot water, and tossed the empty bottle out of the back window of the apartment. Then she snuggled down into her own twin bed and switched off the lights.

The maid was due to come at eight the next morning to clean up the apartment. She would find two figures, one dead, one drugged.

Two of the tablets constituted the heaviest prescribed dose. The six tablets Anita had taken began to worry her. Perhaps she had really taken too many. She wondered if she could call a drug store and find out if—A moment later she was asleep. . . .

Louise Marlow, tired from the long airplane ride, paid off the taxicab in front of the apartment house.

The cab driver helped her with her bags to the entrance door. Louise Marlow inserted the key which Fay Allison had sent her, smiled her thanks to the driver, and picked up her bags.

Sixty-five years old, white-headed, steely-eyed, square of shoulder and broad of beam, she had a salty philosophy of her own. Her love was big enough to encompass those who were dear to her with a protecting umbrella. Her hatred was bitter enough to goad her enemies into confused retreat.

With casual disregard for the fact that it was now one o'clock in the morning, she marched down the corridor to the elevator, banged her bags into the cage, and punched the button for the sixth floor.

The elevator moved slowly upward, then shuddered to a stop. The door slid slowly open and Aunt Louise, picking up her bags, walked down the half-darkened corridor.

At length she found the apartment she wanted, inserted her key, opened the door, and groped for a light switch. She clicked it on, and called, "It's me, Fay!"

There was no answer.

Aunt Louise dragged her bags in, pushed the door shut, called out cheerfully, "Don't shoot," and then added by way of explanation, "I picked up a cancellation on an earlier plane, Fay."

The continued silence bothered her. She moved over to the bedroom.

"Wake up, Fay. It's your Aunt Louise!"

She turned on the bedroom light, smiled down at the two sleepers, said, "Well, if you're going to sleep right through everything, I'll make up a bed on the davenport and say hello to you in the morning."

146

Then something in the color of Fay Allison's face caused the keen eyes to become hard with concentration.

Aunt Louise went over and shook Fay Allison, then turned to Anita Bonsal and started shaking her.

The motion finally brought Anita back to semiconsciousness from drugged slumber. "Who is it?" she asked thickly.

"I'm Fay Allison's Aunt Louise. I got here ahead of time. What's happened?"

Anita Bonsal knew in a drowsy manner that this was a complicating circumstance that she had not foreseen, and despite the numbing effect of the drug on her senses, managed to make the excuse which was to be her first waking alibi.

"Something happened," she said thickly. "The chocolate . . . We drank chocolate and it felt like . . . I can't remember . . . can't remember . . . I want to go to sleep."

She let her head swing over on a limp neck and became a dead weight in Louise Marlow's arms.

Aunt Louise put her back on the bed, snatched up a telephone directory, and thumbed through the pages until she found the name *Perry Mason, Attorney.*

There was a night number: Westfield 6-5943.

Louise Marlow dialed the number.

The night operator on duty at the switchboard of the Drake Detective Agency, picked up the receiver and said, "Night number of Mr. Perry Mason. Who is this talking, please?"

"This is Louise Marlow talking. I haven't met Perry Mason but I know his secretary, Della Street. I want you to get in touch with her and tell her that I'm at Keystone 9-7600. I'm in a mess and I want her to call me back here just as quick as she can. . . . Yes, that's right! You tell her it's Louise Marlow talking and she'll get busy. I think I may need Mr. Mason before I get done; but I want to talk with Della right now."

Louise Marlow hung up and waited.

Within less than a minute she heard the phone ring, and Della Street's voice came over the line as Aunt Louise picked up the receiver.

"Why, Louise Marlow, whatever are *you* doing in town?"

"I came to attend the wedding of my niece, Fay Allison," Aunt Louise said. "Now, listen, Della. I'm at Fay's apartment. She's been drugged and I can't wake her up. Her roommate, Anita Bonsal, has also been drugged. Someone's tried to poison them!"

"I want to get a doctor who's good, and who can keep his mouth shut. Fay's getting married tomorrow. Someone's tried to kill her, and I propose to find out what's behind it. If anything should get into the newspapers about this, I'll wring someone's neck. I'm at the Mandrake Arms, Apartment 604. Rush a doctor up here, and then you'd better get hold of Perry Mason and—"

Della Street said, "I'll send a good doctor up right away, Mrs. Marlow. You sit tight. I'm getting busy."

When Aunt Louise answered the buzzer, Della Street said, "Mrs. Marlow, this is Perry Mason. This is 'Aunt Louise,' Chief. She's an old friend from my home town."

Louise Marlow gave the famous lawyer her hand and a smile. She kissed Della, said, "You haven't changed a bit, Della. Come on in."

"What does the doctor say?" Mason asked.

"He's working like a house afire. Anita is conscious. Fay is going to pull through, all right. Another hour and it would have been too late."

"What happened?" Mason asked.

"Someone dumped sleeping medicine in the powdered chocolate, or else in the sugar."

"Any suspicions?" Mason asked.

She said, "Fay was marrying Dane Grover. I gather from her letters he's a wealthy but shy young man who had one bad experience with a girl years ago and had turned bitter and disillusioned, or thought he had.

"I got here around one o'clock, I guess. Fay had sent me the keys. As soon as I switched on the light and looked at Fay's face I knew that something was wrong. I tried to wake her up and couldn't. I finally shook some sense into Anita. She said the chocolate did it. Then I called Della. That's all I know about it."

"The cups they drank the chocolate from?" Mason asked. "Where are they?"

"On the kitchen sink—unwashed."

"We may need them for evidence," Mason said.

"Evidence, my eye!" Louise Marlow snorted. "I don't want the police in on this. You can imagine what'll happen if some sob sister spills a lot of printer's ink about a bride-to-be trying to kill herself."

"Let's take a look around," Mason said.

The lawyer moved about the apartment. He paused as he came to street coats thrown over the back of a chair, then again as he looked at the two purses.

"Which one is Fay Allison's?" he asked.

"Heavens, I don't know. We'll have to find out," Aunt Louise said.

Mason said, "I'll let you two take the lead. Go through them carefully. See if you can find anything that would indicate whether anyone might have been in the apartment shortly before they started drinking the chocolate. Perhaps there's a letter that will give us a clue, or a note."

The doctor, emerging from the bedroom, said, "I want to boil some water for a hypo."

"How are they coming?" Mason asked, as Mrs. Marlow went to the kitchen.

"The brunette is all right," the doctor said, "and I think the blonde will be soon."

"When can I question them?"

The doctor shook his head. "I wouldn't advise it. They are groggy, and there's some evidence that the brunette is rambling and contradictory in her statements. Give her another hour and you can get some facts."

The doctor, after boiling water for his hypo, went back to the bedroom.

Della Street moved over to Mason's side and said in a low voice, "Here's something I don't understand, Chief. Notice the keys to the apartment house are stamped with the numbers of the apartments. Both girls have keys to this apartment in their purses. Fay Allison also has a key stamped 702. What would she be doing with the key to another apartment?"

Mason's eyes narrowed for a moment in speculation. "What does Aunt Louise say?"

"She doesn't know."

"Anything else to give a clue?"

"Not the slightest thing anywhere."

Mason said, "Okay, I'm going to take a look at 702. You'd better come along, Della."

Mason made excuses to Louise Marlow: "We want to look around on the outside," he said. "We'll be back in a few minutes."

He and Della took the elevator to the seventh floor, walked down to Apartment 702, and Mason pushed the bell button.

They could hear the sound of the buzzer in the apartment, but there was no sound of motion inside.

Mason said, "It's a chance we shouldn't take, but I'm going to take a peek, just for luck."

He fitted the key to the door, clicked back the lock, and gently opened the door.

The blazing light from the living-room streamed through the open door, showed the body lying on the floor, the drinking glass which had rolled from the dead fingers.

The door from an apartment across the hall jerked open. A young woman with disheveled hair, a bathrobe around her, said angrily, "After you've pressed a buzzer for five minutes at this time of the night, you should have sense enough to—"

"We have," Mason interrupted, pulling Della Street into the apartment and kicking the door shut behind them.

Della Street, clinging to Mason's arm, saw the sprawled figure on the floor, the crimson lipstick on the forehead, looked at the overturned chair by the table, the glass which had rolled along the carpet, spilling part of its contents, at the other empty glass standing on the table.

"Careful, Della, we mustn't touch anything."

"Who is he?"

"Apparently he's People's Exhibit A. Do you suppose the nosy dame in the opposite apartment is out of the hall by this time? We'll have to take a chance anyway." He wrapped his hand with his handkerchief, turned the knob on the inside of the door, and pulled it silently open.

The door of the apartment across the hall was closed.

Mason warned Della Street to silence with a gesture. They tiptoed out into the corridor, pulling the door closed behind them.

As the door clicked shut, the elevator came to a stop at the seventh floor. Three men and a woman came hurrying down the corridor.

Mason's voice was low, reassuring: "Perfectly casual, Della. Just friends departing from a late card game."

They caught the curious glances of the four people, and moved slightly to one side until the quartet had passed.

"Well," Della Street said, "they'll certainly know us if they ever see us again. The way that woman looked me over!"

"I know," Mason said, "but we'll hope that—oh—oh! They're going to 702!"

The four paused in front of the door. One of the men pressed the buzzer button.

Almost immediately the door of the opposite apartment jerked open. The woman with the bathrobe shrilled, "I'm suffering from insomnia. I've been trying to sleep, and this—" She broke off as she saw the strangers.

The man who had been pressing the button grinned and said

in a booming voice, "We're sorry, ma'am. I only just gave him one short buzz."

"Well, the other people who went in just before you made enough commotion."

"Other people in here?" the man asked. He hesitated a moment, then went on, "Well, we won't bother him if he's got company."

Mason pushed Della Street into the elevator and pulled the door shut.

"What in the world do we do now?" Della Street asked.

"Now," Mason said, his voice sharp-edged with disappointment, "we ring police headquarters and report a possible homicide. It's the only thing we can do."

There was a phone booth in the lobby. Mason dropped a nickel, dialed police headquarters, and reported that he had found a corpse in Apartment 702 under circumstances indicating probable suicide.

While Mason was in the phone booth, the four people came out of the elevator. There was a distinct aroma of alcohol as they pushed their way toward the door. The woman, catching sight of Della Street standing beside the phone booth, favored her with a feminine appraisal which swept from head to foot.

Mason called Louise Marlow in Apartment 604. "I think you'd better have the doctor take his patients to a sanitarium where they can have complete quiet," he said.

"He seems to think they're doing all right here."

"I distrust doctors who *seem* to think," Mason said. "I would suggest a sanitarium immediately."

Louise Marlow was silent for a full three seconds.

"I think the patients should have *complete quiet*," Mason said.

"Damn it," Louise Marlow sputtered. "When you said it the first time I missed it. The second time I got it. You don't have to let your needle get stuck on the record! I was just trying to figure it out."

Mason heard her slam down the phone at the other end of the line.

Mason grinned, hung up the phone, put the key to 702 in an envelope, addressed the envelope to his office, stamped it, and dropped it in the mailbox by the elevator.

Outside, the four persons in the car were having something of an argument. Apparently there was some sharp difference of opinion as to what action was to be taken next, but as a siren sounded they reached a sudden unanimity of decision. They

151

were starting the car as the police radio car pulled in to the curb. The siren blasted a peremptory summons.

One of the radio officers walked over to the other car, took possession of the ignition keys, and ushered the four people up to the door of the apartment house.

Mason hurried across the lobby to open the locked door.

The officer said, "I'm looking for a man who reported a body."

"That's right. I did. My name's Mason. The body's in 702."

"A body!" the woman screamed.

"Shut up," the radio officer said.

"But we know the—Why, we told you we'd been visiting in 702—We—"

"Yeah, you said you'd been visiting a friend in 702, name of Carver Clements. How was he when you left him?"

There was an awkward silence; then the woman said, "We really didn't get in. We just went to the door. The woman across the way said he had company, so we left."

"Said he had company?"

"That's right. But I think the company had left. It was these two here."

"We'll go take a look," the officer said. "Come on."

Lieutenant Tragg, head of the Homicide Squad, finished his examination of the apartment and said wearily to Mason, "I presume by this time you've thought up a good story to explain how it all happened."

Mason said, "As a matter of fact, I don't know this man from Adam. I had never seen him alive."

"I know," Tragg said sarcastically; "you wanted him as a witness to an automobile accident and just happened to drop around in the wee, small hours of the morning."

"But," Tragg went on, "strange as it may seem, Mason, I'm interested to know how you got in. The woman who has the apartment across the corridor says you stood there and rang the buzzer for as long as two minutes. Then she heard the sound of a clicking bolt just as she opened her door to give you a piece of her mind."

Mason nodded gravely. "I had a key."

"A key! The hell you did! Let's take a look at it."

"I'm sorry; I don't have it now."

"Well, now," Tragg said, "isn't that interesting! And where did you get the key, Mason?"

Mason said, "The key came into my possession in a peculiar manner. I found it."

"Phooey! That key you have is the dead man's key. When we searched the body we found that stuff on the table there. There's no key to this apartment on him."

Mason sparred for time, said, "And did you notice that despite the fact there's a jar of ice cubes on the table, a bottle of whiskey, and a siphon of soda, the fatal drink didn't have any ice in it?"

"How do you know?" Tragg asked.

"Because when this glass fell from his hand and the contents spilled over the floor, it left a single small spot of moisture. If there had been ice cubes in the glass they'd have rolled out for some distance and then melted, leaving spots of moisture."

"I see," Tragg said sarcastically, "and then, having decided to commit suicide, the guy kissed himself on the forehead and—"

He broke off as one of the detectives, walking down the hallway, said, "We've traced that cleaning mark, Lieutenant."

The man handed Tragg a folded slip of paper.

Tragg unfolded the paper. "Well, I'll be—"

Mason met Tragg's searching eyes with calm steadiness.

"And I suppose," Tragg said, "you're going to be surprised at this one: Miss Fay Allison, Apartment 604, in this same building, is the person who owns the coat that was in the closet. Her mark from the dry cleaner is on it. I think, Mr. Mason, we'll have a little talk with Fay Allison, and just to see that you don't make any false moves until we get there, we'll take you right along with us. Perhaps you already know the way."

As Tragg started toward the elevator, a smartly dressed woman in the late thirties or early forties stepped out of the elevator and walked down the corridor, looking at the numbers over the doors.

Tragg stepped forward. "Looking for something?"

She started to sweep past him.

Tragg pulled back his coat, showed her his badge.

"I'm looking for Apartment 702," she said.

"Whom are you looking for?"

"Mr. Carver Clements, if it's any of your business."

"I think it is," Tragg said. "Who are you and how do you happen to be here?"

She said, "I am Mrs. Carver L. Clements, and I'm here because I was informed over the telephone that my husband was secretly maintaining an apartment here."

"And what," Tragg asked, "did you intend to do?"

"I intend to show him that he isn't getting away with anything," she said. "You may as well accompany me. I feel certain that—"

Tragg said, "702 is down the corridor, at the corner on the right. I just came from there. Your husband was killed some time between seven and nine o'clock tonight."

Dark brown eyes grew wide with surprise. "You—you're sure?"

Tragg said, "Someone slipped him a little cyanide in his whiskey and soda. I don't suppose you'd know anything about that?"

She said slowly, "If my husband is dead—I can't believe it. He hated me too much to die. He was trying to force me to make a property settlement, and in order to make me properly submissive, he'd put me through a softening-up process, a period during which I didn't have money enough even to dress decently."

"In other words," Tragg said, "you hated his guts."

She clamped her lips together. "I didn't say that!"

Tragg grinned and said, "Come along with us. We're going down to an apartment on the sixth floor. After that I'm going to take your fingerprints and see if they match up with those on the glass which contained the poison."

Louise Marlow answered the buzzer. She glanced at Tragg, then at Mrs. Clements.

Mason, raising his hat, said with the grave politeness of a stranger, "We're sorry to bother you at this hour, but—"

"*I'll* do the talking," Tragg said.

The formality of Mason's manner was not lost on Aunt Louise, She said, as though she had never seen him before, "Well, this is a strange time—"

Tragg pushed his way forward. "Does Fay Allison live here?"

"That's right," Louise Marlow beamed at him. "She and another girl, Anita Bonsal, share the apartment. They aren't here now, though."

"Where are they?" Tragg asked.

She shook her head. "I'm sure I couldn't tell you."

"And who are you?"

"I'm Louise Marlow, Fay's aunt."

"You're living with them?"

"Heavens, no. I just came up tonight to be here for—for a visit with Fay."

"You said, I believe, that they are not here now?"

"That's right."

Tragg said, "Let's cut out the shadow-boxing and get down to brass tacks, Mrs. Marlow. I want to see both of those girls."

"I'm sorry, but the girls are both sick. They're in the hospital. It's just a case of food poisoning. Only—"

"What's the doctor's name?"

"Now, you listen to me," Louise Marlow said. "I tell you, these girls are too sick to be bothered and—"

Lieutenant Tragg said, "Carver L. Clements, who has an apartment on the floor above here, is dead. It looks like murder. Fay Allison had evidently been living up there in the apartment with him and—"

"What are you talking about!" Louise Marlow exclaimed indignantly. "Why, I—"

"Take it easy," Tragg said. "Her clothes were up there. There's a cleaner's mark that has been traced to her."

"Clothes!" Louise Marlow snorted. "Why, it's probably some junk she gave away somewhere, or—"

"I'm coming to that," Lieutenant Tragg said patiently. "I don't want to do anyone an injustice. I want to play it on the up-and-up. Now, then, there are fingerprints in that apartment, the fingerprints of a woman on a drinking glass, on the handle of a toothbrush, on a tube of tooth paste. I'm not going to get tough unless I have to, but I want to get hold of Fay Allison long enough to take a set of fingerprints. You try holding out on me, and see what the newspapers have to say tomorrow."

Louise Marlow reached an instant decision. "You'll find her at the Crestview Sanitarium," she said, "and if you want to make a little money, I'll give you odds of a hundred to one that—"

"I'm not a betting man," Tragg said wearily. "I've been in this game too long."

He turned to one of the detectives and said, "Keep Perry Mason and his charming secretary under surveillance and away from a telephone until I get a chance at those fingerprints. Okay, boys, let's go."

Paul Drake, head of the Drake Detective Agency, pulled a sheaf of notes from his pocket as he settled down in the big clients' chair in Mason's office.

"It's a mess, Perry," he said.

"Let's have it," Mason said.

Drake said, "Fay Allison and Dane Grover were going to get married today. Last night Fay and Anita Bonsal, who shares the apartment with her, settled down for a nice, gabby little hen party. They made chocolate. Fay had two cups; Anita had one.

Fay evidently got about twice the dose of barbiturate that Anita did. Both girls passed out.

"Next thing Anita knew, Louise Marlow, Fay's aunt, was trying to wake her up. Fay Allison didn't recover consciousness until after she was in the sanitarium.

"Anyhow, Tragg went out and took Fay Allison's fingerprints. They check absolutely with those on the glass. What the police call the murder glass is the one that slipped from Carver Clements's fingers and rolled around the floor. It had been carefully wiped clean of all fingerprints. Police can't even find one of Clements's prints on it. The other glass on the table had Fay's prints. The closet was filled with her clothes. She was living there with him. It's a fine mess.

"Dane Grover is standing by her, but I personally don't think he can stand the gaff much longer. When a man's engaged to a girl and the newspapers scream the details of her affair with a wealthy playboy all over the front pages, you can't expect the man to appear exactly nonchalant. The aunt, Louise Marlow, tells me he's being faced with terrific pressure to repudiate the girl, to break the engagement and take a trip.

"The girls insist it's all part of some sinister over-all plan to frame them, that they were drugged, and all that, but how could anyone have planned it that way? For instance, how could anyone have known they were going to take the chocolate in time to—?"

"The chocolate was drugged?" Mason asked.

Drake nodded. "They'd used up most of the chocolate, but the small amount left in the package is pretty well doped with barbiturate.

"The police theory," Drake went on, "is that Fay Allison had been playing house with Carver Clements. She wanted to get married. Clements wouldn't let her go. She slipped him a little poison. She intended to return and get her things out of the apartment when it got late enough so she wouldn't meet someone in the corridor if she came walking out of 702 with her arms full of clothes. Anita, who had gone out, unexpectedly returned, and that left Fay Allison trapped. She couldn't go up and get her things out of the apartment upstairs without disturbing Anita. So she tried to drug Anita and something went wrong."

"That's a hell of a theory," Mason said.

"Try and get one that fits the case any better," Drake told him. "One thing is certain—Fay Allison was living up there in that Apartment 702. As far as Dane Grover is concerned, that's the thing that will make him throw everything overboard. He's a sensitive chap, from a good family. He doesn't like having his picture in the papers. Neither does his family."

"What about Clements?"

"Successful businessman, broker, speculator. Also a wife who was trying to hook him for a bigger property settlement than Clements wanted to pay. Clements had a big apartment where he lived officially. This place was a playhouse. Only a few people knew he had it. His wife would have given a lot of money to have found out about it."

"What's the wife doing now?"

"Sitting pretty. They don't know yet whether Clements left a will, but she has her community property rights, and Clements's books will be open for inspection now. He'd been juggling things around pretty much, and now a lot of stuff is going to come out—safe-deposit boxes and things of that sort."

"How about the four people who met us in the hall?"

"I have all the stuff on them here," Drake said. "The men were Richard P. Nolin, a sort of partner in some of Clements's business; Manley L. Ogden, an income tax specialist; Don B. Ralston, who acted as dummy for Clements in some business transactions; and Vera Payson, who is someone's girl-friend, but I'm darned if I can find out whose.

"Anyhow, those people knew of the hideout apartment and would go up there occasionally for a poker game. Last night, as soon as the dame across the hall said Clements had company, they knew what that meant, and went away. That's the story. The newspapers are lapping it up. Dane Grover isn't going to stay put much longer. You can't blame him. All he has is Fay Allison's tearful denial. Louise Marlow says we have to do something fast."

Mason said, "Tragg thinks I had Carver Clements's key."

"Where *did* you get it?"

Mason shook his head.

"Well," Drake said, "Carver Clements didn't have a key."

Mason nodded. "That is the only break we have in the case, Paul. We know Clements's key is missing. No one else does, because Tragg won't believe me when I tell him Clements hadn't given me his key."

Drake said, "It won't take Tragg long to figure the answer to that one. If Clements didn't give you the key, only one other person could have given it to you."

Mason said, "We won't speculate too much on that, Paul."

"I gathered we wouldn't," Drake said dryly. "Remember this, Perry, you're representing a girl who's going to be faced with a murder rap. You may be able to beat that rap. It's circumstantial evidence. But, in doing it, you'll have to think out some explanation that will satisfy an embarrassed lover who's being pitied by his friends and ridiculed by the public."

Mason nodded. "We'll push things to a quick hearing in the magistrate's court on a preliminary examination. In the meantime, Paul, find out everything you can about Carver Clements's background. Pay particular attention to Clements's wife. If she had known about that apartment—"

Drake shook his head dubiously. "I'll give it a once-over, Perry, but if she'd even known about that apartment, that would have been all she needed. If she could have raided that apartment with a photographer and had the deadwood on Carver Clements, she'd have boosted her property settlement another hundred grand and walked out smiling. She wouldn't have needed to use any poison."

Mason's strong, capable fingers were drumming gently on the edge of the desk. "There has to be *some* explanation, Paul."

Drake heaved himself wearily to his feet. "That's right," he said without enthusiasm, "and Tragg thinks he has it."

Della Street, her eyes sparkling, entered Mason's private office and said, "He's here, Chief."

"Who's here?" Mason asked.

She laughed. "Don't be like that. As far as this office is concerned, there is only one *he*."

"Dane Grover?"

"That's right."

"What sort?"

"Tall, sensitive-looking. Wavy, dark brown hair, romantic eyes. He's crushed, of course. You can see he's dying ten thousand deaths every time he meets one of his friends. Gertie, at the switchboard, can't take her eyes off of him."

Mason grinned, and said, "Let's get him in, then, before Gertie either breaks up a romance or dies of unrequited love."

Della Street went out, returned after a few moments, ushering Dane Grover into the office.

Mason shook hands, invited Grover to a seat. Grover glanced dubiously at Della Street. Mason smiled. "She's my right hand, Grover. She takes notes for me, and keeps her thoughts to herself."

Grover said, "I suppose I'm unduly sensitive, but I can't stand it when people patronize me or pity me."

Mason nodded.

"I've had them do both ever since the papers came out this morning."

Again, Mason's answer was merely a nod.

"But," Grover went on, "I want you to know that I'll stick."

Mason thought that over for a moment, then held Grover's eyes. "For how long?"

"All the way."

"No matter what the evidence shows?"

Grover said, "The evidence shows the woman I love was living with Carver Clements as his mistress. The evidence simply can't be right. I love her, and I'm going to stick. I want you to tell her that, and I want you to know that. What you're going to have to do will take money. I'm here to see that you have what money you need—all you want, in fact."

"That's fine," Mason said. "Primarily, what I need is a little moral support. I want to be able to tell Fay Allison that you're sticking, and I want some facts."

"What facts?"

"How long have you been going with Fay Allison?"

"A matter of three or four months. Before then I was—well, sort of squiring both of the girls around."

"You mean Anita Bonsal?"

"Yes. I met Anita first. I went with her for a while. Then I went with both. Then I began to gravitate toward Fay Allison. I thought I was just making dates. Actually, I was falling in love."

"And Anita?"

"She's like a sister to both of us. She's been simply grand in this whole thing. She's promised me that she'll do everything she can."

"Could Fay Allison have been living with Carver Clements?"

"She had the physical opportunity, if that's what you mean."

"You didn't see her every night?"

"No."

"What does Anita say?"

"Anita says the charge is ridiculous."

"Do you know of any place where Fay Allison could have had access to cyanide of potassium?"

"That's what I wanted to tell you about, Mr. Mason. Out at my place the gardener uses it. I don't know just what for, but—well,

159

out there the other day, when he was showing Fay around the place—"

"Yes, yes," Mason said impatiently, as Grover paused; "go on."

"Well, I know the gardener told her to be very careful not to touch that sack because it contained cyanide. I remember she asked him a few questions about what he used it for, but I wasn't paying much attention. It's the basis of some sort of spray."

"Has your gardener read the papers?"

Grover nodded.

"Can you trust him?"

"Yes. He's very loyal to all our family. He's been with us for twenty years."

"What's his name?"

"Barney Sheff. My mother—well, rehabilitated him."

"He'd been in trouble? In the pen?"

"That's right. He had a chance to get parole if he could get a job. Mother gave him the job."

"I'm wondering if you have fully explored the possibilities of orchid growing."

"We're not interested in orchid growing. We can buy them and—"

"I wonder," Mason said in exactly the same tone, "if you have fully investigated the possibilities of growing orchids."

"You mean—Oh, you mean we should send Barney Sheff to—"

"Fully investigate the possibilities of growing orchids," Mason said again.

Dane Grover studied Mason silently for a few seconds. Then abruptly he rose from the chair, extended his hand, and said, "I wanted you to understand, Mr. Mason, that I'm going to stick. I brought you some money. I thought you might need it." He carelessly tossed an envelope on the table. And with that he turned and marched out of the office.

Mason reached for the envelope Grover had tossed on his desk. It was well filled with hundred-dollar bills.

Della Street came over to take the money. "When I get so interested in a man," she said, "that I neglect to count the money, you know I'm becoming incurably romantic. How much, Chief?"

"Plenty," Mason said.

Della Street was counting it when the unlisted telephone on her desk rang. She picked up the receiver, and heard Drake's voice on the line. "Hi, Paul," she said.

"Hi, Della. Perry there?"

"Yes."

"Okay," Drake said wearily, "I'm making a progress report. Tell him Lieutenant Tragg nabbed the Grover gardener, a chap by the name of Sheff. They're holding him as a material witness, seem to be all worked up about what they've discovered. Can't find out what it is."

Della Street sat motionless at the desk, holding the receiver.

"Hello, hello," Drake said; "are you there?"

"I'm here," Della said. "I'll tell him." She hung up the phone.

It was after nine o'clock that night when Della Street, signing the register in the elevator, was whisked up to the floor where Perry Mason had his offices. She started to look in on Paul Drake, then changed her mind and kept on walking down the long, dark corridor, the rapid tempo of her heels echoing back at her from the night silence of the hallway.

She rounded the elbow in the corridor, and saw that lights were on in Mason's office.

The lawyer was pacing the floor, thumbs pushed in the armholes of his vest, head shoved forward, wrapped in such concentration that he did not even notice the opening of the door.

The desk was littered with photographs. There were numerous sheets of the flimsy which Paul Drake used in making reports.

Della stood quietly in the doorway, watching the tall, lean-waisted man pacing back and forth. Granite-hard of face, the seething action of his restless mind demanded a physical outlet, and this restless pacing was just an unconscious reflex.

After almost a minute Della Street said, "Hello, Chief. Can I help?"

Mason looked up at her with a start. "What are you doing here?"

"I came up to see if there was anything I could do to help. Had any dinner?" she asked.

He glanced at his wrist watch, said, "Not yet."

"What time is it?" Della Street asked.

He had to look at his wrist watch again in order to tell her. "Nine forty."

She laughed. "I knew you didn't even look the first time you went through the motions. Come on, Chief; you've got to go get something to eat. The case will still be here when you get back."

"How do we know it will?" Mason said. "I've been talking with

Louise Marlow on the phone. She's been in touch with Dane Grover and she knows Dane Grover's mother. Dane Grover says he'll stick. How does *he* know what he'll do? He's never faced a situation like this. His friends, his relatives, are turning the knife in the wound with their sympathy. How can he tell whether he'll stick?"

"Just the same," Della Street insisted, "I think he will. It's through situations such as this that character is created."

"You're just talking to keep your courage up," Mason said. "The guy's undergoing the tortures of the damned. He can't help but be influenced by the evidence. The woman he loves on the night before the wedding trying to free herself from the man who gave her money and a certain measure of security."

"Chief, you simply *have* to eat."

Mason walked over to the desk. "Look at 'em," he said; "photographs! And Drake had the devil's own time obtaining them. They're copies of the police photographs—the body on the floor, glass on the table, an overturned chair, a newspaper half open by a reading chair—an apartment as drab as the sordid affair for which it was used. And somewhere in those photographs I've got to find a clue that will establish the innocence of a woman, not only innocence of murder, but of the crime of betraying the man she loved."

Mason leaned over the desk, picked up the magnifying glass which was on his blotter, and started once more examining the pictures. "Hang it, Della," he said, "I think the thing's here somewhere. That glass on the table, a little whiskey and soda in the bottom, Fay Allison's fingerprints all over it. Then there's the brazen touch of that crimson kiss on the forehead."

"Indicating a woman was with him just before he died?"

"Not necessarily. That lipstick is a perfect imprint of a pair of lips. There was no lipstick on his lips, just there on the forehead. A shrewd man could well have smeared lipstick on his lips, pressed them against Clements's forehead after the poison had taken effect, and so directed suspicion away from himself. This could easily have happened if the man had known some woman was in the habit of visiting Clements in that apartment.

"It's a clue that so obviously indicates a woman that I find myself getting suspicious of it. If there were only something to give me a starting point. If only we had more time."

Della Street walked over to the desk. She said, "Stop it. Come and get something to eat. Let's talk it over."

"Haven't you had dinner?"

162

She smiled, and shook her head. "I knew you'd be working, and that if someone didn't rescue you, you'd be pacing the floor until two or three o'clock in the morning. What's Paul Drake found out?"

She picked up the sheets of flimsy, placed them together, and anchored everything in place with a paperweight. "Come on, Chief."

But he didn't really answer her question until after he had relaxed in one of the booths in their favorite restaurant. He pushed back the plates containing the wreckage of a thick steak, and poured more coffee, then said, "Drake hasn't found out much—just background."

"What, for instance?"

Mason said wearily, "It's the same old seven and six. The wife, Marline Austin Clements, apparently was swept off her feet by the sheer power of Carver Clements's determination to get her. She overlooked the fact that after he had her safely listed as one of his legal chattels, he used that same acquisitive, aggressive tenacity of purpose to get other things he wanted. Marline was left pretty much alone."

"And so?" Della asked.

"And so," Mason said, "in the course of time, Carver Clements turned to other interests. Hang it, Della, we have one thing to work on, only one thing—the fact that Clements had no key on his body.

"You remember the four people who met us in the corridor. They had to get in that apartment house some way. Remember the outer door was locked. Any of the tenants could release the latch by pressing the button of an electric release. But if the tenant of some apartment didn't press the release button, it was necessary to have a key in order to get in.

"Now, then, those four people got in. How? Regardless of what they say now, one of them must have had a key."

"The missing key?" Della asked.

"That's what we have to find out."

"What story did they give the police?"

"I don't know. The police have them sewed up tight. I've got to get one of them on the stand and cross-examine him. Then we'll at least have something to go on."

"So we have to try for an immediate hearing and then go it blind?"

"That's about the size of it."

"Was that key in Fay Allison's purse Clements's missing key?"

"It could have been. If so, either Fay was playing house or the key was planted. In that case, when was it planted, how, and by whom? I'm inclined to think Clements's key must have been on his body at the time he was murdered. It wasn't there when the police arrived. That's the one really significant clue we have to work on."

Della Street shook her head. "It's too deep for me, but I guess you're going to have to wade into it."

Mason lit a cigarette. "Ordinarily I'd spar for time, but in this case I'm afraid time is our enemy, Della. We're going to have to walk into court with all the assurance in the world and pull a very large rabbit out of a very small hat."

She smiled. "Where do we get the rabbit?"

"Back in the office," he said, "studying those photographs, looking for a clue, and—" Suddenly he snapped to attention.

"What is it, Chief?"

"I was just thinking. The glass on the table in 702—there was a little whiskey and soda in the bottom of it, just a spoonful or two."

"Well?" she asked.

"What happens when you drink whiskey and soda, Della?"

"Why—you always leave a little. It sticks to the side of the glass and then gradually settles back."

Mason shook his head. His eyes were glowing now. "You leave ice cubes in the glass," he said, "and then after a while they melt and leave an inch or so of water."

She matched his excitement. "Then there was no ice in the woman's glass?"

"And none in Carver Clements's. Yet there was a jar of ice cubes on the table. Come on, Della; we're going back and *really* study those photographs!"

Judge Randolph Jordan ascended the bench and rapped court to order.

"People versus Fay Allison."

"Ready for the defendant," Mason said.

"Ready for the Prosecution," Stewart Linn announced.

Linn, one of the best of the trial deputies in the district attorney's office, was a steely-eyed individual who had the legal knowledge of an encyclopedia, and the cold-blooded merciless-ness of a steel trap.

Linn was under no illusions as to the resourcefulness of his adversary, and he had all the caution of a boxer approaching a heavyweight champion.

"Call Dr. Charles Keene," he said.

Dr. Keene came forward, qualified himself as a physician and surgeon who had had great experience in medical necropsies, particularly in cases of homicide.

"On the tenth of this month did you have occasion to examine a body in Apartment 702 at the Mandrake Arms?"

"I did."

"What time was it?"

"It was about two o'clock in the morning."

"What did you find?"

"I found the body of a man of approximately fifty-two years of age, fairly well fleshed, quite bald, but otherwise very well preserved for a man of his age. The body was lying on the floor, head toward the door, feet toward the interior of the apartment, the left arm doubled up and lying under him, the right arm flung out, the left side of the face resting on the carpet. The man had been dead for several hours. I fix the time of death as having taken place during a period between seven o'clock and nine o'clock that evening. I cannot place the time of death any closer than that, but I will swear that it took place within those time limits."

"And did you determine the cause of death?"

"Not at that time. I did later."

"What was the cause of death?"

"Poisoning caused by the ingestion of cyanide of potassium."

"Did you notice anything about the physical appearance of the man's body?"

"There was a red smear on the upper part of the forehead, apparently caused by lips that had been heavily coated with lipstick and then pressed against the skin in a somewhat puckered condition. It was as though some woman had administered a last kiss."

"Cross-examine," Linn announced.

"No questions," Mason said.

"Call Benjamin Harlan," Linn said.

Benjamin Harlan, a huge, lumbering giant of a man, promptly proceeded to qualify himself as a fingerprint and identification expert of some twenty years' experience.

Stuart Linn, by skillful, adroit questions, led him through an account of his activities on the date in question. Harlan found no latent fingerprints on the glass which the Prosecution referred to as the "murder glass," indicating this glass had been wiped clean of prints, but there were prints on the glass on the table which the Prosecution referred to as the "decoy glass," on the toothbrush, on the tube of tooth paste, and on various other articles. These latent fingerprints had coincided with the fingerprints taken from the hands of Fay Allison, the defendant.

Harlan also identified a whole series of photographs taken by the police showing the position of the body when it was discovered, the furnishings in the apartment, the table, the overturned chair, the so-called murder glass, which had rolled along the floor, the so-called decoy glass on the table which bore unmistakably the fresh fingerprints of Fay Allison, the bottle of whiskey, the bottle of soda water, the jar containing ice cubes.

"Cross-examine," Linn said triumphantly.

Mason said, "You have had some twenty years' experience as a fingerprint expert, Mr. Harlan?"

"Yes, sir."

"Now, you have heard Dr. Keene's testimony about the lipstick on the forehead of the dead man?"

"Yes, sir."

"And that lipstick, I believe, shows in this photograph which I now hand you?"

"Yes, sir; not only that, but I have a close-up of that lipstick stain which I, myself, took. I have an enlargement of that negative, in case you're interested."

"I'm very much interested," Mason said. "Will you produce the enlargement, please?"

Harlan produced the photograph from his brief-case, showing a section of the forehead of the dead man, with the stain of lips outlined clearly and in microscopic detail.

"What is the scale of this photograph?" Mason asked.

"Life size," Harlan said. "I have a standard of distances by which I can take photographs to a scale of exactly life size."

"Thank you," Mason said. "I'd like to have this photograph received in evidence."

"No objection," Linn said.

"And it is, is it not, a matter of fact that the little lines shown in this photograph are fully as distinctive as the ridges and whorls of a fingerprint?"

"Just what do you mean?"

"Isn't it a fact well known to identification experts that the little wrinkles which form in a person's lips are fully as individual as the lines of a fingerprint?"

166

"It's not a 'well-known' fact."

"But it *is* a fact?"

"Yes, sir, it is."

"So that by measuring the distance between the little lines which are shown on this photograph, indicating the pucker lines of the skin, it would be fully as possible to identify the lips which made this lipstick print as it would be to identify a person who had left a fingerprint upon the scalp of the dead man."

"Yes, sir."

"Now, you have testified to having made imprints of the defendant's fingers and compared those with the fingerprints found on the glass."

"Yes, sir."

"Have you made any attempt to take an imprint of her lips and compare that print with the print of the lipstick on the decedent?"

"No, sir," Harlan said, shifting his position uneasily.

"Why not?"

"Well, in the first place, Mr. Mason, the fact that the pucker lines of lips are so highly individualized is not a generally known fact."

"But *you* knew it."

"Yes, sir."

"And the more skilled experts in your profession know it?"

"Yes, sir."

"Why didn't you do it, then?"

Harlan glanced somewhat helplessly at Stewart Linn.

"Oh, if the Court please," Linn said, promptly taking his cue from that glance, "this hardly seems to be cross-examination. The inquiry is wandering far afield. I will object to the question on the ground that it's incompetent, irrelevant, immaterial, and not proper cross-examination."

"Overruled," Judge Jordan snapped. "Answer the question!"

Harlan cleared his throat. "Well," he said. "I just never thought of it."

"Think of it now," Mason said. "Go ahead and take the imprint right now and right here. . . . Put on plenty of lipstick, Miss Allison. Let's see how your lips compare with those on the dead man's forehead."

"Oh, if the Court please," Linn said wearily, "this hardly seems to be cross-examination. If Mr. Mason wants to make Harlan his own witness and call for this test as a part of the defendant's case, that will be one thing; but this certainly isn't cross-examination."

"It may be cross-examination of Harlan's qualifications as an expert," Judge Jordan ruled.

"Oh, if the Court please! Isn't that stretching a technicality rather far?"

"Your objection was highly technical," Judge Jordan snapped. "It is overruled, and my ruling will stand. Take the impression, Mr. Harlan."

Fay Allison, with trembling hand, daubed lipstick heavily on her mouth. Then, using the make-up mirror in her purse, smoothed off the lipstick with the tip of her little finger.

"Go ahead," Mason said to Harlan; "check on her lips."

Harlan, taking a piece of white paper from his brief-case, moved down to where the defendant was sitting beside Perry Mason and pressed the paper against her lips. He removed the paper and examined the imprint.

"Go ahead," Mason said to Harlan; "make your comparison and announce the results to the Court."

Harlan said, "Of course, I have not the facilities here for making a microscopic comparison, but I can tell from even a superficial examination of the lip lines that these lips did not make that print."

"Thank you," Mason said. "That's all."

Judge Jordan was interested. "These lines appear in the lips only when the lips are puckered, as in giving a kiss?"

"No, Your Honor, they are in the lips all the time, as an examination will show, but when the lips are puckered, the lines are intensified."

"And these lip markings are different with each individual?"

"Yes, Your Honor."

"So that you are now prepared to state to the Court that despite the fingerprints of the defendant on the glass and other objects, her lips definitely could not have left the imprint on the dead man's forehead?"

"Yes, Your Honor."

"That's all," Judge Jordan said.

"Of course," Linn pointed out, "the fact that the defendant did not leave that kiss imprint on the man's forehead doesn't necessarily mean a thing, Your Honor. In fact, he may have met his death *because* the defendant found that lipstick on his forehead. The evidence of the fingerprints is quite conclusive that the defendant was in that apartment."

"The Court understands the evidence. Proceed with your case," Judge Jordan said.

"Furthermore," Linn went on angrily, "I will now show the Court that there was every possibility the print of that lipstick could have been deliberately planted by none other than the attorney for the defendant and his charming and very efficient secretary. I will proceed to prove that by calling Don B. Ralston to the stand."

Ralston came forward and took the stand, his manner that of a man who wishes he were many miles away.

"Your name is Don B. Ralston? You reside at 2935 Creelmore Avenue in this city?"

"Yes, sir."

"And you knew Carver L. Clements in his lifetime?"

"Yes."

"In a business way?"

"Yes, sir."

"Now, on the night—or, rather, early in the morning—of the 10th of this month, did you have occasion to go to Carver Clements's apartment, being Apartment Number 702 in the Mandrake Arms Apartments in this city?"

"I did, yes, sir."

"What time was it?"

"Around—well, it was between one and two in the morning—I would say around one thirty."

"Were you alone?"

"No, sir."

"Who was with you?"

"Richard P. Nolin, who is a business associate—or was a business associate—of Mr. Clements; Manley L. Ogden, who handled some of Mr. Clements's income tax work; and a Miss Vera Payson, a friend of—well, a friend of all of us."

"What happened when you went to that apartment?"

"Well, we left the elevator on the seventh floor, and as we were walking down the corridor, I noticed two people coming down the corridor toward us."

"Now, when you say 'down the corridor,' do you mean from the direction of Apartment 702?"

"That's right, yes, sir."

"And who were these people?"

"Mr. Perry Mason and his secretary, Miss Street."

"And did you actually enter the apartment of Carver Clements?"

"I did not."

"Why not?"

169

"When I got to the door of Apartment 702, I pushed the doorbell and heard the sound of the buzzer on the inside of the apartment. Almost instantly the door of an apartment across the hall opened, and a woman complained that she had been unable to sleep because of people ringing the buzzer of that apartment, and stated, in effect, that other people were in there with Mr. Clements. So we left immediately."

"Now, then, Your Honor," Stewart Linn said, "I propose to show that the two people referred to by the person living in the apartment across the hallway were none other than Mr. Mason and Miss Street, who had actually entered that apartment and were in there with the dead man and the evidence for an undetermined length of time."

"Go ahead and show it," Judge Jordan said.

"Just a moment," Mason said. "Before you do that, I want to cross-examine this witness."

"Cross-examine him, then."

"When you arrived at the Mandrake Arms, Mr. Ralston, the door to the street was locked, was it not?"

"Yes, sir."

"What did you do?"

"We went up to the seventh floor and—"

"I understand that, but how did you get in? How did you get past the entrance door? You had a key, didn't you?"

"No, sir."

"Then how *did* you get in?"

"Why *you* let us in."

"*I* did?"

"Yes."

"Understand," Mason said, "I am not now referring to the time you came up from the street in the custody of the radio officer. I am now referring to the time when you *first* entered that apartment house on the morning of the tenth of this month."

"Yes, sir. I understand. You let us in."

"What makes you say that?"

"Well, because you and your secretary were in Carver Clements's apartment, and—"

"You, yourself, don't *know* we were in there, do you?"

"Well, I surmise it. We met you just after you had left the apartment. You were hurrying down the hall toward the elevator."

Mason said, "I don't want your surmises. You don't even know

I had been in that apartment. I want you to tell us how you got past the locked street door."

"We pressed the button of Carver Clements's apartment, and you—or, at any rate, someone—answered by pressing the button which released the electric door catch on the outer door. As soon as we heard the buzzing sound, which indicated the lock was released, we pushed the door open and went in."

"Let's not have any misunderstanding about this," Mason said. "Who was it pushed the button of Carver Clements's apartment?"

"I did."

"I'm talking now about the button in front of the outer door of the apartment."

"Yes, sir."

"And having pressed that button, you waited until the buzzer announced the door was being opened?"

"Yes, sir."

"How long?"

"Not over a second or two."

Mason said to the witness, "One more question: Did you go right up after you entered the house?"

"We—no, sir, not *right* away. We stopped for a few moments there in the lobby to talk about the type of poker we wanted to play. Miss Payson had lost money on one of these wild poker games where the dealer had the opportunity of calling any kind of game he wants, some of them having the one-eyed Jacks wild, and things of that sort."

"How long were you talking?"

"Oh, a couple of minutes."

"And then went right up?"

"Yes."

"Where was the elevator?"

"The elevator was on one of the upper floors. I remember we pressed the button and it took a little while to come down to where we were."

"That's all," Mason said.

Della Street's fingers dug into his arm. "Aren't you going to ask him about the key?" she whispered.

"Not yet," Mason said, a light of triumph in his eyes. "I know what happened now, Della. Give us the breaks, and we've got this case in the bag. First, make him prove we were in that apartment."

171

Linn said, "I will now call Miss Shirley Tanner to the stand."

The young woman who advanced to the stand was very different from the disheveled and nervous individual who had been so angry at the time Mason and Della Street had pressed the button of Apartment 702.

"Your name is Shirley Tanner, and you reside in Apartment 701 of the Mandrake Arms Apartments?"

"Yes, sir."

"And have for how long?"

She smiled, and said, "Not very long. I put in three weeks apartment hunting and finally secured a sublease on Apartment 701 on the afternoon of the eighth. I moved in on the ninth, which explains why I was tired almost to the point of hysterics."

"You had difficulty sleeping?"

"Yes."

"And on the morning of the tenth did you have any experiences which annoyed you—experiences in connection with the ringing of the buzzer in the apartment next door?"

"I most certainly did, yes, sir."

"Tell us exactly what happened."

"I had been taking sleeping medicine from time to time, but for some reason or other this night I was so nervous the sleeping medicine didn't do me any good. I had been unpacking, and my nerves were all keyed up. I was physically and mentally exhausted but I was too tired to sleep.

"Well, I was trying to sleep, and I think I had just got to sleep, when I was awakened by a continual sounding of the buzzer in the apartment across the hall. It was a low, persistent noise which became very irritating in my nervous state."

"Go on," Linn said. "What did you do?"

"I finally got up and put on a robe and went to the door and flung it open. I was terribly angry at the very idea of people making so much noise at that hour of the morning. You see, those apartments aren't too soundproof and there is a ventilating system over the doors of the apartments. The one over the door of 702 was apparently open and I had left mine open for night ventilation. And then I was angry at myself for getting so upset over the noise. I knew it would prevent me from sleeping at all, which is why I lay still for what seemed an interminable time before I opened the door."

Linn smiled. "And you say you *flung* open the door?"

"Yes, sir."

"What did you find?"

172

"Two people across the hall."

"Did you recognize them?"

"I didn't know them at the time, but I know them now."

"Who were they?"

She pointed a dramatic finger at Perry Mason. "Mr. Perry Mason, the lawyer for the defendant, and the young woman, I believe his secretary, who is sitting there beside him—not the defendant, but the woman on the other side."

"Miss Della Street," Mason said with a bow.

"Thank you," she said.

"And," Linn went on, "what did you see those people do?"

She said, "I saw them enter the apartment."

"Didn't you see how they entered the apartment—I mean, how did they get the door open?"

"They must have used a key. Mr. Mason was just pushing the door open and I—"

"No surmises, please," Linn broke in. "Did you actually see Mr. Mason using a key?"

"Well, I heard him."

"What do you mean?"

"As I was opening my door I heard metal rasping against metal, the way a key does when it scrapes against a lock. And then, when I had my door all the way open, I saw Mr. Mason pushing his way into 702."

"But you only know he must have had a key because you heard the sound of metal rubbing against metal?"

"Yes, and the click of the lock."

"Did you say anything to Mr. Mason and Miss Street?"

"I most certainly did, and then I slammed the door and went back and tried to sleep. But I was so mad by that time I couldn't keep my eyes closed."

"What happened after that?"

"After that, when I was trying to sleep—I would say just a few seconds after that—I heard that buzzer again. This time I was good and mad."

"And what did you do?"

"I swung open the door and started to give these people a piece of my mind."

"People?" Linn asked promptingly.

"There were four people standing there. The Mr. Ralston, who has just testified, two other men, and a woman. They were standing there at the doorway, jabbing away at the button, and I told them this was a sweet time to be calling on someone and making a racket, and that anyway the gentleman already had company, so if he didn't answer his door, it was because he didn't want to."

"Did you at that time see Mr. Mason and Miss Street walking down the corridor?"

"No. I did not. I had my door open only far enough to show me the door of Apartment 702 across the way."

"Thank you," Linn said. "Now, you distinctly saw Mr. Mason and Miss Street enter that apartment?"

"Yes."

"And close the door behind them?"

"Yes."

"Cross-examine!" Linn said triumphantly.

Mason, taking a notebook from his pocket, walked up to stand beside Shirley Tanner. "Miss Tanner," he said, "are you certain that you heard me rub metal against the keyhole of that door?"

"Certain," she said.

"My back was toward you?"

"It was when I first opened my door, yes. I saw your face, however, just after you went in the door. You turned around and looked at me over your shoulder."

"Oh, we'll stipulate," Linn said, with an exaggerated note of weariness in his voice, "that the witness couldn't see through Mr. Mason's back. Perhaps learned counsel was carrying the key in his teeth."

"Thank you," Mason said, turning toward Linn. Then, suddenly stepping forward, he clapped his notebook against Shirley Tanner's face.

The witness screamed and jumped back.

Linn was on his feet. "What are you trying to do?" he shouted.

Judge Jordan pounded with his gavel. "Mr. Mason!" he reprimanded. "That is contempt of court!"

Mason said, "Please let me explain, Your Honor. The Prosecution took the lip-prints of my client. I feel that I am entitled to take the lip-prints of this witness. I will cheerfully admit to being in contempt of court, in the event I am wrong, but I would like to extend this imprint of Shirley Tanner's lips to Mr. Benjamin Harlan, the identification expert, and ask him whether or not the print made by these lips is not the same as that of the lipstick kiss which was found on the dead forehead of Carver L. Clements."

There was a tense, dramatic silence in the courtroom.

Mason stepped forward and handed the notebook to Benjamin Harlan.

From the witness stand came a shrill scream of terror. Shirley Tanner tried to get to her feet. Her eyes were wide and terrified, her face was the color of putty.

She couldn't make it. Her knees buckled. She tried to catch herself, then fell to the floor. . . .

It was when order was restored in the courtroom that Perry Mason exploded his second bombshell.

"Your Honor," he said, "either Fay Allison is innocent or she is guilty. If she is innocent, someone framed the evidence which would discredit her. And if someone did frame that evidence, there is only one person who could have had access to the defendant's apartment, one person who could have transported glasses, toothbrushes, and tooth paste containing Fay Allison's fingerprints, one person who could have transported clothes bearing the unmistakable stamp of ownership of the defendant in this case. . . . Your Honor, I request that Anita Bonsal be called to the stand."

There was a moment's silence.

Anita Bonsal, there in the courtroom, felt suddenly as though she had been stripped stark naked by one swift gesture. One moment, she had been sitting there, attempting to keep pace with the swift rush of developments. The next moment, everyone in the courtroom was seeking her out with staring, prying eyes.

In her sudden surge of panic, Anita did the worst thing she could possibly have done: She ran.

They were after her then, a throng of humanity, motivated only by the mass instinct to pursue that which ran for cover.

Anita dashed to the stairs, went scrambling down them, found herself in another hallway in the Hall of Justice. She dashed the length of that hallway, frantically trying to find the stairs. She could not find them.

An elevator offered her welcome haven.

Anita fairly flung herself into the cage.

"What's the hurry?" the attendant asked.

Shreds of reason were beginning to return to Anita's fear-racked mind. "They're calling my case," she said. "Let me off at—"

"I know," the man said, smiling. "Third floor. Domestic Relations Court."

He slid the cage to a smooth stop at the third floor. "Out to the left," he said. "Department Twelve."

Anita's mind was beginning to work now. She smiled at the elevator attendant, walked rapidly to the left, pushed open a door, and entered the partially filled courtroom. She marched down the center aisle and calmly seated herself in the middle seat in a row of benches.

She was now wrapped in anonymity. Only her breathlessness and the pounding of her pulses gave indication that she was the quarry for which the crowd was now searching.

Then slowly the triumphant smile faded from her face. The realization of the effect of what she had done stabbed her consciousness. She had admitted her guilt. She could flee now to the farthest corners of the earth, but her guilt would always follow her.

Perry Mason had shown that she had not killed Carver Clements, but he had also shown that she had done something which in the minds of all men would be even worse. She had betrayed her friend. She had tried to ruin Fay Allison's reputation. She had attempted the murder of her own roommate by giving her an overdose of sleeping tablets.

How much would Mason have been able to prove? She had no way of knowing. But there was no need for him to prove anything now. Her flight had given Mason all the proof he needed.

She must disappear, and that would not be easy. By evening her photograph would be emblazoned upon the pages of every newspaper in the city. . . .

Back in the courtroom, almost deserted now except for the county officials who were crowding around Shirley Tanner, Mason was asking questions in a low voice.

There was no more stamina left in Shirley Tanner than in a wet dishrag. She heard her own voice answering the persistent drone of Mason's searching questions.

"You knew that Clements had this apartment in 702? . . . You deliberately made such a high offer that you were able to sublease Apartment 701? . . . You were suspicious of Clements and wanted to spy on him?"

"Yes," Shirley said, and her voice was all but inaudible, although it was obvious that the court reporter, standing beside her, was taking down in his notebook all she said.

"You were furious when you realized that Carver Clements had *another* mistress and that all his talk to you about waiting until he could get his divorce was merely bait which you had grabbed?"

Again she said, "Yes." There was no strength in her any more to think up lies.

"You made the mistake of loving him," Mason said. "It wasn't his money you were after, and you administered the poison. How did you do it, Shirley?"

She said, "I'd poisoned the drink I held in my hand. I knew it made Carver furious when I drank, because whiskey makes me lose control of myself, and he never knew what I was going to do when I was drunk."

"I rang his bell, holding that glass in my hand. I leered at him tipsily when he opened the door, and walked on in. I said, 'Hello, Carver darling. Meet your next-door neighbor,' and I raised the glass to my lips."

"He acted just as I knew he would. He was furious. He said, 'You little devil, what're you doing here? I've told you I'll do the drinking for both of us.' He snatched the glass from me and drained it." ·

"What happened?" Mason asked.

"For a moment, nothing," she said. "He went back to the chair and sat down. I leaned over him and pressed that kiss on his head. It was a goodbye kiss. He looked at me, frowned; then suddenly he jumped to his feet and tried to run to the door, but he staggered and fell face forward."

"And what did you do?"

"I took the key to his apartment from his pocket so I could get back in to fix things the way I wanted and get possession of the glass, but I was afraid to be there while he was—dying."

Mason nodded. "You went back to your own apartment, and then, after you had waited a few minutes and thought it was safe to go back, you couldn't, because Anita Bonsal was at the door?"

She nodded, and said, "She had a key. She went in. I supposed, of course, she'd call the police and that they'd come at any time. I didn't dare to go in there then. Finally, I decided the police weren't coming, after all. It was past midnight then."

"So then you went back in there? You were in there when Don Ralston rang the bell. You—"

"Yes," she said. "I went back into that apartment. By that time I had put on a bathrobe and pajamas and ruffled my hair all up. If anyone had said anything to me, if I had been caught, I had a story all prepared to tell them, that I had heard the door open and someone run down the corridor, that I had opened my door and found the door of 702 ajar, and I had just that minute looked in to see what had happened."

"All right," Mason said; "that was your story. What did you do?"

"I went in and wiped all my fingerprints off that glass on the floor. Then the buzzer sounded from the street."

"What did you do?"

She said, "I saw someone had fixed up the evidence just the way I had been going to fix it up. A bottle of whiskey on the table, a bottle of soda, a jar of ice cubes."

"So what did you do?"

She said, "I was rattled, I guess, so I just automatically pushed the button which released the downstairs door catch. Then I ducked back into my own apartment, and hadn't any more than got in when I heard the elevator stop at the seventh floor. I couldn't understand that, because I knew these people couldn't possibly have had time enough to get up to the seventh floor in the elevator. I waited, listening, and heard you two come down the corridor. As soon as the buzzer sounded in the other apartment, I opened the door to chase you away, but you were actually entering the apartment, so I had to make a quick excuse, that the sound of the buzzer had wakened me. Then I jerked the door shut. When the four people came up, I thought you were still in the apartment, and I had to see what was happening."

"How long had you known him?" Mason asked.

She said sadly, "I loved him. I was the one that he wanted to marry when he left his wife. I don't know how long this other romance had been going on. I became suspicious, and one time when I had an opportunity to go through his pockets, I found a key stamped, 'Mandrake Arms Apartment, Number 702.' Then I thought I knew, but I wanted to be sure. I found out who had Apartment 701 and made a proposition for a sublease that couldn't be turned down.

"I waited and watched. This brunette walked down the corridor and used *her* key to open the apartment. I slipped out into the corridor and listened at the door. I heard him give her the same old line he'd given me so many times, and I hated him. I killed him—and I was caught."

Mason turned to Stewart Linn and said, "There you are, young man. There's your murderess, but you'll probably never be able to get a jury to think it's anything more than manslaughter."

A much chastened Linn said, "Would you mind telling me how you figured this out, Mr. Mason?"

Mason said, "Clements's key was missing. Obviously he must have had it when he entered the apartment. Therefore, the murderer must have taken it from his pocket. Why? So he or she could come back. And if what Don Ralston said was true, *someone* must have been in the apartment when he rang the bell from the street, someone who let him in by pressing the buzzer.

"What happened to that someone? I must have been walking down the corridor within a matter of seconds after Ralston had pressed the button on the street door. Yet I saw no one leaving the apartment. *Obviously, then, the person who pressed the buzzer must have had a place to take refuge in a nearby apartment!*"

"Having learned that a young, attractive woman had only that day taken a lease on the apartment opposite, the answer became so obvious it ceased to be a mystery."

Stewart Linn nodded thoughtfully. "It all fits in," he said.

Mason picked up his brief-case, smiled to Della Street. "Come on, Della," he said. "Let's get Fay Allison and—"

He stopped as he saw Fay Allison's face. "What's happened to *your* lipstick?" he asked.

And then his eyes moved over to take in Dane Grover, who was standing by her, his face smeared diagonally across the mouth with a huge, red smear of lipstick.

Fay Allison had neglected to remove the thick coating of lipstick which she had put on when Mason had asked Benjamin Harlan, the identification expert, to take an imprint of her lips. Now, the heavy mark where her mouth had been pressed against the mouth of Dane Grover gave a note of incongruity to the entire proceedings.

On the lower floors a mob of eagerly curious spectators were baying like hounds upon the track of Anita Bonsal. In the courtroom the long, efficient arm of the law was gathering Shirley Tanner into its grasp, and there, amidst the machinery of tragedy, the romance of Fay Allison and Dane Grover picked up where it had left off. . .

It was the gavel of Judge Randolph Jordan that brought them back to the grim realities of justice.

"The Court," announced Judge Jordan, "will dismiss the case against Fay Allison. The Court will order Shirley Tanner into custody, and the Court will suggest to the Prosecutor that a complaint be issued for Anita Bonsal, upon such charge as may seem expedient to the office of the District Attorney. And the

Court does hereby extend its most sincere apologies to the defendant, Fay Allison. And the Court, personally, wishes to congratulate Mr. Perry Mason upon his brilliant handling of this matter."

There was a moment during which Judge Jordan's stern eyes rested upon the lipstick-smeared countenance of Dane Grover. A faint smile twitched at the corners of His Honor's mouth.

The gavel banged once more.

"The Court," announced Judge Randolph Jordan, "is adjourned."

INSPECTOR MAIGRET PURSUES

BY GEORGES SIMENON

Georges Simenon is the pseudonym of Belgian-born mystery writer Georges Sim, who published his first novel, *Au Pont des Arches (Aboard the Ark)*, at seventeen. Between twenty and thirty, he published about 200 popular novels under sixteen pseudonyms and traveled, chiefly in a small boat, all over Europe. In 1973 Mr. Simenon announced that he would write no more novels, leaving his output at about 200 books, including 80 or so detective novels featuring his patient, compassionate, best-selling Maigret. Simenon makes his home at Epalinges, Switzerland.

THE FOUR MEN WERE PACKED IN THE TAXI. It was freezing all over Paris. At half-past seven in the morning the city looked wan; the wind was whipping the powdery frost along the ground. The thinnest of the four men, on one of the flap seats, had a cigarette stuck to his lower lip and handcuffs on his wrists. The most important one, clothed in a thick overcoat, heavy-jawed, a bowler hat on his head, was smoking his pipe and watching the railings of the Bois de Boulogne file past.

"You want me to put on a big dramatic scene?" the handcuffed man suggested politely. "With struggling, frothing at the mouth, insults, and all?"

Taking the cigarette from between the man's lips and opening the door, for they had arrived at the Porte de Bagatelle, Inspector Maigret growled, "Don't overdo it."

The pathways in the Bois were deserted, white as limestone, and as hard. A dozen or so people were standing around at the corner of a bridle path, and a photographer prepared to go into action on the group as it approached.

But, as instructed, P'tit Louis raised his arms in front of his face.

Maigret, looking surly, swung his head from side to side like a bear, taking everything in—the new blocks of flats on the Boulevard Richard-Wallace, their shutters still closed, a few workmen on bikes coming from Puteaux, a lighted tram, two concierges approaching, their hands blue with cold.

"Is this it?" he asked.

The day before he had arranged for the following information to appear in the newspapers:

BAGATELLE MURDER

This time the police will not have been long in clearing up an affair that looked as if it presented insurmountable difficulties. It will be remembered that on Monday morning a park-keeper in the Bois de Boulogne discovered along one of the pathways a hundred yards or so from the Porte de Bagatelle a corpse it was possible to identify on the spot.

It was Ernest Borms, a well-known Viennese doctor who had been in practice in Neuilly for several years. Borms was wearing evening clothes. He must have been attacked during the night of Sunday/Monday, while returning to his flat on the Boulevard Richard-Wallace.

A bullet fired at point-blank range from a small-caliber revolver struck him full in the heart.

Borms, still young and handsome and well turned-out, led a fairly social life.

Scarcely forty-eight hours after the murder Police Headquarters have just made an arrest. Tomorrow morning, between seven and eight o'clock, the man concerned will be conducted to the scene for the purpose of a reconstruction of the crime.

As things turned out, this case was to be referred to at Headquarters as the one perhaps most characteristically Maigret; but when they spoke of it in his hearing, he had a curious way of turning his head away with a groan.

To proceed, everything was ready. Hardly any gaping onlookers, as planned. It was not for nothing that Maigret had chosen this early hour of the morning. Moreover, among the ten or twelve people who were hanging about, could be spotted some plainclothesmen wearing their most innocent air. One of them, Torrence, who loved disguises, was dressed as a milkman. At the sight of him his chief shrugged eloquently. If only P'tit Louis didn't overact. An old customer of theirs who had been picked up the day before for picking pockets in the Métro . . .

"You give us a hand tomorrow morning and we'll see that we aren't too hard on you this time . . ." They had fetched him up from the cells.

"Now, then," growled Maigret, "when you heard the footsteps you were hiding in this corner here, weren't you?"

"As you say, Chief Inspector. I was famished. Stony broke . . . I said to myself, a gent on his way home all dressed up like that must be carrying a walletful. 'Your money or your life!' was what I whispered right into his ear. And I swear it wasn't my fault that the thing went off. I'm quite sure it was the cold made me squeeze the trigger."

11 a.m. Maigret was pacing round his office at Headquarters, smoking solidly and constantly fiddling with the phone.

"Is that you, Chief? Lucas here. I followed the old man who seemed so interested in the reconstruction. Nothing doing there—he's just a lunatic who takes a stroll every morning in the Bois."

"All right, you can come back."

11.15 a.m. "Hullo, is that you, Chief? Torrence. I shadowed the young man you tipped me the wink on. He always hangs round when the plainclothes boys are called in. He's an assistant in a shop on the Champs Elysées. Shall I come back?"

From Janvier no call till five to twelve.

"I've got to be quick, Chief. I'm afraid he'll give me the slip. I'm keeping an eye on him in the mirror of the booth. I'm at the Yellow Dwarf Bar, Boulevard Rochechouart . . . Yes, he spotted me. He's got something on his mind. Crossing the Seine, he threw something in the river. He's tried over and over to shake me off. Will you be coming?"

So began a chase that was to last five days and nights. Among the hurrying crowds, across an unsuspecting Paris, from bar to bar, bistro to bistro, a lone man on the one hand, and on the other Maigret and his detectives, taking it in turn and, in the long run, just as harassed as the man they were following.

Maigret got out of his taxi opposite the Yellow Dwarf at the busy time just before lunch, and found Janvier leaning on the bar. He wasn't troubling to put on any façade of innocence. Quite the opposite.

"Which one is it?"

The detective motioned with his jaw toward a man sitting in the corner at a small table. The man was watching them; his eyes, which were a light blue-gray, gave a foreign cast to his face. Nordic? Slav? More likely a Slav. He was wearing a gray overcoat, a well-cut suit, a soft felt hat. About thirty-five years old, so far as one could judge. He was pale, close-shaven.

"What're you having, Chief? A hot toddy?"

"Toddy let it be. What's *he* drinking?"

"Brandy. It's his fifth this morning. You musn't mind if I sound slurred, but I've had to follow him round all the bistros. He's tough, you know. Look at him—it's been like that all morning. He wouldn't lower his eyes for all the kingdoms of the earth."

It was true. And it was strange. You couldn't call it arrogance or defiance. The man was just looking at them. If he felt any anxiety, it was concealed. It was sadness rather that his face expressed, but a calm, reflective sadness.

"At Bagatelle, when he noticed you were watching him, he went off straight away and I fell into step behind him. He hadn't gone a hundred yards before he turned around. Then, instead of leaving the Bois, as he apparently meant to do, he strode off down the first path he came to. He turned round again. He recognized me. He sat down on a bench, despite the cold, and I stopped. More than once I had the impression he wanted to speak to me, but in the end he only shrugged and set off again.

. "At the Porte Dauphine I almost lost him. He jumped into a taxi and it was just luck that I found one almost immediately. He got out at the Place de l'Opéra, and rushed into the Métro. One behind the other, we changed trains five times before he began to realize he wouldn't shake me off that way . . .

"We went up again into the street. We were at Place Clichy. Since then we have been going from bar to bar. I was waiting for one with a telephone booth where I could keep him in sight. When he saw me phoning, he gave a bitter little laugh. Honestly, you'd have sworn after that he was waiting for you."

"Ring up H.Q. Lucas and Torrence are to hold themselves ready to join me as soon as they're called. And a photographer, too, from the technical branch, with a miniature camera."

"Waiter!" the man called out. "What do I owe you?"

"Three-fifty."

"I bet he's a Pole," Maigret breathed to Janvier. "On our way . . ."

They didn't get far. At Place Blanche they followed the man into a restaurant, sat down at the next table. It was an Italian place, and they ate pasta.

At three, Lucas came to take over from Janvier, who was with Maigret at a *brasserie* opposite the Gare du Nord.

"The photographer?" Maigret asked.

"He's waiting outside to get him as he leaves."

And sure enough, when the Pole left the place, having finished reading the papers, a detective hurried up. At less than three feet he took a shot of him. The man raised his hand quickly to his face, but it was already too late. Then, proving that he knew what was going on, he cast a reproachful look to Maigret.

Aha, my little man, Maigret said to himself, you have some good reason for not revealing where you live. Well, you may be patient, but so am I.

By evening a few snowflakes were fluttering down in the street, the stranger walked on, hands in pockets, waiting for bedtime.

"I'll take over for the night, Chief?" Lucas suggested.

. "No. I'd rather you coped with the photograph. Look at the hotel registrations first. Then see what you can find out in the foreign quarters. That fellow knows his Paris. He didn't arrive yesterday. There must be people who know him."

"How about putting his picture in the papers?"

Maigret eyed his subordinate with scorn. How could Lucas, who had been working with him for so many years, fail to understand? Had the police one single clue? Nothing. Not one piece of evidence. A man killed during the night in the Bois de Boulogne. No weapon is found. No, prints. Dr. Borms lives alone, and his only servant doesn't know where he spent the previous evening. "Do as I say. Get going . . ."

Finally at midnight the man decides to go into a hotel. Maigret follows him in. It is a second- or even third-class hotel.

"I want a room."

"Will you register here, please?"

He registers hesitantly, his fingers stiff with cold. He looks Maigret up and down as if to say, "If you think that's any problem—I can write any name that comes."

And, in fact, he has done so. Nicolas Slaatkovitch, resident of Cracow, arrived the day before in Paris. It is all false, obviously.

Maigret telephones to Headquarters. They hunt through the files of furnished lodgings, the registers of foreigners, they get in touch with the frontier posts. No Nicolas Slaatkovitch.

"And a room for you?" the proprietor asks with distaste, for he senses the presence of a policeman.

"No, thank you. I'll spend the night on the stairs."

It's safer that way. He sits down on a step in front of the door of Room 7. Twice the door opens. The man peers through the gloom, makes out Maigret's silhouette, and ends up by going to bed. In the morning his face is rough with stubble. He hasn't been able to change his shirt. He hasn't even got a comb, and his hair is rumpled.

Lucas has just arrived. "I'll do the next shift, Chief?"

Maigret refuses to leave his stranger. He has watched him pay the bill. He has seen him grow pale. He guesses his thoughts . . .

And a little later, in a bar where, almost side by side, they are breakfasting on white coffee and croissants, the man openly counts up his fortune. One hundred-franc note, two twenty-franc pieces, one of ten, and some small change. He makes a bitter grimace.

Well, he won't get far on that. When he arrived at the Bois de Boulogne, he had come straight from home, for he was freshly shaved, not a speck of dust, not a crease in his clothes. He hadn't even looked to see how much money he had on him.

What he threw in the Seine, Maigret guesses, were his identification papers, perhaps visiting cards. At all costs he wants to prevent their finding out his address.

And so the round of the homeless begins again: the loitering in front of shops or round street traders, the bars one has to go into from time to time, even if it's only to sit down, especially when it's cold outside, the papers one reads in the *brasseries* . . .

One hundred and fifty francs. No more lunchtime restaurant. The man makes do with hard-boiled eggs, which he eats, along with his pint, standing up at the bar counter, while Maigret gulps down sandwiches.

For a long time the man has been thinking about going into a movie his hand fingering the small change in his pocket. Better to stick it out. He walks . . . and walks . . .

There is, incidentally, one detail that strikes Maigret. It is always in the same districts that this exhausting stroll takes place: from the Trinité to Place Clichy, from Place Clichy to Barbès, by way of Rue Caulaincourt . . . from Barbès to the Gare du Nord and Rue Lafayette. Besides, the man's afraid of being recognized, isn't he? Of course he's chosen the districts farthest from his home or hotel, those he didn't usually frequent . . .

Does he, like many foreigners, haunt Montparnasse? The parts around the Panthéon?

His clothes indicate he is reasonably well off. They are comfortable, sober, and well cut. A professional man, no doubt. What's more, he wears a ring, so he's married.

Maigret has had to agree to hand over to Torrence, and has dashed home. Madame Maigret is displeased: her sister has come up from Orléans, she has taken a lot of trouble over the dinner, and her husband, after a shave and a change of clothes, is already off again, and doesn't know when he'll be back.

He drives off to the Quai des Orfèvres. "Lucas hasn't left anything for me?"

Yes, he has. There's a note from the sergeant. He's been round several of the Polish and Russian quarters showing the photograph. Nobody knows the man. Nothing from the political circles, either. As a last resource he has had a large number of copies made of the photograph, and police are now going from door to door in all the districts of Paris, from concierge to concierge; showing the document to bar owners and waiters.

"Hullo, is that Chief Inspector Maigret? This is one of the usherettes at the newsreel theater on the Boulevard de Strasbourg. It's a gentleman—Monsieur Torrence. He's asked me to call you to say he's here, but he didn't want to leave his place in the theater."

Not so stupid, on the stranger's part. He has worked out that it's the best heated place to pass a few hours cheaply—two francs to get in, and you can see the program several times.

A curious intimacy has sprung up between follower and followed, between the man, whose face is now dark with stubble and whose clothes are crumpled, and Maigret, who never for a moment stops trailing him. There is even one rather comic point: they've both caught colds. Their noses are red; they pull out their handkerchiefs almost in time with one another. Once, in spite of himself, the stranger had to smile as he saw Maigret going off into a series of sneezes.

After five consecutive newsreel programs, a dirty hotel on the Boulevard de la Chapelle. Same name on the register. And again Maigret installs himself on the stairs. But as this is a hotel with a casual trade, he is disturbed every ten minutes by couples going up and down; they stare at him curiously, and the women don't find him a reassuring sight.

When he's at the end of his tether, or at the breaking point, will the man decide to go home? In one of the *brasseries*, where he stays long enough to take off his gray coat, Maigret without more ado seizes the garment and looks inside the collar. The coat comes from Old England, the shop on the Boulevard des Italiens. It is a ready-made coat, and the shop must have sold dozens of others like it. One clue, however: it is last year's model, so the stranger has been in Paris for a year at least. And in a year he must have found somewhere to hang out . . .

Maigret has started drinking grog to cure his cold. The other now pays out his money drop by drop. He drinks his coffee straight; he lives on croissants and hard-boiled eggs.

The news from the office is always the same: nothing to report. Nobody recognizes the photograph of the Pole. No one has heard of any missing person.

As to the dead man, nothing there, either. A good practice, he made a lot of money, wasn't interested in politics, went out a lot, and, as he dealt with nervous diseases, most of his patients were women.

There was one experiment Maigret had not yet had the chance of seeing through to the end: how long it would take for a well-bred, well-cared-for, well-dressed man to lose his outward polish.

Four days. As he now knew. To begin with, the unshavenness. The first morning the man looked like a lawyer, or a doctor, or an architect, or a businessman; you could picture him leaving his cosy flat. A four-day growth transformed him to such an extent that if one had now put his pictures in the papers and referred to the Bois de Boulogne affair, everyone would have said, "You can see he's a murderer."

The bitter weather and lack of sleep had reddened his eyelids, and his cheeks were feverish from his cold. His shoes, which were no longer polished, seemed to have lost their shape. His coat weighed on him, and his trousers were baggy round the knees.

Even his walk was no longer the same. He sidled along the wall, he lowered his eyes when people looked at him. Another thing; he turned his head away when he passed a restaurant where one could see people sitting down to large meals . . .

"Your last twenty francs," Maigret worked out, "poor wretch. What now?"

Lucas, Torrence, and Janvier took over from him from time to time, but he left his post as little as possible. He would burst into the Quai des Orfèvres, would see his Chief.

"You'd be well advised to take a rest, Maigret."

It was a peevish Maigret, touchy as if he were torn between contradictory emotions. "Am I or am I not supposed to be finding the murderer?"

"Of course."

"Well then, back to my post." As if resentfully, he would sigh. "I wonder where we'll sleep tonight."

Only twenty francs left. Not even that—when he got back, Torrence said the man had eaten three hard-boiled eggs and drunk two rum coffees in a bar on the corner of the Rue Montmartre.

"Eight francs fifty. That leaves eleven francs fifty."

Maigret admired him. Far from hiding himself, Maigret now tailed him quite openly, sometimes walking right next to him, and he had some difficulty to refrain from speaking to him. "Come now, don't you think it's time to have a proper meal? Somewhere there's a warm home where you're expected. A bed, slippers, a razor. Eh? And a good dinner."

But the man continued to prowl under the arc lamps of Les Halles, like one who no longer knows where to turn. In and out among the heaps of cabbages and carrots, stepping out of the way at the whistle of the train or when the farmers' trucks passed.

"Hasn't even the price of a hotel room."

That evening the National Meteorological Office registered a temperature of eight degrees below zero. The man treated himself to hot sausages from a stall in the streets. Now he would reek of garlic and fat the whole night through.

Once he tried to slip into a shelter and stretch out in the corner. A policeman, whom Maigret wasn't able to stop in time, moved him on. He was hobbling now. Along the quais. The Pont des Arts. As long as he didn't take it into his head to throw himself into the Seine. Maigret didn't feel he had the courage to jump in after him into the black water that was beginning to fill with drift ice.

The man was walking along the towpath level, where the tramps lay grumbling and, under the bridges, all the good places were taken.

In a small street close to the Place Maubert, through the windows of a strange bistro, old men could be seen sleeping with their heads on the tables. Twenty sous, wine included. The man stared in through the gloom. Then, with a fatalistic shrug, he pushed open the door.

Before it closed behind him, Maigret had time to be sickened by the smelly gust that struck him in the face. He preferred to stay outside. He called a policeman, posted him in his place on the pavement while he went to telephone Lucas to take over for the night.

"I've been trying to get you for the last hour, Chief. We've found him! Thanks to a concierge. The fellow's called Stefan Strevzki, an architect, thirty-four years old, born in Warsaw, been in France for three years. Works for a firm in the Faubourg Saint-Honoré. Married to a Hungarian, a magnificent creature named Dora. Living at Passy, Rue de la Pompe, in a twelve-thousand-franc flat. No political interests. The concierge has never seen the dead man. Stefan left the house earlier than usual on Monday morning. She was surprised not to see him return, but she wasn't worried, having ascertained—"

"What time is it?"

"Half-past three. I'm alone at Headquarters. I've had some beer brought up, but it's too cold."

"Listen, Lucas, you're going—yes, I know, too late for the morning ones. But the evening ones . . . understand?"

That morning the man's clothing gave off a muffled odor of poverty. His eyes were sunken. The look he cast at Maigret in the pale morning contained the deepest pathos and reproach.

Had he not been driven, little by little, but for all that a dizzy pace, to the very lowest depths? He turned up the collar of his overcoat. He didn't leave the neighborhood, but he rushed into a bistro that had just opened and downed four quick drinks, as if to rid himself of the appalling aftertaste the night had left in his throat and chest.

So much the worse for him. From now on he no longer had anything. Nothing was left for him but to walk up and down the streets the frost was making slippery. He must be stiff all over. He was limping with his left leg. From time to time he stopped and looked around despairingly.

As soon as he stopped going into cafés where there was a telephone, Maigret could no longer summon a relief. Back again along the quais. Then that mechanical gesture of flipping through the book bargains, turning the pages, pausing to check the authenticity of an engraving or a print.

A freezing wind was sweeping across the Seine. The water tinkled as the barges moved through it, as tiny fragments of ice glittered and jostled against one another. From a distance Maigret caught sight of the windows of his own office. His sister-in-law had gone back to Orléans. As long as Lucas had . . .

He didn't know yet that this dreadful trail was to become a classic, and that for years the older generation of detectives would recount the details to new colleagues. The silliest thing about it all was that it was a ridiculous detail that upset him most: the man had a pimple on his forehead, a pimple that, on close inspection, turned out to be a boil, which was changing from red to purple.

As long as Lucas . . .

At midday the man, who certainly knew his Paris, made for the free soup kitchen that is situated at the end of the Boulevard Saint-Germain. He took his place in the queue of down-and-outers. An old man spoke to him, but he pretended not to understand. Then another, with a pockmarked face, spoke to him in Russian.

Maigret crossed over to the opposite pavement, and paused. When he was driven to have sandwiches in a bistro, he half turned so that the other should not see him eating them through the windows.

The poor wretches moved forward slowly, went in, four or maybe six at a time, to the room where bowls of hot soup were being served. The queue grew longer. From time to time there was a shove from the back, which aroused protests from some of the others.

One o'clock. A newsboy appeared at the far end of the street; he was running, his body sloping forward. *"L'Intransigeant!* Get your *Intran*—" He, too, was in a hurry to get there before the others. He could tell his customers from far off, and he paid no attention to the queue of down-and-outers. "Get your—"

"Pst!" Timidly, the man raised his hand to attract the boy's attention. The others stared at him. So he had still a few sous left to spend on a paper?

Maigret, too, summoned the boy, unfolded the paper, and, to his relief, found what he was looking for—the photograph of a beautiful young woman smiling out of the front page.

STRANGE DISAPPEARANCE

A young Polish woman, Madame Dora Strevzki, who disappeared four days ago from her home in Passy, 17 Rue de la Pompe, has now been reported missing. Her husband, Monsieur Stefan Strevzki, has also been missing from his home since the previous day—i.e., Monday—and the concierge, who reported the disappearance to the police, states . . .

The man had only five or six yards more to go in the queue before he could claim his bowl of steaming soup, when he left his place in the line and was almost run over by a bus. He reached the opposite pavement just as Maigret drew level.

"I'm ready," he said simply. "Take me away. I'll answer all your questions . . ."

They were all standing in the corridor of Headquarters— Lucas, Janvier, Torrence, and others who had not been in on the case but knew about it. As they passed, Lucas made a triumphant signal to Maigret.

A door opened and shut. Beer and sandwiches on the table.

"Take something to eat first."

Not so easy. Mouthfuls stuck in his throat. Then, at last, "Now that she's gone and is somewhere safe . . ."

Maigret couldn't face him: he had to turn away and poke the stove.

"When I read the accounts of the murder in the papers I had already suspected Dora of deceiving me with that man. I knew, too, she wasn't his only mistress. Knowing Dora and her impetuous nature . . . You understand? If he wanted to get rid of her, I knew she was capable of . . . And she always carried an ivory-handled gun in her handbag. When the papers reported that an arrest had been made and there was to be a reconstruction of the crime, I wanted to see . . ."

Maigret would have liked to be able to say to him, as the British police do, "I must warn you that anything you say may be used in evidence against you."

He had kept his coat on and he was still wearing his hat. "Now that she's safe . . . For I suppose . . ." He looked about him anxiously. A suspicion crossed his mind.

"She must have understood when I didn't come home. I knew it would end like that—that Borms wasn't the man for her, that she wouldn't accept the role of a mere plaything, and that she'd come back to me. She went out alone that Sunday evening, as she had been doing recently. She must have killed him then."

Maigret blew his nose. He took a long time over it. A ray of sunlight—the harsh winter sunlight that goes with sharp frost—came in the window. The pimple or boil gleamed on the forehead of the man—as Maigret found he had to go on calling him.

"So your wife killed him. When she found out he had never really cared for her. And you, you realized she had done it. And you didn't want . . ."

He suddenly went up to the Pole. "I'm sorry, old man," he grunted, as if he was talking to an old friend. "I had to find out the truth, hadn't I? It was my duty."

Then he opened the door. "Bring in Madame Dora Strevzki. Lucas, you carry on. I—"

And for the next two days nobody saw him again at Headquarters. His chief telephoned him at home. "Well now, Maigret. You know she's confessed, and—by the way, how's your cold? They tell me—"

"It's nothing, Chief. It's getting better. Another day. How is he?"

"What? Who?"

"He—the man."

"Oh, I see. He's got hold of the best lawyer in Paris He has hopes—you know, *crimes passionels* . . ."

Maigret went back to bed and sank into a grog-and-aspirin stupor. When, later on, he was asked about the investigation, his grumbled "What investigation?" was enough to discourage further questions.

As for the man, he came to see him once or twice a week, and kept him informed of the hopes the defense were holding out.

It wasn't a straightforward acquittal: one year's imprisonment, with sentence suspended.

And the man—it was he who taught Maigret to play chess.

193

THE PURLOINED LETTER

BY EDGAR ALLAN POE

Edgar Allan Poe (b. Boston, January 19, 1809) was the son of a talented actress, Elizabeth Arnold, and her second husband, David Poe, Jr., an actor. Orphaned in Richmond, Virginia, late in 1811, Poe was taken into the home of John Allan, a wealthy merchant who regarded the boy as a genius. Poe entered West Point in 1830 but was expelled. While editing a literary magazine in Richmond in 1836 he entered a strange marriage with the thirteen-year-old Virginia Clemm. His *The Murders in the Rue Morgue*, published in *Graham's Magazine* in April 1841, was the first modern detective story.

AT PARIS, just after dark one gusty evening in the autumn of 18—, I was enjoying the twofold luxury of meditation and meerschaum, in company with my friend, C. Auguste Dupin, in his little back library, or book-closet, *au troisième*, No. 33 Rue Dunôt, Faubourg St. Germain. For one hour at least we had maintained a profound silence; while each, to any casual observer, might have seemed intently and exclusively occupied with the curling eddies of smoke that oppressed the atmosphere of the chamber. For myself, however, I was mentally discussing certain topics which had formed matter for conversation between us at an earlier period of the evening; I mean the affair of the Rue Morgue and the mystery attending the murder of Marie Rogêt. I looked upon it, therefore, as something of a coincidence when the door of our apartment was thrown open and admitted our old acquaintance, Monsieur G——, the Prefect of the Parisian police.

We gave him a hearty welcome; for there was nearly half as much of the entertaining as of the contemptible about the man, and we had not seen him for several years. We had been sitting in the dark, and Dupin now arose for the purpose of lighting a lamp, but sat down again, without doing so, upon G——'s saying that he had called to consult us, or rather to ask the opinion of my friend, about some official business which had occasioned a great deal of trouble.

"If it is any point requiring reflection," observed Dupin, as he forebore to enkindle the wick, "we shall examine it to better purpose in the dark."

"That is another of your odd notions," said the Prefect, who had the fashion of calling everything "odd" that was beyond his comprehension, and thus lived amid an absolute legion of "oddities."

"Very true," said Dupin, as he supplied his visitor with a pipe and rolled toward him a comfortable chair.

"And what is the difficulty now?" I asked. "Nothing more in the assassination way, I hope?"

"Oh, no; nothing of that nature. The fact is, the business is very simple indeed, and I make no doubt that we can manage it sufficiently well ourselves; but then I thought Dupin would like to hear the details of it, because it is so excessively odd."

"Simple and odd?" said Dupin.

"Why, yes; and not exactly that either. The fact is, we have all been a good deal puzzled because the affair is so simple, and yet baffles us altogether."

"Perhaps it is the very simplicity of the thing which puts you at fault," said my friend.

"What nonsense you do talk!" replies the Prefect, laughing heartily.

"Perhaps the mystery is a little too plain," said Dupin.

"Oh, good heavens! who ever heard of such an idea?"

"A little too self-evident."

"Ha! ha! ha!—ha! ha! ha!—ho! ho! ho!" roared our visitor, profoundly amused. "Oh, Dupin, you will be the death of me yet."

"And what, after all, is the matter on hand?" I asked.

"Why, I will tell you," replied the Prefect, as he gave a long, steady, and contemplative puff and settled himself in his chair,—"I will tell you in a few words; but, before I begin, let me caution you that this is an affair demanding the greatest secrecy, and that I should most probably lose the position I now hold were it known that I confided it to anyone at all."

"Proceed," said I.

"Or not," said Dupin.

"Well, then; I have received personal information, from a very high quarter, that a certain document of the last importance has been purloined from the royal apartments. The individual who purloined it is known—this beyond a doubt; he was seen to take it. It is known, also, that it still remains in his possession."

"How is this known?" asked Dupin.

"It is clearly inferred," replied the Prefect, "from the nature of the document and from the non-appearance of certain results which would at once arise from its passing out of the robber's possession, that is to say, from his employing it as he must design in the end to employ it."

"Be a little more explicit," I said.

"Well, I may venture so far as to say that the paper gives its holder a certain power in a certain quarter where such power is immensely valuable." The Prefect was fond of the cant of diplomacy.

"Still I do not quite understand," said Dupin.

"No? Well; the disclosure of the document to a third person, who shall be nameless, would bring in question the honor of a personage of most exalted station; and this fact gives the holder of the document an ascendency over the illustrious personage whose honor and peace are so jeopardized."

"But this ascendency," I interposed, "would depend upon the robber's knowledge of the loser's knowledge of the robber. Who would dare—"

"The thief," said G——, "is the Minister D——, who dares all things, those unbecoming as well as those becoming a man. The method of the theft was not less ingenious than bold. The document in question—a letter, to be frank—had been received by the personage robbed while alone in the royal boudoir. During its perusal she was suddenly interrupted by the entrance of the other exalted personage from whom especially it was her wish to conceal it. After a hurried and vain endeavor to thrust it in a drawer, she was forced to place it, open as it was, upon a table. The address, however, was uppermost, and, the contents thus unexposed, the letter escaped notice. At this juncture enters the Minister D——. His lynx eye immediately perceives the paper, recognizes the handwriting of the address, observes the confusion of the personage addressed, and fathoms her secret. After some business transactions, hurried through in his ordinary manner, he produces a letter somewhat similar to the one in question, opens it, pretends to read it, and then places it in close juxtaposition to the other. Again he converses for some fifteen minutes upon the public affairs. At length, in taking leave, he takes also from the table the letter to which he had no claim. Its rightful owner saw, but, of course, dared not call attention to the fact, in the presence of the third personage, who stood at her elbow. The Minister decamped, leaving his own letter, one of no importance, upon the table."

"Here, then," said Dupin to me, "you have precisely what you demand to make the ascendency complete, the robber's knowledge of the loser's knowledge of the robber."

"Yes," replied the Prefect; "and the power thus attained has, for some months past, been wielded, for political purposes, to a very dangerous extent. The personage robbed is more thoroughly convinced every day of the necessity of reclaiming her letter. But this, of course, cannot be done openly. In fine, driven to despair, she has committed the matter to me."

"Than whom," said Dupin, amid a perfect whirlwind of smoke, "no more sagacious agent could, I suppose, be desired or even imagined."

"You flatter me," replied the Prefect; "but it is possible that some such opinion may have been entertained."

"It is clear," said I, "as you observe, that the letter is still in the possession of the Minister; since it is his possession, and not any employment of the letter, which bestows the power. With the employment the power departs."

"True," said G——; "and upon this conviction I proceeded. My first care was to make thorough search of the Minister's hotel; and here my chief embarrassment lay in the necessity of searching without his knowledge. Beyond all things, I have been warned of the danger which would result from giving him reason to suspect our design."

"But," said I, "you are quite *au fait* in these investigations. The Parisian police have done this thing often before."

"Oh, yes; and for this reason I did not despair. The habits of the Minister gave me, too, a great advantage. He is frequently absent from home all night. His servants are by no means numerous. They sleep at a distance from their master's apartment, and, being chiefly Neapolitans, are readily made drunk. I have keys, as you know, with which I can open any chamber or cabinet in Paris. For three months a night has not passed, during the greater part of which I have not been engaged, personally, in ransacking the D—— Hotel. My honor is interested, and, to mention a great secret, the reward is enormous. So I did not abandon the search until I had become fully satisfied that the thief is a more astute man than myself. I fancy that I have investigated every nook and corner of the premises in which it is possible that the paper can be concealed."

"But is it not possible," I suggested, "that although the letter may be in possession of the Minister, as it unquestionably is, he may have concealed it elsewhere than upon his own premises?"

"This is barely possible," said Dupin. "The present peculiar condition of affairs at court, and especially of those intrigues in which D—— is known to be involved, would render the instant availability of the document, its susceptibility of being produced at a moment's notice, a point of nearly equal importance with its possession."

"Its susceptibility of being produced?" said I.

"That is to say, of being destroyed," said Dupin.

"True," I observed; "the paper is clearly, then, upon the premises. As for its being upon the person of the minister, we may consider that as out of the question."

"Entirely," said the Prefect. "He has been twice waylaid, as if by footpads, and his person rigidly searched under my own inspection."

"You might have spared yourself this trouble," said Dupin. "D——, I presume, is not altogether à fool, and, if not, must have anticipated these waylayings, as a matter of course."

"Not altogether a fool," said G——, "but then he is a poet, which I take to be one remove from a fool."

"True," said Dupin, after a long and thoughtful whiff from his meerschaum, "although I have been guilty of certain doggerel myself."

"Suppose you detail," said I, "the particulars of your search."

"Why, the fact is, we took our time, and we searched everywhere. I have had long experience in these affairs. I took the entire building, room by room; devoting the nights of a whole week to each. We examined, first, the furniture of each apartment. We opened every possible drawer; and I presume you know that, to a properly trained police-agent, such a thing as a 'secret' drawer is impossible. Any man is a dolt who permits a 'secret' drawer to escape him in a search of this kind. The thing is so plain. There is a certain amount of bulk, of space, to be accounted for in every cabinet. Then we have accurate rules. The fiftieth part of a line could not escape us. After the cabinets we took the chairs. The cushions we probed with the fine long needles you have seen me employ. From the tables we removed the tops."

"Why so?"

"Sometimes the top of a table or other similarly arranged piece of furniture is removed by the person wishing to conceal an article; then the leg is excavated, the article deposited within the cavity, and the top replaced. The bottoms and tops of bedposts are employed in the same way."

"But could not the cavity be detected by sounding?" I asked.

"By no means, if, when the article is deposited, a sufficient wadding of cotton be placed around it. Besides, in our case, we were obliged to proceed without noise."

"But you could not have removed, you could not have taken to pieces all articles of furniture in which it would have been possible to make a deposit in the manner you mention. A letter may be compressed into a thin spiral roll, not differing much in shape or bulk from a large knitting-needle, and in this form it might be inserted into the rung of a chair, for example. You did not take to pieces all the chairs?"

"Certainly not, but we did better: we examined the rungs of

every chair in the hotel, and, indeed, the jointings of every description of furniture, by the aid of a most powerful microscope. Had there been any traces of recent disturbance we should not have failed to detect it instantly. A single gram of gimlet-dust, for example, would have been as obvious as an apple. Any disorder in the gluing, any unusual gaping in the joints, would have sufficed to insure detection."

"I presume you looked to the mirrors, between the boards and the plates, and you probed the beds and the bedclothes, as well as the curtains and carpets."

"That of course; and when we had absolutely completed every particle of the furniture in this way, then we examined the house itself. We divided its entire surface into compartments, which we numbered, so that none might be missed; then we scrutinized each individual square inch throughout the premises, including the two houses immediately adjoining, with the microscope, as before."

"The two houses adjoining!" I exclaimed; "you must have had a great deal of trouble."

"We had; but the reward offered is prodigious."

"You included the grounds about the houses?"

"All the grounds are paved with brick. They gave us comparatively little trouble. We examined the moss between the bricks and found it undisturbed."

"You looked among D——'s papers, of course, and into the books of the library?"

"Certainly; we opened every package and parcel; we not only opened every book, but we turned over every leaf in each volume, not contenting ourselves with a mere shake, according to the fashion of some of our police officers. We also measured the thickness of every book-cover with the most accurate measurement, and applied to each the most jealous scrutiny of the microscope. Had any of the bindings been recently meddled with, it would have been utterly impossible that the fact should have escaped observation. Some five or six volumes, just from the hands of the binder, we carefully probed, longitudinally, with the needles."

"You explored the floors beneath the carpets?"

"Beyond doubt. We removed every carpet and examined the boards with the microscope."

"And the paper on the walls?"

"Yes."

"You looked into the cellars?"

"We did."

"Then," I said, "you have been making a miscalculation, and the letter is not upon the premises."

"I fear you are right there," said the Prefect. "And now, Dupin, what would you advise me to do?"

"To make a thorough research of the premises."

"That is absolutely needless," replied G——. "I am not more secure that I breathe than I am that the letter is not at the hotel."

"I have no better advice to give you," said Dupin. "You have, of course, a description of the letter?"

"Oh, yes!" and here the Prefect, producing a memorandum-book, proceeded to read aloud a minute account of the internal, and especially of the external, appearance of the missing document. Soon after finishing the perusal of this description he took his departure, more entirely depressed in spirits than I had ever known the good gentleman before.

In about a month afterward he paid us another visit, and found us occupied very nearly as before. He took a pipe and a chair and entered into some ordinary conversation. At length I said:

"Well, but, G——, what of the purloined letter? I presume you have at last made up your mind that there is no overreaching the Minister?"

"Confound him! say I—yes; I made the re-examination, however, as Dupin suggested, but it was all labor lost, as I knew it would be."

"How much was the reward offered, did you say?" asked Dupin.

"Why, a very great deal, a very liberal reward; I don't like to say how much, precisely; but one thing I will say—that I wouldn't mind giving my individual check for fifty thousand francs to anyone who could obtain me that letter. The fact is, it is becoming of more and more importance every day; and the reward has been lately doubled. If it were trebled, however, I could do no more than I have done."

"Why, yes," said Dupin, drawingly, between the whiffs of his meerschaum, "I really—think, G——, you have not exerted yourself—to the utmost in this matter. You might—do a little more, I think, eh?"

"How? in what way?"

"Why—puff, puff—you might—puff, puff—employ counsel

201

in the matter eh?—puff, puff, puff. Do you remember the story of Abernethy?"

"No; hang Abernethy!"

"To be sure, hang him and welcome. But, once upon a time, a certain rich miser conceived the design of sponging upon this Abernethy for a medical opinion. Getting up, for this purpose, an ordinary conversation in a private company, he insinuated his case to the physician as that of an imaginary individual.

"'We will suppose,' said the miser, 'that his symptoms are such and such; now, Doctor, what would you have directed him to take?'"

"'Take,' said Abernethy, 'why, take advice, to be sure.'"

"But," said the Prefect, a little discomposed, "I am perfectly willing to take advice and to pay for it. I would give fifty thousand francs to anyone who would aid me in the matter."

"In that case," replied Dupin, opening a drawer and producing a checkbook, "you may as well fill me up a check for that amount mentioned. When you have signed it I will hand you the letter."

I was astounded. The Prefect appeared absolutely thunderstricken. For some minutes he remained speechless and motionless, looking incredulously at my friend with open mouth, and eyes that seemed starting from their sockets; then, apparently recovering himself in some measure, he seized a pen, and after several pauses and vacant stares finally filled up and signed a check for fifty thousand francs and handed it across the table to Dupin. The latter examined it carefully and deposited it in his pocketbook; then, unlocking an escritoire, took thence a letter and gave it to the Prefect. This functionary grasped it in a perfect agony of joy, opened it with a trembling hand, cast a rapid glance at its contents, and then, scrambling and struggling to the door, rushed at length unceremoniously from the room and from the house without having uttered a syllable since Dupin had requested him to fill up the check.

When he had gone, my friend entered into some explanation.

"The Parisian police," he said, "are exceedingly able in their way. They are persevering, ingenious, cunning, and thoroughly versed in the knowledge which their duties seem chiefly to demand. Thus, when G—— detailed to us his mode of searching the premises at the Hotel D——, I felt entire confidence in his having made a satisfactory examination, so far as his labors extended."

"'So far as his labors extended?'" said I.

"Yes," said Dupin. "The measures adopted were not only the best of their kind, but carried out to absolute perfection. Had the letter been deposited within the range of their search, these fellows would, beyond a question have found it."

I merely laughed, but he seemed quite serious in all that he said.

"The measures, then," he continued, "were good in their kind and well executed; their defect lay in their being inapplicable to the case and to the man. A certain set of highly ingenious resources are, with the Prefect, a sort of Procrustean bed, to which he forcibly adapts his designs. But he perpetually errs by being too deep or too shallow for the matter in hand; and many a schoolboy is a better reasoner than he. I knew one about eight years of age, whose success at guessing in the game of 'even and odd' attracted universal admiration. This game is simple, and is played with marbles. One player holds in his hand a number of these toys and demands of another whether that number is even or odd. If the guess is right, the guesser wins one; if wrong, he loses one. The boy to whom I allude won all the marbles of the school. Of course he had some principle of guessing; and this lay in mere observation and admeasurement of the astuteness of his opponents. For example, an arrant simpleton is his opponent, and, holding up his closed hand, asks, 'Are they even or odd?' Our schoolboy replies, 'Odd,' and loses; but upon the second trial he wins, for he then says to himself: 'The simpleton had them even upon the first trial, and his amount of cunning is just sufficient to make him have them odd upon the second; I will therefore guess odd'; he guesses odd and wins. Now, with a simpleton a degree above the first, he would have reasoned thus: 'This fellow finds that in the first instance I guessed odd, and in the second he will propose to himself, upon the first impulse, a simple variation from even to odd, as did the first simpleton; but then a second thought will suggest that this is too simple a variation, and finally he will decide upon putting it even as before. I will therefore guess even';—he guesses even and wins. Now this mode of reasoning in the schoolboy, whom his fellows termed 'lucky,'—what, in its last analysis, is it?"

"It is merely," I said, "an identification of the reasoner's intellect with that of his opponent."

"It is," said Dupin; "and upon inquiring of the boy by what means he effected the thorough identification in which his success consisted, I received answer as follows: 'When I wish to find out how wise, or how stupid, or how good, or how wicked is

203

anyone, or what are his thoughts at the moment, I fashion the expression of my face, as accurately as possible, in accordance with the expression of his and then wait to see what thoughts or sentiments arise in my mind or heart, as if to match or correspond with the expression.' This response of the schoolboy lies at the bottom of all the spurious profundity which has been attributed to Rochefoucauld, to La Bruyère, to Machiavelli, and to Campanella."

"And the identification," I said, "of the reasoner's intellect with that of his opponent depends, if I understand you aright, upon the accuracy with which the opponent's intellect is admeasured."

"For its practical value it depends upon this," replied Dupin; "and the Prefect and his cohort fail so frequently, first, by default of this identification, and, secondly, by ill-admeasurement, or rather through non-admeasurement, of the intellect with which they are engaged. They consider only their own ideas of ingenuity; and, in searching for anything hidden, advert only to the modes in which they would have hidden it. They are right in this much, that their own ingenuity is a faithful representative of that of the mass; but when the cunning of tł ˉ individual felon is diverse in character from their own, the felon foils them, of course. This always happens when it is above their own, and very usually when it is below. They have no variation of principle in their investigations; at best, when urged by some unusual emergency, by some extraordinary reward, they extend or exaggerate their old modes of practice without touching their principles. What, for example, in this case of D——, has been done to vary the principle of action? What is all this boring, and probing, and sounding, and scrutinizing with the microscope, and dividing the surface of the building into registered square inches; what is it all but an exaggeration of the application of the one principle or set of principles of search, which are based upon the one set of notions regarding human ingenuity, to which the Prefect, in the long routine of his duty, has been accustomed? Do you not see he has taken it for granted that all men proceed to conceal a letter, not exactly in a gimlet-hole bored in a chair-leg, but, at least, in some out-of-the-way hole or corner suggested by the same tenor of thought which would urge a man to secrete a letter in a gimlet-hole bored in a chair-leg? And do you not see, also, that such recherchés nooks for concealment are adapted only for ordinary occasions, and would be adopted only by ordinary intellects; for, in all cases of concealment, a disposal of it in this *recherché* manner, is, in the very first instance, presumable and presumed; and thus its discovery depends, not at all upon the acumen, but altogether upon the mere care, patience, and determination of the seekers; and where the case is of importance, or, what amounts to the same thing in the policial eyes, when the reward is of magnitude, the qualities in question have never been known to fail. You will now understand what I meant in suggesting that had the purloined letter been hidden anywhere within the limits of the Prefect's examination—in other words, had the principle of its concealment been comprehended within the principles of the Prefect—its discovery would have been a matter altogether beyond question. This functionary, however, has been thoroughly mystified; and the remote source of his defeat lies in the supposition that the Minister is a fool, because he has acquired renown as a poet. All fools are poets; this the Prefect feels; and he is merely guilty of a *non distribution medii* in thence inferring that all poets are fools."

"But is this really the poet?" I asked. "There are two brothers, I know; and both have attained reputation in letters. The Minister, I believe, has written learnedly on the Differential Calculus. He is a mathematician and no poet."

"You are mistaken; I know him well; he is both. As poet and mathematician, he would reason well; as mere mathematician, he could not have reasoned at all, and thus would have been at the mercy of the Prefect."

"You surprise me," I said, "by these opinions, which have been contradicted by the voice of the world. You do not mean to set at naught the well-digested idea of centuries? The mathematical reason has long been regarded as the reason *par excellence.*"

"'*Il y a à parier,*'" replied Dupin, quoting from Chamfort, "'*que toute idée publique, toute convention reçue, est une sottise, car elle a convenue au plus grand nombre.*' The mathematicians, I grant you, have done their best to promulgate the popular error to which you allude, and which is none the less an error for its promulgation as truth. With an art worthy a better cause, for example, they have insinuated the term 'analysis' into application to algebra. The French are the originators of this particular deception; but if a term is of any importance, if words derive any value from applicability, then 'analysis' conveys 'algebra' about as much, as in Latin, '*ambitus*' implies 'ambition,' '*religio*' 'religion,' or '*homines honesti*' a set of honorable men."

"You have a quarrel on hand, I see," said I, "with some of the algebraists of Paris; but proceed."

"I dispute the availability, and thus the value, of that reason which is cultivated in any especial form other than the abstractly logical. I dispute, in particular, the reason educed by mathematical study. The mathematics are the science of form and quantity; mathematical reasoning is merely logic applied to observation upon form and quantity. The great error lies in supposing that even the truths of what is called pure algebra are abstract or general truths. And this error is so egregious that I am confounded at the universality with which it has been received. Mathematical axioms are not axioms of general truth. What is true of relation, of form and quantity, is often grossly false in regard to morals, for example. In this latter science it is very usually untrue that the aggregated parts are equal to the whole. In chemistry, also, the axiom fails. In the consideration of motive it fails; for two motives, each of a given value, have not, necessarily, a value, when united, equal to the sum of their values apart. There are numerous other mathematical truths which are only truths within the limits of relation. But the mathematician argues from his finite truths, through habit, as if they were of an absolutely general applicability, as the world indeed imagines them to be. Bryant, in his very learned *Mythology*, mentions an analogous source of error when he says that 'although the pagan fables are not believed, yet we forget ourselves continually and make inferences from them as existing realities.' With the algebraists, however, who are pagans themselves, the 'pagan fables' are believed, and the inferences are made, not so much through lapse of memory as through an unaccountable addling of the brains. In short, I never yet encountered the mere mathematician who could be trusted out of equal roots, or one who did not clandestinely hold it as a point of his faith that $x^2 + px$ was absolutely and unconditionally equal to q. Say to one of these gentlemen, by way of experiment, if you please, that you believe occasions may occur where $x^2 + px$ is not altogether equal to q, and, having made him understand what you mean, get out of his reach as speedily as convenient, for, beyond doubt, he will endeavor to knock you down.

"I mean to say," continued Dupin, while I merely laughed at his last observations, "that if the Minister had been no more than a mathematician, the Prefect would have been under no necessity of giving me this check. I knew him, however, as both mathematician and poet, and my measures were adapted to his capacity with reference to the circumstances by which he was surrounded. I knew him as a courtier, too, and as a bold intriguant. Such a man, I considered, could not fail to be aware of the ordinary policial modes of action. He could not have failed to anticipate—and events have proved that he did not fail to anticipate—the waylayings to which he was subjected. He must have foreseen, I reflected, the secret investigations of his premises. His frequent absences from home at night, which were hailed by the Prefect as certain aids to his success, I regarded only as ruses to afford opportunity for thorough search to the police, and thus the sooner to impress them with the conviction, to which G——, in fact, did finally arrive—the conviction that the letter was not upon the premises. I felt, also, that the whole train of thought, which I was at some pains in detailing to you just now, concerning the invariable principle of policial action in searches for articles concealed—I felt that this whole train of thought would necessarily pass through the mind of the Minister. It would imperatively lead him to despise all the ordinary nooks of concealment. He could not, I reflected, be so weak as not to see that the most intricate and remote recess of his hotel would be as open as his commonest closets to the eyes, to the probes, to the gimlets, and to the microscopes of the Prefect. I saw, in fine, that he would be driven, as a matter of course, to simplicity, if not deliberately induced to it as a matter of choice. You will remember, perhaps, how desperately the Prefect laughed when I suggested, upon our first interview, that it was just possible this mystery troubled him on account of its being so self-evident."

"Yes," said I, "I remember his merriment well. I really thought he would have fallen into convulsions."

"The material world," continued Dupin, "abounds with very strict analogies to the immaterial and thus some color of truths has been given to the rhetorical dogma that metaphor, or simile, may be made to strengthen an argument as well as to embellish a description. The principle of the *vis inertiæ*, for example, seems to be identical in physics and metaphysics. It is not more true in the former, that a large body is with more difficulty set in motion than a smaller one, and that its subsequent momentum is commensurate with this difficulty, than it is, in the latter, that intellects of the vaster capacity, while more forcible, more constant, and more eventful in their movements than those of inferior grade, are yet the less readily moved, and more embarrassed, and full of hesitation in the first few steps of their progress. Again: have you ever noticed which of the street signs, over the shop doors, are the most attractive of attention?"

"I have never given the matter a thought," I said.

"There is a game of puzzles," he resumed, "which is played upon a map. One party playing requires another to find a given word, the name of town, river, state, or empire—any word, in short, upon the motley and perplexed surface of the chart. A novice in the game generally seeks to embarrass his opponents by giving them the most minutely lettered names; but the adept selects such words as stretch, in large characters, from one end of the chart to the other. These, like the over-largely lettered signs and placards of the street, escape observation by dint of being excessively obvious; and here the physical oversight is precisely analogous with the moral inapprehension by which the intellect suffers to pass unnoticed those considerations which are too obtrusively and too palpably self-evident. But this is a point, it appears, somewhat above or beneath the understanding of the Prefect. He never once thought it probable, or possible, that the Minister had deposited the letter immediately beneath the nose of the whole world by way of best preventing any portion of that world from perceiving it.

"But the more I reflected upon the daring, dashing, and discriminating ingenuity of D——; upon the fact that the document must always have been at hand, if he intended to use it to good purpose; and upon the decisive evidence, obtained by the Prefect, that it was not hidden within the limits of that dignitary's ordinary search, the more satisfied I became that, to conceal this letter, the Minister had resorted to the comprehensive and sagacious expedient of not attempting to conceal it at all.

"Full of these ideas, I prepared myself with a pair of green spectacles, and called one fine morning, quite by accident, at the ministerial hotel. I found D——at home, yawning, lounging, and dawdling, as usual, and pretending to be in the last extremity of *ennui*. He is, perhaps, the most really energetic human being now alive; but that is only when nobody sees him.

"To be even with him, I complained of my weak eyes and lamented the necessity of the spectacles under cover of which I cautiously and thoroughly surveyed the whole apartment, while seemingly intent only upon the conversation of my host.

"I paid especial attention to a large writing-table near which he sat, and upon which lay confusedly some miscellaneous letters and other papers, with one or two musical instruments and a few books. Here, however, after a long and very deliberate scrutiny, I saw nothing to excite particular suspicion.

"At length my eyes, in going the circuit of the room, fell upon a trumpery filigree card-rack of pasteboard that hung dangling by a dirty blue ribbon from a little brass knob just beneath the middle of the mantelpiece. In this rack, which had three or four compartments, were five or six visiting-cards and a solitary letter. This last was much soiled and crumpled. It was torn nearly in two, across the middle, as if a design, in the first instance, to tear it entirely up as worthless had been altered, or stayed, in the second. It had a large black seal, bearing the D—— cipher very conspicuously, and was addressed, in a diminutive female hand, to D——, the Minister, himself. It was thrust carelessly, and even, as it seemed, contemptuously, into one of the uppermost divisions of the rack.

"No sooner had I glanced at this letter than I concluded it to be that of which I was in search. To be sure, it was, to all appearance, radically different from the one of which the Prefect had read us so minute a description. Here the seal was large and black, with the D—— cipher, there it was small and red, with the ducal arms of the S—— family. Here, the address, to the Minister, was diminutive and feminine; there the superscription, to a certain royal personage, was markedly bold and decided; the size alone formed a point of correspondence. But, then, the radicalness of these differences, which was excessive: the dirt; the soiled and torn condition of the paper, so inconsistent with the true methodical habits of D——, and so suggestive of a design to delude the beholder into an idea of the worthlessness of the document—these things, together with the hyperobtrusive situation of this document, full in the view of every visitor, and thus exactly in accordance with the conclusions to which I had previously arrived; these things, I say, were strongly corroborative of suspicion, in one who came with the intention to suspect.

"I protracted my visit as long as possible, and, while I maintained a most animated discussion with the Minister upon a topic which I knew well had never failed to interest and excite him, I kept my attention really riveted upon the letter. In this examination, I committed to memory its external appearance and arrangement in the rack; and also fell, at length, upon a discovery which set at rest whatever trivial doubt I might have entertained. In scrutinizing the edges of the paper, I observed them to be more chafed than seemed necessary. They presented the broken appearance which is manifested when a stiff paper, having been once folded and pressed with a folder, is refolded in a reversed direction, in the same creases or edges which had formed the original fold. This discovery was sufficient. It was clear to me that the letter had been turned, as a glove, inside out, redirected and resealed. I bade the Minister good morning, and took my departure at once, leaving a gold snuff-box upon the table.

"The next morning I called for the snuff-box, when we resumed, quite eagerly, the conversation of the preceding day. While thus engaged, however, a loud report, as if of a pistol, was heard immediately beneath the windows of the hotel, and was succeeded by a series of fearful screams, and the shoutings of a terrified mob. D—— rushed to a casement, threw it open, and looked out. In the meantime I stepped to the card-rack, took the letter, put it in my pocket, and replaced it by a facsimile (so far as regards externals) which I had carefully prepared at my lodgings, imitating the D—— cipher very readily by means of a seal formed of bread.

"The disturbance in the street had been occasioned by the frantic behavior of a man with a musket. He had fired it among a crowd of women and children. It proved, however, to have been without a ball, and the fellow was suffered to go his way as a lunatic or a drunkard. When he had gone, D—— came from the window, whither I had followed him immediately upon securing the object in view. Soon afterward I bade him farewell. The pretended lunatic was a man in my own pay."

"But what purpose had you," I asked, "in replacing the letter by a facsimile? Would it not have been better, at the first visit, to have seized it openly and departed?"

"D——," replied Dupin, "is a desperate man, and a man of nerve. His hotel, too, is not without attendants devoted to his interests. Had I made the wild attempt you suggest, I might never have left the ministerial presence alive. The good people of Paris might have heard of me no more. But I had an object apart from these considerations. You know my political prepossessions. In this matter, I act as a partisan of the lady concerned. For eighteen months the Minister has had her in his power. She has now him in hers, since, being unaware that the letter is not in his possession, he will proceed with his exactions as if it was. Thus will he inevitably commit himself, at once, to his political destruction. His downfall, too, will not be more precipitate than awkward. It is all very well to talk about the *facilis descensus Averni*; but in all kinds of climbing, as Catalani said of singing, it is far more easy to get up than to come down. In the present instance I have no sympathy, at least no pity, for him who descends. He is that *monstrum horrendum*, an unprincipled man of genius. I confess, however, that I should like very well to know the precise character of his thoughts, when, being defied by her whom the Prefect terms 'a certain personage,' he is reduced to opening the letter which I left for him in the card-rack."

"How? Did you put anything particular in it?"

"Why, it did not seem altogether right to leave the interior blank; that would have been insulting. D——, at Vienna once, did me an evil turn, which I told him, quite good-humoredly, that I should remember. So, as I knew he would feel some curiosity in regard to the identity of the person who had outwitted him, I thought it a pity not to give him a clue. He is well acquainted with my MS., and I just copied into the middle of the blank sheets the words

"'—Un dessein si funeste,
    S'il n'est digne d'Atrée, est digne de Thyeste.'
They are to be found in Crébillon's *Atrée*."

TOO MANY HAVE LIVED

BY DASHIELL HAMMETT

Dashiell Hammett worked as a newsboy, freight clerk, railroad laborer, messenger boy, stevedore, advertising manager and Pinkerton detective before becoming a detective-story writer in the late 1920s. He was born in St. Mary's County, Maryland, on May 27, 1894. His most famous fictional detectives are Sam Spade, Nick and Nora Charles, and the Continental Op. He served in World War I and World War II. Because of his politics his books were removed from many libraries during the McCarthy era. He died on January 10, 1961.

THE MAN'S TIE WAS AS ORANGE AS a sunset. He was a large man, tall and meaty, without softness. The dark hair parted in the middle, flattened to his scalp, his firm, full cheeks, the clothes that fit him with noticeable snugness, even the small pink ears flat against the sides of his head—each of these seemed but a differently colored part of one same smooth surface. His age could have been thirty-five or forty-five.

He sat beside Samuel Spade's desk, leaning forward a little over his Malacca stick, and said, "No. I want you to find out what happened to him. I hope you never find him." His protuberant green eyes stared solemnly at Spade.

Spade rocked back in his chair. His face—given a not unpleasantly satanic cast by the v's of his bony chin, mouth, nostrils, and thickish brows—was as politely interested as his voice. "Why?"

The green-eyed man spoke quietly, with assurance, "I can talk to you, Spade. You've the sort of reputation I want in a private detective. That's why I'm here."

Spade's nod committed him to nothing.

The green-eyed man said, "And any fair price is all right with me."

Spade nodded as before. "And with me," he said, "but I've got to know what you want to buy. You want to find out what happened to this—uh—Eli Haven, but you don't care what it is?"

The green-eyed man lowered his voice, but there was no other change in his mien. "In a way I do. For instance, if you found him and fixed it so he stayed away for good, it might be worth more money."

"You mean even if he didn't want to stay away?"

The green-eyed man said, "Especially."

Spade smiled and shook his head. "Probably not enough more money—the way you mean it." He took his long thick-fingered hands from the arms of his chair and turned their palms up. "Well, what's it all about, Colyer?"

Colyer's face reddened a little, but his eyes maintained their unblinking cold stare. "This man's got a wife. I like her. They _ar_ _ row last week and he blew. If I can convince her he's gone _r_ good, there's a chance she'll divorce him."

"I'd want to talk to her," Spade said. "Who is this Eli Haven?"

"He's a bad egg. He doesn't do anything. Writes poetry or something."

"What can you tell me about him that'll help?"

"Nothing Julia, his wife, can't tell you. You're going to talk to her." Colyer stood up. "I've got connections. Maybe I can get something for you through them later."

A small-boned woman of twenty-five or -six opened the apartment door. Her powder-blue dress was trimmed with silver buttons. She was full-bosomed but slim, with straight shoulders and narrow hips, and she carried herself with a pride that would have been cockiness in one less graceful.

Spade said, "Mrs. Haven?"

She hesitated before saying, "Yes."

"Gene Colyer sent me to see you. My name's Spade. I'm a private detective. He wants me to find your husband."

"And have you found him?"

"I told him I'd have to talk to you first."

Her smile went away. She studied his face gravely, feature by feature, then she said, "Certainly," and stepped back, drawing the door back with her.

When they were seated in facing chairs in a cheaply furnished room overlooking a playground where children were noisy, she asked, "Did Gene tell you why he wanted Eli found?"

"He said if you knew he was gone for good maybe you'd listen to reason."

She said nothing.

"Has he ever gone off like this before?"

"Often."

"What's he like?"

"He's a swell man," she said dispassionately, "when he's sober; and when he's drinking he's all right except with women and money."

"That leaves him a lot of room to be all right in. What does he do for a living?"

"He's a poet," she replied, "but nobody makes a living at that."

"Well?"

"Oh, he pops in with a little money now and then. Poker, races, he says. I don't know."

"How long've you been married?"

"Four years, almost." She smiled mockingly.

"San Francisco all the time?"

214

"No, we lived in Seattle the first year and then came here."

"He from Seattle?"

She shook her head. "Some place in Delaware."

"What place?"

"I don't know."

Spade drew his thickish brows together a little. "Where are you from?"

She said sweetly, "You're not hunting for me."

"You act like it," he grumbled. "Well, who are his friends?"

"Don't ask me!"

He made an impatient grimace. "You know some of them," he insisted.

"Sure. There's a fellow named Minera and a Louis James and somebody he calls Conny."

"Who are they?"

"Men," she replied blandly. "I don't know anything about them. They phone or drop by to pick him up, or I see him around town with them. That's all I know."

"What do they do for a living? They can't all write poetry."

She laughed. "They could try. One of them, Louis James, is a—a member of Gene's staff, I think. I honestly don't know any more about them than I've told you."

"Think they'd know where your husband is?"

She shrugged. "They're kidding me if they do. They still call up once in a while to see if he's turned up."

"And these women you mentioned?"

"They're not people I know."

Spade scowled thoughtfully at the floor, asked, "What'd he do before he started not making a living writing poetry?"

"Anything—sold vacuum cleaners, hoboed, went to sea, dealt blackjack, railroaded, canning houses, lumber camps, carnivals, worked on a newspaper—anything."

"Have any money when he left?"

"Three dollars he borrowed from me."

"What'd he say?"

She laughed. "Said if I used whatever influence I had with God while he was gone he'd be back at dinnertime with a surprise for me."

Spade raised his eyebrows. "You were on good terms?"

"Oh, yes. Our last fight had been patched up a couple of days before."

"When did he leave?"

"Thursday afternoon; three o'clock, I guess."

"Got any photographs of him?"

"Yes." She went to a table by one of the windows, pulled a drawer out, and turned toward Spade with a photograph in her hand.

Spade looked at the picture of a thin face with deep-set eyes, a sensual mouth, and a heavily lined forehead topped by a disorderly mop of coarse blond hair.

He put Haven's photograph in his pocket and picked up his hat. He turned toward the door, halted. "What kind of poet is he? Pretty good?"

She shrugged. "That depends on who you ask."

"Any of it around here?"

"No." She smiled. "Think he's hiding between pages?"

"You never can tell what'll lead to what. I'll be back some time. Think things over and see if you can't find some way of loosening up a little more. 'Bye."

He walked down Post Street to Mulford's book store and asked for a volume of Haven's poetry.

"I'm sorry," the girl said. "I sold my last copy last week—" she smiled—"to Mr. Haven himself. I can order it for you."

"You know him?"

"Only through selling him books."

Spade pursed his lips, asked, "What day was it?" He gave her one of his business cards. "Please. It's important."

She went to a desk, turned the pages of a red-bound salesbook, and came back to him with the book open in her hand. "It was last Wednesday," she said, "and we delivered it to a Mr. Roger Ferris, 1981 Pacific Avenue."

"Thanks a lot," he said.

Outside, he hailed a taxicab and gave the driver Mr. Roger Ferris' address.

The Pacific Avenue house was a four-story graystone set behind a narrow strip of lawn. The room into which a plump-faced maid ushered Spade was large and high-ceilinged.

Spade sat down, but when the maid had gone away he rose and began to walk around the room. He halted at a table where there were three books. One of them had a salmon-colored jacket on which was printed in red an outline drawing of a bolt of lightning striking the ground between a man and a woman, and in black the words *Colored Light, by Eli Haven.*

Spade picked up the book and went back to his chair.

There was an inscription on the flyleaf—heavy, irregular characters written with blue ink:

To good old Buck, who knew his colored lights, in memory of them there days.

Eli

Spade turned the pages at random and idly read a verse:

STATEMENT

Too many have lived
As we live
For our lives to be
Proof of our living.
Too many have died
As we die
For their deaths to be
Proof of our dying.

He looked up from the book as a man in dinner clothes came into the room. He was not a tall man, but his erectness made him seem tall even when Spade's six feet and a fraction of an inch were standing before him. He had bright blue eyes undimmed by his fifty-some years, a sunburnt face in which no muscle sagged, a smooth, broad forehead, and thick, short, nearly white hair. There was dignity in his countenance, and amiability.

He nodded at the book Spade still held. "How do you like it?"

Spade grinned, said, "I guess I'm just a mug," and put the book down. "That's what I came to see you about, though, Mr. Ferris. You know Haven?"

"Yes, certainly. Sit down, Mr. Spade." He sat in a chair not far from Spade's. "I knew him as a kid. He's not in trouble, is he?"

Spade said, "I don't know. I'm trying to find him."

Ferris spoke hesitantly, "Can I ask why?"

"You know Gene Colyer?"

"Yes." Ferris hesitated again, then said, "This is in confidence. I've a chain of motion picture houses through northern California, you know, and a couple of years ago when I had some labor trouble I was told that Colyer was the man to get in touch with to have it straightened out. That's how I happened to meet him."

"Yes," Spade said dryly, "A lot of people happen to meet Gene that way."

"But what's he got to do with Eli?"

217

"Wants him found. How long since you've seen him?"

"Last Thursday he was here."

"What time did he leave?"

"Midnight—a little after. He came over in the afternoon around half-past three. We hadn't seen each other for years. I persuaded him to stay for dinner—he looked pretty seedy—and lent him some money."

"How much?"

"A hundred and fifty—all I had in the house."

"Say where he was going when he left?"

Ferris shook his head. "He said he'd phone me the next day."

"Did he phone you the next day?"

"No."

"And you've known him all his life?"

"Not exactly, but he worked for me fifteen or sixteen years ago when I had a carnival company—Great Eastern and Western Combined Shows—with a partner for a while and then by myself. I always liked the kid."

"How long before Thursday since you'd seen him?"

"Lord knows," Ferris replied. "I'd lost track of him for years. Then, Wednesday, out of a clear sky, that book came, with no address or anything, just that stuff written in the front, and the next morning he called me up. I was tickled to death to know he was still alive and doing something with himself. So he came over that afternoon and we put in about nine hours talking about old times."

"Tell you much about what he'd been doing since then?"

"Just that he'd been knocking around, doing one thing and another, taking the breaks as they came. He didn't complain much; I had to make him take the hundred and fifty."

Spade stood up. "Thanks ever so much, Mr. Ferris. I—"

Ferris interrupted him. "Not at all, and if there's anything I can do, call on me."

Spade looked at his watch. "Can I phone my office?"

"Certainly; there's a phone in the next room, to the right."

Spade said "Thanks" and went out. When he returned he was rolling a cigarette. His face was wooden.

"Any news?" Ferris asked.

"Yes. Colyer's called the job off. He says Haven's body's been found in some bushes on the other side of San Jose, with three bullets in it." He smiled, adding mildly, "He *told* me he might be able to find out something through his connections."

218

Morning sunshine, coming through the curtains that screened Spade's office windows, put two fat, yellow rectangles on the floor and gave everything in the room a yellow tint.

He sat at his desk, staring meditatively at a newspaper. He did not look up when Effie Perine came in from the outer office.

She said, "Mrs. Haven is here."

He raised his head then and said, "That's better. Push her in."

Mrs. Haven came in quickly. Her face was white and she was shivering in spite of her fur coat. She came straight to Spade and asked, "Did Gene kill him?"

Spade said, "I don't know."

"I've got to know," she cried.

Spade took her hands. "Here, sit down." He led her to a chair. He asked, "Colyer tell you he'd called the job off?"

She stared at him in amazement. "He what?"

"He left word here last night that your husband had been found and he wouldn't need me any more."

She hung her head and her words were barely audible. "Then he did."

Spade shrugged. "Maybe only an innocent man could've afforded to call it off then, or maybe he was guilty, but had brains enough and nerve enough to—"

She was not listening to him. She was leaning toward him, speaking earnestly, "But, Mr. Spade, you're not going to drop it like that? You're not going to let him stop you?"

While she was speaking his telephone bell rang. He said, "Excuse me," and picked up the receiver. "Yes? . . . Uh-huh . . . So?" He pursed his lips. "I'll let you know." He pushed the telephone aside slowly and faced Mrs. Haven again. "Colyer's outside."

"Does he know I'm here?" she asked quickly.

"Couldn't say." He stood up, pretending he was not watching her closely. "Do you care?"

She pinched her lower lip between her teeth, said "No" hesitantly.

"Fine. I'll have him in."

She raised a hand as if in protest, then let it drop, and her white face was composed. "Whatever you want," she said.

Spade opened the door, said, "Hello, Colyer. Come on in. We were just talking about you."

Colyer nodded and came into the office holding his Malacca stick in one hand, his hat in the other. "How are you this morning, Julia? You ought to've phoned me. I'd've driven you back to town."

"I—I didn't know what I was doing."

Colyer looked at her for a moment longer, then shifted the focus of his expressionless green eyes to Spade's face. "Well, have you been able to convince her I didn't do it?"

"We hadn't got around to that," Spade said. "I was just trying to find out how much reason there was for suspecting you. Sit down."

Colyer sat down somewhat carefully, asked, "And?"

"And then you arrived."

Colyer nodded gravely. "All right, Spade," he said; "you're hired again to prove to Mrs. Haven that I didn't have anything to do with it."

"Gene" she exclaimed in a choked voice and held her hands out toward him appealingly. "I don't think you did—I don't want to think you did—but I'm so afraid." She put her hands to her face and began to cry.

Colyer went over to the woman. "Take it easy," he said. "We'll kick it out together."

Spade went into the outer office, shutting the door behind him. Effie Perine stopped typing a letter.

He grinned at her, said, "Somebody ought to write a book about people sometime—they're peculiar," and went over to the water cooler. "You've got Wally Kellogg's number. Call him up and ask him where I can find Tom Minera."

He returned to the inner office.

Mrs. Haven had stopped crying. She said, "I'm sorry."

Spade said, "It's all right." He looked sidewise at Colyer. "I still got my job?"

"Yes." Colyer cleared his throat. "But if there's nothing special right now, I'd better take Mrs. Haven home."

"Okay, but there's one thing: according to the *Chronicle* you identified him. How come you were down there?"

"I went down when I heard they'd found a body," Colyer replied deliberately. "I told you I had connections."

Spade said, "All right; be seeing you," and opened the door for them.

When the corridor door closed behind them, Effie Perine said, "Minera's at the Buxton on Army Street."

Spade said, "Thanks." He went into the inner office to get his hat. On his way out he said, "If I'm not back in a couple of months tell them to look for my body there."

Spade walked down a shabby corridor to a battered green door marked *411*. The murmur of voices came through the door, but no words could be distinguished. He stopped listening and knocked.

An obviously disguised male voice asked, "What is it?"

"I want to see Tom. This is Sam Spade."

A pause, then: "Tom ain't here."

Spade put a hand on the knob and shook the frail door. "Come on, open up," he growled.

Presently the door was opened by a thin dark man of twenty-five or -six who tried to make his beady dark eyes guileless while saying, "I didn't think it was your voice at first." The slackness of his mouth made his chin seem even smaller than it was. His green-striped shirt, open at the neck, was not clean. His gray pants were carefully pressed.

"You've got to be careful these days," Spade said solemnly, and went through the doorway into a room where two men were trying to seem uninterested in his arrival.

One of them leaned against the window sill filing his finger-nails. The other was tilted back in a chair with his feet on the edge of a table and a newspaper spread between his hands. They glanced at Spade in unison and went on with their occupations.

Spade said cheerfully "Always glad to meet any friends of Tom Minera's."

Minera finished shutting the door and said awkwardly. "Uh—yes—Mr. Spade, meet Mr. Conrad and Mr. James."

Conrad, the man at the window, made a vaguely polite gesture with the nail file in his hand. He was a few years older than Minera, of average height, sturdily built, with a thick-featured, dull-eyed face.

James lowered his paper for an instant to look coolly, appraisingly, at Spade and say, "How'r'ye, brother?" Then he returned to his reading. He was as sturdily built as Conrad, but taller, and his face had a shrewdness the other's lacked.

"Ah," Spade said, "and friends of the late Eli Haven."

The man at the window jabbed a finger with his nail file, and cursed it bitterly. Minera moistened his lips, and then spoke rapidly, with a whining note in his voice, "But on the level, Spade, we hadn't none of us seen him for a week."

Spade seemed mildly amused by the dark man's manner.

"What do you think he was killed for?"

"All I know is what the paper says: his pockets was all turned inside out and there wasn't much as a match on him." He drew

221

down the ends of his mouth. "But far as I know he didn't have no dough. He didn't have none Tuesday night."

Spade, speaking softly, said, "I hear he got some Thursday night."

Minera, behind Spade, caught his breath audibly.

James said, "I guess you ought to know. I don't."

"He ever work with you boys?"

James slowly put aside his newspaper and took his feet off the table. His interest in Spade's question seemed great enough, but almost impersonal. "Now what do you mean by that?"

Spade pretended surprise, "But you boys must work at something?"

Minera came around to Spade's side. "Aw, listen, Spade," he said. "This guy Haven was just a guy we knew. We didn't have nothing to do with rubbing him out; we don't know nothing about it. You know, we—"

Three deliberate knocks sounded at the door.

Minera and Conrad looked at James, who nodded, but by then Spade, moving swiftly, had reached the door and was opening it.

Roger Ferris was there.

Spade blinked at Ferris, Ferris at Spade. Then Ferris put out his hand and said, "I *am* glad to see you."

"Come on in," Spade said.

"Look at this, Mr. Spade." Ferris' hand trembled as he took a slightly soiled envelope from his pocket.

Ferris' name and address were typewritten on the envelope. There was no postage stamp on it. Spade took out the enclosure, a narrow slip of cheap white paper, and unfolded it. On it was typewritten:

You had better come to Room 411 Buxton Hotel on Army St at 5 PM this afternoon on account of Thursday night.

There was no signature.

Spade said, "It's a long time before five o'clock."

"It is," Ferris agreed with emphasis. "I came as soon as I got that. It was Thursday night Eli was at my house."

Minera was jostling Spade, asking, "What is all this?"

Spade held the note up for the dark man to read. He read it and yelled, "Honest, Spade, I don't know nothing about that letter."

"Does anybody?" Spade asked.

Conrad said "No" hastily.

James said, "What letter?"

Spade looked dreamily at Ferris for a moment, then said, as if speaking to himself, "Of course, Haven was trying to shake you down."

Ferris' face reddened. "What?"

"Shakedown," Spade repeated patiently; "Money, blackmail."

"Look here, Spade," Ferris said earnestly; "you don't really believe what you said? What would he have to blackmail me on?"

" 'To good old Buck',"—Spade quoted the dead poet's inscription—" 'who knew his colored lights, in memory of them there days.' " He looked somberly at Ferris from beneath slightly raised brows. "What colored lights? What's the circus and carnival slang term for kicking a guy off a train while it's going? Red-lighting. Sure, that's it—red lights. Who'd you red-light, Ferris, that Haven knew about?"

Minera went over to a chair, sat down, put his elbows on his knees, his head between his hands, and stared blankly at the floor. Conrad was breathing as if he had been running.

Spade addressed Ferris, "Well?"

Ferris wiped his face with a handkerchief, put the handkerchief in his pocket, and said simply, "It was a shakedown."

"And you killed him."

Ferris' blue eyes, looking into Spade's yellow-gray ones, were clear and steady, as was his voice. "I did not," he said. "I swear I did not. Let me tell you what happened. He sent me the book, as I told you, and I knew right away what that joke he wrote in the front meant. So the next day, when he phoned me and said he was coming over to talk over old times and to try to borrow some money for old times' sake, I knew what he meant again, and I went down to the bank and drew out ten thousand dollars. You can check that up. It's the Seamen's National."

"I will," Spade said.

"As it turned out, I didn't need that much. He wasn't very big-time, and I talked him into taking five thousand. I put the other five back in the bank next day. You can check that up."

"I will," Spade said.

"I told him I wasn't going to stand for any more taps, this five thousand was the first and last. I made him sign a paper saying he'd helped in the—in what I'd done—and he signed it. He left sometime around midnight, and that's the last I ever saw of him."

Spade tapped the envelope that Ferris had given him. "And how about this note?"

"A messenger boy brought it at noon, and I came right over.

Eli had assured me he hadn't said anything to anybody, but I didn't know. I had to face it, whatever it was."

Spade turned to the others, his face wooden. "Well?"

Minera and Conrad looked at James, who made an impatient grimace and said, "Oh, sure, we sent him the letter. Why not? We was friends of Eli's, and we hadn't been able to find him since he went to put the squeeze to this baby, and then he turns up dead, so we kind of like to have the gent come over and explain things."

"You knew about the squeeze?"

"Sure. We was all together when he got the idea."

"How'd he happen to get the idea?" Spade asked.

James spread the fingers of his left hand. "We'd been drinking and talking—you know the way a bunch of guys will, about all they'd seen and done—and he told a yarn about once seeing a guy boot another off a train into a cañon, and he happens to mention the name of the guy that done the booting—Buck Ferris. And somebody says, 'What's this Ferris look like?' Eli tells him what he looked like then, saying he ain't seen him for fifteen years; and whoever it is whistles and says, 'I bet that's the Ferris that owns about half the movie joints in the state. I bet you he'd give something to keep that back trail covered!' "

"Well, the idea kind of hit Eli. You could see that. He thought a little while and then he got cagey. He asked what this movie Ferris' first name is, and when the other guy tells him, 'Roger,' he makes out he's disappointed and says, 'No, it ain't him. His first name was Martin.' We all give him the ha-ha and he finally admits he's thinking of seeing the gent, and when he called me up Thursday around noon and says he's throwing a party at Pogey Hecker's that night, it ain't no trouble to figure out what's what.'

"What was the name of the gentleman who was red-lighted?"

"He wouldn't say. He shut up tight. You couldn't blame him."

"Then nothing. He never showed up at Pogey's. We tried to get him on the phone around two o'clock in the morning, but his wife said he hadn't been home, so we stuck around till four or five and then decided he had given us a run-around, and made Pogey charge the bill to him, and beat it. I ain't seen him since—dead or alive."

Spade said mildly. "Maybe. Sure you didn't find Eli later that morning, take him riding, swap him bullets for Ferris' five thou, dump him in the—?"

A sharp double knock sounded on the door.

Spade's face brightened. He went to the door and opened it.

A young man came in. He was very dapper, and very well proportioned. He wore a light topcoat and his hands were in its pockets. Just inside the door he stepped to the right, and stood with his back to the wall.

By that time another young man was coming in. He stepped to the left. Though they did not actually look alike, their common dapperness, the similar trimness of their bodies, and their almost identical positions—back to wall, hands in pockets, cold, bright eyes studying the occupants of the room—gave them the appearance of twins.

Then Gene Colyer came in. He nodded at Spade, but paid no attention to the others in the room, though James said, "Hello, Gene."

"Anything new?" Colyer asked Spade.

Spade nodded. "It seems this gentleman"—jerked a thumb at Ferris—"was—"

"Any place we can talk?"

"There's a kitchen back here."

Colyer snapped a "Smear anybody that pops" over his shoulder at the two dapper young men and followed Spade into the kitchen. He sat on the one kitchen chair and stared with unblinking green eyes at Spade while Spade told him what he had learned.

When the private detective had finished, the green-eyed man asked, "Well, what do you make of it?"

Spade looked thoughtfully at the other. "You've picked up something. I'd like to know what it is."

Colyer said, "They found the gun in a stream a quarter of a mile from where they found him. It's James's—got the mark on it where it was shot out of his hand once in Vallejo."

"That's nice," Spade said.

"Listen. A kid named Thurston says James comes to him last Wednesday and gets him to tail Haven. Thurston picks him up Thursday afternoon, puts him in at Ferris', and phones James. James tells him to take a plant on the place and let him know where Haven goes when he leaves, but some nervous woman in the neighborhood puts in a ruble about the kid hanging around, and the cops chase him along about ten o'clock."

Spade pursed his lips and stared thoughtfully at the ceiling.

Colyer's eyes were expressionless, but sweat made his round face shiny, and his voice was hoarse. "Spade," he said, "I'm going to turn him in."

Spade switched his gaze from the ceiling to the protuberant green eyes.

"I've never turned in one of my people before," Colyer said, "but this one goes. Julia's *got* to believe I hadn't anything to do with it if it's one of my people and I turn him in, hasn't she?"

Spade nodded slowly. "I think so."

Colyer suddenly averted his eyes and cleared his throat. When he spoke again it was curtly. "Well, he goes."

Minera, James, and Conrad were seated when Spade and Colyer came out of the kitchen. Ferris was walking the floor. The two dapper young men had not moved.

Colyer went over to James. "Where's your gun, Louis?" he asked.

James moved his right hand a few inches toward his left breast, stopped it, and said, "Oh, I didn't bring it."

With his gloved hand—open—Colyer struck James on the side of the face, knocking him out of his chair.

James straightened up, mumbling, "I didn't mean nothing." He put a hand to the side of his face. "I know I oughtn't've done it, Chief, but when he called up and said he didn't like to go up against Ferris without something and didn't have any of his own, I said, 'All right,' and sent it over to him."

Colyer said, "And you sent Thurston over to him, too."

"We were just kind of interested in seeing if he did go through with it," James mumbled.

"And you couldn't've gone there yourself, or sent somebody else?"

"After Thurston had stirred up the whole neighborhood?"

Colyer turned to Spade. "Want us to help you take them in, or want to call the wagon?"

"We'll do it regular," Spade said, and went to the wall telephone. When he turned away from it his face was wooden, his eyes dreamy. He made a cigarette, lit it, and said to Colyer, "I'm silly enough to think your Louis has got a lot of right answers in that story of his."

James took his hand down from his bruised cheek and stared at Spade with astonished eyes.

Colyer growled, "What's the matter with you?"

"Nothing," Spade said softly, "except I think you're a little too anxious to slam it on him." He blew smoke out. "Why, for instance, should he drop his gun there when it had marks on it that people knew?"

Colyer said, "You think he's got brains."

226

"If these boys killed him, knew he was dead, why do they wait till the body's found and things are stirred up before they go after Ferris again? What'd they turn his pockets inside out for if they hijacked him? That's a lot of trouble and only done by folks that kill for some other reason and want to make it look like robbery." He shook his head. "You're too anxious to slam it on him. Why should they—?"

"That's not the point right now," Colyer said. "The point is, why do you keep saying I'm too anxious to slam it on him?"

Spade shrugged. "Maybe to clear yourself with Julia as soon as possible and as clear as possible, maybe even to clear yourself with the police, and then you've got clients."

Colyer said, "What?"

Spade made a careless gesture with his cigarette. "Ferris," he said blandly. "He killed him, of course."

Colyer's eyelids quivered, though he did not actually blink.

Spade said, "First, he's the last person we know of who saw Eli alive, and that's always a good bet. Second, he's the only person I talked to before Eli's body turned up who cared whether they were holding out on me or not. The rest of you just thought I was hunting for a guy who'd gone away. He knew I was hunting for a man he'd killed, so he had to put himself in the clear. He was even afraid to throw that book away, because it had been sent up by the book store and could be traced, and there might be clerks who'd seen the inscription. Third, he was the only one who thought Eli was just a sweet, clean, lovable boy—for the same reasons. Fourth, that story about a blackmailer showing up at three o'clock in the afternoon, making an easy touch for five grand, and then sticking around till midnight is just silly, no matter how good the booze was. Fifth, the story about the paper Eli signed is still worse, though a forged one could be fixed up easy enough. Sixth, he's got the best reason of anybody we know for wanting Eli dead."

Colyer nodded slowly. "Still—"

"Still nothing," Spade said. "Maybe he did the ten-thousand-out-five-thousand-back trick with his bank, but that was easy. Then he got this feeble-minded blackmailer in his house, stalled him along until the servant had gone to bed, took the borrowed gun away from him, shoved him downstairs into his car, took him for a ride—maybe took him already dead, maybe shot him down there by the bushes—frisked him clean to make identification harder and to make it look like robbery, tossed the gun in the water, and came home—"

227

He broke off to listen to the sound of a siren in the street. He looked then, for the first time since he had begun to talk, at Ferris.

Ferris' face was ghastly white, but he held his eyes steady.

Spade said, "I've got a hunch, Ferris, that we're going to find out about that red-lighting job, too. You told me you had your carnival company with a partner for a while when Eli was working for you, and then by yourself. We oughtn't to have a lot of trouble finding out about your partner—whether he disappeared, or died a natural death, or is still alive."

Ferris had lost some of his erectness. He wet his lips and said, "I want to see my lawyer. I don't want to talk till I've seen my lawyer."

Spade said, "It's all right with me. You're up against it, but I don't like blackmailers myself. I think Eli wrote a good epitaph for them in that book back there—'Too many have lived.' "

THE MAN IN THE PASSAGE

BY GILBERT K. CHESTERTON

Gilbert Keith Chesterton, essayist, man-of-letters and creator of Father Brown, was born on May 29, 1874, in London. He did not distinguish himself at St. Paul's or at Slade, the art school of University College, London, though he became a light comic draftsman of some merit and later illustrated a number of books by himself and with E. C. Bentley and Hilaire Belloc. As a widely read and heard journalist, debater and after-dinner speaker, even his opponents granted him credit for his wit, his humanity and personal kindness, his love of liberty and gift of paradox.

Two men appeared simultaneously at the two ends of a sort of passage running along the side of the Apollo Theater in the Adelphi. The evening daylight in the streets was large and luminous, opalescent and empty. The passage was comparatively long and dark, so each man could see the other as a mere black silhouette at the other end. Nevertheless, each man knew the other, even in that inky outline, for they were both men of striking appearance, and they hated each other.

The covered passage opened at one end on one of the steep streets of the Adelphi, and at the other on a terrace overlooking the sunset-colored river. One side of the passage was a blank wall, for the building it supported was an old unsuccessful theater restaurant, now shut up. The other side of the passage contained two doors, one at each end. Neither was what was commonly called the stage door; they were a sort of special and private stage doors, used by very special performers, and in this case by the star actor and actress in the Shakespearean performance of the day. Persons of that eminence often like to have such private exits and entrances, for meeting friends or avoiding them.

The two men in question were certainly two such friends, men who evidently knew the doors and counted on their opening, for each approached the door at the upper end with equal coolness and confidence. Not, however, with equal speed; but the man who walked fast was the man from the other end of the tunnel, so they both arrived before the secret stage door almost at the same instant. They saluted each other with civility, and waited a moment before one of them, the sharper walker, who seemed to have the shorter patience, knocked at the door.

In this and everything else each man was opposite and neither could be called inferior. As private persons, both were handsome, capable, and popular. As public persons, both were in the first public rank. But everything about them, from their glory to their good looks, was of a diverse and incomparable kind. Sir Wilson Seymour was the kind of man whose importance is known to everybody who knows. The more you mixed with the innermost ring in every polity or profession, the more often you met Sir Wilson Seymour. He was the one intelligent man on twenty unintelligent committees—on every sort of subject, from the reform of the Royal Academy to the project of bimetallism for Greater Britain. In the arts especially he was omnipotent. He was so unique that nobody could quite decide whether he was a great aristocrat who had taken up art, or a great artist whom the aristocrats had taken up. But you could not meet him for five minutes without realizing that you had really been ruled by him all your life.

His appearance was "distinguished" in exactly the same sense; it was at once conventional and unique. Fashion could have found no fault with his high silk hat; yet it was unlike anyone else's hat—a little higher, perhaps, and adding something to his natural height. His tall, slender figure had a slight stoop, yet it looked the reverse of feeble. His hair was silver-gray, but he did not look old; it was worn longer than the common, yet he did not look effeminate; it was curly, but it did not look curled. His carefully pointed beard made him look more manly and militant rather than otherwise, as it does in those old admirals of Velasquez with whose dark portraits his house was hung. His gray gloves were a shade bluer, his silver-knobbed cane a shade longer than scores of such gloves and canes flapped and flourished about the theaters and the restaurants.

The other man was not so tall, yet would have struck nobody as short, but merely as strong and handsome. His hair also was curly, but fair and cropped close to a strong, massive head—the sort of head you break a door with, as Chaucer said of the Miller's. His military mustache and the carriage of his shoulders showed him a soldier, but he had a pair of those peculiar, frank, and piercing blue eyes which are more common in sailors. His face was somewhat square, his jaw was square; his shoulders were square, even his jacket was square. Indeed, in the wild school of caricature then current, Mr. Max Beerbohm had represented him as a proposition in the fourth book of Euclid.

For he also was a public man, though with quite another sort of success. You did not have to be in the best society to have heard of Captain Cutler, of the siege of Hong-Kong and the great march across China. You could not get away from hearing of him wherever you were; his portrait was on every other post card; his maps and battles in every other illustrated paper; songs in his honor in every other music-hall turn or on every other barrel organ. His fame, though probably more temporary, was ten times more wide, popular, and spontaneous than the other man's. In thousands of English homes he appeared enormous above England, like Nelson. Yet he had infinitely less power in England than Sir Wilson Seymour.

The door was opened to them by an aged servant or "dresser," whose broken-down face and figure and black, shabby coat and trousers contrasted queerly with the glittering interior of the great actress's dressing room. It was fitted and filled with looking glasses at every angle of refraction, so that they looked like the hundred facets of one huge diamond—if one could get inside a diamond. The other features of luxury—a few flowers, a few colored cushions, a few scraps of stage costume—were multiplied by all the mirrors into the madness of the Arabian Nights, and danced and changed places perpetually as the shuffling attendant shifted a mirror outwards or shot one back against the wall.

They both spoke to the dingy dresser by name, calling him Parkinson, and asking for the lady as Miss Aurora Rome. Parkinson said she was in the other room, but he would go and tell her. A shade crossed the brow of both visitors; for the other room was the private room of the great actor with whom Miss Aurora was performing, and she was of the kind that does not inflame admiration without inflaming jealousy. In about half a minute, however, the inner door opened, and she entered as she always did, even in private life, so that the very silence seemed to be a roar of applause, and one well deserved. She was clad in a somewhat strange garb of peacock green and peacock blue satins, that gleamed like blue and green metals, such as delight children and esthetes, and her heavy, hot brown hair framed one of those magic faces which are dangerous to all men, but especially to boys and to men growing gray. In company with her male colleague, the great American actor, Isidore Bruno, she was producing a particularly poetical and fantastic interpretation of *Midsummer Night's Dream*, in which the artistic prominence was given to Oberon and Titania, or in other words to Bruno and herself.

Set in dreamy and exquisite scenery, moving in mystical dances, the green costume, like burnished beetle wings, expressed all the elusive individuality of an elfin queen. But when personally confronted in what was still broad daylight, a man looked only at her face.

She greeted both men with the beaming and baffling smile which kept so many males at the same just dangerous distance from her. She accepted some flowers from Cutler, which were as tropical and expensive as his victories; and another sort of present from Sir Wilson Seymour, offered later on and more non-chalantly by that gentleman. For it was against his breeding to show eagerness, and against his conventional unconventionality to give anything so obvious as flowers. He had picked up a trifle, he said, which was rather a curiosity; it was an ancient Greek dagger of the Mycenean Epoch, and might have been well worn in the time of Theseus and Hippolyta. It was made of brass like all the Heroic weapons, but, oddly enough, sharp enough to prick anyone still. He had really been attracted to it by the leaflike shape; it was as perfect as a Greek vase. If it was of any interest to Miss Rome or could come in anywhere in the play, he hoped she would—

The inner door burst open and a big figure appeared, who was more of a contrast to the explanatory Seymour than even Captain Cutler. Nearly six-foot-six, and of more than theatrical thews and muscles, Isidore Bruno, in the gorgeous leopard skin and golden-brown garments of Oberon, looked like a barbaric god. He leaned on a sort of hunting spear, which across a theater looked a slight, silvery wand, but which in the small and comparatively crowded room looked as plain as a pikestaff—and as menacing. His vivid, black eyes rolled volcanically, his bronze face, handsome as it was, showed at that moment a combination of high cheekbones with set white teeth, which recalled certain American conjectures about his origin in the Southern plantations.

"Aurora," he began, in that deep voice like a drum of passion that had moved so many audiences, "will you—"

He stopped indecisively because a sixth figure had suddenly presented itself just inside the doorway—a figure so incongruous in the scene as to be almost comic. It was a very short man in the black uniform of the Roman secular clergy, and looking (especially in such a presence as Bruno's and Aurora's) rather like the wooden Noah out of an ark. He did not, however, seem conscious of any contrast, but said with dull civility, "I believe Miss Rome sent for me."

A shrewd observer might have remarked that the emotional temperature rather rose at so unemotional an interruption. The detachment of a professional celebate seemed to reveal to the others that they stood round the woman as a ring of amorous rivals; just as a stranger coming in with frost on his coat will reveal that a room is like a furnace. The presence of the one man who did not care about her increased Miss Rome's sense that everybody else was in love with her, and each in a somewhat

233

dangerous way: the actor with all the appetite of a savage and a spoiled child; the soldier with all the simple selfishness of a man of will rather than mind; Sir Wilson with that daily hardening concentration with which old Hedonists take to a hobby; nay, even the abject Parkinson, who had known her before her triumphs, and who followed her about the room with eyes or feet, with the dumb fascination of a dog.

A shrewd person might also have noted a yet odder thing. The man like a black wooden Noah (who was not wholly without shrewdness) noted it with a considerable but contained amusement. It was evident that the great Aurora, though by no means indifferent to the admiration of the other sex, wanted at this moment to get rid of all the men who admired her and be left alone with the man who did not—did not admire her in that sense, at least; for the little priest did admire and even enjoy the firm feminine diplomacy with which she went about her task. There was, perhaps, only one thing that Aurora Rome was clever about, and that was one half of humanity—the other half. The little priest watched, like a Napoleonic campaign, the swift precision of her policy for expelling all while banishing none. Bruno, the big actor, was so babyish that it was easy to send him off in brute sulks, banging the door. Cutler, the British officer, was pachydermatous to ideas, but punctilious about behavior. He would ignore all hints, but he would die rather than ignore a definite commission from a lady. As to old Seymour he had to be treated differently; he had to be left to the last. The only way to move him was to appeal to him in confidence as an old friend, to let him into the secret of the clearance. The priest did really admire Miss Rome as she achieved all these three objects in one selected action.

She went across to Captain Cutler and said in her sweetest manner, "I shall value all these flowers because they must be your favorite flowers. But they won't be complete, you know, without *my* favorite flower. *Do* go over to that shop around the corner and get me some lilies-of-the-valley and then it will be *quite lovely*."

The first object of her diplomacy, the exit of the enraged Bruno, was at once achieved. He had already handed his spear in a lordly style like a scepter to the piteous Parkinson, and was about to assume one of the cushioned seats like a throne. But at this open appeal to his rival there glowed in his opal eyeballs all the sensitive insolence of the slave; he knotted his enormous brown fists for an instant, and then, dashing open the door, disappeared into his own apartments beyond. But meanwhile Miss Rome's experiment in mobilizing the British Army had not succeeded so simply as seemed probable. Cutler had indeed risen stiffly and suddenly, and walked towards the door, hatless, as if at a word of command. But perhaps there was something ostentatiously elegant about the languid figure of Seymour leaning against one of the looking glasses, that brought him up short at the entrance, turning his head this way and that like a bewildered bulldog.

"I must show this stupid man where to go," said Aurora in a whisper to Seymour, and ran out to the threshold to speed the parting guest.

Seymour seemed to be listening, elegant and unconscious as was his posture, and he seemed relieved when he heard the lady call out some last instructions to the Captain, and then turn sharply and run laughing down the passage towards the other end, the end on the terrace above the Thames. Yet a second or two after, Seymour's brow darkened again. A man in his position has so many rivals, and he remembered that at the other end of the passage was the corresponding entrance to Bruno's private room. He did not lose his dignity; he said some civil words to Father Brown about the revival of Byzantine architecture in the Westminster Cathedral, and then, quite naturally, strolled out himself into the upper end of the passage. Father Brown and Parkinson were left alone, and they were neither of them men with a taste for superfluous conversation. The dresser went round the room, pulling out looking glasses and pushing them in again, his dingy dark coat and trousers looking all the more dismal since he was still holding the festive fairy spear of King Oberon. Every time he pulled out the frame of a new glass, a new black figure of Father Brown appeared; the absurd glass chamber was full of Father Browns, upside down in the air like angels, turning somersaults like acrobats, turning their backs to everybody like very rude persons.

Father Brown seemed quite unconscious of this cloud of witnesses, but followed Parkinson with an idly attentive eye till he took himself and his absurd spear into the farther room of Bruno. Then he abandoned himself to such abstract meditations as always amused him—calculating the angles of the mirrors, the angles of each refraction, the angle at which each must fit into the wall . . . when he heard a strong but strangled cry.

He sprang to his feet and stood rigidly listening. After the same instant Sir Wilson Seymour burst back into the room, white

235

as ivory. "Who's that man in the passage?" he cried. "Where's that dagger of mine?"

Before Father Brown could turn in his heavy boots, Seymour was plunging about the room looking for the weapon. And before he could possibly find that weapon or any other, a brisk running of feet broke upon the pavement outside, and the square face of Cutler was thrust into the same doorway. He was still grotesquely grasping a bunch of lilies-of-the-valley. "What's this?" he cried. "What's that creature down the passage? Is this some of your tricks?"

"My tricks!" exclaimed his pale rival, and made a stride towards him.

In the instant of time in which all this happened, Father Brown stepped out into the top of the passage, looked down it, and at once walked briskly towards what he saw.

At this the other two men dropped their quarrel and darted after him, Cutler calling out, "What are you doing? Who are you?"

"My name is Brown," said the priest sadly, as he bent over something and straightened himself again. "Miss Rome sent for me, and I came as quickly as I could. I have come too late."

The three men looked down, and in one of them at least the life died in that late light of afternoon. It ran along the passage like a path of gold, and in the midst of it Aurora Rome lay lustrous in her robes of green and gold, with her dead face turned upwards. Her dress was torn away as in a struggle, leaving the right shoulder bare, but the wound from which the blood was welling was on the other side. The brass dagger lay flat and gleaming a yard or so away.

There was a blank stillness for a measurable time; so that they could hear far off a flower girl's laugh outside Charing Cross, and someone whistling furiously for a taxicab in one of the streets off the Strand. Then the Captain, with a movement so sudden that it might have been passion or playacting, took Sir Wilson Seymour by the throat.

Seymour looked at him steadily without either fight or fear. "You need not kill me," he said, in a voice quite cold. "I shall do that on my own account."

The Captain's hand hesitated and dropped; and the other added with the same icy candor, "If I find I haven't the nerve to do it with that dagger, I can do it in a month with drink."

"Drink isn't good enough for me," replied Cutler, "but I'll

236

have blood for this before I die. Not yours—but I think I know whose."

And before the others could appreciate his intention he snatched up the dagger, sprang at the other door at the lower end of the passage, burst it open, bolt and all, confronted Bruno in his dressing room. As he did so, old Parkinson tottered in his wavering way out of the door and caught sight of the corpse lying in the passage. He moved shakily towards it; looked at it weakly with a working face; then moved shakily back into the dressing room again, and sat down suddenly on one of the richly cushioned chairs. Father Brown instantly ran across to him, taking no notice of Cutler and the colossal actor, though the room already rang with their blows and they began to struggle for the dagger. Seymour, who retained some practical sense, was whistling for the police at the end of the passage.

When the police arrived it was to tear the two men from an almost apelike grapple; and, after a few formal inquiries, to arrest Isidore Bruno upon a charge of murder, brought against him by his furious opponent. The idea that the great national hero of the hour had arrested a wrongdoer with his own hand doubtless had its weight with the police, who are not without elements of the journalist. They treated Cutler with a certain solemn attention, and pointed out that he had got a slight slash on the hand. Even as Cutler bore him back across tilted chair and table, Bruno had twisted the dagger out of his grasp and disabled him just below the wrist. The injury was really slight, but till he was removed from the room the half-savage prisoner stared at the running blood with a steady smile.

"Looks a cannibal sort of chap, don't he?" said the constable confidentially to Cutler.

Cutler made no answer, but said sharply a moment after, "We must attend to the . . . death . . ." and his voice escaped from articulation.

"The two deaths," came in the voice of the priest from the farther side of the room. "This poor fellow was gone when I got across to him." And he stood looking down at old Parkinson, who sat in a black huddle on the gorgeous chair. He also had paid his tribute, not without eloquence, to the woman who had died.

The silence was first broken by Cutler, who seemed not untouched by a rough tenderness. "I wish I was him," he said huskily. "I remember he used to watch her wherever she walked more than—anybody. She was his air, and he's dried up. He's just dead."

"We are all dead," said Seymour, in a strange voice, looking down the road.

They took leave of Father Brown at the corner of the road, with some random apologies for any rudeness they might have shown. Both their faces were tragic, but also cryptic.

The mind of the little priest was always a rabbit warren of wild thoughts that jumped too quickly for him to catch them. Like the white tail of a rabbit, he had the vanishing thought that he was certain of their grief, but not so certain of their innocence.

"We had better all be going," said Seymour heavily. "We have done all we can to help."

"Will you understand my motives," asked Father Brown quietly, "if I say you have done all you can to hurt?"

They both started as if guiltily, and Cutler said sharply, "To hurt?"

"To hurt yourselves," answered the priest. "I would not add to your troubles if it weren't common justice to warn you. You've done nearly everything you could do to hang yourselves, if this actor should be acquitted. They'll be sure to subpoena me; I shall be bound to say that after the cry was heard each of you rushed into the room in a wild state and began quarreling about a dagger. As far as my words on oath can go, either of you might have done it. You hurt yourselves with that; and then Captain Cutler must hurt himself with the dagger."

"Hurt myself!" exclaimed the Captain, with contempt. "A silly little scratch."

"Which drew blood,'" replied the priest, nodding. "We know there's blood on the brass now. And so we shall never know whether there was blood on it before."

There was a silence; and then Seymour said, with an emphasis quite alien to his daily accent, "But I saw a man in the passage."

"I know you did," answered the cleric Brown, with a face of wood; "so did Captain Cutler. That's what seems so improbable."

Before either could make sufficient sense of it even to answer, Father Brown had politely excused himself and gone stumping up the road with his stumpy old umbrella.

As modern newspapers are conducted, the most honest and most important news is the police news. If it be true that in the twentieth century more space was given to murder than to politics, it was for the excellent reason that murder is a more serious subject. But even this would hardly explain the enormous omnipresence and widely distributed detail of "The Bruno Case," or "The Passage Mystery," in the Press of London and the excitement that for some weeks the Press really told the truth; and the reports of examination and cross-examination, if interminable, even if intolerable, are at least reliable coincidence of persons. The victim was a popular actor; and the accused had been caught red-handed, as it were, by the most popular soldier of the patriotic season. In those extraordinary circumstances the Press was paralyzed into probity and accuracy; and the rest of this somewhat singular business can practically be recorded from the reports of Bruno's trial.

The trial was presided over by Mr. Justice Monkhouse, one of those who are jeered at as humorous judges, but who are generally much more serious than the serious judges, for their levity comes from a living impatience of professional solemnity; while the serious judge is really filled with frivolity, because he is filled with vanity. All the chief actors being of a worldly importance, the barristers were well balanced; the prosecutor for the Crown was Sir Walter Cowdray, a heavy but weighty advocate of the sort that knows how to seem English and trustworthy, and how to be rhetorical with reluctance. The prisoner was defended by Mr. Patrick Butler, K.C., who was mistaken for a mere *flâneur* by those who misunderstand the Irish character—and those who had not been examined by him. The medical evidence involved no contradictions, the doctor whom Seymour had summoned on the spot, agreeing with the eminent surgeon who had later examined the body. Aurora Rome had been stabbed with some sharp instrument such as a knife or dagger; some instrument, at least, of which the blade was short. The wound was just over the heart, and she had died instantly. When the first doctor saw her she could hardly have been dead for twenty minutes. Therefore, when Father Brown found her, she could hardly have been dead for three.

Some official detective evidence followed, chiefly concerned with the presence or absence of any proof of a struggle: the only suggestion of this was the tearing of the dress at the shoulder, and this did not seem to fit in particularly well with the direction and finality of the blow. When these details had been supplied, though not explained, the first of the important witnesses was called.

Sir Wilson Seymour gave evidence as he did everything else that he did at all—not only well, but perfectly. Though himself much more of a public man than the judge, he conveyed exactly the fine shade of self-effacement before the King's Justice; and though everyone looked at him as they would at the Prime Minister or the Archbishop of Canterbury, they could have said nothing of his part in it but that it was that of a private gentleman, with an accent on the noun. He was also refreshingly lucid, as he was on the committees. He had been calling on Miss Rome at the theater; he had met Captain Cutler there; they had been joined for a short time by the accused, who had then returned to his own dressing room; they had then been joined by a Roman Catholic priest, who asked for the deceased lady and said his name was Brown. Miss Rome had then gone just outside the theater to the entrance of the passage, in order to point out to Captain Cutler a flower shop at which he was to buy her some more flowers; and the witness had remained in the room, exchanging a few words with the priest. He had then distinctly heard the deceased, having sent the Captain on his errand, turn round laughing and run down the passage towards its other end, where was the prisoner's dressing room. In idle curiosity as to the rapid movements of his friends, he had strolled out to the head of the passage himself and looked down it towards the prisoner's door. Did he see anything in the passage? Yes, he saw something in the passage.

Sir Walter Cowdray allowed an impressive interval, during which the witness looked down, and for all his usual composure seemed to have more than his usual pallor. Then the barrister said in a lower voice, which seemed at once sympathetic and creepy, "Did you see it distinctly?"

Sir Wilson Seymour, however moved, had his excellent brains in full working order. "Very distinctly as regards its outline, but quite indistinctly—indeed not at all—as regards the details inside the outline. The passage is of such length that anyone in the middle of it appears quite black against the light at the other end." The witness lowered his steady eyes once more and added, "I had noticed the fact before, when Captain Cutler first entered it." There was another silence, and the judge leaned forward and made a note.

"Well," said Sir Walter patiently, "what was the outline like? Was it, for instance, like the figure of the murdered woman?"

"Not in the least," answered Seymour quietly.

"What did it look to you like?"

"It looked to me," replied the witness, "like a tall man."

Everyone in court kept his eyes riveted on his pen or his umbrella handle or his book or his boots or whatever he happened to be looking at. They seemed to be holding their eyes away from the prisoner by main force; but they felt his figure in the dock, and they felt it as gigantic. Tall as Bruno was to the eye, he seemed to swell taller and taller when all eyes had been torn away from him.

Cowdray was resuming his seat with his solemn face, smoothing his black silk robes and white silk whiskers. Sir Wilson was leaving the witness box, after a few final particulars to witnesses, when the counsel for the defense sprang up and stopped him.

"I shall only detain you a moment," said Mr. Butler, who was a rustic-looking person with red eyebrows and an expression of partial slumber. "Will you tell his lordship how you knew it was a man?"

A faint, refined smile seemed to pass over Seymour's features. "I'm afraid it is the vulgar test of trousers," he said. "When I saw daylight between the long legs I was sure it was a man, after all."

Butler's sleepy eyes opened as suddenly as some silent explosion. "After all!" he repeated slowly. "So you did think first it was a woman?" The red brows quivered.

Seymour looked troubled for the first time. "It is hardly a point of fact," he said, "but if his lordship would like me to answer for my impression, of course I shall do so. There was something about the thing that was not exactly a woman and yet was not quite a man; somehow the curves were different. And it had something that looked like long hair."

"Thank you," said Mr. Butler, K.C., and sat down suddenly, as if he had got what he wanted.

Captain Cutler was a far less plausible and composed witness than Sir Wilson, but his account of the opening incidents was solidly the same. He described the return of Bruno to his dressing room, the dispatching of himself to buy a bunch of lilies-of-the-valley, his return to the upper end of the passage, the thing he saw in the passage, his suspicion of Seymour, and his struggle with Bruno. But he could give little artistic assistance about the black figure that he and Seymour had seen. Asked about its outline, he said he was no art critic—with a somewhat too obvious sneer at Seymour. Asked if it was a man or a woman, he said it looked more like a beast—with a too obvious snarl at the prisoner. But the man was plainly shaken with sorrow and sincere anger, and Cowdray quickly excused him from confirming facts that were already fairly clear.

The defending counsel also was again brief in his cross-examination; although (as was his custom) even in being brief, he seemed to take a long time about it. "You used a rather remarkable expression," he said, looking at Cutler sleepily. "What do you mean by saying that it looked more like a beast than a man or a woman?"

Cutler seemed seriously agitated. "Perhaps I oughtn't to have said that," he said, "but when the brute has huge humped shoulders like a chimpanzee, and bristles sticking out of its head like a pig—"

Mr. Butler cut short his curious impatience in the middle. "Never mind whether its hair was like a pig's," he said. "Was it like a woman's?"

"A woman's!" cried the soldier. "Great Scott, no!"

"The last witness said it was," commented the counsel, with unscrupulous swiftness. "And did the figure have any of those serpentine and semi-feminine curves to which eloquent allusion has been made? No? No feminine curves? The figure, if I understand you, was rather heavy and square than otherwise?"

"He may have been bending forward," said Cutler, in a hoarse and rather faint voice.

"Or again, he may not," said Mr. Butler, and sat down suddenly for the second time.

The third witness called by Sir Walter Cowdray was the little Catholic clergyman, so little compared with the others, that his head seemed hardly to come above the box, so that it was like cross-examining a child. But unfortunately Sir Walter had somehow got it into his head (mostly by some ramifications of his family's religion) that Father Brown was on the side of the prisoner, because the prisoner was wicked and foreign and even partly black. Therefore, he took Father Brown up sharply whenever that proud pontiff tried to explain anything; and told him to answer yes or no, and merely tell the plain facts. When Father Brown began, in his simplicity, to say who he thought the man in the passage was, the barrister told him that he did not want his theories.

"A black shape was seen in the passage. And you say you saw the black shape. Well, what shape was it?"

Father Brown blinked as under rebuke; but he had long known the literal nature of obedience. "The shape," he said, "was short and thick, but had two sharp, black projections curved upwards on each side of the head or top, rather like horns, and—"

"Oh, the devil with horns, no doubt," ejaculated Cowdray, sitting down in triumphant jocularity.

"No," said the priest dispassionately. "I know who it was."

Those in court had been wrought up to an irrational but real sense of some monstrosity. They had forgotten the figure in the dock and thought only of the figure in the passage. And the figure in the passage, described by three capable and respectable men who had all seen it, was a shifting nightmare: one called it a woman, and the other a beast, and the other a devil . . .

The judge was looking at Father Brown with level and piercing eyes. "You are a most extraordinary witness," he said, "but there is something about you that makes me think you are trying to tell the truth. Well, who was the man you saw in the passage?"

"He was myself," said Father Brown.

Butler, K.C., sprang to his feet in an extraordinary stillness, and said quite calmly, "Your lordship will allow me to cross-examine?" And then, without stopping, he shot at Brown the apparently disconnected question, "You have heard about this dagger; you know the experts say the crime was committed with a short blade?"

"A short blade," assented Brown, nodding solemnly like an owl, "but a very long hilt."

Before the audience could quite dismiss the idea that the priest had really seen himself doing murder with a short dagger with a long hilt (which seemed somehow to make it more horrible), he had himself hurried on to explain.

"I mean daggers aren't the only thing with short blades. Spears have short blades. And spears catch at the end of the steel just like daggers, if they're that sort of fancy spear they have in theaters; like the spear poor old Parkinson killed his wife with, just when she'd sent for me to settle their family troubles—and I came just too late, God forgive me! But he died penitent—he just died of being penitent. He couldn't bear what he'd done."

The general impression in court was that the little priest, who was gabbling away, had literally gone mad in the box. But the judge still looked at him with bright and steady eyes of interest; and the counsel for the defense went on with his questions, unperturbed.

"If Parkinson did it with that pantomine spear," asked Butler, "he must have thrust from four yards away. How do you account for signs of struggle, like the dress dragged off the shoulder?" He had slipped into treating this mere witness as an expert; but no one noticed it now.

"The poor lady's dress was torn," said the witness, "because it was caught in a panel that slid to just behind her. She struggled to free herself, and as she did so Parkinson came out of the prisoner's room and lunged with the spear."

"A panel?" repeated the barrister in a curious voice.

"It was a looking glass on the other side," explained Father Brown. "When I was in the dressing room I noticed that some of them could probably be slid out into the passage."

There was another vast and unnatural silence, and this time it was the judge who spoke. "So you really mean that, when you looked down that passage, the man you saw was yourself—in a mirror?"

"Yes, my lord; that was what I was trying to say," said Brown, "but they asked me for the shape; and our hats have corners just like horns, and so I—"

The judge leaned forward, his old eyes yet more brilliant, and said in specially distinct tones, "Do you really mean to say that when Sir Wilson Seymour saw that wild what-you-call-him with curves and a woman's hair and a man's trousers, what he saw was Sir Wilson Seymour?"

"Yes, my lord," said Father Brown.

"And you mean to say that when Captain Cutler saw that chimpanzee with humped shoulders and hog's bristles, he simply saw himself?"

"Yes, my lord."

The judge leaned back in his chair with a luxuriance in which it was hard to separate the cynicism and the admiration. "And can you tell us why," he asked, "you should know your own figure in a looking glass, when two such distinguished men don't?"

Father Brown blinked even more painfully than before; then he stammered, "Really, my lord, I don't know . . . unless it's because I don't look at it so often."

244

THE FOOTSTEPS THAT RAN

BY DOROTHY L. SAYERS

Dorothy Leigh Sayers was the daugher of the Reverend H. Sayers, headmaster of the Cathedral Choir School, Oxford, and grand-niece of Percival Leigh, "the Professor" of *Punch*. She was one of the first women to obtain a degree from Oxford. The East-Anglian fen country where she was raised is the setting for *The Nine Tailors*, regarded by many as her best book. Her nobleman-detective Lord Peter Wimsey is one of detective fiction's finest. Miss Sayers is also highly regarded as an anthologist. She died on December 17, 1957.

MR. BUNTER withdrew his head from beneath the focusing cloth.

"I fancy that will be quite adequate, sir," he said deferentially, "unless there are any further patients, if I may call them so, which you would wish put on record."

"Not today," replied the doctor. He took the last stricken rat gently from the table, and replaced it in its cage with an air of satisfaction. "Perhaps on Wednesday, if Lord Peter can kindly spare your services once again——"

"What's that?" murmured his lordship, withdrawing his long nose from the investigation of a number of unattractive-looking glass jars. "Nice old dog," he added vaguely. "Wags his tail when you mention his name, what? Are these monkey-glands, Hartman, or a southwest elevation of Cleopatra's duodenum?"

"You don't know anything, do you?" said the young physician, laughing. "No use playing your bally-fool-with-an-eyeglass tricks on me, Wimsey. I'm up to them. I was saying to Bunter that I'd be no end grateful if you'd let him turn up again three days hence to register the progress of the specimens—always supposing they do progress, that is."

"Why ask, dear old thing?" said his lordship. "Always a pleasure to assist a fellow-sleuth, don't you know. Trackin' down murderers—all in the same way of business and all that. All finished? Good egg! By the way, if you don't have that cage mended you'll lose one of your patients—Number 5. The last wire but one is workin' loose—assisted by the intelligent occupant. Jolly little beasts, ain't they? No need of dentists—wish I was a rat—wire much better for the nerves than that fizzlin' drill."

Dr. Hartman uttered a little exclamation.

"How in the world did you notice that, Wimsey? I didn't think you'd even looked at the cage."

"Built noticin'—improved by practice," said Lord Peter quietly. "Anythin' wrong leaves a kind of impression on the eye; brain trots along afterwards with the warnin'. I saw that when we came in. Only just grasped it. Can't say my mind was glued on the matter. Shows the victim's improvin', anyhow. All serene, Bunter?"

"Everything perfectly satisfactory, I trust, my lord," replied the manservant. He had packed up his camera and plates, and was quietly restoring order in the little laboratory, whose fittings—compact as those of an ocean liner—had been disarranged for the experiment.

"Well," said the doctor, "I am enormously obliged to you, Lord Peter, and to Bunter too. I am hoping for a great result from these experiments, and you cannot imagine how valuable an assistance it will be to me to have a really good series of photographs. I can't afford this sort of thing—yet," he added, his rather haggard young face wistful as he looked at the great camera, "and I can't do the work at the hospital. There's no time; I've got to be here. A struggling G.P. can't afford to let his practice go, even in Bloomsbury. There are times when even a half-crown visit makes all the difference between making both ends meet and having an ugly hiatus."

"As Mr. Micawber said," replied Wimsey, "'Income twenty pounds, expenditure nineteen, nineteen, six—result: happiness; expenditure twenty pounds, ought, six—result: misery.' Don't prostrate yourself in gratitude, old bean; nothin' Bunter loves like messin' round with pyro and hyposulphite. Keeps his hand in. All kinds of practice welcome. Fingerprints and process plates spell seventh what-you-may-call-it of bliss, but focal-plane work on scurvy-ridden rodents (good phrase!) acceptable if no crime forthcoming. Crimes have been rather short lately. Been eatin' our heads off, haven't we, Bunter? Don't know what's come over London. I've taken to prying into my neighbor's affairs to keep from goin' stale. Frightened the postman into a fit the other day by askin' him how his young lady at Croydon was. He's a married man, livin' in Great Ormond Street."

"How did you know?"

"Well, I didn't really. But he lives just opposite to a friend of mine—Inspector Parker; and his wife—not Parker's; he's unmarried; the postman's, I mean—asked Parker the other day whether the flyin' shows at Croydon went on all night. Parker, bein' flummoxed, said 'No,' without thinkin'. Bit of a give-away, what? Thought I'd give the poor devil a word in season, don't you know. Uncommonly thoughtless of Parker."

The doctor laughed. "You'll stay to lunch, won't you?" he said. "Only cold meat and salad, I'm afraid. My woman won't come Sundays. Have to answer my own door. Deuced unprofessional, I'm afraid, but it can't be helped."

"Pleasure," said Wimsey, as they emerged from the laboratory and entered the dark little flat by the back door. "Did you build this place on?"

"No," said Hartman; "the last tenant did that. He was an artist. That's why I took the place. It comes in very useful, ramshackle as it is, though this glass roof is a bit sweltering on a hot day like this. Still, I had to have something on the ground floor, cheap, and it'll do till times get better."

"Till your vitamin experiments make you famous, eh?" said Peter cheerfully. "You're goin' to be the comin' man, you know. Feel it in my bones. Uncommonly neat little kitchen you've got, anyhow."

"It does," said the doctor. "The lab makes it a bit gloomy, but the woman's only here in the daytime."

He led the way into a narrow little dining-room, where the table was laid for a cold lunch. The one window at the end farthest from the kitchen looked out into Great James Street. The room was little more than a passage, and full of doors—the kitchen door, a door in the adjacent wall leading into the entrance-hall, and a third on the opposite side, through which his visitor caught a glimpse of a moderate-sized consulting-room.

Lord Peter Wimsey and his host sat down to table, and the doctor expressed a hope that Mr. Bunter would sit down with them. That correct person, however, deprecated any such suggestion.

"If I might venture to indicate my own preference, Sir," he said, "it would be to wait upon you and his lordship in the usual manner."

"It's no use," said Wimsey. "Bunter likes me to know my place. Terrorizin' sort of man, Bunter. Can't call my soul my own. Carry on, Bunter; we wouldn't presume for the world."

Mr. Bunter handed the salad, and poured out the water with a grave decency appropriate to a crusted old tawny port.

It was a Sunday afternoon in that halcyon summer of 1921. The sordid little street was almost empty. The ice-cream man alone seemed thriving and active. He leaned luxuriously on the green post at the corner, in the intervals of driving a busy trade. Bloomsbury's swarm of able-bodied and able-voiced infants were still; presumably within-doors, eating steamy Sunday din- ners inappropriate to the tropical weather. The only disturbing sounds came from the flat above, where heavy footsteps passed rapidly to and fro.

"Who's the merry-and-bright bloke above?" enquired Lord Peter presently. "Not an early riser, I take it. Not that anybody is on a Sunday mornin'. Why an inscrutable Providence ever inflicted such a ghastly day on people livin' in town I can't

248

imagine. I ought to be in the country, but I've got to meet a friend at Victoria this afternoon. Such a day to choose. . . . Who's the lady? Wife or accomplished friend? Gather she takes a properly submissive view of woman's duties in the home, either way. That's the bedroom overhead, I take it."

Hartman looked at Lord Peter in some surprise.

"'Scuse my beastly inquisitiveness, old thing," said Wimsey. "Bad habit. Not my business."

"How did you ——?"

"Guesswork," said Lord Peter, with disarming frankness. "I heard the squawk of an iron bedstead on the ceiling and a heavy fellow get out with a bump, but it may quite well be a couch or something. Anyway, he's been potterin' about in his stocking feet over these few feet of floor for the last half-hour, while the woman has been clatterin' to and fro, in and out of the kitchen and away into the sittin'-room, with her high heels on, ever since we've been here. Hence deduction as to domestic habits of the first-floor tenants."

"I thought," said the doctor, with an aggrieved expression, "you'd been listening to my valuable exposition of the beneficial effects of Vitamin B, and Lind's treatment of scurvy with lemons in 1755."

"I was listenin'," agreed Lord Peter hastily, "but I heard the footsteps as well. Fellow's toddled into the kitchen—only wanted the matches, though; he's gone off into the sittin'-room and left her to carry on the good work. What was I sayin'? Oh, yes! You see, as I was sayin' before, one hears a thing or sees it without knowin' or thinkin' about it. Then afterwards one starts meditatin', and it all comes back, and one sorts out one's impressions. Like those plates of Bunter's. Picture's all there, l—la—what's the word I want, Bunter?"

"Latent, my lord."

"That's it. My right-hand man, Bunter; couldn't do a thing without him. The picture's latent till you put the developer on. Same with the brain. No mystery. Little grey matter's all you want to remember things with. As a matter of curiosity, was I right about those people above?"

"Perfectly. The man's a gas-company's inspector. A bit surly, but devoted (after his own fashion) to his wife. I mean, he doesn't mind hulking in bed on a Sunday morning and letting her do the chores, but he spends all the money he can spare on giving her pretty hats and fur coats and what not. They've only been married about six months. I was called in to her when she had a touch of 'flu in the spring, and he was almost off his head with anxiety. She's a lovely little woman, I must say—Italian. He picked her up in some eating-place in Soho, I believe. Glorious dark hair and eyes: Venus sort of figure; proper contours in all the right places; good skin—all that sort of thing. She was a bit of a draw to that restaurant while she was there, I fancy. Lively. She had an old admirer round here one day—awkward little Italian fellow with a knife—active as a monkey. Might have been unpleasant, but I happened to be on the spot, and her husband came along. People are always laying one another out in these streets. Good for business, of course, but one gets tired of tying up broken heads and slits in the jugular. Still, I suppose the girl can't help being attractive, though I don't say she's what you might call stand-offish in her manner. She's sincerely fond of Brotherton, I think, though—that's his name."

Wimsey nodded inattentively. "I suppose life is a bit monotonous here," he said.

"Professionally, yes. Births and drunks and wife-beatings are pretty common. And all the usual ailments, of course. God!" cried the doctor explosively, "if only I could get away, and do my experiments!"

"Ah!" said Peter, "where's that eccentric old millionaire with a mysterious disease, who always figures in the novels? A lightning diagnosis—a miraculous cure—'God bless you, doctor; here are five thousand pounds'—Harley Street——"

"That sort doesn't live in Bloomsbury," said the doctor.

"It must be fascinatin', diagnosin' things," said Peter thoughtfully. "How d'you do it? I mean, is there a regular set of symptoms for each disease, like callin' a club to show you want your partner to go no trumps? You don't just say: 'This fellow's got a pimple on his nose, therefore he has fatty degeneration of the heart——'"

"I hope not," said the doctor drily.

"Or is it more like gettin' a clue to a crime?" went on Peter. "You see somethin'—a room, or a body, say, all knocked about anyhow, and there's a damn sight of symptoms of somethin' wrong, and you've got just to pick out the ones which tell the story?"

"That's more like it," said Dr. Hartman. "Some symptoms are significant in themselves—like the condition of the gums in scurvy, let us say—others in conjunction with——"

He broke off, and both sprang to their feet as a shrill scream sounded suddenly from the flat above, followed by a heavy thud.

250

A man's voice cried out lamentably; feet ran violently to and fro; then, as the doctor and his guests stood frozen in consternation, came the man himself—falling down the stairs in his haste, hammering at Hartman's door.

"Help! Help! Let me in! My wife! He's murdered her!"

They ran hastily to the door and let him in. He was a big, fair man, in his shirt-sleeves and stockings. His hair stood up, and his face was set in bewildered misery.

"She is dead—dead. He was her lover," he groaned. "Doctor! I have lost my wife! My Maddalena——" He paused, looked wildly for a moment, and then said hoarsely, "someone's been in—somehow—stabbed her—murdered her. I'll have the law on him, doctor. Come quickly—she was cooking the chicken for my dinner—Ah-h-h!"

He gave a long, hysterical shriek, which ended in a hiccupping laugh. The doctor took him roughly by the arm and shook him. "Pull yourself together, Mr. Brotherton," he said sharply. "Perhaps she is only hurt. Stand out of the way!"

"Only hurt?" said the man, sitting heavily down on the nearest chair. "No—no—she is dead—little Maddalena—Oh, my God!"

Dr. Hartman had snatched a roll of bandages and a few surgical appliances from the consulting-room, and he ran upstairs, followed closely by Lord Peter. Bunter remained for a few moments to combat hysterics with cold water. Then he stepped across to the dining-room window and shouted.

"Well, wot is it?" cried a voice from the street.

"Would you be so kind as to step in here a minute, officer?" said Mr. Bunter. "There's been murder done."

When Brotherton and Bunter arrived upstairs with the constable, they found Dr. Hartman and Lord Peter in the little kitchen. The doctor was kneeling beside the woman's body. At their entrance he looked up, and shook his head.

"Death instantaneous," he said. "Clean through the heart. Poor child. She cannot have suffered at all. Oh, constable, it is very fortunate you are here. Murder appears to have been done—though I'm afraid the man has escaped. Probably Mr. Brotherton can give us some help. He was in the flat at the time."

The man had sunk down on a chair, and was gazing at the body with a face from which all meaning seemed to have been struck out. The policeman produced a notebook.

"Now, sir," he said, "don't let's waste any time. Sooner we can

251

get to work the more likely we are to catch our man. Now, you was 'ere at the time, was you?"

Brotherton stared a moment, then, making a violent effort, he answered steadily:

"I was in the sitting-room, smoking and reading the paper. My—*she*—was getting the dinner ready in here. I heard her give a scream, and I rushed in and found her lying on the floor. She didn't have time to say anything. When I found she was dead, I rushed to the window, and saw the fellow scrambling away over the glass roof there. I yelled at him, but he disappeared. Then I ran down——"

"'Arf a mo'," said the policeman. "Now, see 'ere, sir, didn't you think to go after 'im at once?"

"My first thought was for her," said the man. "I thought maybe she wasn't dead. I tried to bring her round——" His speech ended in a groan.

"You say he came in through the window," said the policeman.

"I beg your pardon, officer, interrupted Lord Peter, who had been apparently making a mental inventory of the contents of the kitchen. "Mr. Brotherton suggested that the man went *out* through the window. It's better to be accurate."

"It's the same thing," said the doctor. "It's the only way he could have come in. These flats are all alike. The staircase door leads into the sitting-room, and Mr. Brotherton was there, so the man couldn't have come that way."

"And," said Peter, "he didn't get in through the bedroom window, or we should have seen him. We were in the room below. Unless, indeed, he let himself down from the roof. Was the door between the bedroom and the sitting-room open?" he asked suddenly, turning to Brotherton.

The man hesitated a moment. "Yes," he said finally. "Yes, I'm sure it was."

"Could you have seen the man if he had come through the bedroom window?"

"I couldn't have helped seeing him."

"Come, come, sir," said the policeman, with some irritation, "better let *me* ask the questions. Stands to reason the fellow wouldn't get in through the bedroom window in full view of the street."

"How clever of you to think of that," said Wimsey. "Of course not. Never occurred to me. Then it must have been this window, as you say."

"And, what's more, here's his marks on the window-sill," said the constable triumphantly, pointing to some blurred traces among the London soot. "That's right. Down he goes by that drain-pipe, over the glass roof down there—what's that the roof of?"

"My laboratory," said the doctor. "Heavens! to think that while we were at dinner this murdering villain——"

"Quite so, sir," agreed the constable. "Well, he'd get away over the wall into the court be'ind. 'E'll 'ave been seen there, no fear; you needn't anticipate much trouble in layin' 'ands on 'im, sir. I'll go round there in 'arf a tick. Now then, sir"—turning to Brotherton—"'ave you any idea wot this party might have looked like?"

Brotherton lifted a wild face, and the doctor interposed.

"I think you ought to know, constable," he said, "that there was—well, not a murderous attack, but what might have been one, made on this woman before—about eight weeks ago—by a man named Marinetti—an Italian waiter—with a knife."

"Ah!" The policeman licked his pencil eagerly. "Do you know this party as 'as been mentioned?" he enquired of Brotherton.

"That's the man," said Brotherton, with concentrated fury. "Coming here after my wife—God curse him! I wish to God I had him dead here beside her!"

"Quite so," said the policeman. "Now, sir"—to the doctor—"'ave you got the weapon wot the crime was committed with?"

"No," said Hartman, "there was no weapon in the body when I arrived."

"Did *you* take it out?" pursued the constable, to Brotherton.

"No," said Brotherton, "he took it with him."

"Took it with 'im," the constable entered the fact in his notes. "Phew! Wonderful 'ot it is in 'ere, ain't it, sir?" he added, mopping his brow.

"It's the gas-oven, I think," said Peter mildly. "Uncommon hot thing, a gas-oven, in the middle of July. D'you mind if I turn it out? There's the chicken inside, but I don't suppose you want——"

Brotherton groaned, and the constable said: "Quite right, sir. A man wouldn't 'ardly fancy 'is dinner after a thing like this. Thank you, sir. Well now, doctor, wot kind of weapon do you take this to 'ave been?"

"It was a long, narrow weapon—something like an Italian stiletto, I imagine," said the doctor, "about six inches long. It was thrust in with great force under the fifth rib, and I should say it had pierced the heart centrally. As you see, there has been practically no bleeding. Such a wound would cause instant

253

death. Was she lying just as she is now when you first saw her, Mr. Brotherton?"

"On her back, just as she is," replied the husband.

"Well, that seems clear enough," said the policeman. "This 'ere Marinetti, or wotever 'is name is, 'as a grudge against the poor young lady——"

"I believe he was an admirer," put in the doctor.

"Quite so," agreed the constable. "Of course, these foreigners are like that—even the decentest of 'em. Stabbin' and such-like seems to come nateral to them, as you might say. Well, this 'ere Marinetti climbs in 'ere, sees the poor young lady standin' 'ere by the table all alone, gettin' the dinner ready; 'e comes in be'ind, catches 'er round the waist, stabs 'er—easy job, you see; no corsets nor nothink—she shrieks out, 'e pulls 'is stiletty out of 'er an' makes tracks. Well, now we've got to find 'im, and by your leave, sir, I'll be gettin' along. We'll 'ave 'im by the 'eels before long, sir, don't you worry. I'll 'ave to put a man in charge 'ere, sir, to keep folks out, but that needn't worry you. Good mornin', gentlemen."

"May we move the poor girl now?" asked the doctor.

"Certainly. Like me to 'elp you, sir?"

"No. Don't lose any time. We can manage." Dr. Hartman turned to Peter as the constable clattered downstairs. "Will you help me, Lord Peter?"

"Bunter's better at that sort of thing," said Wimsey, with a hard mouth.

The doctor looked at him in some surprise, but said nothing, and he and Bunter carried the still form away. Brotherton did not follow them. He sat in a grief-stricken heap, with his head buried in his hands. Lord Peter walked about the little kitchen, turning over the various knives and utensils, peering into the sink bucket, and apparently taking an inventory of the bread, butter, condiments, vegetables, and so forth which lay about in preparation for the Sunday meal. There were potatoes in the sink, half peeled, a pathetic witness to the quiet domestic life which had been so horribly interrupted. The colander was filled with green peas. Lord Peter turned these things over with an inquisitive finger, gazed into the smooth surface of a bowl of drippings as though it were a divining-crystal, ran his hands several times right through a bowl of flour—then drew his pipe from his pocket and filled it slowly.

The doctor returned, and put his hand on Brotherton's shoulder.

"Come," he said gently, "we have laid her in the other bed-room. She looks very peaceful. You must remember that, except for that moment of terror when she saw the knife, she suffered nothing. It is terrible for you, but you must try not to give way. The police——"

"The police can't bring her back to life," said the man savagely. "She's dead. Leave me alone, curse you! Leave me alone I say!"

He stood up, with a violent gesture.

"You must not sit here," said Hartman firmly. "I will give you something to take, and you must try to keep calm. Then we will leave you, but if you don't control yourself——"

After some further persuasion, Brotherton allowed himself to be led away.

"Bunter," said Lord Peter, as the kitchen door closed behind them, "do you know why I am doubtful about the success of those rat experiments?"

"Meaning Dr. Hartman's, my lord?"

"Yes. Dr. Hartman has a theory. In any investigation, my Bunter, it is most damnably dangerous to have a theory."

"I have heard you say so, my lord."

"Confound you—you know it as well as I do! What is wrong with the doctor's theories, Bunter?"

"You wish me to reply, my lord, that he only sees the facts which fit in with the theory."

"Thought-reader!" exclaimed Lord Peter bitterly.

"And that he supplies them to the police, my lord."

"Hush!" said Peter, as the doctor returned.

"I have got him to lie down," said Dr. Hartman, "and I think the best thing we can do is to leave him to himself."

"D'you know," said Wimsey, "I don't cotton to that idea, somehow."

"Why? Do you think he's likely to destroy himself?"

"That's as good a reason to give as any other, I suppose," said Wimsey, "when you haven't got any reason which can be put into words. But my advice is, don't leave him for a moment."

"But why? Frequently, with a deep grief like this, the presence of other people is merely an irritant. He begged me to leave him."

"Then for God's sake go back to him," said Peter.

"Really, Lord Peter," said the doctor, "I think I ought to know what is best for my patient."

"Doctor," said Wimsey, "this is not a question of your patient. A crime has been committed."

"But there is no mystery."

"There are twenty mysteries. For one thing, when was the window-cleaner here last?"

"The window-cleaner?"

"Who shall fathom the ebony-black enigma of the window-cleaner?" pursued Peter lightly, putting a match to his pipe. "You are quietly in your bath, in a state of more or less innocent nature, when an intrusive head appears at the window, like the ghost of Hamilton Tighe, and a gruff voice, suspended between earth and heaven, says, 'Good morning sir.' Where do window-cleaners go between visits? Do they hibernate, like busy bees? Do they——"

"Really, Lord Peter," said the doctor, "don't you think you're going a bit beyond the limit?"

"Sorry you feel like that," said Peter, "but I really want to know about the window-cleaner. Look how clear these panes are."

"He came yesterday, if you want to know," said Dr. Hartman, rather stiffly.

"You are sure?"

"He did mine at the same time."

"I thought as much," said Lord Peter. "In that case, it is absolutely imperative that Brotherton should not be left alone for a moment. Bunter! Confound it all, where's that fellow got to?"

The door into the bedroom opened.

"My lord?" Mr. Bunter unobtrusively appeared, as he had unobtrusively stolen out to keep an unobtrusive eye on the patient.

"Good," said Wimsey. "Stay where you are." His lackadaisical manner had gone, and he looked at the doctor as four years previously he might have looked at a refractory subaltern.

"Dr. Hartman," he said, "something is wrong. Cast your mind back. We were talking about symptoms. Then came the scream. Then came the sound of feet running. *Which direction did they run in?*"

"I'm sure I don't know."

"Don't you? Symptomatic though. doctor. They have been troubling me all the time, subconsc usly. Now I know why. They ran *from the kitchen*."

"Well?"

"Well! And now the window-cleaner——"

"What about him?"

"Could you swear that it wasn't the window-cleaner who made those marks on the sill?"

"And the man Brotherton saw——"

"Have we examined your laboratory for his footsteps?"

"But the weapon? Wimsey, this is madness! Someone took the weapon."

"I know. But did you think the edge of the wound was clean enough to have been made by a smooth stiletto? It looked ragged to me."

"Wimsey, what are you driving at?"

"There's a clue here in the flat—and I'm damned if I can remember it. I've seen it—I know I've seen it. It'll come to me presently. Meanwhile, don't let Brotherton——"

"What?"

"Do whatever it is he's going to do."

"But what is it?"

"If I could tell you that I could show you the clue. Why couldn't he make up his mind whether the bedroom door was open or shut? Very good story, but not quite thought out. Anyhow—I say, doctor, make some excuse, and strip him, and bring me his clothes. And send Bunter to me."

The doctor stared at him, puzzled. Then he made a gesture of acquiescence and passed into the bedroom. Lord Peter followed him, casting a ruminating glance at Brotherton as he went. Once in the sitting-room, Lord Peter sat down on a red velvet armchair, fixed his eyes on a gilt-framed oleograph, and became wrapped in contemplation.

Presently Bunter came in, with his arms full of clothing. Wimsey took it, and began to search it, methodically enough, but listlessly. Suddenly he dropped the garments, and turned to the manservant.

"No," he said, "this is a precaution, Bunter mine, but I'm on the wrong track. It wasn't here I saw—whatever I did see. It was in the kitchen. Now, what was it?"

"I could not say, my lord, but I entertain a conviction that I was also in a manner of speaking, conscious—not consciously conscious, my lord, if you understand me, but still conscious of an incongruity."

"Hurray!" said Wimsey suddenly. "Cheer-oh! for the subconscious what's-his-name! Now let's remember the kitchen. I cleared out of it because I was gettin' obfuscated. Now then. Begin at the door. Fryin'-pans and sauce-pans on the wall. Gas-stove—oven goin'—chicken inside. Rack of wooden spoons on the wall, gas-lighter, pan-lifter. Stop me when I'm gettin' hot. Mantelpiece. Spice-boxes and stuff. Anything wrong with them?

No. Dresser. Plates. Knives and forks—all clean; flour dredger—milk-jug—sieve on the wall—nutmeg-grater. Three-tier steamer. Looked inside—no grisly secrets in the steamer."

"Did you look in all the dresser drawers, my lord?"

"No. That could be done. But the point is, I *did* notice somethin'. What did I notice? That's the point. Never mind. On with the dance—let joy be unconfined! Knife-board. Knife-powder. Kitchen table. Did you speak?"

"No," said Bunter, who had moved from his attitude of wooden deference.

"Table stirs a chord. Very good. On table. Choppin'-board. Remains of ham and herb stuffin'. Packet of suet. Another sieve. Several plates. Butter in a glass dish. Bowl of drippin'—"

"Ah!"

"Drippin'——! Yes, there was——"

"Something unsatisfactory, my lord——"

"About the drippin'! Oh, my head! What's that they say in *Dear Brutus*, Bunter? 'Hold on to the workbox.' That's right. Hold on to the drippin'. Beastly slimy stuff to hold on to——Wait!"

There was a pause.

"When I was a kid," said Wimsey, "I used to love to go down into the kitchen and talk to old cookie. Good old soul she was, too. I can see her now, gettin' chicken ready, with me danglin' my legs on the table. *She* used to pluck an' draw 'em herself. I revelled in it. Little beasts boys are, ain't they, Bunter? Pluck it, draw it, wash it, stuff it, tuck its little tail through its little what-you-may-call-it, truss it, grease the dish——Bunter?"

"My lord!"

"Hold on to the dripping!"

"The bowl, my lord——"

"The bowl—visualize it—what was wrong?"

"It was full, my lord!"

"Got it—got it—*got* it! The bowl was full—smooth surface. Golly! I knew there was something queer about it. Now why shouldn't it be full? Hold on to the——"

"The bird was in the oven."

"Without dripping!"

"Very careless cookery, my lord."

"The bird—in the oven—no dripping. Bunter! Suppose it was never put in till after she was dead? Thrust in hurriedly by someone who had something to hide—horrible!"

"But with what object, my lord?"

"Yes, why? That's the point. One more mental association with the bird. It's just coming. Wait a moment. Pluck, draw, wash, stuff, tuck up, truss——By God!"

"My lord?"

"Come on, Bunter. Thank Heaven we turned off the gas!"

He dashed through the bedroom, disregarding the doctor and the patient, who sat up with a smothered shriek. He flung open the oven door and snatched out the baking-tin. The skin of the bird had just begun to discolour. With a little gasp of triumph, Wimsey caught the iron ring that protruded from the wing, and jerked out—*the six-inch spiral skewer*.

The doctor was struggling with the excited Brotherton in the doorway. Wimsey caught the man as he broke away, and shook him into the corner with a jiu-jitsu twist.

"Here is the weapon," he said.

"Prove it, blast you!" said Brotherton savagely.

"I will," said Wimsey. "Bunter, call in the policeman at the door. Doctor, we shall need your microscope."

In the laboratory the doctor bent over the microscope. A thin layer of blood from the skewer had been spread upon the slide.

"Well?" said Wimsey impatiently.

"It's all right," said Hartman. "The roasting didn't get anywhere near the middle. My God, Wimsey, yes, you're right—round corpuscles, diameter $1/3621$—mammalian blood—probably human——"

"Her blood," said Wimsey.

"It was very clever, Bunter," said Lord Peter, as the taxi trundled along on the way to his flat in Piccadilly. "If that fowl had gone on roasting a bit longer the blood-corpuscles might easily have been destroyed beyond all hope of recognition. It all goes to show that the unpremeditated crime is usually the safest."

"And what does your lordship take the man's motive to have been?"

"In my youth," said Wimsey meditatively, "they used to make me read the Bible. Trouble was, the only books I ever took to naturally were the ones they weren't over and above keen on. But I got to know the Song of Songs pretty well by heart. Look it up, Bunter; at your age it won't hurt you; it talks sense about jealousy."

"I have perused the work in question, your lordship," replied Mr. Bunter, with a sallow blush. "It says, if I remember rightly: *'Jealousy is cruel as the grave.'*"

THE PENCIL

BY RAYMOND CHANDLER

Raymond Chandler was educated abroad and first wrote verse, essays, book reviews and special articles for British newspapers. After World War I, in which he served in the Canadian and British forces, he returned to America and started writing for the pulps. It wasn't until 1939, when he was 51 years old, that Chandler published his first novel, *The Big Sleep*. Most of his fiction thereafter dealt with corrupt businessmen, policemen and politicians. He died on March 26, 1959, at the age of seventy.

HE WAS A SLIGHTLY FAT MAN with a dishonest smile that pulled the corners of his mouth out half an inch leaving the thick lips tight and his eyes bleak. For a fattish man he had a slow walk. Most fat men are brisk and light on their feet. He wore a gray herringbone suit and a handpainted tie with part of a diving girl visible on it. His shirt was clean, which comforted me, and his brown loafers, as wrong as the tie for his suit, shone from a recent polishing.

He sidled past me as I held the door between the waiting room and my thinking parlor. Once inside, he took a quick look around. I'd have placed him as a mobster, second grade, if I had been asked. For once I was right. If he carried a gun, it was inside his pants. His coat was too tight to hide the bulge of an underarm holster.

He sat down carefully and I sat opposite and we looked at each other. His face had a sort of foxy eagerness. He was sweating a little. The expression on my face was meant to be interested but not clubby. I reached for a pipe and the leather humidor in which I kept my Pearce's tobacco. I pushed the cigarettes at him.

"I don't smoke." He had a rusty voice. I didn't like it any more than I liked his clothes, or his face. While I filled the pipe he reached inside his coat, prowled in a pocket, came out with a bill, glanced at it, and dropped it across the desk in front of me. It was a nice bill and clean and new. One thousand dollars.

"Ever save a guy's life?"

"Once in a while, maybe."

"Save mine."

"What goes?"

"I heard you leveled with the customers, Marlowe."

"That's why I stay poor."

"I still got two friends. You make it three and you'll be out of the red. You got five grand coming if you pry me loose."

"From what?"

"You're talkative as hell this morning. Don't you pipe who I am?"

"Nope."

"Never been east, huh?"

"Sure—but I wasn't in your set."

"What set would that be?"

I was getting tired of it. "Stop being so damn cagey or pick up your grand and be missing."

"I'm Ikky Rossen. I'll be missing but good unless you can figure something out. Guess."

"I've already guessed. You tell me and tell me quick. I don't have all day to watch you feeding me with an eye-dropper."

"I ran out on the Outfit. The high boys don't go for that. To them it means you got info you figure you can peddle, or you got independent ideas, or you lost your moxie. Me, I lost my moxie. I had it up to here." He touched his Adam's apple with the forefinger of a stretched hand. "I done bad things. I scared and hurt guys. I never killed nobody. That's nothing to the Outfit. I'm out of line. So they pick up the pencil and they draw a line. I got the word. The operators are on the way. I made a bad mistake. I tried to hole up in Vegas. I figured they'd never expect me to lie up in their own joint. They outfigured me. What I did's been done before, but I didn't know it. When I took the plane to L.A. there must have been somebody on it. They know where I live."

"Move."

"No good now. I'm covered."

I knew he was right.

"Why haven't they taken care of you already?"

"They don't do it that way. Always specialists. Don't you know how it works?"

"More or less. A guy with a nice hardware store in Buffalo. A guy with a small dairy in K.C. Always a good front. They report back to New York or somewhere. When they mount the plane west or wherever they're going, they have guns in their brief cases. They're quiet and well-dressed and they don't sit together. They could be a couple of lawyers or income-tax sharpies—anything at all that's well-mannered and inconspicuous. All sorts of people carry brief cases. Including women."

"Correct as hell. And when they land they'll be steered to me, but not from the airfield. They got ways. If I go to the cops, somebody will know about me. They could have a couple Mafia boys right on the City Council for all I know. The cops will give me twenty-four hours to leave town. No use. Mexico? Worse than here. Canada? Better but still no good. Connections there too."

"Australia?"

"Can't get a passport. I been here twenty-five years—illegal. They can't deport me unless they can prove a crime on me. The Outfit would see they didn't. Suppose I got tossed into the freezer. I'm out on a writ in twenty-four hours. And my nice friends got a car waiting to take me home—only not home."

I had my pipe lit and going well. I frowned down at the one-grand note. I could use it very nicely. My checking account could kiss the sidewalk without stooping.

"Let's stop horsing," I said. "Suppose—just suppose—I could figure an out for you. What's your next move?"

"I know a place—if I could get there without bein' tailed. I'd leave my car here and take a rent car. I'd turn it in just short of the county line and buy a secondhand job. Halfway to where I'm going I trade it on a new last-year's model, a leftover—this is just the right time of year. Good discount, new models out soon. Not to save money—less show off. Where I'd go is a good-sized place but still pretty clean."

"Uh-huh," I said. "Wichita, last I heard. But it might have changed."

He scowled at me. "Get smart, Marlowe, but not too damn smart."

"I'll get as smart as I want to. Don't try to make rules for me. If I take this on, there aren't any rules. I take it for this grand and the rest if I bring it off. Don't cross me. I might leak information. If I get knocked off, put just one red rose on my grave. I don't like cut flowers. I like to see them growing. But I could take one, because you're such a sweet character. When's the plane in?"

"Sometime today. It's nine hours from New York. Probably come in about 5:30 p.m."

"Might come by San Diego and switch or by San Francisco and switch. A lot of planes from both places. I need a helper."

"Damn you, Marlowe—"

"Hold it. I know a girl. Daughter of a Chief of Police who got broken for honesty. She wouldn't leak under torture."

"You got no right to risk her," Ikky said angrily.

I was so astonished my jaw hung halfway to my waist. I closed it slowly and swallowed.

"Good God, the man's got a heart."

"Women ain't built for the rough stuff," he said grudgingly.

I picked up the thousand-dollar note and snapped it. "Sorry. No receipt," I said. "I can't have my name in your pocket. And there won't be any rough stuff if I'm lucky. They'd have me outclassed. There's only one way to work it. Now give me your address and all the dope you can think of—names, descriptions of any operators you have ever seen in the flesh."

He did. He was a pretty good observer. Trouble was, the

Outfit would know what he had seen. The operators would be strangers to him.

He got up silently and put his hand out. I had to shake it, but what he had said about women made it easier. His hand was moist. Mine would have been in his spot. He nodded and went out silently.

It was a quiet street in Bay City, if there are any quiet streets in this beatnik generation when you can't get through a meal without some male or female stomach-singer belching out a kind of love that is as old-fashioned as a bustle or some Hammond organ jazzing it up in the customer's soup.

The little one-story house was as neat as a fresh pinafore. The front lawn was cut lovingly and very green. The smooth composition driveway was free of grease spots from standing cars, and the hedge that bordered it looked as though the barber came every day.

The white door had a knocker with a tiger's head, a go-to-hell window, and a dingus that let someone inside talk to someone outside without even opening the little window.

I'd have given a mortgage on my left leg to live in a house like that. I didn't think I ever would.

The bell chimed inside and after a while she opened the door in a pale-blue sports shirt and white shorts that were short enough to be friendly. She had gray-blue eyes, dark red hair, and fines bones in her face. There was usually a trace of bitterness in the gray-blue eyes. She couldn't forget that her father's life had been destroyed by the crooked power of a gambling-ship mobster, that her mother had died too.

She was able to suppress the bitterness when she wrote nonsense about young love for the shiny magazines, but this wasn't her life. She didn't really have a life. She had an existence without much pain and enough money to make it safe. But in a tight spot she was as cool and resourceful as a good cop. Her name was Anne Riordan.

She stood to one side and I passed her pretty close. But I have rules too. She shut the door and parked herself on a sofa and went through the cigarette routine, and here was one doll who had the strength to light her own cigarette.

I stood looking around. There were a few changes, not many.

"I need your help," I said.

"The only time I ever see you."

"I've got a client who is an ex-hood, used to be a troubleshooter for the Outfit, the Syndicate, the big mob, or whatever name you want to use for it. You know damn well it exists and is as rich as Midas. You can't beat it because not enough people want to, especially the million-a-year lawyers who work for it."

"My God, are you running for office somewhere? I never heard you sound so pure."

She moved her legs around, not provocatively—she wasn't the type—but it made it difficult for me to think straight just the same.

"Stop moving your legs around," I said. "Or put a pair of slacks on."

"Damn you, Marlowe. Can't you think of anything else?"

"I'll try. I like to think that I know at least one pretty and charming female who doesn't have round heels." I swallowed and went on. "The man's name is Ikky Rossen." He's not beautiful and he's not anything that I like—except one thing. He got mad when I said I needed a girl helper. He said women were not made for the rough stuff. That's why I took the job. To a real mobster, a woman means no more than a sack of flour. They use women in the usual way, but if it's advisable to get rid of them they do it without a second thought."

"So far you've told me a whole lot of nothing. Perhaps you need a cup of coffee or a drink."

"You're sweet but I don't in the morning—except sometimes, and this isn't one of them. Coffee later. Ikky has been penciled."

"Now what's that?"

"You have a list. You draw a line through a name with a pencil. The guy is as good as dead. The Outfit has reasons. They don't do it just for kicks any more. They don't get any kick. It's just bookkeeping to them."

"What on earth can I do? I might even have said, what can *you* do?"

"I can try. What you can do is help me spot their plane and see where they go—the operators assigned to the job."

"Yes, but how can you do anything?"

"I said I could try. If they took a night plane they are already here. If they took a morning plane they can't be here before five or so. Plenty of time to get set. You know what they look like?"

"Oh, sure. I meet killers every day. I have them in for whiskey sours and caviar on hot toast." She grinned. While she was grinning I took four long steps across the tan-figured rug and lifted her and put a kiss on her mouth. She didn't fight me but she didn't go all trembly either. I went back and sat down.

"They'll look like anybody who's in a quiet well-run business or profession. They'll have quiet clothes and they'll be polite—when they want to be. They'll have brief cases with guns in them that have changed hands so often they can't possibly be traced. When and if they do the job, they'll drop the guns. They'll probably use revolvers, but they could use automatics. They won't use silencers because silencers can jam a gun and the weight makes it hard to shoot accurately. They won't sit together on the plane, but once off of it they may pretend to know each other and simply not have noticed during the flight. They may shake hands with appropriate smiles and walk away and get in the same taxi. I think they'll go in the same taxi. I think they'll go to a hotel first. But very soon they will move into something from which they can watch Ikky's movements and get used to his schedule. They won't be in any hurry unless Ikky makes a move. That would tip them off that Ikky has been tipped off. He has a couple of friends left—he says."

"Will they shoot him from this room or apartment across the street—assuming there is one?"

"No. They'll shoot him from three feet away. They'll walk up behind and say 'Hello, Ikky.' He'll either freeze or turn. They'll fill him with lead, drop the guns, and hop into the car they have waiting. Then they'll follow the crash car off the scene."

"Who'll drive the crash car?"

"Some well-fixed and blameless citizen who hasn't been rapped. He'll drive his own car. He'll clear the way, even if he has to accidentally on purpose crash somebody, even a police car. He'll be so damn sorry he'll cry all the way down his monogrammed shirt. And the killers will be long gone."

"Good heavens," Anne said. "How can you stand your life? If you did bring it off, they'll send operators after you."

"I don't think so. They don't kill a legit. The blame will go to the operators. Remember, these top mobsters are businessmen. They want lots and lots of money. They only get really tough when they figure they have to get rid of somebody, and they don't crave that. There's always a chance of a slipup. Not much of a chance. No gang killing has ever been solved here or anywhere else except two or three times. The top mobster is awful big and awful tough. When he gets too big, too tough—pencil."

She shuddered a little. "I think I need a drink myself."

I grinned at her. "You're right in the atmosphere, darling. I'll weaken."

She brought a couple of Scotch highballs. When we were drinking them I said, "If you spot them or think you spot them, follow to where they go—if you can do it safely. Not otherwise. If it's a hotel—and ten to one it will be—check in and keep calling me until you get me."

She knew my office number and I was still on Yucca Avenue. She knew that too.

"You're the damndest guy," she said. "Women do anything you want them to. How come I'm still a virgin at twenty-eight?"

"We need a few like you. Why don't you get married?"

"To what? Some cynical chaser who has nothing left? I don't know any really nice men—except you. I'm no pushover for white teeth and a gaudy smile."

I went over and pulled her to her feet. I kissed her long and hard. "I'm honest," I almost whispered. "That's something. But I'm too shop-soiled for a girl like you. I've thought of you, I've wanted you, but that sweet clear look in your eyes tells me to lay off."

"Take me," she said softly. "I have dreams too."

"I couldn't. I've had too many women to deserve one like you. We have to save a man's life. I'm going."

She stood up and watched me leave with a grave face.

The women you get and the women you don't get—they live in different worlds. I don't sneer at either world. I live in both myself.

At Los Angeles International Airport you can't get close to the planes unless you're leaving on one. You see them land, if you happen to be in the right place, but you have to wait at a barrier to get a look at the passengers. The airport buildings don't make it any easier. They are strung out from here to breakfast time, and you can get calluses walking from TWA to American.

I copied an arrival schedule off the boards and prowled around like a dog that has forgotten where he put his bone. Planes came in, planes took off, porters carried luggage, passengers sweated and scurried, children whined, the loudspeaker overrode all the other noises.

I passed Anne a number of times. She took no notice of me.

At 5:45 they must have come. Anne disappeared. I gave it half an hour, just in case she had some other reason for fading. No. She was gone for good. I went out to my car and drove some long crowded miles to Hollywood and my office. I had a drink and sat. At 6:45 the phone rang.

267

"I think so," she said. "Beverly-Western Hotel. Room 410. I couldn't get any names. You know the clerks don't leave registration cards lying around these days. I didn't like to ask any questions. But I rode up in the elevator with them and spotted their room. I walked right on past them when the bellman put a key in their door, and went down to the mezzanine and then downstairs with a bunch of women from the tea room. I didn't bother to take a room."

"What were they like?"

"They came up the ramp together but I didn't hear them speak. Both had brief cases, both wore quiet suits, nothing flashy. White shirts, starched, one blue tie, one black striped with gray. Black shoes. A couple of businessmen from the East Coast. They could be publishers, lawyers, doctors, account executives—no, cut the last; they weren't gaudy enough. You wouldn't look at them twice."

"Faces?"

"Both medium-brown hair, one a bit darker than the other. Smooth faces, rather expressionless. One had gray eyes, the one with the lighter hair had blue eyes. Their eyes were interesting. Very quick to move, very observant, watching everything near them. That might have been wrong. They should have been a bit preoccupied with what they came out for or interested in California. They seemed more occupied with faces. It's a good thing I spotted them and not you. You don't look like a cop, but you don't look like a man who is not a cop. You have marks on you."

"Phooey. I'm a damn good-looking heart wrecker."

"Their features were strictly assembly line. Each picked up a flight suitcase. One suitcase was gray with two red and white stripes up and down, about six or seven inches from the ends, the other a blue and white tartan. I didn't know there was such a tartan."

"There is, but I forget the name of it."

"I thought you knew everything."

"Just almost everything. Run along home now."

"Do I get a dinner and maybe a kiss?"

"Later, and if you're not careful you'll get more than you want."

"You'll take over and follow them?"

"If they're the right men, they'll follow me. I already took an apartment across the street from Ikky—that block on Poynter with six lowlife apartment houses on the block. I'll bet the incidence of chippies is very high."

"It's high everywhere these days."

"So long, Anne. See you."

"When you need help."

She hung up. I hung up. She puzzles me. Too wise to be so nice. I guess all nice women are wise too.

I called Ikky. He was out. I had a drink from the office bottle, smoked for half an hour, and called again. This time I got him.

I told him the score up to then, and said I hoped Anne had picked the right men. I told him about the apartment I had taken.

"Do I get expenses?" I asked.

"Five grand ought to cover the lot."

"If I earn it and get it. I heard you had a quarter of a million," I said at a wild venture.

"Could be, pal, but how do I get at it? The high boys know where it is. It'll have to cool a long time."

I said that was all right. I had cooled a long time myself. Of course, I didn't expect to get the other four thousand, even if I brought the job off. Men like Ikky Rossen would steal their mother's gold teeth. There seemed to be a little good in him somewhere—but little was the operative word.

I spent the next half hour trying to think of a plan. I couldn't think of one that looked promising. It was almost eight o'clock and I needed food. I didn't think the boys would move that night. Next morning they would drive past Ikky's place and scout the neighborhood.

I was ready to leave the office when the buzzer sounded from the door of my waiting room. I opened the communicating door. A small tight-looking man was standing in the middle of the floor rocking on his heels with his hands behind his back. He smiled at me, but he wasn't good at it. He walked toward me.

"You Philip Marlowe?"

"Who else? What can I do for you?"

He was close now. He brought his right hand around fast with a gun in it. He stuck the gun in my stomach.

"You can lay off Ikky Rossen," he said in a voice that matched his face, "or you can get your belly full of lead."

He was an amateur. If he had stayed four feet away, he might have had something. I reached up and took the cigarette out of my mouth and held it carelessly.

269

"What makes you think I know any Ikky Rossen?"

He laughed and pushed his gun into my stomach.

"Wouldn't you like to know!" The cheap sneer, the empty triumph of that feeling of power when you hold a fat gun in a small hand.

"It would be fair to tell me."

As his mouth opened for another crack, I dropped the cigarette and swept a hand. I can be fast when I have to. There are boys that are faster, but they don't stick guns in your stomach.

I got my thumb behind the trigger and my hand over his. I kneed him in the groin. He bent over with a whimper. I twisted his arm to the right and I had his gun. I hooked a heel behind his heel and he was on the floor.

He lay there blinking with surprise and pain, his knees drawn up against his stomach. He rolled from side to side groaning. I reached down and grabbed his left hand and yanked him to his feet. I had six inches and forty pounds on him. They ought to have sent a bigger, better trained messenger.

"Let's go into my thinking parlor," I said. "We could have a chat and you could have a drink to pick you up. Next time don't get near enough to a prospect for him to get your gun hand. I'll just see if you have any more iron on you."

He hadn't. I pushed him through the door and into a chair. His breath wasn't quite so rasping. He grabbed out a handkerchief and mopped at his face.

"Next time," he said between his teeth. "Next time."

"Don't be an optimist. You don't look the part."

I poured him a drink of Scotch in a paper cup, set it down in front of him. I broke his .38 and dumped the cartridges into the desk drawer. I clicked the chamber back and laid the gun down.

"You can have it when you leave—if you leave."

"That's a dirty way to fight," he said, still gasping.

"Sure. Shooting a man is so much cleaner. Now, how did you get here?"

"Nuts."

"Don't be a fool. I have friends. Not many, but some. I can get you for armed assault, and you know what would happen then. You'd be out on a writ or on bail and that's the last anyone would hear of you. The biggies don't go for failures. Now who sent you and how did you know where to come?"

"Ikky was covered," he said sullenly. "He's dumb. I trailed him

270

here without no trouble at all. Why would he go see a private eye? People want to know."

"More."

"Go to hell."

"Come to think of it, I don't have to get you for armed assault. I can smash it out of you right here and now."

I got up from the chair and he put out a flat hand.

"If I get knocked about, a couple of real tough monkeys will drop around. If I don't report back, same thing. You ain't holding no real high cards. They just look high," he said.

"You haven't anything to tell. If this Ikky came to see me, you don't know why, nor whether I took him on. If he's a mobster, he's not my type of client."

"He come to get you to try and save his hide."

"Who from?"

"That'd be talking."

"Go right ahead. Your mouth seems to work fine. And tell the boys any time I front for a hood, that will be the day."

You have to lie a little once in a while in my business. I was lying a little. "What's Ikky done to get himself disliked? Or would that be talking?"

"You think you're a lot of man," he sneered, rubbing the place where I had kneed him. "In my league you wouldn't make pinch runner."

I laughed in his face. Then I grabbed his right wrist and twisted it behind his back. He began to squawk. I reached into his breast pocket with my left hand and hauled out a wallet. I let him go. He reached for his gun on the desk and I bisected his upper arm with a hard cut. He fell into the customer's chair and grunted.

"You can have your gun," I told him. "When I give it to you. Now be good or I'll have to bounce you just to amuse myself."

In the wallet I found a driver's license made out to Charles Hickon. It did me no good at all. Punks of his type always have slangy aliases. They probably called him Tiny, or Slim, or Marbles, or even just "you." I tossed the wallet back to him. It fell to the floor. He couldn't even catch it.

"Hell," I said, "there must be an economy campaign on, if they send you to do more than pick up cigarette butts."

"Nuts."

"All right, mug. Beat it back to the laundry. Here's your gun."

He took it, made a business of shoving it into his waistband,

271

stood up, gave me as dirty a look as he had in stock, and strolled to the door, nonchalant as a hustler with a new mink stole.

He turned at the door and gave me the beady eye. "Stay clean, tinhorn. Tin bends easy."

With this blinding piece of repartee he opened the door and drifted out.

After a little while I locked my other door, cut the buzzer, made the office dark, and left. I saw no one who looked like a lifetaker. I drove to my house, packed a suitcase, drove to a service station where they were almost fond of me, stored my car, and picked up a rental Chevrolet.

I drove this to Poynter Street, dumped my suitcase in the sleazy apartment I had rented early in the afternoon, and went to dinner at Victor's. It was nine o'clock, too late to drive to Bay City and take Anne to dinner.

I ordered a double Gibson with fresh limes and drank it, and I was as hungry as a schoolboy.

On the way back to Poynter Street I did a good deal of weaving in and out and circling blocks and stopping, with a gun on the seat beside me. As far as I could tell, no one was trying to tail me.

I stopped on Sunset at a service station and made two calls from the box. I caught Bernie Ohls just as he was leaving to go home.

"This is Marlowe, Bernie. We haven't had a fight in years. I'm getting lonely."

"Well, get married. I'm chief investigator for the Sheriff's Office now. I rank acting captain until I pass the exam. I don't hardly speak to private eyes."

"Speak to this one. I need help. I'm on a ticklish job where I could get killed."

"And you expect me to interfere with the course of nature?"

"Come off it, Bernie. I haven't been a bad guy. I'm trying to save an ex-mobster from a couple of executioners."

"The more they mow each other down, the better I like it."

"Yeah. If I call you, come running or send a couple of good boys. You'll have had time to teach them."

We exchanged a couple of mild insults and hung up. I dialed Ikky Rossen's number. His rather unpleasant voice said, "Okay, talk."

"Marlowe. Be ready to move out about midnight. We've spotted your boy friends and they are holed up at the Beverly-

Western. They won't move to your street tonight. Remember, they don't know you've been tipped."

"Sounds chancy."

"Good God, it wasn't meant to be a Sunday School picnic. You've been careless, Ikky. You were followed to my office. That cuts the time we have."

He was silent for a moment. I heard him breathing. "Who by?" he asked.

"Some little tweezer who stuck a gun in my belly and gave me the trouble of taking it away from him. I can only figure they sent a punk on the theory they don't want me to know too much, in case I don't know it already."

"You're in for trouble, friend."

"When not? I'll come over to your place about midnight. Be ready. Where's your car?"

"Out front."

"Get it on a side street and make a business of locking it up. Where's the back door of your flop?"

"In back. Where would it be? On the alley."

"Leave your suitcase there. We walk out together and go to your car. We drive by the alley and pick up the suitcase or cases."

"Suppose some guy steals them?"

"Yeah. Suppose you get dead. Which do you like better?"

"Okay," he grunted. "I'm waiting. But we're taking big chances."

"So do race drivers. Does that stop them? There's no way to get out but fast. Douse your lights about ten and rumple the bed well. It would be good if you could leave some baggage behind. Wouldn't look so planned."

He grunted okay and I hung up. The telephone box was well lighted outside. They usually are in service stations. I took a good long gander around while I pawed over the collection of giveaway maps inside the station. I saw nothing to worry me. I took a map of San Diego just for the hell of it and got into my rented car.

On Poynter I parked around the corner and went up to my second-floor sleazy apartment and sat in the dark watching from my window. I saw nothing to worry about. A couple of medium-class chippies came out of Ikky's apartment house and were picked up in a late-model car. A man about Ikky's height and build went into the apartment house. Various other people came and went. The street was fairly quiet. Since they put in the

Hollywood Freeway nobody much uses the off-the-boulevard streets unless they live in the neighborhood.

It was a nice fall night—or as nice as they get in Los Angeles' climate—clearish but not even crisp. I don't know what's happened to the weather in our overcrowded city, but it's not the weather I knew when I came to it.

It seemed like a long time to midnight. I couldn't spot anybody watching anything, and no couple of quiet-suited men paged any of the six apartment houses available. I was pretty sure they'd try mine first when they came, but I wasn't sure if Anne had picked the right men, and if the tweezer's message back to his bosses had done me any good or otherwise.

In spite of the hundred ways Anne could be wrong, I had a hunch she was right. The killers had no reason to be cagey if they didn't know Ikky had been warned. No reason but one. He had come to my office and been tailed there. But the Outfit, with all its arrogance of power, might laugh at the idea he had been tipped off or come to me for help. I was so small they would hardly be able to see me.

At midnight I left the apartment, walked two blocks watching for a tail, crossed the street, and went into Ikky's dive. There was no locked door, and no elevator. I climbed steps to the third floor and looked for his apartment. I knocked lightly. He opened the door with a gun in his hand. He probably looked scared.

There were two suitcases by the door and another against the far wall. I went over and lifted it. It was heavy enough. I opened it—it was unlocked.

"You don't have to worry," he said. "It's got everything a guy could need for three-four nights, and nothing except some clothes that I couldn't glom off in any ready-to-wear place."

I picked up one of the other suitcases. "Let's stash this by the back door."

"We can leave by the alley too."

"We leave by the front door. Just in case we're covered—though I don't think so—we're just two guys going out together. Just one thing. Keep both hands in your coat pockets and the gun in your right. If anybody calls out your name behind you, turn fast and shoot. Nobody but a lifetaker will do it. I'll do the same."

"I'm scared," he said in his rusty voice.

"Me too, if it helps any. But we have to do it. If you're braced, they'll have guns in their hands. Don't bother asking them ques-

274

tions. They wouldn't answer in words. If it's just my small friend, we'll cool him and dump him inside the door. Got it?"

He nodded, licking his lips. We carried the suitcases down and put them outside the back door. I looked along the alley. Nobody, and only a short distance to the side street. We went back in and along the hall to the front. We walked out on Poynter Street with all the casualness of a wife buying her husband a birthday tie.

Nobody made a move. The street was empty.

We walked around the corner to Ikky's rented car. He unlocked it. I went back with him for the suitcases. Not a stir. We put the suitcases in the car and started up and drove to the next street.

A traffic light not working, a boulevard stop or two, the entrance to the Freeway. There was plenty of traffic on it even at midnight. California is loaded with people going places and making speed to get there. If you don't drive eighty miles an hour, everybody passes you. If you do, you have to watch the rear-view mirror for highway patrol cars. It's the rat race of rat races.

Ikky did a quiet seventy. We reached the junction to Route 66 and he took it. So far nothing. I stayed with him to Pomona.

"This is far enough for me," I said. "I'll grab a bus back if there is one, or park myself in a motel. Drive to a service station and we'll ask for the bus stop. It should be close to the Freeway."

He did that and stopped midway on a block. He reached for his pocketbook and held out four thousand-dollar bills.

"I don't really feel I've earned all that. It was too easy."

He laughed with a kind of wry amusement on his pudgy face. "Don't be a sap. I have it made. You didn't know what you was walking into. What's more, your troubles are just beginning. The Outfit has eyes and ears everywhere. Perhaps I'm safe if I'm damn careful. Perhaps I ain't as safe as I think I am. Either way, you did what I asked. Take the dough. I got plenty."

I took it and put it away. He drove to an all-night service station and we were told where to find the bus stop. "There's a cross-country Greyhound at 2:25 a.m.," the attendant said, looking at a schedule. "They'll take you, if they got room."

Ikky drove to the bus stop. We shook hands and he went gunning down the road toward the Freeway. I looked at my watch and found a liquor store still open and bought a pint of Scotch. Then I found a bar and ordered a double with water.

275

My troubles were just beginning, Ikky had said. He was so right.

I got off at the Hollywood bus station, grabbed a taxi, and drove to my office. I asked the driver to wait a few moments. At that time of night he was glad to. The night man let me into the building.

"You work late, Mr. Marlowe. But you always did, didn't you?"

"It's that sort of business," I said. "Thanks, Jimmy."

Up in my office I pawed the floor for mail and found nothing but a longish narrowish box, Special Delivery, with a Glendale postmark.

It contained nothing at all but a freshly sharpened pencil—the mobster's mark of death.

I didn't take it too hard. When they mean it, they don't send it to you. I took it as a sharp warning to lay off. There might be a beating arranged. From their point of view, that would be good discipline. "When we pencil a guy, any guy that tries to help him is in for a smashing." That could be the message.

I thought of going to my house on Yucca Avenue. Too lonely. I thought of going to Anne's place in Bay City. Worse. If they got wise to her, real hoods would think nothing of beating her up too.

It was the Poynter Street flop for me—easily the safest place now. I went down to the waiting taxi and had him drive me to within three blocks of the so-called apartment house. I went upstairs, undressed, and slept raw. Nothing bothered me but a broken spring—that bothered my back.

I lay until 3:30 pondering the situation with my massive brain. I went to sleep with a gun under the pillow, which is a bad place to keep a gun when you have one pillow as thick and soft as a typewriter pad. It bothered me, so I transferred it to my right hand. Practice had taught me to keep it there even in sleep.

I woke up with the sun shining. I felt like a piece of spoiled meat. I struggled into the bathroom and doused myself with cold water and wiped off with a towel you couldn't have seen if you held it sideways. This was a really gorgeous apartment. All it needed was a set of Chippendale furniture to be graduated into the slum class.

There was nothing to eat and if I went out, Miss-Nothing Marlowe might miss something. I had a pint of whiskey. I looked at it and smelled it, but I couldn't take it for breakfast on an empty stomach, even if I could reach my stomach, which was floating around near the ceiling.

I looked into the closets in case a previous tenant might have left a crust of bread in a hasty departure. Nope. I wouldn't have liked it anyhow, not even with whiskey on it. So I sat at the window. An hour of that and I was ready to bite a piece off a bellhop's arm.

I dressed and went around the corner to the rented car and drove to an eatery. The waitress was sore too. She swept a cloth over the counter in front of me and let me have the last customer's crumbs in my lap.

"Look, sweetness," I said, "don't be so generous. Save the crumbs for a rainy day. All I want is two eggs three minutes—no more—a slice of your famous concrete toast, a tall glass of tomato juice with a dash of Lee and Perrins, a big happy smile, and don't give anybody else any coffee. I might need it all."

"I got a cold," she said. "Don't push me around. I might crack you one on the kisser."

"Let's be pals. I had a rough night too."

She gave me a half smile and went through the swing door sideways. It showed more of her curves, which were ample, even excessive. But I got the eggs the way I liked them. The toast had been painted with melted butter past its bloom.

"No Lee and Perrins," she said, putting down the tomato juice. "How about a little Tabasco? We're fresh out of arsenic too."

I used two drops of Tabasco, swallowed the eggs, drank two cups of coffee, and was about to leave the toast for a tip, but I went soft and left a quarter instead. That really brightened her. It was a joint where you left a dime or nothing. Mostly nothing.

Back on Poynter Street nothing had changed. I got to my window again and sat. At about 8:30 the man I had seen go into the apartment house across the way—the one about the same height and build as Ikky—came out with a small brief case and turned east. Two men got out of a dark-blue sedan. They were of the same height and very quietly dressed and had soft hats pulled low over their foreheads. Each jerked out a revolver.

"Hey, Ikky!" one of them called out.

The man turned. "So long, Ikky," the other man said.

Gunfire racketed between the houses. The man crumpled and lay motionless. The two men rushed for their car and were off, going west. Halfway down the block I saw a limousine pull out and start ahead of them.

In no time at all they were completely gone.

It was a nice swift clean job. The only thing wrong with it was that they hadn't given it enough time for preparation.

They had shot the wrong man.

I got out of there fast, almost as fast as the two killers. There was a smallish crowd grouped around the dead man. I didn't have to look at him to know he was dead—the boys were pros. Where he lay on the sidewalk on the other side of the street I couldn't see him—people were in the way. But I knew just how he would look and I already heard sirens in the distance. It could have been just the routine shrieking from Sunset, but it wasn't. So somebody had telephoned. It was too early for the cops to be going to lunch.

I strolled around the corner with my suitcase and jammed into the rented car and beat it away from there. The neighborhood was not my piece of shortcake any more. I could imagine the questions.

"Just what took you over there, Marlowe? You got a flop of your own, ain't you?"

"I was hired by an ex-mobster in trouble with the Outfit. They'd sent killers after him!"

"Don't tell us he was trying to go straight."

"I don't know. But I liked his money."

"Didn't do much to earn it, did you?"

"I got him away last night. I don't know where he is now, and I don't want to know."

"You got him away?"

"That's what I said."

"Yeah—only he's in the morgue with multiple bullet wounds. Try something better. Or somebody's in the morgue."

And on and on. Policeman's dialogue. It comes out of an old shoebox. What they say doesn't mean anything, what they ask doesn't mean anything. They just keep boring in until you are so exhausted you flip on some detail. Then they smile happily and rub their hands, and say, "Kind of careless there, weren't you? Let's start all over again."

The less I had of that, the better. I parked in my usual parking slot and went up to the office. It was full of nothing but stale air. Every time I went into the dump I felt more and more tired. Why the hell hadn't I got myself a government job ten years ago? Make it fifteen years. I had brains enough to get a mail-order law degree. The country's full of lawyers who couldn't write a complaint without the book.

So I sat in my office chair and disadmired myself. After a while

I remembered the pencil. I made certain arrangements with a .45 gun, more gun than I ever carry—too much weight. I dialed the Sheriff's Office and asked for Bernie Ohls. I got him. His voice was sour.

"Marlowe. I'm in trouble—real trouble," I said.

"Why tell me?" he growled. "You must be used to it by now."

"This kind of trouble you don't get used to. I'd like to come over and tell you."

"You in the same office?"

"The same."

"Have to go over that way. I'll drop in."

He hung up. I opened two windows. The gentle breeze wafted a smell of coffee and stale fat to me from Joe's Eats next door. I hated it, I hated myself, I hated everything.

Ohls didn't bother with my elegant waiting room. He rapped on my own door and I let him in. He scowled his way to the customer's chair.

"Okay. Give."

"Ever hear of a character named Ikky Rossen?"

"Why would I? Record?"

"An ex-mobster who got disliked by the mob. They put a pencil through his name and sent the usual two tough boys on a plane. He got tipped and hired me to help him get away."

"Nice clean work."

"Cut it out, Bernie." I lit a cigarette and blew smoke in his face. In retaliation he began to chew a cigarette. He never lit one, but he certainly mangled them.

"Look," I went on. "Suppose the man wants to go straight and suppose he doesn't. He's entitled to his life as long as he hasn't killed anyone. He told me he hadn't."

"And you believed the hood, huh? When do you start teaching Sunday School?"

"I neither believed him nor disbelieved him. I took him on. There was no reason not to. A girl I know and I watched the planes yesterday. She spotted the boys and tailed them to a hotel. She was sure of what they were. They looked it right down to their black shoes. This girl—"

"Would she have a name?"

"Only for you."

"I'll buy, if she hasn't cracked any laws."

"Her name is Anne Riordan. She lives in Bay City. Her father was once Chief of Police there. And don't say that makes him a crook, because he wasn't."

"Uh-huh. Let's have the rest. Make a little time too."

"I took an apartment opposite Ikky. The killers were still at the hotel. At midnight I got Ikky out and drove with him as far as Pomona. He went on in his rented car and I came back by Greyhound. I moved into the apartment on Poynter Street, right across from his dump."

"Why—if he was already gone?"

I opened the middle desk drawer and took out the nice sharp pencil. I wrote my name on a piece of paper and ran the pencil through it.

"Because someone sent me this. I didn't think they'd kill me, but I thought they planned to give me enough of a beating to warn me off any more pranks."

"They knew you were in on it?"

"Ikky was tailed here by a little squirt who later came around and stuck a gun in my stomach. I knocked him around a bit, but I had to let him go. I thought Poynter Street was safer after that. I live lonely."

"I get around," Bernie Ohls said. "I hear reports. So they gunned the wrong guy."

"Same height, same build, same general appearance. I saw them gun him. I couldn't tell if it was the two guys from the Beverly-Western. I'd never seen them. It was just two guys in dark suits with hats pulled down. They jumped into a blue Pontiac sedan, about two years old, and lammed off, with a big Caddy running crash for them."

Bernie stood up and stared at me for a long moment. "I don't think they'll bother with you now," he said. "They've hit the wrong guy. The mob will be very quiet for a while. You know something? This town is getting to be almost as lousy as New York, Brooklyn, and Chicago. We could end up real corrupt."

"We've made a hell of a good start."

"You haven't told me anything that makes me take action, Phil. I'll talk to the city homicide boys. I don't guess you're in any trouble. But you saw the shooting. They'll want that."

"I couldn't identify anybody, Bernie. I didn't know the man who was shot. How did *you* know it was the wrong man?"

"You told me, stupid."

"I thought perhaps the city boys had a make on him."

"They wouldn't tell me, if they had. Besides, they ain't hardly had time to go out for breakfast. He's just a stiff in the morgue to them until the ID comes up with something. But they'll want to talk to you, Phil. They just love their tape recorders."

He went out and the door whooshed shut behind him. I sat there wondering if I had been a dope to talk to him. Or to take on Ikky's troubles. Five thousand green men said no. But they can be wrong too.

Somebody banged on my door. It was a uniform holding a telegram. I receipted for it and tore it loose.

It said: ON MY WAY TO FLAGSTAFF. MIRADOR MOTOR COURT. THINK I'VE BEEN SPOTTED. COME FAST.

I tore the wire into small pieces and burned them in my big ashtray.

I called Anne Riordan.

"Funny thing happened," I told her, and told her about the funny thing.

"I don't like the pencil," she said. "And I don't like the wrong man being killed—probably some poor bookkeeper in a cheap business or he wouldn't be living in that neighborhood. You should never have touched it, Phil."

"Ikky had a life. Where he's going he might make himself decent. He can change his name. He must be loaded or he wouldn't have paid me so much."

"I said I didn't like the pencil. You'd better come down here for a while. You can have your mail readdressed—if you get any mail. You don't have to work right away anyhow. And L.A. is oozing with private eyes."

"You don't get the point. I'm not through with the job. The city dicks have to know where I am, and if they do, all the crime reporters will know too. The cops might even decide to make me a suspect. Nobody who saw the shooting is going to put out a description that means anything. The American people know better than to be witnesses to gang killings."

"All right, but my offer stands."

The buzzer sounded in the outside room. I told Anne I had to hang up. I opened the communicating door and a well-dressed—I might say elegantly dressed—middle-aged man stood six feet inside the outer door. He had a pleasantly dishonest smile on his face. He wore a white Stetson and one of those narrow ties that go through an ornamental buckle. His cream-colored flannel suit was beautifully tailored.

He lit a cigarette with a gold lighter and looked at me over the first puff of smoke.

"Mr. Philip Marlowe?"

I nodded.

"I'm Foster Grimes from Las Vegas. I run the Rancho Esperanza on South Fifth. I hear you got a little involved with a man named Ikky Rossen."

"Won't you come in?"

He strolled past me into my office. His appearance told me nothing—a prosperous man who liked or felt it good business to look a bit western. You see them by the dozen in the Palm Springs winter season. His accent told me he was an easterner, but not New England. New York or Baltimore, likely. Long Island, the Berkshires—no, too far from the city.

I showed him the customer's chair with a flick of the wrist and sat down in my antique swivelsqueaker. I waited.

"Where is Ikky now, if you know?"

"I don't know, Mr. Grimes."

"How come you messed with him?"

"Money."

"A damned good reason," he smiled. "How far did it go?"

"I helped him leave town. I'm telling you this, although I don't know who the hell you are, because I've already told an old friend-enemy of mine, a top man in the Sheriff's Office."

"What's a friend-enemy?"

"Law men don't go around kissing me, but I've known him for years, and we are as much friends as a private star can be with a law man."

"I told you who I was. We have a unique set-up in Vegas. We own the place except for one lousy newspaper editor who keeps climbing our backs and the backs of our friends. We let him live because letting him live makes us look better than knocking him off. Killings are not good business any more."

"Like Ikky Rossen."

"That's not a killing. It's an execution. Ikky got out of line."

"So your gun boys had to rub the wrong guy. They could have hung around a little to make sure."

"They would have, if you'd kept your nose where it belonged. They hurried. We don't appreciate that. We want cool efficiency."

"Who's this great big fat 'we' you keep talking about?"

"Don't go juvenile on me, Marlowe."

"Okay. Let's say I know."

"Here's what we want. He reached into his pocket and drew out a loose bill. He put it on the desk on his side. "Find Ikky and tell him to get back in line and everything is okay. With an innocent bystander gunned, we don't want any trouble or any extra publicity. It's that simple. You get this now," he nodded at the bill. It was a grand. Probably the smallest bill they had. "And another when you find Ikky and give him the message. If he holds out—curtains."

"Suppose I say take your grand and blow your nose with it?"

"That would be unwise." He flipped out a Colt Woodsman with a short silencer on it. A Colt Woodsman will take one without jamming. He was fast too, fast and smooth. The genial expression on his face didn't change.

"I never left Vegas," he said calmly. "I can prove it. You're dead in your office chair and nobody knows anything. Just another private eye that tried the wrong pitch. Put your hands on the desk and think a little. Incidentally, I'm a crack shot even with this damned silencer."

I flipped the nicely sharpened pencil across to him. He grabbed for it after a swift change of the gun to his left hand—very swift. He held the pencil up so that he could look at it without taking his eyes off me.

I said, "It came to me by Special Delivery mail. No message, no return address. Just the pencil. Think I've never heard about the pencil, Mr. Grimes?"

He frowned and tossed the pencil down. Before he could shift his long lithe gun back to his right hand I dropped mine under the desk and grabbed the butt of the .45 and put my finger hard on the trigger.

"Look under the desk, Mr. Grimes. You'll see a .45 in an openend holster. It's fixed there and it's pointing at your belly. Even if you could shoot me through the heart, the .45 would still go off from a convulsive movement of my hand. And your belly would be hanging by a shred and you would be knocked out of that chair. A .45 slug can throw you back six feet. Even the movies learned that at last."

"Looks like a Mexican stand-off," he said quietly. He holstered his gun. He grinned. "Nice work, Marlowe. We could use a man like you. I suggest that you find Ikky and don't be a drip. He'll listen to reason. He doesn't really want to be on the run for the rest of his life."

"Tell me something, Mr. Grimes. Why pick on me? Apart from Ikky, what did I ever do to make you dislike me?"

Not moving, he thought a moment, or pretended to. "The Larsen case. You helped send one of our boys to the gas chamber. That we don't forget. We had you in mind as a fall guy for Ikky. You'll aways be a fall guy, unless you play it our way. Something will hit you when you least expect it."

"A man in my business is always a fall guy, Mr. Grimes. Pick up your grand and drift out quietly. I might decide to do it your way, but I have to think about it. As for the Larsen case, the cops did all the work. I just happened to know where he was. I don't guess you miss him terribly."

"We don't like interference." He stood up. He put the grand note casually back in his pocket. While he was doing it I let go of the .45 and jerked out my Smith and Wesson five-inch .38.

He looked at it contemptuously. "I'll be in Vegas, Marlowe—in fact, I never left Vegas. You can catch me at the Esperanza. No, we don't give a damn about Larsen personally. Just another gun handler. They come in gross lots. We *do* give a damn that some punk private eye fingered him."

He nodded and went out by my office door.

I did some pondering. I knew Ikky wouldn't go back to the Outfit. He wouldn't trust them enough even if he got the chance. But there was another reason now. I called Anne Riordan again.

"I'm going to look for Ikky. I have to. If I don't call you in three days, get hold of Bernie Ohls. I'm going to Flagstaff, Arizona. Ikky says he will be there."

"You're a fool," she wailed. "It's some sort of trap."

"A Mr. Grimes of Vegas visited me with a silenced gun. I beat him to the punch, but I won't always be that lucky. If I find Ikky and report to Grimes, the mob will let me alone."

"You'd condemn a man to death?" Her voice was sharp and incredulous.

"No. He won't be there when I report. He'll have to hop a plane to Montreal, buy forged papers, and plane to Europe. He may be fairly safe there. But the Outfit has long arms and Ikky won't have a dull life staying alive. He hasn't any choice. For him it's either hide or get the pencil."

"So clever of you, darling. What about your own pencil?"

"If they meant it, they wouldn't have sent it. Just a bit of scare technique."

"And you don't scare, you wonderful handsome brute."

"I scare. But it doesn't paralyze me. So long. Don't take any lovers until I get back."

"Damn you, Marlowe!"

284

She hung up on me. I hung up on myself.

Saying the wrong thing is one of my specialties.

I beat it out of town before the homicide boys could hear about me. It would take them quite a while to get a lead. And Bernie Ohls wouldn't give a city dick a used paper bag. The Sheriff's men and the City Police cooperate about as much as two tomcats on a fence.

I made Phoenix by evening and parked myself in a motor court on the outskirts. Phoenix was damned hot. The motor court had a dining room, so I had dinner. I collected some quarters and dimes from the cashier and shut myself in a phone booth and started to call the Mirador in Flagstaff.

How silly could I get? Ikky might be registered under any name from Cohen to Cordileone, from Watson to Woichehovski. I called anyway and got nothing but as much of a smile as you can get on the phone.

So I asked for a room the following night. Not a chance unless someone checked out, but they would put me down for a cancellation or something. Flagstaff is too near the Grand Canyon. Ikky must have arranged in advance. That was something to ponder too.

I bought a paperback and read it. I set my alarm watch for 6:30. The paperback scared me so badly that I put two guns under my pillow. It was about a guy who bucked the hoodlum boss of Milwaukee and got beaten up every fifteen minutes. I figured that his head and face would be nothing but a piece of bone with a strip of skin hanging from it. But in the next chapter he was as gay as a meadow lark.

Then I asked myself why I was reading this drivel when I could have been memorizing *The Brothers Karamazov*. Not knowing any good answers, I turned the light out and went to sleep.

At 6:30 I shaved, showered, had breakfast, and took off for Flagstaff. I got there by lunchtime, and there was Ikky in the restaurant eating mountain trout. I sat down across from him. He looked surprised to see me.

I ordered mountain trout and ate it from the outside in, which is the proper way. Boning spoils it a little.

"What gives?" he asked me with his mouth full. A delicate eater.

"You read the papers?"

"Just the sports section."

"Let's go to your room and talk about it."

We paid for our lunches and went along to a nice double. The motor courts are getting so good that they make a lot of hotels look cheap. We sat down and lit cigarettes.

"The two hoods got up too early and went over to Poynter Street. They parked outside your apartment house. They hadn't been briefed carefully enough. They shot a guy who looked a little like you."

"That's a hot one," he grinned. "But the cops will find out, and the Outfit will find out. So the tag for me stays on."

"You must think I'm dumb," I said. 'I am."

"I thought you did a first-class job, Marlowe. What's dumb about that?"

"What job did I do?"

"You got me out of there pretty slick."

"Anything about it you couldn't have done yourself?"

"With luck—no. But it's nice to have a helper."

"You mean sucker."

His face tightened. And his rusty voice growled. "I don't catch. And give me back some of that five grand, will you? I'm shorter than I thought."

"I'll give it back to you when you find a hummingbird in a salt shaker."

"Don't be like that." He almost sighed, and flicked a gun into his hand. I didn't have a flick. I was holding one in my side pocket.

"I oughtn't to have boobed off," I said. "Put the heater away. It doesn't pay any more than a Vegas slot machine."

"Wrong. Them machines pay the jackpot every so often. Otherwise—no customers."

"Every so seldom, you mean. Listen, and listen good."

He grinned. His dentist was tired waiting for him.

"The set-up intrigued me," I went on, debonair as Philo Vance in an S.S. Van Dine story and a lot brighter in the head. "First off, could it be done? Second, if it could be done, where would I be? But gradually I saw the little touches that flawed the picture. Why would you come to me at all? The Outfit isn't naive. Why would they send a little punk like this Charles Hickon or whatever name he uses on Thursdays? Why would an old hand like you let anybody trail you to a dangerous connection?"

"You slay me, Marlowe. You're so bright I could find you in the dark. You're so dumb you couldn't see a red, white, and blue giraffe. I bet you were back there in your unbrain emporium playing with that five grand like a cat with a bag of catnip. I bet you were kissing the notes."

"Not after you handled them. Then why the pencil that was sent to me? Big dangerous threat. It reinforced the rest. But like I told your choir boy from Vegas, they don't send them when they mean them. By the way, he had a gun too. A Woodsman .22 with a silencer. I had to make him put it away. He was nice about that. He started waving grands at me to find out where you were and tell him. A well-dressed, nice-looking front man for a pack of dirty rats. The Women's Christian Temperance Association and some bootlicking politicans gave them the money to be big, and they learned how to use it and make it grow. Now they're pretty well unstoppable. But they're still a pack of dirty rats. And they're always where they can't make a mistake. That's inhuman. Any man has a right to a few mistakes. Not the rats. They have to be perfect all the time. Or else they get stuck with *you*."

"I don't know what the hell you're talking about. I just know it's too long."

"Well, allow me to put it in English. Some poor jerk from the East Side gets involved with the lower echelons of a mob. You know what an echelon is, Ikky?"

"I been in the Army," he sneered.

"He grows up in the mob, but he's not all rotten. He's not rotten enough. So he tries to break loose. He comes out here and gets himself a cheap job of some sort and changes his name or names and lives quietly in a cheap apartment house. But the mob by now has agents in many places. Somebody spots him and recognizes him. It might be a pusher, a front man for a bookie joint, a night girl. So the mob, or call them the Outfit, say through their cigar smoke: 'Ikky can't do this to us. It's a small operation because he's small. But it annoys us. Bad for discipline. Call a couple of boys and have them pencil him.' But what boys do they call? A couple they're tired of. Been around too long. Might make a mistake or get chilly toes. Perhaps they like killing. That's bad too. That makes for recklessness. The best boys are the ones that don't care either way. So although they don't know it, the boys they call are on their way out. But it would be kind of cute to frame a guy they already don't like, for fingering a hood named Larsen. One of these puny little jokes the Outfit takes big. 'Look, guys, we even got time to play footsie with a private eye.' So they send a ringer."

"The Torrence brothers ain't ringers. They're real hard boys. They proved it—even if they did make a mistake."

"Mistake nothing. They got Ikky Rossen. You're just a singing commercial in this deal. And as of now you're under arrest for murder. You're worse off than that. The Outfit will habeas corpus you out of the clink and blow you down. You've served your purpose and you failed to finger me into a patsy."

His finger tightened on the trigger. I shot the gun out of his hand. The gun in my coat pocket was small, but at that distance accurate. And it was one of my days to be accurate.

He made a faint moaning sound and sucked at his hand. I went over and kicked him hard in the chest. Being nice to killers is not part of my repertoire. He went over backward and stumbled four or five steps. I picked up his gun and held it on him while I tapped all the places—not just pockets or holsters—where a man could stash a second gun. He was clean—that way anyhow.

"What are you trying to do to me?" he whined. "I paid you. You're clear. I paid you damn well."

"We both have problems there. Your's is to stay alive." I took a pair of cuffs out of my pocket and wrestled his hands behind him and snapped them on. His hand was bleeding. I tied his show handkerchief around it and then went to the telephone and called the police.

I had to stick around for a few days, but I didn't mind that as long as I could have trout caught eight or nine thousand feet up. I called Annie and Bernie Ohls. I called my answering service. The Arizona D.A. was a young keen-eyed man and the Chief of Police was one of the biggest men I ever saw.

I got back to L.A. in time and took Anne to Romanoff's for dinner and champagne.

"What I can't see," she said over a third glass of bubbly, "is why they dragged you into it, why they set up the fake Ikky Rossen. Why didn't they just let the two lifetakers do their job?"

"I couldn't really say. Unless the big boys feel so safe they're developing a sense of humor. And unless this Larsen guy who went to the gas chamber was bigger than he seemed to be. Only three or four important mobsters have made the electric chair or the rope or the gas chamber. None that I know of in the life-imprisonment states like Michigan. If Larsen was bigger than anyone thought, they might have had my name on a waiting list."

"But why wait?" she asked me. "They'd go after you quickly."

"They can afford to wait. Who's going to bother them? Except when they make a mistake."

"Income tax rap?"

"Yeah, like Capone. Capone may have had several hundred men killed, and killed a few of them himself, personally. But it took the Internal Revenue boys to get him. But the Outfit won't make that mistake often."

"What I like about you, apart from your enormous personal charm, is that when you don't know an answer you make one up."

"The money worries me," I said. "Five grand of their dirty money. What do I do with it?"

"Don't be a jerk all your life. You earned the money and you risked your life for it. You can buy Series E Bonds—they'll make the money clean. And to me that would be part of the joke."

"*You* tell *me* one good sound reason why they pulled the switch."

"You have more of a reputation than you realize. And suppose it was the false Ikky who pulled the switch? He sounds like one of these over-clever types that can't do anything simple."

"The Outfit will get him for making his own plans—if you're right."

"If the D.A. doesn't. And I couldn't care less about what happens to him. More champagne, please."

They extradited "Ikky" and he broke under pressure and named the two gunmen—after I had already named them, the Torrence brothers. But nobody could find them. They never went home. And you can't prove conspiracy on one man. The law couldn't even get him for accessory after the fact. They couldn't prove he knew the real Ikky had been gunned.

They could have got him for some trifle, but they had a better idea. They left him to his friends. They just turned him loose.

Where is he now? My hunch says nowhere.

Anne Riordan was glad it was all over and I was safe. Safe—that isn't a word you use in my trade.

THE PROVERBIAL MURDER

BY JOHN DICKSON CARR

John Dickson Carr, the popular writer of mysteries in the literate English tradition under his own name as well as the pseudonyms Carter Dickson and Carr Dickson, was born in Uniontown, Pennsylvania, on November 30, 1906. His earliest heroes were Sherlock Holmes, d'Artagnan and the Wizard of Oz. He lived in England from 1931 to 1948 and collaborated with Adrian Conan Doyle on *The Life of Sir Arthur Conan Doyle*. His works stress the intellectual and puzzle elements in the solution of crime and they often have a historical setting.

THE TIMBERED COTTAGE, which belonged to Herr Dr. Ludwig Meyer and which was receiving attention from the man with the field-glasses, stood some distance down in the valley.

In clear moonlight, the valley was washed clean of color except at one point, where a light showed in a window to the right of Dr. Meyer's door. It was a diamond-paned window with two leaves, now closed. The lamplight streamed out through it, touching grass and rose-beds.

At a desk beside the window, Dr. Meyer sat at his endless writing. "A Dissertation on the Theory of the Atom," was its official title. The white cretonne curtains of the window were not drawn. From this angle the watchers had an awkward, sideways view of him.

Some quarter of a mile away, on the edge of the hill, the man with the field-glasses lay flat on his face. His back ached and his arms felt cramped. Momentarily he lowered the glasses and peered round.

"S-ss-t!" he whispered. "What are you doing? Don't light a cigarette!"

His companion's voice sounded aggrieved. "Why not? Nobody can see it up here."

"It's orders, that's all."

"And, anyway," grumbled the other, "it's two o'clock in the morning. Our bloke's not coming tonight: that's certain. Unless he's already gone in by the back door?"

"Lewes is covering the back door and the other side. Listen!"

He held up his hand. Nothing stirred in the valley. There was no noise except, far away, the faint drag and thunder of the surf at Lynmouth.

It was mellow September weather, yet the man with the field-glasses, Detective-Inspector Ballard, of the Special Branch attached to the Metropolitan Police, felt an unaccountable shiver. Lifting the glasses again, he raked the path leading up to the cottage. He looked at the lighted window. Beyond the edge of a cretonne curtain, he could just make out a part of the bony profile, the thick spectacles, the fishlike movements of the mouth, as Dr. Meyer filled page after page of neat handwriting.

"If you ask me," grumbled Sergeant Buck, "the A.C.'s barking up the wrong tree this time. This Meyer is a distinguished scientist—a real refugee—"

"No."

"But where's your evidence?"

"In cases of this kind," returned Ballard, lowering the glasses to rub his aching eyes, "you can't afford to go by the rules of legal evidence. The A.C. isn't sure; but he thinks the tip-off came from Meyer's wife."

Sergeant Buck whistled.

"A good German hausfrau tip off the English?"

"That's just it. She's not German: she's English. There are some very funny things going on in this country at the moment, my lad. If we can nab the man who's coming to see Meyer tonight, we'll catch somebody high up. We can—"

"Listen!" said Buck.

It was unnecessary to ask anyone to listen. The report of the firearm crashed and rolled in that little valley. It was an illusion, but Ballard almost imagined he could hear the wiry *whing* of the bullet.

Both men jumped to their feet. Ballard, his knee-joints painful from their cramped position, whisked up the glasses again and scanned the front of the cottage. His gaze came to rest on the window.

"Poachers?" suggested Buck.

"That was no poacher," said Inspector Ballard. "That was an Army rifle. And it didn't miss either. Come on!"

The pigmy picture rose in his mind as he scrambled down the hill: the flutter of the cretonne curtain, the bald head fallen forward across the desk. Neither he nor Buck made any effort at concealment. The echoes hardly seemed to have settled in the valley when they arrived in front of the house. Holding his companion back, Ballard pointed.

The lighted window was not far up from the ground. First of all Ballard noticed the bullet-hole in the glass, close to the lead joining of one of the diamond-panes. It was a neatly drilled hole, with hardly any starring of the glass, such as is made by a smallish, high-velocity riflebullet (say a .256) fired from some distance away.

Then they both saw what was inside, lying limply across the desk with a mark on the left temple; and they both hurried for the front door.

The door-knocker was stiff and rusty, giving only a padded sound which Ballard had to supplement by banging his fist on the door. It seemed interminable minutes before the bar was drawn back on the inside, and the door opened.

A white-faced woman, carrying a paraffin lamp and with a dressing-gown hastily pulled round her, peered out at them. She was perhaps thirty-five, some ten or fifteen years younger than Ludwig Meyer. Though not pretty, she was attractive in a pink-and-white fashion; blue-eyed, with heavy, rich-brushed fair hair over her shoulders.

"Mrs. Meyer?"

"Yes?" She moistened her lips.

"We're police officers, ma'am. I'm afraid something has happened to your husband."

Slowly Harriet Meyer held up the lamp. Just as slowly, she turned round and looked towards the door of the room on the right of the hall. The lamp wabbled in her hand, its golden light spilling and breaking among shadows.

"I—I heard it," she said. "I wondered."

Gritting her teeth, she turned round and walked towards the door of that room. With a word of apology Ballard brushed past her.

"Well," said Sergeant Buck, after a pause, "there's nothing we can do for *him*, sir."

There was not. They stood in a long, low-ceilinged room, its walls lined with improvised bookshelves. The smell of burning oil from the lamp on the desk by the window competed with a fog of rank tobacco-smoke. A long china-bowled pipe lay on the desk near the dead man's hand. The fountain pen had slipped from his fingers. His face and shoulders lay against the paper-strewn desk; but, as the creaking of their footsteps jarred the floor, he slowly slid off and fell with an unnerving thump on his side. It was a grotesque mimicry of life which made Harriet Meyer cry out.

"Steady, ma'am," said Ballard.

Circling the body, he went to the window and tried to peer out. But in the dazzle between lamp and moonlight he could see nothing. The bullet-hole in the glass, he noted, had tiny splinters—the little shell-shaped grooves on the edge of the opening—which showed that the bullet had been fired from outside.

Inspector Ballard drew a deep breath and turned round.

"Tell us about it, ma'am," he said.

Late on the following afternoon, Colonel Penderel sat in a

wicker chair on the lawn before The Red Lodge, and looked gloomily at his shoes.

Everything about Red Lodge, like Colonel Penderel himself, was of a brushed trimness. The lawn was of that smooth green which seems to have lighter stripes in it; the house, of mellow red brick under mellow September sunshine, opened friendly doors to all the world.

But Hubert Penderell, a long lean man with big shoes, and wiry wintry-looking hair like his cropped moustache, slouched down in the chair. He clenched his big-knuckled fist, stared at it, and brought it down on the arm of the chair. Then he glanced round—and stopped guiltily as he caught sight of a brown-haired girl in a sleeveless white tennis-frock, who had just come round the side of the house with a tennis racket under her arm.

The girl did not hesitate. She studied him for a moment, out of blue eyes wide-spaced above a short straight nose. A colored silk scarf was tied round her head. Then she marched across the lawn, swinging the tennis racket as though she were going to hit somebody with it.

"Daddy," she said abruptly, "what on earth *is* it?"

Colonel Penderel said nothing.

"There *is* something," she insisted. "There has been, ever since that police-superintendent came here this morning. What is it? Have you been getting into trouble with your car again?"

Colonel Penderel raised his head.

"Professor Meyer's been shot," he answered with equal abruptness. "Somebody plugged him through the window last night with a .303 service-rifle.—Nancy, how would you like to see your old man arrested for murder?"

He had tried to say the last words whimsically. But he was not a very good actor, and his conception of the whimsical was somewhat heavy-handed.

Nancy Penderel backed away.

"What on earth are you talking about?"

"Fact," said the Colonel, giving a slight flick to his shoulders. He peered round the lawn, hunching up his shoulders. "That superintendent (Willet, his name is) wanted to know if I owned a rifle. I said yes: the one we all used to shoot with, on our own range. He said, where was it kept? I said, in the garden-shed. He said, could he see it? I said, certainly."

Nancy was having difficulty in adjusting her wits to this.

"He said, can I borrow this?" the Colonel concluded, hunching up his shoulders still further, and avoiding her eye. "He took it away with him. It can't be the rifle that killed Meyer. But if by any chance it should happen to be—?"

"Dr. Meyer?" Nancy breathed. "Dr. Meyer *dead?*"

Colonel Penderel jumped to his feet.

"I didn't like the blighter." His tone was querulous. "Everybody knows it. We had a rare old row only three days ago. Not because he was a German, mind. After all, I've got a German staying here as my guest, haven't I? But—well, there it is. And another thing. That garden-shed has a Yale lock. *I've* got the only key."

There was another wicker chair near her father's. Nancy groped across to it, and sat down.

She felt no sense of danger or tragedy. It was merely that she could not understand. It was as though, in the midst of a dinner, the cloth were suddenly twitched off and all the dishes with their contents overturned.

It was a pleasant afternoon. She had just finished playing three sets of tennis with Carl Kuhn. There couldn't, she assured herself, be anything really wrong: nothing that could blacken the daylight or spoil her week. Yet she watched her father tramping up and down the lawn, in his old chequered brown-and-black sports coat, more disturbed than she had ever seen him.

"But it's absurd!" Nancy cried. "We can't take it seriously. Everybody knows you. The local police know you."

"Ah," said Colonel Penderel. "Yes. The local police know me. But the fellows who've taken this over aren't local. They're down here from Scotland Yard."

"Scotland Yard?"

"Special Branch. Look here, mouse." He approached closer, and lowered his voice. "Keep this under your hat. Don't mention it to your mother, whatever you do. But this fellow Meyer *was* a wrong 'un. A spy."

"Impossible! That doddery little man?"

"Fact. Willet wouldn't say much, naturally. But I did gather they've got the goods on him, and his papers prove it. Damn it, you can't trust anybody nowadays, can you?"

Colonel Penderel's face darkened. He rubbed his hands together with a dry, rustling sound.

"If that's what he was—I say, good luck to the man who plugged him! But I didn't do it. Can you imagine me sneaking up on a man (that's what worries me, mouse) and letting drive at him when he wasn't looking?"

295

"No, of course not." Nancy was beginning to reflect. "If anybody killed him, I'm betting it was that simpering blonde wife of his."

"Harriet Meyer? Great Scott, no!"

"Why not? She's fifteen years younger than he is. And they live all alone in that house, without even a maid to help with the work."

Colonel Penderel was honest enough not to pursue this. He shook his head.

"There are reasons why not, mouse. Which you might understand, or you might not. . . ."

"Daddy, stop treating me like a child! Why couldn't she have done it?"

"First, because the bullet that killed Meyer came from outside. Second, because there were Special Branch men watching every side of the house, and nobody went out or in at any time—certainly not Harriet Meyer. Third, they made an immediate search of the house, and there was no weapon in it except an old 16-bore shotgun which couldn't possibly have fired a rifle-bullet."

"S-ss-t!" said Nancy warningly.

Colonel Penderel whirled round.

The latch of the front gate was being lifted. Detective-Inspector Ballard, nondescript and fortyish, might have been any businessman; but to the two watchers he had policeman written all over him. He came up the brick path smiling pleasantly, and raised his hat.

And, at the same time, Carl Kuhn strolled out of the open front door.

Carl Kuhn, in his late twenties, was one of these teutonic types which seem all the more Nordic for being dark instead of fair. He was a middle-sized, stockily built, amiable young man with a ruddy complexion and a vast fund of chuckles. His heavy black hair grew low on his forehead; a narrow moustache followed the line of his wide mouth. Wearing white flannels, a sports coat, and a silk scarf, he came sauntering across the lawn to put his hands on the back of Nancy's chair.

But nobody looked at him.

"Good afternoon," Ballard said pleasantly. "Colonel Penderel," said the owner of that name, looking very hard at him. "This is my daughter. And Mr. Kuhn."

Ballard gave them a brief glance.

296

"Colonel Penderel, I am a police-officer investigating the murder of Dr. Ludwig Meyer," continued Ballard; and Kuhn, who had started to light a cigarette, flicked up his head and blew two jets of smoke through his nostrils like an amiable dragon. "I wonder if I could have a word with you in private, sir?"

"Say it," said the Colonel.

"Pardon?"

"If you've got anything to say to me," pursued the Colonel, sitting down deliberately and taking tight hold of the arms of the chair, "say it. Here. Now. In front of these people."

"You're sure that's what you'd prefer, sir?"

Ballard's own deliberate gaze moved round the group. He took a notebook out of his pocket.

"Well, sir, you own a rifle. This morning you loaned that rifle to Superintendent Willet."

"Yes?"

"Certain tests," said Ballard, "were made with this .303 rifle by the ballistics-consultant to the Devonshire County Constabulary." He looked at his notebook. " 'Number of grooves: five and a half. Direction of twist: right-hand. Individual markings—' Never mind the technicalities, though." His manner remained expressionless, almost kindly. "The fact is, sir, that the bullet which killed Dr. Meyer was fired from your rifle."

From behind the house came the drowsy whir of a lawn-mower.

Not even yet had Nancy Penderel a full sense of danger or even death. The sheer incredibility of the thing flooded her mind. She thought of the garden-shed by the tennis-court; and of the miniature rifle-range, sandbags backed by sheet-iron, which her father had constructed at the end of the meadow.

"I see," observed Colonel Penderel. His manner was stiff and impassive. He lifted one hand as though to whack it down on the arm of the chair, but he lowered it gently instead. "Someone stole it, then. Or—am I by any chance under arrest?"

Ballard smiled, though his eyes did not move.

"Hardly that, sir. All we know is that your rifle *was* used."

Throughout this, Carl Kuhn had been shifting from one foot to the other as though in a hopping agony of indecision. He took short, quick puffs at his cigarette.

"You are not saying," he exploded, in English not far from perfect, "that this man Meyer was shot yesterday afternoon?"

Ballard glanced at him quickly.

"Yesterday afternoon? What makes you say that?"

"Because," returned Kuhn, "yesterday afternoon I took a walk in the direction of that house. It is not more than a quarter of a mile from here. And I heard a rifle-shot. I looked over the edge of the hill, and saw this Meyer standing in front of the house. He seemed very angry. But he was not dead then. No, no, no!"

He illustrated this story by cupping his hands over his eyes, and other elaborate gestures. Ballard stared at him.

"But what did you do, sir? Didn't you go closer to see what had happened?"

"No."

"Why not?"

"His blood," said Kuhn, holding himself very stiffly, "was not my blood. His race was not my race. I would have nothing to do with him. But there!" Kuhn's tension relaxed, and he smiled. "Not to talk politics in this house we have agreed. Is it not so, Colonel Penderel?"

"Yes, it's so," admitted the Colonel, shifting. "I didn't care anything about the fellow's race or politics. I just didn't like him." He eyed Ballard. "I suppose you've heard all about that?"

Ballard was silent for a moment.

"Knowledge hereabouts is pretty general, sir. Is it true that on Tuesday you threatened to kill him?"

The Colonel went rather white.

"I threatened to wring his neck, if that's what you mean?"

"Why?"

"I didn't like his manners. He browbeat the tradespeople and threw his weight about wherever he went. He was supposed to have come out of Germany penniless, but he had everything he wanted. At a garden-party here on Tuesday—when my wife was trying to conciliate him—he said calmly that the English had no taste, no education, no manners, and no knowledge of science."

"Ach, so?" murmured Kuhn.

"I didn't say anything at the time. I just walked part of the way home with him, and told him a few things. There was a hell of a row, yes."

"Oh, this is absurd!" Nancy protested; but Ballard very gently and persuasively silenced her.

"Dr. Meyer," Ballard said without comment, "was shot at about two o'clock in the morning, with a rifle taken from the garden-shed here. . . . "

"Which was locked," said the Colonel stonily, "and to which I've got the only key."

"Daddy!" cried Nancy.

"And," persisted the Colonel, "at two o'clock in the morning I was asleep. I don't sleep in the same room as my wife; and I can't produce an alibi. Furthermore, the rifle *was* in that shed as late as nine o'clock in the evening; I know, because I put away the garden-sprinkler then. The window won't open and there's no way into the shed except by the door. Now you know everything. But I didn't kill Meyer."

Ballard was about to speak when there was an interruption.

Round the side of the house, at a blundering and near-sighted gait, lumbered a twenty-stone man in a white linen suit. He wore eyeglasses on a broad black ribbon, carried a crutch-handled stick, and seemed to be muttering down the slope of his several chins.

Colonel Penderel jumped up.

"Fell!" he shouted, "Gideon Fell! What in the name of sanity are you doing here?"

Dr. Fell woke up. He beamed all over his face like Old King Cole. He swept off his broad-brimmed white hat and ducked them a sort of bow. Then, wheezing gently after the exertion of this, he scowled.

"I trust," he said, "you will forgive my informal entrance by way of the back garden. I was—ahem—examining your miniature rifle-range."

Inspector Ballard intervened quickly.

"You're acquainted with Dr. Fell, Colonel?"

"Lord, yes! One of my oldest. . . . Here, sit down! Have a drink. Have something. You don't happen to have heard what's going on here, do you?"

Dr. Fell seemed uncomfortable.

"Not to put too fine a point on it," he answered, "yes. I came down here to discuss a point of practical science, the use of thermite in a safe-breaking case, with Dr. Meyer. My second visit. I find him—" He spread out his hand, widening the fingers. "Sir Herbert Armstrong wired to ask if I would—um—lend a little consulting assistance."

"Glad of any help, sir," smiled Ballard.

"Not as glad as I am," said the Colonel. "You see, Fell, they think I did it."

"Nonsense!" roared Dr. Fell.

"Well, what do *you* think?"

A mulish expression overspread Dr. Fell's face.

"Proverbs," he said. "Proverbs! I don't know. Before I express my opinion, there are two things about which I must have some information. I must know all about the wildcat and the moss."

They stared at him.

"The what, sir?" demanded Inspector Ballard.

"The wildcat," said Dr. Fell, "and the moss."

Grunting acceptance of the chair which Colonel Penderel set out for him, he lowered his vast bulk into it. He got out a red bandanna handkerchief and mopped his face.

"When I last visited Dr. Meyer," he went on, "I noticed on the mantelpiece in his study a big figure of a stuffed wildcat."

"That's right," agreed the Colonel.

"But when I went there today, the wildcat was gone. I asked Mrs. Meyer about this, and she informed me that three days ago he took the stuffed wildcat out into the garden and burned it."

"Burned it? Why should he do that?"

"Precisely," said Dr. Fell, flourishing the handkerchief, "the shrewd, crafty question I asked myself. Why? Then there is the question of the moss. Somebody has been pulling up large quantities of moss from the vicinity of that house."

It was Nancy Penderel's first sight of the man about whom she had heard so much from her father. Her first impulse, on seeing Dr. Fell, was to laugh. She looked again, and was not so sure.

"Mark you," the doctor went on suddenly, "it was always *dry* moss. Very dry moss. The picker would have no traffic with anything damp. Archons of Athens! If only—"

He shook his head, sunk deep in mazy meditations. Inspector Ballard hesitated.

"Are you sure either of those two things has any bearing on the matter, sir?"

"Not at all. But we must look for some clue or retire to Bedlam. My first thought, of course, was that the stuffed wildcat might have been used as a kind of safe: a receptacle for papers. Since our evidence proves that Dr. Meyer was a Germany espionage-agent. . . ."

"S-ss-t!" warned Inspector Ballard.

But Dr. Fell merely blinked at him.

"My good sir,"—he spoke with some testiness,—"you can't keep it dark. Everybody in North Devon knows about it. At the pub, where I had the pleasure of lowering several pints before

300

coming on here, the talk was of nothing else. Somebody has been industriously spreading it."

He looked thoughtful.

"But observe! Dr. Meyer burns the safe, but leaves the papers. A version (I suppose) of locking the stable door after the horse is stolen. And a rolling stone gathers no moss. And—" He blinked at Carl Kuhn. "You, sir. You are the other German I've heard so much about?"

Kuhn had been shifting excitedly from one foot to the other. His color was higher. His surprise seemed deep and genuine. Once he made a gesture like one who removes an invisible hat and stands to attention.

"At your service, Doctor," he said.

Dr. Fell scowled. "You're not providing us with still another proverb, I hope?"

"Another proverb?"

"That birds of a feather flock together?"

Kuhn was very serious. "No. I regret what has happened. I deeply regret it. But—do not judge too harshly. Such tasks are often glorious. I misjudged him."

Colonel Penderel stared at him. So did Nancy. She had a confused idea that her ordered world was crumpling around her.

"Glorious!" she repeated. "That little worm was a spy, doing heaven knows what, and you say 'such things are often glorious?' "

Kuhn's color was still higher.

"Perhaps I express myself badly in English."

"No, you don't, either! You've spent half your life in England. I've known you since you were ten years old. You're more English than German anyway."

"I regret, no," said Kuhn. "I *am* a German." He drew himself up, but his anxious eyes regarded first Nancy and then the Colonel. "This does not interfere with our long friendship?"

"Hanged if I know *what* it does," muttered Colonel Penderel, after a pause. "It seems to me we've got a parable here instead of a proverb; but never mind. What I do know is that we're in an unholy mess." He frowned. "You didn't happen to kill Meyer yourself, did you?"

"Is it likely?" Kuhn asked simply.

"Don't you think," said Nancy, "you've got rather a nerve?"

"Little one, you do not understand!" Kuhn seemed in agony. "Ach, now, let us forget this! It is no business of ours. Instead

301

they should inquire who was firing at Herr Meyer yesterday afternoon—"

Dr. Fell spoke in such a sharp voice that they all swung round.

"What's that? Who was firing at him yesterday afternoon?"

Kuhn repeated his story. As he did so, Inspector Ballard's expression was one of growing suspicion; but Dr. Fell, with a sort of half-witted enlightenment dawning in his eyes, merely shaded those eyes with his hand.

"How did you happen to be there, Mr. Kuhn?" asked Ballard.

"I was going for a walk. That is all."

"In the direction of Professor Meyer's house?"

"No, no, that was quite by chance. Man must go somewhere when he walks."

"A point," observed Dr. Fell, "which is sometimes open to dispute. And last night?"

"Now that is very odd." Suddenly Kuhn knocked his knuckles against his forehead. "I had forgotten. Excuse. You say that Herr Meyer was shot at two o'clock in the morning?"

"Yes."

"Towser!" said Kuhn with powerful relief. "The dog! He was restless! He kept barking!"

"That's true," breathed Nancy.

"So! Listen to me. I was disturbed. I could not sleep. Finally I rise to my feet and put my head out of the window. I saw McCabe, the gardener, going along the path in his dressing-gown. I called and asked if he could quiet the dog, and he said he was going to do it. The stable-clock, I heard, was just striking two."

There was a silence. Kuhn's anxious eyes turned towards the Inspector.

"I see," said Ballard, making a note. "Alibi, eh?"

"If you wish to call it so, yes. The man McCabe will tell you what I say is true. It was bright moonlight: I saw him and he saw me."

"Inspector," remarked Dr. Fell, without taking his hand away from his eyes, "I think you'd better accept that."

"Accept the alibi?"

"Yes," said Dr. Fell. With infinite labor he propelled himself to his feet on his crutch-handled stick. "Because it isn't necessary. I know how Professor Meyer really died. As a matter of fact, you told me."

"*I* told you?" repeated Ballard.

"And if you'd care to come with me to the house," pursued Dr.

Fell, "I think I can show you." He looked curiously at Colonel Penderel. "If I remember correctly, my lad, you used to be something of an authority on firearms. You'd better come along too."

"Is the answer," asked Colonel Penderel, "as easy as that?"

"The answer," said Dr. Fell, "*is* another proverb."

In late afternoon light, the timbered cottage in the valley stood deserted and rather sinister. The bullet-hole in the diamond-paned glass looked itself like a scar on a body.

Repeated knockings on the door roused nobody. Dr. Fell tried the knob, and found that it was open. He beckoned Inspector Ballard inside for a short whispered conference, after which the Inspector disappeared. Then Dr. Fell, his face very red, invited the other three in.

Colonel Penderel walked in boldly. Nancy and Carl Kuhn followed with more hesitation. The German was obviously upset, and muttered something to himself as he crossed the threshold.

In the long, low-ceilinged study there was still a smell of stale tobacco-smoke. Ludwig Meyer's body had been removed. Of his murder there now remained no trace except a spot of brown, dried blood on the papers which littered his desk. They were the sheets of his latest scientific treatise, which he would not now complete.

Dr. Fell, his underlip drawn up over his bandit's moustache, stood in the doorway. His eyes moved left towards the mantelpiece in the narrower wall of the oblong, and right towards the window in the wall facing it. He lumbered across to the desk, where he turned round.

"Here," he said, tapping the desk, "is where Meyer was sitting. Here,"—he picked up a few sheets of manuscript, and dropped them,—"is Meyer's last book. Here,"—he drew open a drawer of the desk,—"was the evidence which proved, so very obviously, that Meyer was an espionage-agent. By thunder, but wasn't it obvious!"

He closed the drawer with a bang. Only the sun entered. The bang of the drawer shook and disturbed dust-motes against the sunlight. Dr. Fell reached across and fingered the cretonne curtain. It was very warm in here, so warm that Nancy Penderel's head swam.

"I have a particular question to ask," continued Dr. Fell. He

303

looked at the Colonel. "Why is everybody so sure that the bullet which killed Meyer was fired from your rifle?"

Colonel Penderel put a hand to his forehead.

"See here, Fell," he began querulously, but checked himself. "It *was* fired from my rifle, wasn't it?"

"Oh, yes. I merely ask the question. Why is everyone so sure of that?"

"Because of the distinctive marks of rifling left on the bullet," returned the other.

"True. Palpably and painfully true. Harrumph. Now, then: you've built a miniature rifle-range in the meadow behind your house, haven't you?"

"You ought to know," retorted the Colonel, regarding him with some exasperation. "You said you'd been looking at it."

"And what do you use to catch the bullets there?"

"Soft sand."

"So that," said Dr. Fell, "the many rounds fired into that sand would be lying about all over the place?"

"Yes."

"Yes. And each bullet, though keeping exactly its original shape, would bear the distinctive marking of your rifle. Wouldn't it?"

The door of the study banged open, making them all jump. Inspector Ballard entered and gave Dr. Fell a significant glance, and nodded.

Dr. Fell drew a deep breath, shutting his eyes for a moment before he went on.

"You see," he said, "this crime is very much more ingenious than it looks. A certain person who is listening to me now has created something of an artistic masterpiece.

"Those bullets, for instance. A bullet, selected for its most distinctive markings, could be fished out of that soft sand. It could easily be fitted into a loaded cartridge-case and fired again. Couldn't it?"

"Not without . . . " Colonel Penderel began, but Dr. Fell stopped him.

"Then there is this question of the window-curtain." The doctor leaned across and flicked it with his thumb and forefinger. But he was not looking at it; he was looking at Inspector Ballard.

"You, Inspector, were watching this house last night with a pair of field-glasses. On the second the shot was fired, you

304

jumped up and focused your glasses on this window. At least, so you told me this morning?"

"Yes, sir. That's right."

"And, when the shot was fired, you saw this curtain flutter. Is that correct too?"

In Ballard's mind the picture returned with sharp clearness of light and shadow. He nodded.

"It is a flat impossibility," said Dr. Fell, "for any shot fired from some distance away outside a closed window to agitate a curtain *inside* that window. There is only one thing which could have caused it: the expansion of gases from the muzzle of a firearm when the shot was fired in this room."

Supporting himself on his stick, he lumbered across to the door, which was an inch or two open. He opened it fully into the little hall.

Just outside, her fingers pressed to her cheeks, stood Harriet Meyer. Her startled expression, with the upper lip slightly lifted to expose the teeth, was caught as though by a camera.

"Come in, Mrs. Meyer," said Dr. Fell. "Will you tell us how you killed your husband, or shall I?"

She struck out at him with a slap like a cat's. When he tried to catch her arm, she backed away swiftly to the other side of the room. There she stood against the bookshelves: her blue eyes as shallow as a doll's, but her breast rising and falling heavily.

Again Dr. Fell drew a weary breath.

"Colonel Penderel," he continued, "will tell you that a .303 bullet can be fired from a 16-bore shotgun, such as the one in this house. When you say it 'can't possibly' be done, you don't really mean that. What you mean is that it can't be fired without leaving traces, and it can't be fired with accuracy.

"But accuracy, at more or less point-blank range, isn't necessary. And there is one way of firing it, out of a smooth-barrelled shotgun, so that it leaves no traces. You'll find that method fully outlined in Gross's *Criminal Investigation*."

Colonel Penderel eyes opened wide, and then narrowed.

"Moss!" he said. "By the Lord Harry, dry moss! I must have been half-witted. Wrap the bullet in dry moss. It doesn't touch the inside of the gun, and no marks are left. The combustion ignites and destroys the moss: so that there's nothing left except a fouled barrel. When I was musketry instructor . . ."

Nancy was pointing wordlessly to the window.

Dr. Fell nodded again.

"Oh, yes," he agreed, contemplating the bullet-hole. "Made yesterday afternoon, as you've guessed. Made by a bullet out of a real rifle, probably a .256. Made, of course, to set the stage.

"While her husband was occupied elsewhere, this lady calculated all angles, stood back some distance, and fired a clean hole through the window—lodging the bullet in a stuffed wildcat on the mantelpiece. If you will just note the line of fire, here, you'll see what happened.

"She could explain to Professor Meyer that she had been practicing, and made a wild shot. We can't blame him for being 'enraged.' But it was an accident. Later she could burn the stuffed figure and hide the rifle outside the house. Then she was ready for real business that night.

"She and her husband lived alone here. There was nobody to notice that inconspicuous hole in the window—until the time came for it to be noticed. There would be (as she had arranged) police-officers round the house, to trap a mythical spyhead who was supposed to be calling on Dr. Meyer. They would not come close until they heard a shot. But when they heard a shot, it would be too late."

Still Harriet Meyer had not spoken. Her eyes, with the poised look of one who cannot decide whether to fight or run, moved round the room.

"She had only," said Dr. Fell, "to walk in here. Meyer would turn round (you note the position of the door) so that his left temple would be exposed. Any after-smell of smokeless powder, which is very slight, would go unnoticed in the fog of rank tobacco-smoke.

"The crime was all outlined for her, of course. In any good German scientist's house you are likely to find a copy of Hans Gross's *System der Kriminalistik*. There's one, I think, in the shelf just over her head now."

They heard Harriet Meyer's fingernails scratch against the books. Two voices spoke almost together.

"Frau Meyer—" began Kuhn.

"But she's English!" cried Nancy.

"Of course she is," said Dr. Fell, and rapped the ferrule of his stick sharply against the floor. "Confound it, don't you realize that's what makes her so dangerous?"

Harriet Meyer threw back her head and laughed.

"Don't you see," thundered Dr. Fell, "that poor old Meyer,

306

objectionable as he was, wasn't a spy at all? That he was just what he pretended to be? That this charming lady here, a convert to what some call the modern ideology, was the real spy?

"The Special Branch thought they were hot on Meyer's track, because all trails led to his house. They were getting too close. So she had to sacrifice him. She tipped off the police and planned Meyer's murder, leaving incriminating evidence which was far too incriminating to be true, and bringing the police themselves as witnesses to her innocence. By thunder, I admire her!"

Harriet Meyer was still laughing. But it was a choked, vicious sort of laughter which turned her listeners cold. And it stopped, with a whistling inhalation of breath, as Inspector Ballard walked towards her.

Her eyes searched him. Then she seemed to make up her mind. She straightened up, her heels together. Her hand flashed outwards, palm uppermost, in salute. Then, striking at him with the same hand, she ran for the door.

Dr. Fell seized Ballard's arm.

"Let her go," he said quietly. "The house is surrounded. She won't get far. You have that shotgun safely locked up?"

"Yes; but—"

"The traces of burnt moss in the barrel should be good enough. These clever people usually overlook something."

The room was very hot. Again Dr. Fell got out his bandanna handkerchief and mopped his face. Carl Kuhn hurried across to the window and peered out.

"You would not," said Dr. Fell softly, "like her to get away?"

"I cannot say," said Kuhn, whose face had lost its color. "I do not know. She is a compatriot of yours, not mine. It is none of my affair."

Dr. Fell stowed away his handkerchief.

"Sir," he said gravely, "I know nothing against you. I believe you to be an honest man."

Kuhn ducked his head, and his heels came together.

"Even if you were not, you fly your own colors and present yourself for what you are. But there,"—he pointed his stick in the direction Harriet Meyer had taken,—"there goes a portent and a warning. The alien we can deal with. But the hypnotized zealot among ourselves, the bat and the owl and the mole who would ruin us with the best intentions, is another thing. It has happened before. It may happen again. It is what we have to fear; and, by God, *all* we have to fear!"

In silence he put on his broadbrimmed white hat.

"And now you must excuse me," he added, "I have no relish for cases such as this."

"I said it was Harriet," Nancy told him. "I always thought she was queerer than he was. And yet, you know, I didn't *really* think so either. What did you mean when you told us the answer to this whole business was a proverb?"

Dr. Fell made a hideous face.

"Oh, that?" he said. "I wondered if she might be our quarry when I heard about her denouncing her husband to the police. Haven't I heard somewhere that people who live in glass houses shouldn't throw stones?"

MIDNIGHT BLUE

BY ROSS MACDONALD

Ross Macdonald is the pseudonym of Ken Millar, who was born in California on December 13, 1915, and raised in Ontario, Canada. He served in the Navy in World War II and received his doctorate (thesis on Coleridge) from the University of Michigan in 1951. His most famous character, private detective Lew Archer, has appeared in eighteen novels, one novelette, nine short stories, a television movie and series, and, renamed Harper, in two popular motion pictures. He lives in Santa Barbara, California, with his wife, mystery writer Margaret Millar.

IT HAD RAINED in the canyon during the night. The world had the colored freshness of a butterfly just emerged from the chrysalis stage and trembling in the sun. Actual butterflies danced in flight across free spaces of air or played a game of tag without any rules among the tree branches. At this height there were giant pines among the eucalyptus trees.

I parked my car where I usually parked it, in the shadow of the stone building just inside the gates of the old estate. Just inside the posts, that is—the gates had long since fallen from their rusted hinges. The owner of the country house had died in Europe, and the place had stood empty since the war. It was one reason I came here on the occasional Sunday when I wanted to get away from the Hollywood rat race. Nobody lived within two miles.

Until now, anyway. The window of the gatehouse overlooking the drive had been broken the last time that I'd noticed it. Now it was patched up with a piece of cardboard. Through a hole punched in the middle of the cardboard, bright emptiness watched me—human eye's bright emptiness.

"Hello," I said.

A grudging voice answered, "Hello."

The gatehouse door creaked open, and a white-haired man came out. A smile sat strangely on his ravaged face. He walked mechanically, shuffling in the leaves, as if his body was not at home in the world. He wore faded denims through which his clumsy muscles bulged like animals in a sack. His feet were bare.

I saw when he came up to me that he was a huge old man, a head taller than I was and a foot wider. His smile was not a greeting or any kind of smile that I could respond to. It was the stretched, blind grimace of a man who lived in a world of his own, a world that didn't include me.

"Get out of here. I don't want trouble. I don't want nobody messing around."

"No trouble," I said. "I came up to do a little target shooting. I probably have as much right here as you have."

His eyes widened. They were as blue and empty as holes in his head through which I could see the sky.

"Nobody has the rights here that I have. I lifted up mine eyes

310

unto the hills and the voice spoke and I found sanctuary. Nobody's going to force me out of my sanctuary."

I could feel the short hairs bristling on the back of my neck. Though my instincts didn't say so, he was probably a harmless nut. I tried to keep my instincts out of my voice.

"I won't bother you. You don't bother me. That should be fair enough."

"You bother me just *being* here. I can't stand people. I can't stand cars. And this is twice in two days you come up harrying me and harassing me."

"I haven't been here for a month."

"You're an Ananias liar." His voice whined like a rising wind. He clenched his knobbed fists and shuddered on the verge of violence.

"Calm down, old man," I said. "There's room in the world for both of us."

He looked around at the high green world as if my words had snapped him out of a dream.

"You're right," he said in a different voice. "I have been blessed, and I must remember to be joyful. Creation belongs to all of us poor creatures." His smiling teeth were as long and yellow as an old horse's. His roving glance fell on my car. "And it wasn't you who come up here last night. It was a different automobile. I remember."

He turned away, muttering something about washing his socks, and dragged his horny feet back into the gatehouse. I got my targets, pistol, and ammunition out of the trunk, and locked the car up tight. The old man watched me through his peephole, but he didn't come out again.

Below the road, in the wild canyon, there was an open meadow backed by a sheer bank which was topped by the crumbling wall of the estate. It was my shooting gallery. I slid down the wet grass of the bank and tacked a target to an oak tree, using the butt of my heavy-framed .22 as a hammer.

While I was loading it, something caught my eye—something that glinted red, like a ruby among the leaves. I stooped to pick it up and found that it was attached. It was a red-enameled fingernail at the tip of a white hand. The hand was cold and stiff.

I let out a sound that must have been loud in the stillness. A jaybird erupted from a manzanita, sailed up to a high limb of the oak, and yelled down curses at me. A dozen chickadees flew out of the oak and settled in another at the far end of the meadow.

Panting like a dog, I scraped away the dirt and wet leaves that

311

had been loosely piled over the body. It was the body of a girl wearing a midnight-blue sweater and skirt. She was a blonde, about 17. The blood that congested her face made her look old and dark. The white rope with which she had been garroted was sunk almost out of sight in the flesh of her neck. The rope was tied at the nape in what is called a granny's knot, the kind of knot that any child can tie.

I left her where she lay and climbed back up to the road on trembling knees. The grass showed traces of the track her body had made where someone had dragged it down the bank. I looked for tire marks on the shoulder and in the rutted, impacted gravel of the road. If there had been any, the rain had washed them out.

I trudged up the road to the gatehouse and knocked on the door. It creaked inward under my hand. Inside there was nothing alive but the spiders that had webbed the low black beams. A dustless rectangle in front of the stone fireplace showed where a bedroll had lain. Several blackened tin cans had evidently been used as cooking utensils. Gray embers lay on the cavernous hearth. Suspended above it from a spike in the mantel was a pair of white cotton work socks. The socks were wet. Their owner had left in a hurry.

It wasn't my job to hunt him. I drove down the canyon to the highway and along it for a few miles to the outskirts of the nearest town. There a drab green box of a building with a flag in front of it housed the Highway Patrol. Across the highway was a lumberyard deserted on Sunday.

"Too bad about Ginnie," the dispatcher said when she had radioed the local sheriff. She was a thirtyish brunette with fine black eyes and dirty fingernails. She had on a plain white blouse, which was full of her.

"Do you know Ginnie?"

"My young sister knows her. They go—they went to high school together. It's an awful thing when it happens to a young person like that. I knew she was missing—I got the report when I came on at eight—but I kept hoping that she was just off on a lost weekend, like. Now there's nothing to hope for, is there?" Her eyes were liquid with feeling. "Poor Ginnie. And poor Mr. Green."

"Her father?"

"That's right. He was in here with her high school counselor not more than an hour ago. I hope he doesn't come back right away. I don't want to be the one that has to tell him."

"How long has the girl been missing?"

"Just since last night. We got the report here about three a.m., I think. Apparently she wandered away from a party at Cavern Beach. Down the pike a ways." She pointed south toward the canyon mouth.

"What kind of party was it?"

"Some of the kids from the Union High School—they took some wienies down and had a fire. The party was part of graduation week. I happen to know about it because my young sister Alice went. I didn't want her to go, even if it was supervised. That can be a dangerous beach at night. All sorts of bums and scroungers hang out in the caves. Why, one night when I was a kid I saw a naked man down there in the moonlight. He didn't have a woman with him, either."

She caught the drift of her words, did a slow blush, and checked her loquacity. I leaned on the plywood counter between us.

"What sort of girl was Ginnie Green?"

"I wouldn't know. I never really knew her."

"Your sister does."

"I don't let my sister run around with girls like Ginnie Green. Does that answer your question?"

"Not in any detail."

"It seems to me you ask a lot of questions."

"I'm naturally interested, since I found her. Also I'm a private detective."

"Looking for a job?"

"I can always use a job."

"So can I, and I've got one and I don't intend to lose it." She softened the words with a smile. "Excuse me; I have work to do."

She turned to her short-wave and sent out a message to the patrol cars that Virginia Green had been found. Virginia Green's father heard it as he came in the door. He was a puffy gray-faced man with red-rimmed eyes. Striped pajama bottoms showed below the cuffs of his trousers. His shoes were muddy, and he walked as if he had been walking all night.

He supported himself on the edge of the counter, opening and shutting his mouth like a beached fish. Words came out, half strangled by shock.

"I heard you say she was dead, Anita."

313

The woman raised her eyes to his. "Yes. I'm awfully sorry, Mr. Green."

He put his face down on the counter and stayed there like a penitent, perfectly still. I could hear a clock somewhere, snipping off seconds, and in the back of the room the L.A. police signals like muttering voices coming in from another planet. Another planet very much like this one, where violence measured out the hours.

"It's my fault," Green said to the bare wood under his face. "I didn't bring her up properly. I haven't been a good father."

The woman watched him with dark and glistening eyes ready to spill. She stretched out an unconscious hand to touch him, pulled her hand back in embarrassment when a second man came into the station. He was a young man with crew-cut brown hair, tanned and fit-looking in a Hawaiian shirt. Fit-looking except for the glare of sleeplessness in his eyes and the anxious lines around them.

"What is it, Miss Brocco? What's the word?"

"The word is bad." She sounded angry. "Somebody murdered Ginnie Green. This man here is a detective and he just found her body up in Trumbull Canyon."

The young man ran his fingers through his short hair and failed to get a grip on it, or on himself. "My God! That's terrible!"

"Yes," the woman said. "You were supposed to be looking after her, weren't you?"

They glared at each other across the counter. The tips of her breasts pointed at him through her blouse like accusing fingers. The young man lost the glaring match. He turned to me with a wilted look.

"My name is Connor, Franklin Connor, and I'm afraid I'm very much to blame in this. I'm a counselor at the high school, and I was supposed to be looking after the party, as Miss Brocco said."

"Why didn't you?"

"I didn't realize. I mean, I thought they were all perfectly happy and safe. The boys and girls had pretty well paired off around the fire. Frankly, I felt rather out of place. They aren't children, you know. They were all seniors, they had cars. So I said good night and walked home along the beach. As a matter of fact, I was hoping for a phone call from my wife."

"What time did you leave the party?"

314

"It must have been nearly eleven. The ones who hadn't paired off had gone home."

"Who did Ginnie pair off with?"

"I don't know. I'm afraid I wasn't paying too much attention to the kids. It's graduation week, and I've had a lot of problems—"

The father, Green, had been listening with a changing face. In a sudden yammering rage his impulsive grief and guilt exploded outward.

"It's your business to know! By God, I'll have your job for this. I'll make it *my* business to run you out of town."

Connor hung his head and looked at the stained tile floor. There was a thin spot in his short brown hair, and his scalp gleamed through it like bare white bone. It was turning into a bad day for everybody, and I felt the dull old nagging pull of other people's trouble, like a toothache you can't leave alone.

The sheriff arrived, flanked by several deputies and an HP sergeant. He wore a Western hat and a rawhide tie and a blue gabardine business suit which together produced a kind of gun-smog effect. His name was Pearsall.

I rode back up the canyon in the right front seat of Pearsall's black Buick, filling him in on the way. The deputies' Ford and an HP car followed us, and Green's new Oldsmobile convertible brought up the rear.

The sheriff said, "The old guy sounds like a loony to me."

"He's a loner, anyway."

"You never can tell about them hoboes. That's why I give my boys instructions to roust 'em. Well, it looks like an open-and-shut case."

"Maybe. Let's keep our minds open anyway, Sheriff."

"Sure. Sure. But the old guy went on the run. That shows consciousness of guilt. Don't worry, we'll hunt him down. I got men that know these hills like you know your wife's geography."

"I'm not married."

"Your girl friend, then." He gave me a sideways leer that was no gift. "And if we can't find him on foot, we'll use the air squadron."

"You have an air squadron?"

"Volunteers, mostly local ranchers. We'll get him." His tires squealed on a curve. "Was the girl raped?"

"I didn't try to find out. I'm not a doctor. I left her as she was."

The sheriff grunted. "You did the right thing at that."

Nothing had changed in the high meadow. The girl lay waiting to have her picture taken. It was taken many times, from

315

several angles. All the birds flew away. Her father leaned on a tree and watched them go. Later he was sitting on the ground.

I volunteered to drive him home. It wasn't pure altruism. I'm incapable of it. I said when I had turned his Oldsmobile, "Why did you say it was your fault, Mr. Green?"

He wasn't listening. Below the road four uniformed men were wrestling a heavy covered aluminum stretcher up the steep bank. Green watched them as he had watched the departing birds, until they were out of sight around a curve.

"She was so young," he said to the back seat.

I waited, and tried again. "Why did you blame yourself for her death?"

He roused himself from his daze. "Did I say that?"

"In the Highway Patrol office you said something of the sort."

He touched my arm. "I didn't mean I killed her."

"I didn't think you meant that. I'm interested in finding out who did."

"Are you a cop—a policeman?"

"I have been."

"You're not with the locals."

"No. I happen to be a private detective from Los Angeles. The name is Archer."

He sat and pondered this information. Below and ahead the summer sea brimmed up in the mouth of the canyon.

"You don't think the old tramp did her in?" Green said.

"It's hard to figure out how he could have. He's a strong looking old buzzard, but he couldn't have carried her all the way up from the beach. And she wouldn't have come along with him of her own accord."

It was a question, in a way.

"I don't know," her father said. "Ginnie was a little wild— she'd do a thing *because* it was wrong, *because* it was dangerous. She hated to turn down a dare, especially from a man."

"There were men in her life?"

"She was attractive to men. You saw her, even as she is." He gulped. "Don't get me wrong. Ginnie was never a *bad* girl. She was a little headstrong, and I made mistakes. That's why I blame myself."

"What sort of mistakes, Mr. Green?"

"All the usual ones, and some I made up on my own." His voice was bitter. "Ginnie didn't have a mother, you see. Her mother left me years ago, and it was as much my fault as hers. I tried to bring her up myself. I didn't give her proper supervision. I run a restaurant in town, and I don't get home nights till after midnight. Ginnie was pretty much on her own since she was in grade school. We got along fine when I was there, but I usually wasn't there.

"The worst mistake I made was letting her work in the restaurant over the weekends. That started about a year ago. She wanted the money for clothes, and I thought the discipline would be good for her. I thought I could keep an eye on her, you know. But it didn't work out. She grew up too fast, and the night work played hell with her studies.

"I finally got the word from the school authorities. I fired her a couple of months ago, but I guess it was too late. We haven't been getting along too well since then. Mr. Connor said she resented my indecision, that I gave her too much responsibility and then took it away again."

"You've talked her over with Connor?"

"More than once, including last night. He was her academic counselor, and he was concerned about her grades. We both were. Ginnie finally pulled through, after all, thanks to him. She was going to graduate. Not that it matters now, of course."

Green was silent for a time. The sea expanded below us like a second blue dawn. I could hear the roar of the highway. Green touched my elbow again, as if he needed human contact.

"I oughtn't to've blown my top at Connor. He's a decent boy, he means well. He gave my daughter hours of free tutoring this last month. And he's got troubles of his own, like he said."

"What troubles?"

"I happen to know his wife left him, same as mine. I shouldn't have borne down so hard on him. I have a lousy temper, always have had." He hesitated, then blurted out as if he had found a confessor, "I said a terrible thing to Ginnie at supper last night. She always has supper with me at the restaurant. I said if she wasn't home when I got home last night that I'd wring her neck."

"And she wasn't home," I said. And somebody wrung her neck, I didn't say.

The light at the highway was red. I glanced at Green. Tear tracks glistened like snail tracks on his face.

"Tell me what happened last night."

"There isn't anything much to tell," he said. "I got to the house about twelve thirty, and, like you said, she wasn't home. So I called Al Brocco's house. He's my night cook, and I knew his youngest daughter Alice was at the moonlight party on the beach. Alice was home all right."

"Did you talk to Alice?"

"She was in bed asleep. Al woke her up, but I didn't talk to her. She told him she didn't know where Ginnie was. I went to bed, but I couldn't sleep. Finally I got up and called Mr. Connor. That was about one thirty. I thought I should get in touch with the authorities, but he said no, Ginnie had enough black marks against her already. He came over to the house and we waited for a while and then we went down to Cavern Beach.

"There was no trace of her. I said it was time to call in the authorities, and he agreed. We went to his beach house, because it was nearer, and called the sheriff's office from there. We went back to the beach with a couple of flashlights and went through the caves. He stayed with me all night. I give him that."

"Where are these caves?"

"We'll pass them in a minute. I'll show you if you want. But there's nothing in any of the three of them."

Nothing but shadows and empty beer cans, the odor of rotting kelp. I got sand in my shoes and sweat under my collar. The sun dazzled my eyes when I half walked, half crawled, from the last cave.

Green was waiting beside a heap of ashes.

"This is where they had the wienie roast," he said.

I kicked the ashes. A half-burned sausage rolled along the sand. Sand fleas hopped in the sun like fat on a griddle. Green and I faced each other over the dead fire. He looked out to sea. A seal's face floated like a small black nose cone beyond the breakers. Farther out a water skier slid between unfolding wings of spray.

Away up the beach two people were walking towards us. They were small and lonely and distinct as Chirico figures in the long white distance.

Green squinted against the sun. Red-rimmed or not, his eyes were good. "I believe that's Mr. Connor. I wonder who the woman is with him."

They were walking as close as lovers, just above the white margin of the surf. They pulled apart when they noticed us, but they were still holding hands as they approached.

"It's Mrs. Connor," Green said in a low voice.

"I thought you said she left him."

"That's what he told me last night. She took off on him a

couple of weeks ago, couldn't stand a high school teacher's hours. She must have changed her mind."

She looked as though she had a mind to change. She was a hard-faced blonde who walked like a man. A certain amount of style took the curse off her stiff angularity. She had on a madras shirt, mannishly cut, and a pair of Capri pants that hugged her long slim legs.

Connor looked at us in complex embarrassment. "I thought it was you from a distance, Mr. Green. I don't believe you know my wife."

"I've seen her in my place of business." He explained to the woman, "I run the Highway Restaurant in town."

"How do you do," she said aloofly, then added in an entirely different voice, "You're Virginia's father, aren't you? I'm so sorry."

The words sounded queer. Perhaps it was the surroundings; the ashes on the beach, the entrances to the caves, the sea, and the empty sky which dwarfed us all. Green answered her solemnly.

"Thank you, ma'am. Mr. Connor was a strong right arm to me last night, I can tell you." He was apologizing. And Connor responded, "Why don't you come to our place for a drink? It's just down the beach. You look as if you could use one, Mr. Green. You too," he said to me. "I don't believe I know your name."

"Archer. Lew Archer."

He gave me a hard hand. His wife interposed, "I'm sure Mr. Green and his friend won't want to be bothered with us on a day like this. Besides, it isn't even noon yet, Frank."

She was the one who didn't want to be bothered. We stood around for a minute, exchanging grim, nonsensical comments on the beauty of the day. Then she led Connor back in the direction they had come from. Private Property, her attitude seemed to say: Trespassers will be fresh-frozen.

I drove Green to the Highway Patrol station. He said that he was feeling better, and could make it home from there by himself. He thanked me profusely for being a friend in need to him, as he put it. He followed me to the door of the station, thanking me.

The dispatcher was cleaning her fingernails with an ivory-handled file. She glanced up.

"Did they catch him yet?"

"I was going to ask you the same question, Miss Brocco."

"No such luck. But they'll get him," she said with female vindictiveness. "The sheriff called out his air squadron, and he sent to Ventura for bloodhounds."

"Big deal."

She bridled. "What do you mean by that?"

"I don't think the old man of the mountain killed her. If he had, he wouldn't have waited till this morning to go on the lam. He'd have taken off right away."

"Then why did he go on the lam at all?" The word sounded strange in her prim mouth.

"I think he saw me discover the body, and realized he'd be blamed."

She considered this, bending the long nail file between her fingers. "If the old tramp didn't do it, who did?"

"You may be able to help me answer that question."

"Me help you? How?"

"You know Frank Connor, for one thing."

"I know him. I've seen him about my sister's grades a few times."

"You don't seem to like him much."

"I don't like him, I don't dislike him. He's just blah to me."

"Why? What's the matter with him?"

Her tight mouth quivered, and let out words. "I don't know what's the matter with him. He can't keep his hands off of young girls."

"How do you know that?"

"I heard it."

"From your sister Alice?"

"Yes. The rumor was going around the school, she said."

"Did the rumor involve Ginnie Green?"

She nodded. Her eyes were as black as fingerprint ink.

"Is that why Connor's wife left him?"

"I wouldn't know about that. I never even laid eyes on Mrs. Connor."

"You haven't been missing much."

There was a yell outside, a kind of choked ululation. It sounded as much like an animal as a man. It was Green. When I reached the door, he was climbing out of his convertible with a heavy blue revolver in his hand.

"I saw the killer," he cried out exultantly.

"Where?"

He waved the revolver toward the lumberyard across the road. "He poked his head up behind that pile of white pine.

320

When he saw me, he ran like a deer. I'm going to get him."

"No. Give me the gun."

"Why? I got a license to carry it. And use it."

He started across the four-lane highway, dodging through the moving patterns of the Sunday traffic as if he were playing parcheesi on the kitchen table at home. The sounds of brakes and curses split the air. He had scrambled over the locked gate of the yard before I got to it. I went over after him.

Green disappeared behind a pile of lumber. I turned the corner and saw him running halfway down a long aisle walled with stacked wood and floored with beaten earth. The old man of the mountain was running ahead of him. His white hair blew in the wind of his own movement. A burlap sack bounced on his shoulders like a load of sorrow and shame.

"Stop or I'll shoot!" Green cried.

The old man ran on as if the devil himself were after him. He came to a cyclone fence, discarded his sack, and tried to climb it. He almost got over. Three strands of barbed wire along the top of the fence caught and held him struggling.

I heard a tearing sound, and then the sound of a shot. The huge old body espaliered on the fence twitched and went limp, fell heavily to the earth. Green stood over him breathing through his teeth.

I pushed him out of the way. The old man was alive, though there was blood in his mouth. He spat it onto his chin when I lifted his head.

"You shouldn't ought to of done it. I come to turn myself in. Then I got ascairt."

"Why were you scared?"

"I watched you uncover the little girl in the leaves. I knew I'd be blamed. I'm one of the chosen. They always blame the chosen. I been in trouble before."

"Trouble with girls?" At my shoulder Green was grinning terribly.

"Trouble with cops."

"For killing people?" Green said.

"For preaching on the street without a license. The voice told me to preach to the tribes of the wicked. And the voice told me this morning to come in and give my testimony."

"What voice?"

"The great voice." His voice was little and weak. He coughed red.

"He's as crazy as a bedbug," Green said.

"Shut up." I turned back to the dying man. "What testimony do you have to give?"

"About the car I seen. It woke me up in the middle of the night, stopped in the road below my sanctuary."

"What kind of car?"

"I don't know cars. I think it was one of them foreign cars. It made a noise to wake the dead."

"Did you see who was driving it?"

"No. I didn't go near. I was ascairt."

"What time was this car in the road?"

"I don't keep track of time. The moon was down behind the trees."

Those were his final words. He looked up at the sky with his sky-colored eyes, straight into the sun. His eyes changed color.

Green said, "Don't tell them. If you do, I'll make a liar out of you. I'm a respected citizen in this town. I got a business to lose. And they'll believe me ahead of you, mister."

"Shut up."

He couldn't. "The old fellow was lying, anyway. You know that. You heard him say yourself that he heard voices. That proves he's a psycho. He's a psycho killer. I shot him down like you would a mad dog, and I did right."

He waved the revolver.

"You did wrong, Green, and you know it. Give me that gun before it kills somebody else."

He thrust it into my hand suddenly. I unloaded it, breaking my fingernails in the process, and handed it back to him empty. He nudged up against me.

"Listen, maybe I did do wrong. I had provocation. It doesn't have to get out. I got a business to lose."

He fumbled in his hip pocket and brought out a thick sharkskin wallet. "Here. I can pay you good money. You say that you're a private eye; you know how to keep your lip buttoned."

I walked away and left him blabbering beside the body of the man he had killed. They were both vicious, in a sense, but only one of them had blood on his hands.

Miss Brocco was in the HP parking lot. Her bosom was jumping with excitement.

"I heard a shot."

322

"Green shot the old man. Dead. You better send in for the meat wagon and call off your bloody dogs."

The words hit her like slaps. She raised her hand to her face, defensively. "Are you mad at me? Why are you mad at me?"

"I'm mad at everybody."

"You still don't think he did it."

"I know damned well he didn't. I want to talk to your sister."

"Alice? What for?"

"Information. She was on the beach with Ginnie Green last night. She may be able to tell me something."

"You leave Alice alone."

"I'll treat her gently. Where do you live?"

"I don't want my little sister dragged into this filthy mess."

"All I want to know is who Ginnie paired off with."

"I'll ask Alice. I'll tell you."

"Come on, Miss Brocco, we're wasting time. I don't need your permission to talk to your sister, after all. I can get the address out of the phone book if I have to."

She flared up then and then flared down.

"You win. We live on Orlando Street, 224. That's on the other side of town. You will be nice to Alice, won't you? She's bothered enough as it is about Ginnie's death."

"She really was a friend of Ginnie's, then?"

"Yes. I tried to break it up. But you know how kids are—two motherless girls, they stick together. I tried to be like a mother to Alice."

"What happened to your own mother?"

"Father—I mean, she died." A greenish pallor invaded her face and turned it to old bronze. "Please. I don't want to talk about it. I was only a kid when she died."

She went back to her muttering radios. She was quite a woman, I thought as I drove away. Nubile but unmarried, probably full of untapped Mediterranean passions. If she worked an eight-hour shift and started at eight, she'd be getting off about four.

It wasn't a large town, and it wasn't far across it. The highway doubled as its main street. I passed the Union High School. On the green playing field beside it a lot of kids in mortarboards and gowns were rehearsing their graduation exercises. A kind of pall seemed to hang over the field. Perhaps it was in my mind.

Farther along the street I passed Green's Highway Restaurant. A dozen cars stood in its parking space. A couple of white-

323

uniformed waitresses were scooting around behind the plate-glass windows.

Orlando Street was a lower-middle-class residential street bisected by the highway. Jacaranda trees bloomed like low small purple clouds among its stucco and frame cottages. Fallen purple petals carpeted the narrow lawn in front of the Brocco house.

A thin dark man, wiry under his T-shirt, was washing a small red Fiat in the driveway beside the front porch. He must have been over fifty, but his long hair was as black as an Indian's. His Sicilian nose was humped in the middle by an old break.

"Mr. Brocco?"

"That's me."

"Is Alice home?"

"She's home."

"I'd like to speak to her."

He turned off his hose, pointing its dripping nozzle at me like a gun.

"You're a little old for her, ain't you?"

"I am a detective investigating the death of Ginnie Green."

"Alice don't know nothing about that."

"I've just been talking to your older daughter at the Highway Patrol office. She thinks Alice may know something."

He shifted on his feet. "Well, if Anita says it's all right."

"It's okay, Dad," a girl said from the front door. "Anita just called me on the telephone. Come in, Mister—Archer, isn't it?"

"Archer."

She opened the screen door for me. It opened directly into a small square living room containing worn green frieze furniture and a television set which the girl switched off. She was a handsome, serious-looking girl, a younger version of her sister with ten years and ten pounds subtracted and a pony tail added. She sat down gravely on the edge of a chair, waving her hand at the chesterfield. Her movements were languid. There were blue depressions under her eyes. Her face was sallow.

"What kind of questions do you want to ask me? My sister didn't say."

"Who was Ginnie with last night?"

"Nobody. I mean, she was with me. She didn't make out with any of the boys." She glanced from me to the blind television set, as if she felt caught between. "It said on the television that she was with a man, that there was medical evidence to prove it. But I didn't see her with no man. Any man."

"Did Ginnie go with men?"

324

She shook her head. Her pony tail switched and hung limp. She was close to tears.

"You told Anita she did."

"I did not!"

"Your sister wouldn't lie. You passed on a rumor to her—a high school rumor that Ginnie had had something to do with one man in particular."

The girl was watching my face in fascination. Her eyes were like a bird's eyes, bright and shallow and fearful.

"Was the rumor true?"

She shrugged her thin shoulders. "How would I know?"

"You were good friends with Ginnie."

"Yes. I was." Her voice broke on the past tense. "She was a real nice kid, even if she was kind of boy crazy."

"She was boy crazy, but she didn't make out with any of the boys last night?"

"Not while I was there."

"Did she make out with Mr. Connor?"

"No. He wasn't there. He went away. He said he was going home. He lives up the beach."

"What did Ginnie do?"

"I don't know. I didn't notice."

"You said she was with you. Was she with you all evening?"

"Yes." Her face was agonized. "I mean no."

"Did Ginnie go away, too?"

She nodded.

"In the same direction Mr. Connor took? The direction of his house?"

Her head moved almost imperceptibly downward.

"What time was that, Alice?"

"About eleven o'clock, I guess."

"And Ginnie never came back from Mr. Connor's house?"

"I don't know. I don't know for certain that she went there."

"But Ginnie and Mr. Connor were good friends?"

"I guess so."

"How good? Like a boy friend and a girl friend?"

She sat mute, her birdlike stare unblinking.

"Tell me, Alice."

"I'm afraid."

"Afraid of Mr. Connor?"

"No. Not him."

"Has someone threatened you—told you not to talk?"

Her head moved in another barely perceptible nod.

325

"Who threatened you, Alice? You'd better tell me for your own protection. Whoever did threaten you is probably a murderer."

She burst into frantic tears. Brocco came to the door.

"What goes on in here?"

"Your daughter is upset. I'm sorry."

"Yeah, and I know who upset her. You better get out of here or you'll be sorrier."

He opened the screen door and held it open, his head poised like a dark and broken ax. I went out past him. He spat after me. The Broccos were a very emotional family.

I started back toward Connor's beach house on the south side of town but ran into a diversion on the way. Green's car was parked in the lot beside his restaurant. I went in.

The place smelled of grease. It was almost full of late Sunday lunchers seated in booths and at the U-shaped breakfast bar in the middle. Green himself was sitting on a stool behind the cash register counting money. He was counting it as if his life and his hope of heaven depended on the colored paper in his hands.

He looked up, smiling loosely and vaguely. "Yes, sir?" Then he recognized me. His face went through a quick series of transformations and settled for a kind of boozy shame. "I know I shouldn't be here working on a day like this. But it keeps my mind off my troubles. Besides, they steal you blind if you don't watch 'em. And I'll be needing the money."

"What for, Mr. Green?"

"The trial." He spoke the word as if it gave him a bitter satisfaction.

"Whose trial?"

"Mine. I told the sheriff what the old guy said. And what I did. I know what I did. I shot him down like a dog, and I had no right to. I was crazy with my sorrow, you might say."

He was less crazy now. The shame in his eyes was clearing. But the sorrow was still there in their depths, like stone at the bottom of a well.

"I'm glad you told the truth, Mr. Green."

"So am I. It doesn't help him, and it doesn't bring Ginnie back. But at least I can live with myself."

"Speaking of Ginnie," I said. "Was she seeing quite a lot of Frank Connor?"

"Yeah. I guess you could say so. He came over to help her with

326

her studies quite a few times. At the house, and at the library. He didn't charge me, either."

"That was nice of him. Was Ginnie fond of Connor?"

"Sure she was. She thought very highly of Mr. Connor."

"Was she in love with him?"

"In love? Hell, I never thought of anything like that. Why?"

"Did she have dates with Connor?"

"Not to my knowledge," he said. "If she did, she must have done it behind my back." His eyes narrowed to two red swollen slits. "You think Frank Connor had something to do with her death?"

"It's a possibility. Don't go into a sweat now. You know where that gets you."

"Don't worry. But what about this Connor? Did you get something on him? I thought he was acting queer last night."

"Queer in what way?"

"Well, he was pretty tight when he came to the house. I gave him a stiff snort, and that straightened him out for a while. But later on, down on the beach, he got almost hysterical. He was running around like a rooster with his head chopped off."

"Is he a heavy drinker?"

"I wouldn't know. I never saw him drink before last night at my house." Green narrowed his eyes. "But he tossed down a triple bourbon like it was water. And remember this morning, he offered us a drink on the beach. A drink in the morning, that isn't the usual thing, especially for a high school teacher."

"I noticed that."

"What else have you been noticing?"

"We won't go into it now," I said. "I don't want to ruin a man unless and until I'm sure he's got it coming."

He sat on his stool with his head down. Thought moved murkily under his knitted brows. His glance fell on the money in his hands. He was counting tens.

"Listen, Mr. Archer. You're working on this case on your own, aren't you? For free?"

"So far."

"So go to work for me. Nail Connor for me and I'll pay you whatever you ask."

"Not so fast," I said. "We don't know that Connor is guilty. There are other possibilities."

"Such as?"

"If I tell you, can I trust you not to go on a shooting spree?"

"Don't worry," he repeated. "I've had that."

"Where's your revolver?"

"I turned it in to Sheriff Pearsall. He asked for it."

We were interrupted by a family group getting up from one of the booths. They gave Green their money and their sympathy. When they were out of hearing, I said, "You mentioned that your daughter worked here in the restaurant for a while. Was Al Brocco working here at the same time?"

"Yeah. He's been my night cook for six-seven years. Al is a darned good cook. He trained as a chef on the Italian line." His slow mind, punchy with grief, did a double-take. "You wouldn't be saying that he messed around with Ginnie?"

"I'm asking you."

"Shucks, Al is old enough to be her father. He's all wrapped up in his own girls, Anita in particular. He worships the ground she walks on. She's the mainspring of that family."

"How did he get on with Ginnie?"

"Very well. They kidded back and forth. She was the only one who could ever make him smile. Al is a sad man, you know. He had a tragedy in his life."

"His wife's death?"

"It was worse than that," Green said. "Al Brocco killed his wife with his own hand. He caught her with another man and put a knife in her."

"And he's walking around loose?"

"The other man was a Mex," Green said in an explanatory way. "A wetback. He couldn't even talk the English language. The town hardly blamed Al, the jury gave him manslaughter. But when he got out of the pen, the people at the Pink Flamingo wouldn't give him his old job back—he used to be chef there. So I took him on. I felt sorry for his girls, I guess, and Al's been a good worker. A man doesn't do a thing like that twice, you know."

He did another slow mental double-take. His mouth hung open.

"Let's hope not."

"Listen here," he said. "You go to work for me, eh? You nail the guy, whoever he is. I'll pay you. I'll pay you now. How much do you want?"

I took a hundred dollars of his money and left him trying to comfort himself with the rest of it. The smell of grease stayed in my nostrils.

Connor's house clung to the edge of a low bluff about halfway between the HP station and the mouth of the canyon where the thing had begun: a semi-cantilevered redwood cottage with a closed double garage fronting the highway. From the grape-stake-fenced patio in the angle between the garage and the front door a flight of wooden steps climbed to the flat roof which was railed as a sun deck. A second set of steps descended the fifteen or twenty feet to the beach.

I tripped on a pair of garden shears crossing the patio to the garage window. I peered into the interior twilight. Two things inside interested me: a dismasted flattie sitting on a trailer, and a car. The sailboat interested me because its cordage resembled the white rope that had strangled Ginnie. The car interested me because it was an imported model, a low-slung Triumph two-seater.

I was planning to have a closer look at it when a woman's voice screeched overhead like a gull's, "What do you think you're doing?"

Mrs. Connor was leaning over the railing on the roof. Her hair was in curlers. She looked like a blonde Gorgon. I smiled up at her, the way that Greek whose name I don't remember must have smiled.

"Your husband invited me for a drink, remember? I don't know whether he gave me a rain check or not."

"He did not! Go away! My husband is sleeping!"

"Shh. You'll wake him up. You'll wake up the people in Forest Lawn."

She put her hand to her mouth. From the expression on her face she seemed to be biting her hand. She disappeared for a moment, and then came down the steps with a multicolored silk scarf over her curlers. The rest of her was sheathed in a white satin bathing suit. Against it her flesh looked like brown wood.

"You get out of here," she said. "Or I shall call the police."

"Fine. Call them. I've got nothing to hide."

"Are you implying that we have?"

"We'll see. Why did you leave your husband?"

"That's none of your business."

"I'm making it my business, Mrs. Connor. I'm a detective investigating the murder of Ginnie Green. Did you leave Frank on account of Ginnie Green?"

"No. No! I wasn't even aware—" Her hand went to her mouth again. She chewed on it some more.

"You weren't aware that Frank was having an affair with Ginnie Green?"

"He wasn't."

"So you say. Others say different."

"What others? Anita Brocco? You can't believe anything *that* woman says. Why, her own father is a murderer, everybody in town knows that."

"Your own husband may be another, Mrs. Connor. You might as well come clean with me."

"But I have nothing to tell you."

"You can tell me why you left him."

"That is a private matter, between Frank and me. It has nothing to do with anybody but us." She was calming down, setting her moral forces in a stubborn, defensive posture.

"There's usually only the one reason."

"I had my reasons. I said they were none of your business. I chose for reasons of my own to spend a month with my parents in Long Beach."

"When did you come back?"

"This morning."

"Why this morning?"

"Frank called me. He said he needed me." She touched her thin breast absently, pathetically, as if perhaps she hadn't been needed in the past.

"Needed you for what?"

"As his wife," she said. "He said there might be tr—" Her hand went to her mouth again. She said around it, "Trouble."

"Did he name the kind of trouble?"

"No."

"What time did he call you?"

"Very early, around seven o'clock."

"That was more than an hour before I found Ginnie's body."

"He knew she was missing. He spent the whole night looking for her."

"Why would he do that, Mrs. Connor?"

"She was his student. He was fond of her. Besides, he was more or less responsible for her."

"Responsible for her death?"

"How dare you say a thing like that?"

"If he dared to do it, I can dare to say it."

330

"He didn't!" she cried. "Frank is a good man. He may have his faults, but he wouldn't kill anyone. I know him."

"What are his faults?"

"We won't discuss them."

"Then may I have a look in your garage?"

"What for? What are you looking for?"

"I'll know when I find it." I turned toward the garage door.

"You musn't go in there," she said intensely. "Not without Frank's permission."

"Wake him up and we'll get his permission."

"I will not. He got no sleep last night."

"Then I'll just have a look without his permission."

"I'll kill you if you go in there."

She picked up the garden shears and brandished them at me—a sick-looking lioness defending her overgrown cub. The cub himself opened the front door of the cottage. He slouched in the doorway groggily, naked except for white shorts.

"What goes on, Stella?"

"This man has been making the most horrible accusations."

His blurred glance wavered between us and focused on her. "What did he say?"

"I won't repeat it."

"I will, Mr. Connor. I think you were Ginnie Green's lover, if that's the word. I think she followed you to this house last night, around midnight. I think she left it with a rope around her neck."

Connor's head jerked. He started to make a move in my direction. Something inhibited it, like an invisible leash. His body slanted toward me, static, all the muscles taut. It resembled an anatomy specimen with the skin off. Even his face seemed mostly bone and teeth.

I hoped he'd swing on me and let me hit him. He didn't. Stella Connor dropped the garden shears. They made a noise like the dull clank of doom.

"Aren't you going to deny it, Frank?"

"I didn't kill her. I swear I didn't. I admit that we—that we were together last night, Ginnie and I."

"Ginnie and I?" the woman repeated incredulously.

His head hung down. "I'm sorry, Stella. I didn't want to hurt you more than I have already. But it has to come out. I took up with the girl after you left. I was lonely and feeling sorry for myself. Ginnie kept hanging around. One night I drank too

331

much and let it happen. It happened more than once. I was so flattered that a pretty young girl—"

"You fool!" she said in a deep harsh voice.

"Yes, I'm a moral fool. That's no surprise to you, is it?"

"I thought you respected your pupils, at least. You mean to say you brought her into our own house, into our own bed?"

"You'd left. It wasn't ours any more. Besides, she came of her own accord. She wanted to come. She loved me."

She said with grinding contempt, "You poor groveling ninny. And to think you had the gall to ask me to come back here, to make you look respectable."

I cut in between them. "Was she here last night, Connor?"

"She was here. I didn't invite her. I wanted her to come, but I dreaded it, too. I knew that I was taking an awful chance. I drank quite a bit to numb my conscience—"

"What conscience?" Stella Connor said.

"I have a conscience," he said without looking at her. "You don't know the hell I've been going through. After she came, after it happened last night, I drank myself unconscious."

"Do you mean after you killed her?" I said.

"I didn't kill her. When I passed out, she was perfectly all right. She was sitting up drinking a cup of instant coffee. The next thing I knew, hours later, her father was on the telephone and she was gone."

"Are you trying to pull the old blackout alibi? You'll have to do better than that."

"I can't. It's the truth."

"Let me into your garage."

He seemed almost glad to be given an order, a chance for some activity. The garage wasn't locked. He raised the overhead door and let the daylight into the interior. It smelled of paint. There were empty cans of marine paint on a bench beside the sailboat. Its hull gleamed virgin white.

"I painted my flattie last week," he said inconsequentially.

"You do a lot of sailing?"

"I used to. Not much lately."

"No," his wife said from the doorway. "Frank changed his hobby to women. Wine and women."

"Lay off, eh?" His voice was pleading.

She looked at him from a great and stony distance.

I walked around the boat, examining the cordage. The starboard jib line had been sheared off short. Comparing it with the port line, I found that the missing piece was approximately a yard long. That was the length of the piece of white rope that I was interested in.

"Hey!" Connor grabbed the end of the cut line. He fingered it as it if was a wound in his own flesh. "Who's been messing with my lines? Did you cut it, Stella?"

"I never go near your blessed boat," she said.

"I can tell you where the rest of that line is, Connor. A line of similar length and color and thickness was wrapped around Ginnie Green's neck when I found her."

"Surely you don't believe I put it there?"

I tried to, but I couldn't. Small-boat sailers don't cut their jib lines, even when they're contemplating murder. And while Connor was clearly no genius, he was smart enough to have known that the line could easily be traced to him. Perhaps someone else had been equally smart.

I turned to Mrs. Connor. She was standing in the doorway with her legs apart. Her body was almost black against the daylight. Her eyes were hooded by the scarf on her head.

"What time did you get home, Mrs. Connor?"

"About ten o'clock this morning. I took a bus as soon as my husband called. But I'm in no position to give him an alibi."

"An alibi wasn't what I had in mind. I suggest another possibility—that you came home twice. You came home unexpectedly last night, saw the girl in the house with your husband, waited in the dark till the girl came out, waited with a piece of rope in your hands—a piece of rope you'd cut from your husband's boat in the hope of getting him punished for what he'd done to you. But the picture doesn't fit the frame, Mrs. Connor. A sailor like your husband wouldn't cut a piece of line from his own boat. And even in the heat of murder he wouldn't tie a granny's knot. His fingers would automatically tie a reef knot. That isn't true of a woman's fingers."

She held herself upright with one long rigid arm against the door frame.

"I wouldn't do anything like that. I wouldn't do that to Frank."

"Maybe you wouldn't in daylight, Mrs. Connor. Things have different shapes at midnight."

"And hell hath no fury like a woman scorned? Is that what you're thinking? You're wrong. I wasn't here last night. I was in bed in my father's house in Long Beach. I didn't even know about that girl and Frank."

"Then why did you leave him?"

333

"He was in love with another woman. He wanted to divorce me and marry her. But he was afraid—afraid that it would affect his position in town. He told me on the phone this morning that it was all over with the other woman. So I agreed to come back to him." Her arm dropped on her side.

"He said that it was all over with Ginnie?"

Possibilities were racing through my mind. There was the possibility that Connor had been playing reverse English, deliberately and clumsily framing himself in order to be cleared. But that was out of far left field.

"Not Ginnie," his wife said. "The other woman was Anita Brocco. He met her last spring in the course of work and fell in love—what *he* calls love. My husband is a foolish, fickle man."

"Please, Stella. I said it was all over between me and Anita, and it is."

She turned on him in quiet savagery. "What does it matter now? If it isn't one girl it's another. Any kind of female flesh will do to poultice your sick little ego."

Her cruelty struck inward and hurt her. She stretched out her hand toward him. Suddenly her eyes were blind with tears.

"Any flesh but mine, Frank," she said brokenly.

Connor paid no attention.

He said to me in a hushed voice, "My God, I never thought. I noticed her car last night when I was walking home along the beach."

"Whose car?"

"Anita's red Fiat. It was parked at the viewpoint a few hundred yards from here." He gestured vaguely toward town. "Later, when Ginnie was with me, I thought I heard someone in the garage. But I was too drunk to make a search." His eyes burned into mine. "You say a woman tied that knot?"

"All we can do is ask her."

We started toward my car together. His wife called after him, "Don't go, Frank. Let him handle it."

He hesitated, a weak man caught between opposing forces.

"I need you," she said. "We need each other."

I pushed him in her direction.

It was nearly four when I got to the HP station. The patrol cars had gathered like homing pigeons for the change in shift. Their uniformed drivers were talking and laughing inside.

Anita Brocco wasn't among them. A male dispatcher, a

334

fat-faced man with pimples, had taken her place behind the counter.

"Where's Miss Brocco?" I asked.

"In the Ladies' Room. Her father is coming to pick her up any minute."

She came out wearing lipstick and a light beige coat. Her face turned beige when she saw my face. She came toward me in slow motion, leaned with both hands flat on the counter. Her lipstick looked like fresh blood on a corpse.

"You're a handsome woman, Anita," I said. "Too bad about you."

"Too bad." It was half a statement and half a question. She looked down at her hands.

"Your fingernails are clean now. They were dirty this morning. You were digging in the dirt in the dark last night, weren't you?"

"No."

"You were, though. You saw them together and you couldn't stand it. You waited in ambush with a rope, and put it around her neck. Around your own neck, too."

She touched her neck. The talk and laughter had subsided around us. I could hear the tick of the clock again, and the muttering signals coming in from inner space.

"What did you use to cut the rope with, Anita? The garden shears?"

Her red mouth groped for words and found them. "I was crazy about him. She took him away. It was all over before it started. I didn't know what to do with myself. I wanted him to suffer."

"He's suffering. He's going to suffer more."

"He deserves to. He was the only man—" She shrugged in a twisted way and looked down at her breast. "I didn't want to kill her, but when I saw them together—I saw them through the window. I saw her take off her clothes and put them on. Then I thought of the night my father—when he—when there was all the blood in Mother's bed. I had to wash it out of the sheets."

The men around me were murmuring. One of them, a sergeant, raised his voice.

"Did you kill Ginnie Green?"

"Yes."

"Are you ready to make a statement?" I said.

"Yes. I'll talk to Sheriff Pearsall. I don't want to talk here, in front of my friends." She looked around doubtfully.

"I'll take you downtown."

"Wait a minute." She glanced once more at her empty hands. "I left my purse in the—in the back room. I'll go and get it."

She crossed the office like a zombie, opened a plain door, closed it behind her. She didn't come out. After a while we broke the lock and went in after her.

Her body was cramped on the narrow floor. The ivory-handled nail file lay by her right hand. There were bloody holes in her white blouse and in the white breast under it. One of them had gone as deep as her heart.

Later Al Brocco drove up in her red Fiat and came into the station.

"I'm a little late," he said to the room in general. "Anita wanted me to give her car a good cleaning. Where is she, anyway?"

The sergeant cleared his throat to answer Brocco.

All us poor creatures, as the old man of the mountain had said that morning.

ONE MORNING
THEY'LL HANG HIM

BY MARGERY ALLINGHAM

Margery Allingham was born in London in 1904, the
eldest child of H. J. Allingham, whose serials appeared in
the popular weeklies of the day. In 1927 she married
Philip Youngman Carter, an artist, and the following
year she wrote *The Crime at Black Dudley*, her first novel
featuring the mild, bespectacled Albert Campion. Her
novels before 1934 were mostly pure entertainment;
those written later place her in the forefront of the generation of detection writers who attempted to fuse the
police novel and the novel of character and psychology.

IT WAS TYPICAL of Detective Inspector Kenny, at that time D.D.I. of the L. Division, that, having forced himself to ask a favor, he should set about with the worst grace possible. When at last he took the plunge, he heaved his two hundred pounds off Mr. Campion's fireside couch and set down his empty glass with a clatter.

"I don't know if I needed that at three in the afternoon," he said ungratefully, his small blue eyes baleful, "but I've been up since two this morning dealing with women, tears, minor miracles, and this perishing rain." He rubbed his broad face, and presented it scarlet and exasperated at Mr. Campion's back. "If there's one thing that makes me savage it's futility!" he added.

Mr. Albert Campion, who had been staring idly out of the window watching the rain on the roofs, did not glance round. He was still the lean, somewhat ineffectual-looking man to whom the Special Branch had turned so often in the last twenty years. His very fair hair had bleached into whiteness and a few lines had appeared round the pale eyes which were still, as always, covered by large horn-rimmed spectacles, but otherwise he looked much as Kenny first remembered him—"Friendly and a little simple—the old snake!"

"So there's futility in Barraclough Road too, is there?" Campion's light voice sounded polite rather than curious.

Kenny drew a sharp breath of annoyance.

"The Commissioner has 'phoned you? He suggested I should look you up. It's not a great matter—just one of those stupid little snags which has some perfectly obvious explanation. Once it's settled the whole case is open-and-shut. As it is, we can't keep the man at the station indefinitely."

Mr. Campion picked up the early edition of the evening paper from his desk.

"This is all I know," he said, holding it out. "Mr. Oates didn't 'phone. There you are, in the Stop Press. *Rich Widow shot in Barraclough Road West. Nephew at police station helping investigation.* What's the difficulty? His help is not altogether wholehearted, perhaps?"

To his surprise an expression remarkably like regret flickered round Kenny's narrow lips.

"Ruddy young fool," he said, and sat down abruptly. "I tell you, Mr. Campion, this thing is in the bag. It's just one of those ordinary, rather depressing little stories which most murder cases are. There's practically no mystery, no chase—nothing but a wretched little tragedy. As soon as you've spotted what I've missed, I shall charge this chap and he'll go before the magistrates and be committed for trial. His counsel will plead insanity and the jury won't have it. The Judge will sentence him, he'll appeal, their Lordships will dismiss it. The Home Secretary will sign the warrant and one morning they'll take him out and they'll hang him." He sighed. "All for nothing," he said. "All for nothing at all. It'll probably be raining just like it is now," he added inconsequentially.

Mr. Campion's eyes grew puzzled. He knew Kenny for a conscientious officer and, some said, a hard man. This philosophic strain was unlike him.

"Taken a fancy to him?" he inquired.

"Who? Me? I certainly haven't." The Inspector was grim. "I've got no sympathy for youngsters who shoot up their relatives however selfish the old besoms may be. No, he's killed her and he must take what's coming to him, but it's hard on—well, on some people. Me, for one." He took out a large old-fashioned notebook and folded it carefully in half. "I stick to one of these," he remarked virtuously. "None of your backs of envelopes for me. My record is kept as neatly as when I was first on the beat, and it can be handed across the court whenever a know-all counsel asks to see it." He paused. "I sound like an advertisement, don't I? Well, Mr. Campion, since I'm here, just give your mind to this, if you will. I don't suppose it'll present any difficulty to you."

"One never knows," murmured Mr. Campion idiotically. "Start with the victim."

Kenny returned to his notebook.

"Mrs. Mary Alice Cibber, aged about seventy or maybe a bit less. She had heart trouble which made her look frail and, of course, I didn't see her until she was dead. She had a nice house in Barraclough Road, a good deal too big for her, left her by her husband who died ten years ago. Since then she's been alone except for a maid who cleared off in the war and now for another old party who calls herself a companion. *She* looks older still, poor old girl, but you can see she's been kept well under—" he put his thumb down expressively—"by Mrs. C. who appears to have been a dictator in her small way. She was the sort of woman who lived for two chairs and a salad bowl."

"I beg your pardon?"

"Antiques." He was mildly contemptuous. "The house is crammed with them, all three floors and the attic, everything kept as if it was brand-new. The old companion says she loved it more than anything on earth. Of course she hadn't much else *to* love, not a relation in the world except the nephew—"

"Whose future you see so clearly?"

"The man who shot her," the Inspector agreed. "He's a big, nervy lad, name of Woodruff, the son of the old lady's brother. His mother, father, and two young sisters all got theirs in the blitz on Portsmouth. Whole family wiped out."

"I see." Campion began to catch some of Kenny's depression. "Where was he when that happened?"

"In the Western Desert." The D.D.I.'s protruberant eyes were dark with irritation. "I told you this was just an ordinary miserable slice of life. It goes on the same way. This boy, Richard Woodruff—he's only twenty-eight now—did very well in the war. He was in the landings in Sicily and went through the fighting in Italy where he got the M.C. and was promoted major. Then he copped in for the breakthrough in France and just before the finish he became a casualty. A bridge blew up with him on it—or something of the sort, my informant didn't know exactly—and he seems to have become what the boys call 'bomb happy.' It used to be 'shell shock' in my day. As far as I can gather, he always had been quick-tempered, but this sent him over the edge. He sounds to me as if he wasn't safe for a while. That may help him in his defense, of course."

"Yes." Campion sounded depressed. "Where's he been since then?"

"On a farm mostly. He was training to be an architect before the war but the motherly old Army knew what was best for him and when he came out of the hospital they bunged him down to Dorset. He's just got away. Some wartime buddy got him a job in an architect's office under the old pals' act and he was all set to take it up." He paused and his narrow mouth, which was not entirely insensitive, twisted bitterly. "Ought to have started Monday," he said.

"Oh dear," murmured Mr. Campion inadequately. "Why did he shoot his aunt? Pure bad temper?"

Kenny shook his head.

"He had a reason. I mean one can see why he was angry. He hadn't anywhere to live, you see. As you know London is crowded, and rents are fantastic. He and his wife were paying through the nose for a cupboard of a bed-sitting room off the Edgware Road."

"His wife?" The lean man in the horn-rims was interested. "Where did she come from? You're keeping her very quiet."

To Campion's surprise the Inspector did not speak at once. Instead he grunted and there was regret, and surprise at it, in his little smile. "I believe I would if I could," he said sincerely. "He found her on the farm. They've been married six weeks. I don't know if you've ever seen love, Mr. Campion? It's very rare—the kind I mean." He put out his hands deprecatingly. "It seems to crop up—when it does—among the most unexpected people, and when you do see it, well, it's very impressive." He succeeded in looking thoroughly ashamed of himself. "I shouldn't call myself a sentimental man," he said.

"No." Campion was reassuring. "You got his war history from her, I suppose?"

"I had to, but we're confirming it. He's shut up as a watch—or a hand grenade. 'Yes' and 'No' and 'I did not shoot her'—that's about all his contribution amounted to, and he's had a few hours of expert treatment. The girl is quite different. She's down there too. Won't leave. We put her in the waiting room finally. She's not difficult—just sits there."

"Does she know anything about it?"

"No." Kenny was quite definite. "She's nothing to look at," he went on presently, as if he felt the point should be made. "She's just an ordinary nice little country girl, a bit too thin and a bit too brown, natural hair and inexpert make-up, and yet with this— this blazing, radiant steadfastness about her!" He checked himself. "Well, she's fond of him," he amended.

"Believes he's God," Campion suggested.

Kenny shook his head. "She doesn't care if he isn't," he said sadly. "Well, Mr. Campion, some weeks ago these two approached Mrs. Cibber about letting them have a room or two at the top of her house. That must have been the girl's idea; she's just the type to have old-fashioned notions about blood being thicker than water. She made the boy write. The old lady ignored the question but asked them both to an evening meal last night. That invitation was sent a fortnight ago, so you can see there was no eager bless-you-my-children about it."

"Only that she had to have notice if she was giving a party. The

341

old companion explained that to me. There was the silver to get out and clean, and the best china to be washed, and so on. Oh, there was nothing simple and homely about the household!" He sounded personally affronted. "When they got there, of course there was a blazing row."

"Hard words or flying crockery?"

Kenny hesitated. "In a way, both," he said slowly. "It seems to have been a funny sort of flare-up. I had two accounts of it—one from the girl and one from the companion. I think they are both trying to be truthful but they both seem to have been completely foxed by it. They both agree that Mrs. Cibber began it. She waited until there were three oranges and a hundredweight of priceless early Worcester dessert service on the table, and then let fly. Her theme seems to have been the impudence of Youth in casting its eyes on its inheritance before Age was in its grave, and so on and so on. She then made it quite clear that they hadn't a solitary hope of getting what they wanted, and conveyed that she did not care if they slept in the street so long as her precious furniture was safely housed. There's no doubt about it that she was very aggravating and unfair."

"Unfair?"

"Ungenerous. After all she knew the man quite well. He used to go and stay with her by himself when he was a little boy." Kenny returned to his notes. "Woodruff then lost his temper in his own way which, if the exhibition he gave in the early hours of this morning is typical, is impressive. He goes white instead of red, says practically nothing, but looks as if he's about to 'incandesce'—if I make myself plain."

"Entirely." Mr. Campion was deeply interested. This new and human Kenny was an experience. "I take it he then fished out a gun and shot her?"

"Lord, no! If he had, he'd have a chance at least of Broadmoor. No. He just got up and asked her if she had any of his things, because if so he'd take them and not inconvenience her with them any longer. It appears that when he was in hospital some of his gear had been sent to her, as his next of kin. She said yes, she had, and it was waiting for him in the boot cupboard. The old companion, Miss Smith, was sent trotting out to fetch it and came staggering in with an old officers' hold-all, bursted at the sides and filthy. Mrs. Cibber told her nephew to open it and see if she'd robbed him, and he did as he was told. Of course, one of the first things he saw among the ragged bush shirts and old photographs was a revolver and a clip of ammunition." He paused and shook his head. "Don't ask me how it got there. You know what hospitals were like in the war. Mrs. Cibber went on taunting the man in her own peculiar way, and he stood there examining the gun and presently loading it, almost absently. You can see the scene?"

Campion could. The pleasant, perhaps slightly overcrowded room was vivid in his mind, and he saw the gentle light on the china and the proud, bitter face of the woman.

"After that," said Kenny, "the tale gets more peculiar, although both accounts agree. It was Mrs. C. who laughed and said, 'I suppose you think I ought to be shot?' Woodruff did not answer but he dropped the gun in his side pocket. Then he packed up the hold-all and said 'Goodbye.'" He hesitated. "Both statements say that he then said something about *the sun having gone down*. I don't know what that meant, or if both women mistook him. Anyway, there's nothing to it. He has no explanation to offer. Says he doesn't remember saying it. However, after that he suddenly picked up one of his aunt's beloved china fruit-bowls and simply dropped it on the floor. It fell on a rug, as it happened, and did not break, but old Mrs. Cibber nearly passed out, and the girl hurried him off home."

"With the gun?"

"With the gun." Kenny shrugged his heavy shoulders. "As soon as the girl heard that Mrs. Cibber had been shot, she jumped up with a tale that he had *not* taken it. She said she'd sneaked it out of his pocket and put it on the window sill. The lamest story you ever heard! She's game and she's ready to say absolutely anything, but she won't save him, poor kid. He was seen in the district at midnight."

Mr. Campion put a hand through his sleek hair. "Ah. That rather tears it."

"Oh, it does. There's no question that he did it. It hardly arises. What happened was this. The young folk got back to their bed-sitting room about ten to nine. Neither of them will admit it, but it's obvious that Woodruff was in one of those boiling but sulky rages which made him unfit for human society. The girl left him alone—I should say she has a gift for handling him—and she says she went to bed while he sat up writing letters. Quite late, she can't or won't say when, he went out to the post. He won't say anything. We may or may not break him down, he's a queer chap. However, we have a witness who saw him somewhere about midnight at the Kilburn end of Barraclough Road. Woodruff stopped him and asked if the last eastbound 'bus had

343

gone. Neither of them had a watch, but the witness is prepared to swear it was just after midnight—which is important because the shot was fired at two minutes before twelve. We've gotten that time fixed."

Mr. Campion, who had been making notes, looked up in mild astonishment.

"You got that witness very promptly," he remarked. "Why did he come forward?"

"He was a plainclothesman off duty," said Kenny calmly. "One of the local men who had been out to a reunion dinner. He wasn't tight but he had decided to walk home before his wife saw him. I don't know why he hadn't a watch"—Kenny frowned at this defect—"anyway, he hadn't, or it wasn't going. But he was alert enough to notice Woodruff. He's a distinctive chap, you know. Very tall and dark, and his manner was so nervy and excitable that the dick thought it worth reporting."

Campion's teeth appeared in a brief smile.

"In fact, he recognized him at once as a man who looked as though he'd done a murder?"

"No." The Inspector remained unruffled. "No, he said he looked like a chap who had just got something off his mind and was pleased with himself."

"I see. And meanwhile the shot was fired at two minutes to twelve."

"That's certain." Kenny brightened and became businesslike. "The man next door heard it and looked at his watch. We've got his statement and the old lady's companion. Everyone else in the street is being questioned, but nothing has come in yet. It was a cold wet night and most people had their windows shut; besides, the room where the murder took place was heavily curtained. So far, these two are the only people who seem to have heard anything at all. The man next door woke up and nudged his wife who had slept through it. But then he may have dozed again, for the next thing he remembers is hearing screams for help. By the time he got to the window, the companion was out in the street in her dressing gown, wedged in between the lamp post and the mail box, screeching her little gray head off. The rain was coming down in sheets."

"When exactly was this?"

"Almost immediately after the shot, according to the companion. She had been in bed for some hours and had slept. Her room is on the second floor, at the back. Mrs. Cibber had not come up with her but had settled down at her bureau in the

344

drawing-room, as she often did in the evening. Mrs. C. was still very upset by the scene at the meal, and did not want to talk. Miss Smith says she woke up and thought she heard the front door open. She won't swear to this, and at any rate she thought nothing of it, for Mrs. Cibber often slipped out to the mail box with letters before coming to bed. Exactly how long it was after she woke that she heard the shot she does not know, but it brought her scrambling out of bed. She agrees she might have been a minute or two finding her slippers and a wrapper, but she certainly came down right away. She says she found the street door open, letting in the rain, and the drawing-room door, which is next to it, wide open as well, and the lights in there full on." He referred to his notes and began to read aloud. "'I smelled burning'—she means cordite—'and I glanced across the room to see poor Mrs. Cibber on the floor with a dreadful hole in her forehead. I was too frightened to go near her, so I ran out of the house shouting "Murder! Thieves!"'"

"That's nice and old-fashioned. Did she see anybody?"

"She says not, and I believe her. She was directly under the only lamp post for fifty yards and it was certainly raining hard."

Mr. Campion appeared satisfied but unhappy. When he spoke his voice was very gentle.

"Do I understand that your case is that Woodruff came back, tapped on the front door, and was admitted by his aunt; after some conversation, which must have taken place in lowered tones since the companion upstairs did not hear it, he shot her and ran away, leaving all the doors open?"

"Substantially, yes. Although he may have shot her as soon as he saw her."

"In that case she'd have been found dead in the hall."

Kenny blinked. "Yes, I suppose she would. Still, they couldn't have talked much."

"Why?"

The Inspector made a gesture of distaste. "This is the bit which gets under my skin," he said. "They could hardly have spoken long—*because she'd forgiven him*. She had written to her solicitor—the finished letter was on her writing pad ready for the post. She'd written to say she was thinking of making the upper part of her house into a home for her nephew, and asked if there was a clause in her lease to prevent it. She also said she wanted the work done quickly, as she had taken a fancy to her new niece and hoped in time there might be children. It's pathetic, isn't it?" His eyes were wretched. "That's what I meant by

345

futility. She'd forgiven him, see? She wasn't a mean old harridan, she was just quick-tempered. I told you this isn't a mystery tale, this is ordinary sordid life."

Mr. Campion looked away.

"Tragic," he said. "Yes. A horrid thing. What do you want me to do?"

Kenny sighed. "Find the gun," he murmured.

The lean man whistled.

"You'll certainly need that if you're to be sure of a conviction. How did you lose it?"

"He ditched it somewhere. He didn't get rid of it in Barraclough Road because the houses come right down to the street, and our chaps were searching for it within half an hour. At the end of the road he caught the last 'bus, which ought to come along at midnight but was a bit late last night, I'm morally certain. These drivers make up time on the straight stretch by the park; it's more than their jobs are worth, so you never get them to admit it. Anyhow, he didn't leave the gun on the 'bus, and it's not in the house where his room is. It's not in the old lady's house at 81 Barraclough Road because I've been over that house myself." He peered at the taller man hopefully. "Where would you hide a gun in this city at night, if you were all that way from the river? It's not so easy, is it? If it had been anywhere obvious it would have turned up by now."

"He may have given it to someone."

"And risked blackmail?" Kenny laughed. "He's not as dumb as that. You'll have to see him. He says he never had it—but that's only natural. Yet where did he put it, Mr. Campion? It's only a little point but, as you say, it's got to be solved."

Campion grimaced.

"Anywhere, Kenny. Absolutely anywhere. In a drain—"

"They're narrow gratings in Barraclough Road."

"In a sandbin or a static water tank—"

"There aren't any in that district."

"He threw it down in the street and someone, who felt he'd rather like to have a gun, picked it up. Your area isn't peopled solely with the lawabiding, you know."

Kenny became more serious. "That's the real likelihood," he admitted gloomily. "But all the same, I don't believe he's the type to throw away a gun casually. He's too intelligent, too cautious. Do you know how this war has made some men cautious even when they're being the most reckless? He's one of those. He's hidden it. Where? Mr. Oates said you'd know if anyone did."

346

Campion ignored this blatant flattery. He stood staring absently out of the window for so long that the Inspector was tempted to nudge him, and when at last he spoke, his question did not sound promising.

"How often did he stay with his aunt when he was a child?"

"Quite a bit, I think, but there's no kid's hiding-place there that only he could have known, if that's what you're after." Kenny could hardly conceal his disappointment. "It's not that kind of house. Besides, he hadn't the time. He got back about twenty past twelve; a woman in the house confirms it—she met him on the stairs. He was certainly spark-out when we got there at a quarter after four this morning. They were both sleeping like kids when I first saw them. She had one skinny little brown arm round his neck. He just woke up in a rage, and she was more astounded than frightened, I swear—"

Mr. Campion had ceased to listen.

"Without the gun the only real evidence you've got is the plainclothesman's story of meeting him," he said. "And even you admit that gallant officer was walking for his health after a party. Imagine a good defense lawyer enlarging on that point."

"I have," the Inspector agreed, dryly. "That's why I'm here. You must find the gun for us, sir. Can I fetch you a raincoat? Or," he added, a faintly smug expression flickering over his broad face, "will you just sit in your armchair and do it there?"

To his annoyance his elegant host appeared to consider the question.

"No, perhaps I'd better come with you," he said at last. "We'll go to Barraclough Road first, if you don't mind. And if I might make a suggestion, I should send Woodruff and his wife back to their lodgings—suitably escorted, of course. If the young man was going to crack, I think he would have done so by now, and the gun, wherever it is, can hardly be at the police station."

Kenny considered. "He may give himself away and lead us to it," he agreed, although without enthusiasm. "I'll telephone. Then we'll go anywhere you say, but as I told you I've been over the Barraclough Road house myself and if there's anything there it's high time I retired."

Mr. Campion merely looked foolish, and the Inspector sighed and let him have his way.

He came back from the telephone smiling wryly.

"That's settled." he announced. "He's been behaving like a good soldier interrogated by the enemy, silly young fool—after all, we're only trying to hang him! The girl has been asking for him to be fed, and reporters are crawling up the walls. Our boys won't be sorry to get rid of 'em for a bit. They'll be looked after. We shan't lose 'em. Now, if you've set your heart on the scene of the crime, Mr. Campion, we'll go."

In the taxi he advanced a little idea.

"I was thinking of that remark he is alleged to have made," he said, not without shame. "You don't think that it could have been 'Your sun has gone down,' and that we could construe it as a threat within the meaning of the act?"

Campion regarded him owlishly.

"We could, but I don't think we will. That's the most enlightening part of the whole story, don't you think?"

If Inspector Kenny agreed he did not say so, and they drove to the top of Barraclough Road in silence. There Campion insisted on stopping at the first house next to the main thoroughfare. The building had traded on its proximity to the shopping centre and had been converted into a dispensing chemist's. Campion was inside for several minutes, leaving Kenny in the cab. When he came out he offered no explanation other than to observe fatuously that they had a "nice time," and settled back without troubling to look out at the early Victorian stucco three-story houses which lined the broad road.

A man on duty outside, and a handful of idlers gaping apathetically at the drawn blinds, distinguished 81 Barraclough Road. Kenny rang the bell and the door was opened after a pause by a flurried old lady with a duster in her hand.

"Oh, it's you, Inspector," she said hastily. "I'm afraid you've found me in a muddle. I've been trying to tidy up a little. *She* couldn't have borne the place left dirty after everyone had been trampling over it. Yet I don't mean to say that you weren't all very careful."

She led them into a spotless dining room which glowed with old mahogany and limpid silver, and the wan afternoon light showed them her reddened eyes and worn navy-blue house-dress. She was a timid-looking person, not quite so old as Kenny had suggested, with very neat gray hair and a skin which had never known cosmetics. Her expression was closed and secret with long submission, and her shoulder blades stuck out a little under the cloth of her dress. Her hands still trembled slightly from the shock of the evening before.

Kenny introduced Campion. "We shan't be long, Miss Smith," he said cheerfully. "Just going to have another little look around."

Campion smiled at her reassuringly. "It's difficult to get help these days?" he suggested pleasantly.

"Oh, it is," she said earnestly. "And Mrs. Cibber wouldn't trust just anyone with her treasures. They are so very good." Her eyes filled with tears. "She was so fond of them."

"I daresay she was. That's a beautiful piece, for instance." Campion glanced with expert interest at the serpentine sideboard with its genuine handles and toilet cupboard.

"Beautiful," echoed Miss Smith dutifully. "And the chairs, you see?"

"I do." He eyed the Trafalgar set with the cherry-leather seats. "Is this where the quarrel took place?"

She nodded and trembled afresh. "Yes. I—I shall never forget it, never."

"Was Mrs. Cibber often bad-tempered?"

The woman hesitated, and her firm small mouth moved without words.

"Was she?"

She shot a swift unhappy glance at him.

"She was quick," she said. "Yes, I think I ought to say she was quick. Now, would you like to see the rest of the house or—?"

Campion glanced at his watch and compared it with the Tompion bracket clock on the mantelshelf.

"I think we've just time," he said, idiotically. "Upstairs first, Inspector."

The next thirty-five minutes reduced Kenny to a state of jitters rare in him. After watching Campion with breathless interest for the first five, it slowly dawned on him that the expert had forgotten the crime in his delight at discovering a treasure trove. Even Miss Smith, who betrayed a certain proprietorial pride, flagged before Campion's insatiable interest. Once or twice she hinted that perhaps they ought to go down, but he would not hear of it. By the time they had exhausted the third floor and were on the steps to the attic, she became almost firm. There was really nothing there but some early Georgian children's toys, she said.

"But I must just see the toys. I've got a 'thing' on toys, Kenny." Campion sounded ecstatic. "Just a minute—"

A vigorous tattoo on the front door interrupted him and Miss Smith, whose nerves were suffering, emitted a little squeak.

"Oh, dear. Somebody at the door. I must go down."

"No, no." Campion was uncharacteristically effusive. "I'll see who it is and come back. I shan't be a moment."

He flung himself downstairs with boyish enthusiasm, Miss Smith behind him, and Kenny, seeing escape at last, following quickly.

They reached the hall just in time to see him closing the door. "Only the post," he said, holding out a package. "Your library book, Miss Smith."

"Oh, yes," she came forward, hand outstretched. "I was expecting that."

"I rather thought you were." His voice was very soft and suddenly menacing. He held the cardboard book box high over his head with one hand, and with the other released the flap which closed it. The soft gleam of metal appeared in the light from the transom, and a service revolver crashed heavily to the parquet floor.

For a long minute there was utter silence.

Miss Smith appeared frozen in mid air, her hands clawing at the box.

Then, most dreadfully, she began to scream . . .

A little over an hour later Kenny sat on a Trafalgar chair in a room which still seemed to quiver and shudder with terrible sound. He was pale and tired-looking. His shirt was torn and there were three livid nail scratches down his face.

"God," he said, breathing hard. "God, can you beat that?"

Mr. Campion sat on the priceless table and scratched his ear.

"It was a bit more than I bargained for," he murmured. "It didn't occur to me that she'd become violent. I'm afraid they may be having trouble in the van. Sorry. I ought to have thought of it."

The C.I.D. man grunted. "Seems to me you thought of plenty," he muttered. "It came as a shock to me—I don't mind admitting it since I can't very well help it. When did it come to you? Did you have it from the start?"

"Oh, Lord, no." Campion sounded apologetic. "It was that remark of Woodruff's you quoted about the sun going down. That's what set me on the train of thought. Weren't you ever warned as a kid, Kenny, and by an aunt perhaps, never to let the sun go down on your wrath?"

"I've heard it, of course. What do you mean? It was a sort of saying between them?"

"I wondered if it was. They knew each other well when he was a child, and they were both quick-tempered people. It seemed to me that he was reminding her that the sun *had* gone down, and he showed her he could have smashed her precious bowl if he liked. It would have broken, you know, if he hadn't taken care it shouldn't. I wondered if, like many quick-tempered people, they

350

got sorry just as quickly. Didn't you think it odd, Kenny, that directly after the row they should *both* have settled down to write letters?"

The detective stared at him.

"She wrote to her solicitor," he began slowly. "And he—? Good Lord! You think he wrote to her to say he was sorry?"

"Almost certainly, but we shall never find his letter. That's in the kitchen stove by now. He came back to deliver it, pushed it through the door, and hurried off looking, just as your plainclothesman said, as if he'd got something off his chest. Then he could sleep. The sun had not gone down on his wrath." He slid off the table and stood up. "The vital point is, of course, that *Mrs. Cibber knew he would.* She sat up waiting for it."

Kenny sucked in his breath.

"And Miss Smith knew?"

"Of course, she knew. Mrs. Cibber hadn't the kind of temperament one can keep a secret. Miss Smith knew from the moment that Mrs. Cibber received the initial letter that the nephew would get his way in the end—*unless she could stop it somehow!* She was the one with the bee in her bonnet about the furniture. I realized that as soon as you said the whole house was kept like a bandbox. No woman with a weak heart can keep a three-story house like a palace, or compel another to do it—unless the other wants to. Miss Smith was the one with the mania. Who was to get the house if the nephew died in the war? Mrs. Cibber must have made some provision."

Kenny rubbed his head with both hands. "I knew!" he exploded. "The lawyer's clerk told me this morning when I rang up to find out if Woodruff was the heir. I was so keen to confirm that point that I discounted the rest. If he died the companion was to have it for her lifetime."

Campion looked relieved.

"I thought so. There you are, you see. She had to get rid of them both—Woodruff and his new wife. With a young and vigorous woman in the house there was a danger of the companion becoming—well, redundant. Don't you think?"

Kenny was fingering his notebook.

"You think she'd planned it for a fortnight?"

"She'd thought of it for a fortnight. She didn't see how to do it until the row occurred last night. When she found the gun on the window sill, where young Mrs. Woodruff left it, and Mrs. Cibber told her that the boy would come back, the plan was obvious." He shivered. "Do you realize that she must have been waiting, probably on the stairs, with the gun in one hand and the book box addressed to herself in the other, listening for Woodruff's letter to slide under the door? As soon as she heard it, she had to fly down and get it and open the door. Then she had to walk into the drawing-room, shoot the old lady as she turned to see who it was, and put the gun in the book box. The instant she was certain Mrs. Cibber was dead, she then had to run out screaming to her place between the lamp post and the mail box and—*post the package!*"

Kenny put down his pencil and looked up.

"Now there," he said with honest admiration, "there I hand it to you. How in the world did you get on to that?"

"You suggested it."

"*I* did?" Kenny was pleased in spite of himself. "When?"

"When you kept asking me where one could hide a gun in a London street with no wide gratings and no sandbins. There was only the mail box. I guessed she'd posted it to herself—no one else would have been safe. Even the dead letter office eventually gives up its dead. That's why I was so keen to get her to the top of the house—as far away from the front door as possible." He sighed. "The book box was misguided genius. The gun was an old Luger, did you notice? Loot. That's why he never had to turn it in. It just fitted in the box. She must have had a thrill when she discovered that."

Kenny shook his head wonderingly. "Well, blow me down!" he said inelegantly. "Funny that *I* put you onto it!"

Mr. Campion was in bed that night when the telephone rang. It was Kenny again.

"I say, Mr. Campion?"

"Yes?"

"Sorry to bother you at this time of night but there's something worrying me. You don't mind, do you?"

"Think nothing of it."

"Well. Everything is all right. Smith has been certified by three medicos. The little girl is very happy comforting her boy, who seems to be upset about his aunt's death. The Commissioner is very pleased. But I can't get off to sleep. Mr. Campion, *how did you know what time the afternoon post is delivered in Barraclough Road?*"

The lean man stifled a yawn.

"Because I went into the chemist's shop on the corner and asked," he said. "Elementary, my dear Kenny."